M.D.

M.D.

A NOVEL BY

Neil Ravin

Delacorte Press/Seymour Lawrence

Published by
Delacorte Press/Seymour Lawrence
1 Dag Hammarskjold Plaza
New York, N.Y. 10017

Lyrics from "Just Like Tom Thumb's Blues" by Bob Dylan: © 1965
by Warner Bros. Inc. All Rights Reserved. Used by Permission.

Manufactured in the United States of America

First printing

Designed by Laura Bernay

Library of Congress Cataloging in Publication Data

Ravin, Neil.
M.D. : a novel.

I. Title.
PS3568.A84M2   813'.54   80-25779
ISBN 0-440-05468-0

For Jean Ziman Ravin,
Kindness to sons and doctors

Humankind cannot bear very much reality.
                                    —T. S. Eliot

BOOK I

The First Month

1

July 10

Mrs. Tilly died Monday. Or perhaps Tuesday. Ryan wasn't sure. His watch had stopped at 11:00 P.M., when the nurse called. It might have been past midnight when Mrs. Tilly belched up a liter of blood over Ryan's shoes. Not that the time mattered to Ryan. It mattered for the death certificate.

Mrs. Tilly had liked Ryan, and as a parting kindness had died with a sense of timing, beginning her swift slide out of this world before midnight, before Ryan had gotten to bed, so he did not have to be jarred out of a numbed sleep by the raucous phone in the on-call room. Awakenings like that were always followed by a blinding headache. Ryan was grateful to Mrs. Tilly for dying when she did.

He would have been more grateful had she hung on until the next night, when he was off. But nobody's perfect. Ryan felt intensely guilty for thinking like that.

She arrested while he was wringing her life's blood out of his socks, and Ryan considered his options. As for poor Mrs. Tilly, there were no options. That had already been decided at chart rounds, when Ryan's resident had gone over her chart and concluded resuscitation would be doing Mrs. Tilly a grave disservice. Ryan's options were Monday or Tuesday, and blue or black ink for the death certificate. It had been a bad night. Bad nights were nights with surprises. Ryan had expected Mrs. Tilly to hang on for weeks. Ryan thought about the colors. It was better than thinking about Mrs. Tilly. He used blue, and Tuesday.

The secretary in Administration paged at eight. She told Ryan he had to redo the certificate on Tilly.

3

Ryan sighed. Last night he had taken perverse delight in using blue ink. This morning he had a numbing headache, and the good fight was no fun.

"I'll think about it."

"The body cannot be released until the certificate is filled out. The undertaker has already called once."

"The certificate is filled out," said Ryan, pressing his throbbing temples, trying to sound like a recording. "I distinctly remember doing it."

"In blue ink, Dr. Ryan."

"Then you admit, it's filled out."

"We've been through this before, Dr. Ryan," she said. She had a way of turning *doctor* into a pejorative. "Blue ink is not legal on death certificates."

"It's legal on charts," said Ryan. "Charts are legal."

"Dr. Ryan"—the secretary's voice swelled with reason, tempered by tones of waning patience—"the body cannot be released unless the death certificate is in order. This could delay the funeral. Think of the family."

It was a tactic Ryan knew well, after only a week. The authorities simply resorted to the emotional club when straightforward commands failed. Ryan told himself to calm down, to put that secretary's mother-superior voice in perspective, to ignore her. But judicious behavior on four hours' sleep did not come easily. He had collected himself so many times that night. He had to be polite to the nurses who hounded him with patients' complaints. The nurses knew more than he did at this point, and he needed them. But he didn't need the secretary with the prickly voice. She needed *him* to fill out that certificate. He hung up.

Ryan considered the three certificates he had filled out the night before: one in red, one in blue, and one in standard black. Of the three, the red had the most character. He had gotten carried away with the red one: it was a masterful piece of calligraphy, with two different lettering styles for the two different sections of the certificate—gothic for the primary diagnosis (primary biliary cirrhosis), italic for the terminal event (cardiac arrest). Italic wasn't easy with those hospital ball-points. Ryan

4

had finished it off with a John Hancock–style signature, all flourish. He had even added a numeral to his name: William Ryan III, M.D., although he was not the third, nor even the second. He knew he was right. Color was irrelevant in the eyes of the law; at least, it ought to be. He hadn't used pencil, after all.

The secretary's supervisor paged while Ryan wasn't redoing the death certificate. He was busy botching another attempt at restarting an IV, so he didn't answer. Then the chief resident, Frank Wright, paged.

"Ryan, what is this about red and blue death certificates?"

Ryan presented what he thought was a compelling case for his right to use blue ink. The chief resident did not care about cases, compelling or otherwise. Ryan was creating problems, and the chief resident had enough problems.

"Ryan," said Frank Wright, the chief resident. "Go down and redo the certificate."

Ryan struggled to say "Yes, sir." He really wanted simply to acquiesce, as silently as possible. "In your particular case," Arch had told him, "silence *is* golden." Arch should know. Arch had known him for six years. Arch was correct: Ryan could not afford to lose sight of the big picture. Ryan had to avoid offending people.

But somehow Ryan's principles kept reasserting themselves, almost against his will.

It was a sort of incontinence of rectitude, and it had gotten him into trouble in medical school more than once. It hadn't helped him get his internship, either.

"People don't like hearing they're wrong," said Arch. "And even less, that you're right. Don't be so right."

Ryan said, "Okay."

"And Ryan," said the chief resident.

"Yes?"

"Next time you get all lathered up, pick something with a little more scope."

"Scope?"

"Scope."

2

July turned Manhattan into a tropical city. Arch, Ryan's roommate, devoted his waking hours to the pursuit of air conditioning. His main problem, the nadir of his daily existence, was the forty-minute ride downtown on buses, frequently un-air-conditioned, and always packed tightly as cattle cars. He devoted considerable effort to avoiding that crush, leaving the town house with Ryan at seven in the morning and staying downtown in a cool bar until eight in the evening.

When he got home Tuesday evening, the town house was stifling. He worked his way up to Ryan's study, turning on air conditioners. Ryan was at his desk, in his jogging shorts, in the trancelike state he entered whenever he read inspiring biography. This evening, he was immobile with *Claude Bernard: Master of Experimental Physiology.*

"Ryan?"

No answer.

"You okay?"

Ryan started.

"Thought you might have died," said Arch, "in the heat."

"Just reading," said Ryan absently.

"And forgetting to turn on the air conditioners?"

"Guess so," said Ryan, putting down his book. "It's getting dark out."

Ten minutes later they were jogging east, toward the river. Ryan was telling Arch about the death certificates.

"You should've gone to law school," said Arch, already a little winded.

6

"Law's all haggling," said Ryan.

"Precisely," laughed Arch, breathlessly. "Perfect match of temperament and profession."

They passed a squat red brick building, which was caddy-corner to the shimmering, white Manhattan Hospital.

"The Whipple Annex," said Ryan. "Where I have the pleasure of spending this coming August and September."

"Looks like a county jail."

"It's not till August," said Ryan. "Maybe it'll collapse by then."

"Where are the air conditioners?" asked Arch, getting to the heart of the matter.

"No air conditioning."

"Jesus!"

They jogged past The Manhattan Hospital, its white stone going purple in the twilight.

"Everyone has to rotate there," said Ryan of Whipple. "How bad could two months be?"

"Without air conditioning." Arch shook his head at the enormity of it.

"It's medicine, wherever you do it: tropics, the Tower, wherever."

Ryan said things like that. "It's medicine." He had been saying things like that since his first year in medical school. It was one of those attitudes to which he remained loyal.

Ryan thought constancy a virtue. He prided himself on it. He had moved through college in a straight line toward medical school with a singleness of purpose that appalled all who knew him. Even his truncated football career was a means to the end: Ryan thought football would make him seem more well rounded, a more appealing applicant.

In fact, he played very well, and had some good times, for which he felt intensely guilty, because, after all, he wasn't at college to have a good time. He was there to get past it.

Ryan had decided to become a doctor in high school, when he broke his leg and was confined with a copy of *Not as a Stranger* and with daytime TV, from which he learned doctors lead the most romantic lives.

Ryan's youth had been cursed by overwhelming success. Not so much success, as the absence of defeat. He was elected, respected, and an undetected monomaniac about not screwing up. In short, he was afraid to risk. His high school yearbook had his number: most likely to succeed. What they did not say was most likely to drive himself crazy trying. He had nightmares about letting everyone down.

Six years later, four years of sustained collegiate effort, landed him in medical school, his personal promised land. Then a funny thing happened: medical school evaporated. After the great, long push to get in, it just disappeared, and Ryan was suddenly faced with being an intern.

Ryan knew that he had not always been an intern. Something must have preceded; but trying to recall what it was was like trying to remember life in the womb.

Arch, on the other hand, had no trouble remembering life before Ryan's "medical phase." Of course, Arch had his own perspective: he had been born to a life of comfort, and was determined to maintain it. He lived for his good meals, luxuriant sleeps, and lovely women. And he had watched, both bewildered and horrified, as Ryan had systematically deprived himself of all three.

Ryan had been something of an ascetic during his collegiate struggle toward medical school, but since medical school it took constant vigilance to keep him anywhere near balance.

Arch was a calming presence: his drooping eyelids, oversized body, and unhurried pace projected an imperturbability which could be very reassuring. Arch knew Ryan needed that.

Arch had the metabolism of a three-toed sloth, and a body like a giant pillow. And he had his grandfather's town house, complete with air conditioners and all the comforts of home. Around him buzzed Ryan, with the metabolism of a hummingbird, intriguing to watch.

3

July 12

For two days after the flap over the death certificates Ryan behaved himself, turning cheek to those little annoyances wrought by administrators, page operators, and clerks. But it wasn't easy.

Finally he came up against the classic immovable object, in the form of a head nurse, and he tottered quickly toward playing the irresistible force.

Arch's admonitions were ringing in his engorged ears: low profile, big picture, nonconfrontation.

The head nurse on B-7 had decided that dope addicts were stealing needles and syringes, so she locked them up at night.

"You don't count needles and syringes, how could you know any were missing?" Ryan asked her.

She knew, but she wasn't telling.

She knows I know she couldn't know, but she still says she knows.

It soon became a practical thorn in Ryan's nocturnal flesh. He couldn't do blood cultures at night with the needles locked up. He tried squirreling some away during the day, but he lost them even more quickly than black pens. And he'd sit on them. And he'd pull them out of his pockets in the cafeteria, trying to find change for coffee.

Ryan decided to reason with her. She could not be expecting that. Yes, junkies might well be sneaking up six flights of stairs, past other floors, to steal needles from B-7. But wasn't it better that they have clean needles? The head nurse considered. No, they ought to be using their own filthy needles. Let them wallow in their habit.

So Ryan called the chief resident, who was still mad about the death certificates.

"Ryan," said Frank Wright, "you can't fight everybody all the time. You have to pick your spots. Remember: scope."

So Ryan went to see the hospital president, down to the air-conditioned office. He made it as far as the secretary. She peered across her spotless desk at grimy Ryan, who, in the asepsis of this fountain of power, rejoiced in his own fecal-stained white uniform. No, he did not have an appointment. He would have to wait. He chose the cleanest chair, and settled in for the seige.

The president would be busy all morning. Ryan could understand that. Ryan was busy this morning, too. He answered his pages from her phone. She wiped the receiver each time he used it. Ryan liked the office. It was cooler than B-7 in sticky July. And it had *National Geographic.* He was reading and seething about the slaughter of baby seals when an administrator intruded.

The administrator was no older than Ryan, and wore a bloodless, three-piece suit. He was clean-cut, well scrubbed, with a composed smile and soothing voice. Ryan disliked him immediately. He made Ryan feel suddenly soiled. It was the sweaty feeling of organic-chemistry labs in college, where Ryan was busy enough investing in deferred gratification to tolerate his own stench.

But here was Ryan, still waiting to be gratified, grubby again, and there was the administrator, a happy lackey, smelling of after-shave, sent to keep smelly Ryan in his place. Ryan got so demoralized, he left with only a few wilted threats. He would take drastic action.

Maxwell Baptist was sitting on the sofa in his office, across from Diana Hayes, the chief of Cardiac Diagnostics, when the phone on the coffee table between them buzzed.

"Yes?" said Baptist, annoyed. His talk with Dr. Hayes had already been interrupted once.

10

"Sorry to bother you again," said his secretary, "but Jack Hughes is on the line."

"Who?"

"The president's administrative assistant, the one you said looked prepubescent."

"Oh, yes. Put him on. . . . Yes," said Baptist. "Yes, we'll take care of it. My apologies."

Baptist pushed down the lever on the phone to signal his secretary, and looked up at Dr. Hayes, who recrossed her superb legs.

"Sorry," said Baptist, to Dr. Hayes, then, "Ginny, get me the chief resident on the phone. Yes, page him."

Frank Wright, chief res, was on the line before Baptist could turn his attention back to Diana Hayes. Baptist was writing a name on a note card.

"Frank, one of the new interns was down in the president's office this morning making a ruckus. He needs a talking to." Baptist looked at his note card and said, "William Ryan," then hung up.

"What was an intern doing in the president's office?" asked Dr. Hayes.

"Some foolishness," said Baptist, reaching for his pipe, and lighting it. "Some nurses had locked up his syringes. Some kind of prank."

"But why did he go to the president of the hospital about something like that?"

"Diana," said Baptist, "when I start trying to fathom the reasoning of interns, I'll know it's time to retire."

"Perhaps," said Diana Hayes, smiling, "he thought he was going right to the top."

Baptist's eyes narrowed involuntarily. Then he forced himself to laugh.

Frank Wright decided to handle the order from the chief of medicine the way he was beginning to handle more and more orders from the chief: he would do nothing about it. He did ask

Ryan what all the fuss was about, this time, and nodded his way through an impassioned recitation of charges. Ryan was right of course. The supplies would be unlocked every third night, when Ryan was on: twenty needles and ten syringes, for Ryan's blood cultures. When he ran out, he could drop down to B-6, where the supplies weren't locked.

4

They were seniors in college before Arch got to know Ryan well.
There had been speculation about Ryan among the football
players since sophomore year. He had been a walk-on who made
the team, unrecruited, as a flanker. He was friendly enough, but
he was a bona fide phantom. He invariably declined when asked
to join teammates for a beer, and nobody knew where he lived
or with whom. He never lingered in the locker room, just
dressed in his khaki pants and preppie tweed jacket and disappeared. Some of the engineers on the team said he studied in
the science library. Nobody knew whom he dated or where he
hung out when he wasn't at practice or in the library. He just
came out to the stadium and caught passes, then vanished.

All this aroused Arch's curiosity, but not sufficiently to move
him to investigate. Arch thought Ryan was probably stuck up. It
was the preppie clothes. Arch wore what most of the players
wore around campus: gray T-shirts with Brown Football printed
on the front and jeans. Ryan wore Top-Siders and tweed. Not
Arch's style. Arch had gone to prep school but considered himself a jock. It was only since coming to college that he had begun
to perceive that he could be more. Like many big men, Arch was
late in discovering that he was bright.

During spring term of junior year Arch sauntered into An-
thropology 124 (New Guinea Tribalism—popularly known as
Cannibals for Animals). In darted Ryan. Seeing Arch, he took a
desk beside him. Arch was surprised by such overt friendliness.

"You an anthro major?" he asked Ryan.

"Human bio."

13

"Premed?"

"Yeah."

That explained a lot.

Ryan seemed very relaxed, for Ryan. He even said "sure" when Arch suggested they stop for coffee after class.

"Heard you never stopped for coffee," Arch remarked, when they got to the Brown Bear Room.

"Pressure's off now."

"Pressure?"

"Finished organic chem, physics, calculus last term. It's all downhill now—just anthro, bio, and soft sciences. My fate's sealed, far as med school goes."

Ryan was drinking coffee, trying to look relaxed, but he hadn't got the hang of it. He kept glancing at his watch and bouncing his foot.

"Yeah, you've really calmed down," said Arch dryly. "You going to play this fall?"

"No way. This fall I'll be pounding the pavement at any med school that will interview me. Will you play?"

"Of course," said Arch, amazed. Arch was a jock, what else could he do? "Of course, I still gotta book."

"What for?"

"Law school." Arch had only vaguely considered law school up to that moment, but faced with Ryan's utter directedness, he felt compelled to be more decisive about his own plans.

"Where?"

"Anywhere good. Columbia maybe. Got relatives in New York."

"That where you come from?"

"New York and Palm Beach."

"Go to high school in New York?"

"Andover."

"Oh," said Ryan, looking down at his coffee.

"Where'd you go?"

"Robert E. Lee Senior High," said Ryan. "Arlington, Virginia."

"That where you grew up?"

"Yes," said Ryan. "Funny place to be from."

"Why?"

"Big thing in Arlington, Virginia, is the cemetery. Arlington National . . ."

"I know."

"I started out where most people think of ending up."

Ryan's father was a building contractor. Worked his way up. No college. Arch gathered the family had not been well off financially until very recently. Ryan was the third of three sons, the only one they could afford to send to the Ivy League.

"Shanty Irish," said Ryan, a little more than half serious. "My oldest brother is really the one with the most smarts. He had to go to the University of Virginia, though. Didn't cost much."

"Nothing wrong with the University of Virginia."

"Dad's from Rhode Island originally. To him the University of Virginia meant nothing except that Brendan, that's my brother, got to be the first one in our family to graduate from college. But Brown, anything in the Ivy League, that's what Dad really wanted for his kids."

"What's Brendan do now?"

"Works with Dad."

Ryan had worked summers, construction, in the family business.

"They call me the poet," he said a little ruefully, "not real down-to-earth. I never was much good in the business."

"But you made Brown. And premed."

"Dad doesn't know about the premed."

"He'll approve?"

"If I get in," smiled Ryan. "He'd better. He'll have to pay for it."

By the end of spring term, Arch and Ryan were spending a lot of time together. (Arch had never spent so much time in the library, a habit Ryan couldn't break.) Senior year, they rented an apartment off campus. Arch tried initially to enliven what he considered Ryan's bleak social life. But Ryan kept slipping off to the library. It wasn't that Ryan was afraid of women. He charmed many of Arch's girl friends. But he was incapable of calling up

15

a coed for a straightforward date. For Ryan dates just had to evolve. Conversations in the library lounge, continued over coffee, a walk in the campus night, home to bed. He was a senior before the full sequence was actually accomplished.

"Waste of a college education," Arch would mutter whenever Ryan failed to call the number Arch had pressed into his hand. But eventually Arch noticed coeds slipping discreetly out of Ryan's room in the early morning.

"You had me worried. Veritable monk," Arch told Ryan with relief.

They both applied to schools all over the East Coast. Arch got Columbia Law and Ryan got the university medical school at The Manhattan Hospital, and Johns Hopkins. Arch's grandfather was giving up his town house to move to Florida, but didn't really want to sell, which worked out perfectly. Money was never a problem in Arch's family. The town house was located in the East Sixties, a good distance from Columbia, but only blocks from Manhattan Hospital. "It's a sign," said Arch. "The man upstairs thinks we're a good team." They went down to look over the town house. Ryan was sold.

They set the place up the week after graduation.

"This is the last free summer of our lives," said Arch. "Let's go to Europe."

Ryan was all for it, but cooled suddenly.

"We'll go to Ireland," said Arch, hoping to appeal to Ryan on an emotional level.

"Big deal."

"You're not interested in your roots? Ryan, the anthro maven, not interested in roots?"

"I'm not proud to be Irish, if that's what you mean. I've got more in common with Joe DiMaggio than with the average Irishman. Besides, ethnic pride is no great virtue. It's all tribalism."

Ryan didn't have the money to go. It came out eventually. He would have loved to go.

"I ought to be earning this summer, not spending."

"No problem," said Arch, who got him a job in one of his grandfather's restaurants. Ryan worked double shifts June and July, and they were flush by August.

"I can't believe you would have gone back to Virginia and worked construction the last free summer of your youth," said Arch.

"Not happily. I'm down there two days and go stir crazy. Nighttime's the worst. Sit on the porch and listen to the crickets. Once in a while a car goes by down the road. Deadsville."

They started out in London, then headed for Scotland. They were enchanted by Edinburgh.

"See that building," said Ryan as they looked down on Princes Street from the castle high above. "Someday I'll have a clinic there, and you, a barrister of international repute, will have an adjoining office, right there."

In September they started school, Ryan with his cadavers and Arch with his contracts. Three years later Arch was finished and passed the bar. The following June he went to the medical school graduation with Ryan's mother.

She had come up Friday and stayed the weekend in the town house. The ceremony was Monday. Ryan's father flew up that morning, arriving in time to see Ryan stride off the stage, diploma in hand.

"You made it!" said Ryan, pumping his father's hand.

"Brendan can take care of the business for one day," said his father, examining the diploma. "Besides, the business paid for this thing. Wanted to see it. Not what we'd imagined for you. But damned fine achievement. Always worried you couldn't get your head out of the clouds. But here's proof. You've made something of yourself."

Of course Ryan had learned a few things in medical school, and one thing was that writing M.D. after your name does not make you a physician. The making of something real was yet to come. He decided then and there not to go home until he had achieved that.

5

July 14, Morning Rounds

"That gomer needs manual disimpaction," said Iggy.

Iggy Bart was Ryan's resident on B-7. Iggy had two interns to shepherd, Ryan and a Californian named Biotto, who wore a gold necklace and yellow-tinted glasses.

"Gomer?" said Biotto, blankly.

"Four years of med school, and you have to ask?" said Iggy, staring at the button pinned, in defiance of regulations, to Biotto's white hospital tunic. It said SAVE THE WHALES. "Where'd you go to med school?"

"San Francisco."

"Figures," said Iggy. Iggy was skeleton-thin, and wore an Oleg Cassini shirt and tie under his white jacket. A Gucci belt cinched his white hospital pants. Iggy drew a deep breath and began the gomer-orientation lecture.

"Gomerhood is a syndrome, a state of being, a level of existence, somewhere between animal and vegetable.

"The truly classic gomer is unmistakable, an *Aügenblick* diagnosis, which is to say, the diagnosis can be made in the blink of an eye.

"For example, you discover an eighty-year-old man drinking from a toilet bowl: *Aügenblick.*

"Sometimes, it only becomes clear with time: you're taking a history in a six-bedded room, and notice that you're hearing two answers to every question you ask, one from the patient you're talking to, and one from the gomer in the far corner. To establish the patient in the corner as a true gomer, just ask him a direct question. If he sits there staring at you, he's a gomer.

"Sometimes, the history is the best clue: he's been in a nursing home for six months and been shipped to the hospital four times during that period, dehydrated.

"A sure sign: the admitting resident calls from the E.R., and the first thing he says is 'Sorry about this admission.' He's admitting you a gomer.

"Gomers are usually over seventy, but gomerosis may be present at any age—acute and chronic gomerosis is well described. We had a thirty-year-old gomer up here last month—motorcycle accident, head injury—couldn't find his way to the bathroom. Kept peeing on his roommate. We catheterized him, put him in full restraints, but he managed to pull out the Foley, *with* the anchor balloon fully inflated. A bona fide gomer, age thirty."

Biotto and Ryan listened silently, each concluding that Iggy Bart had to be the most callous man alive. Biotto had political feelings about health food, and had been in therapy since age six. He was heavily into his patients as whole humans.

Ryan managed to say nothing. But he resolved to be kind to gomers, who were, after all, still people. By the end of the week, however, Ryan felt the inexorable gravitation toward Iggy's point of view. Gomers may not be a scourge visited upon struggling interns, but they were no blessing either. Whenever a gomer was shipped in from a nursing home, after twenty days without a bowel movement, it was always the intern who wound up with his gloved finger up the patient's rectum, hauling out great chunks of hideously malodorous feces. Biotto refused, one Friday, to end his week by disimpacting a gomer.

They were on morning rounds, with the medical students, nurses, and interns trying to get to see all the patients at Iggy's breakneck pace, before Iggy had to leave the floor for Morning Report at the department office. Biotto was balking.

"This just isn't caring medicine," he said in a whine. "I hardly know Mr. Jones, I can't just stick my finger up his rectum. . . . It's so dehumanizing."

"Have you seen his flat plate?" asked Iggy impatiently.

"No."

"Go look at it," said Iggy. "He's got a belly full of stool; every

19

centimeter is packed. He'll feel more human as soon as you haul it out."

"But I mean it's dehumanizing for me," said Biotto. "I just can't relate to turning into a surrogate bowel movement, a digital laxative. It just blows my mind. A complete turn-off."

"Biotto," said Iggy, "I can understand how you feel. But just remember"—Iggy paused to meet Biotto's yellow-tinted eyes with his own hollowed-out pair—"it's the patient who suffers."

Within the first two weeks of internship every intern had learned to hate that phrase. Biotto and Ryan shuddered whenever it was trotted out. "It's the patient who'll suffer" meant "It's your turn to suffer again."

Iggy had been in the class ahead of Ryan in medical school, and had a reputation for insight. Ryan didn't know much more about him than that, then. Now Ryan spent fourteen hours a day trailing after him. The interns arrived at 7:30 in the morning to draw bloods. When there were medical students around to help, they were finished by 8:00. That's when Iggy arrived, and rounds began. The students, interns, the head nurse, and Iggy moved bed to bed, room to room, down the hall, relentlessly.

Iggy allowed each intern thirty seconds to interview his patient and sixty to examine him, then took two minutes listing the tests and X-ray studies needed to complete the patient's investigation. Then they all moved on. It wasn't easy to interview a patient in thirty seconds. Few patients are inclined to confine any answer to less than twenty-five minutes, which meant the interview had to be directed. "Chest pain? Short of breath?" When the patient had exhausted his allotted time, he was silenced by a tongue depressor and "Say, 'Ah!' " and examined.

The group always reached the nursing station, at the middle of the hall, by 8:30, and they made the far end of the hall by 8:50, at which point Iggy ran back to the nursing station, scooped the charts on the new patients from the metal chart rack, and disappeared off to Morning Report, at the department office, leaving Ryan and Iggy with long lists of things to do. Ryan usually went right to the phone; his calls could take half an hour.

"First the telephone, then the stethoscope, then the X-ray

20

requisition, then the brain, in that order," Iggy had said. "The intern's most important equipment."

Biotto had other ideas.

"I'm not going to be turned into a computer," said Biotto, "and I'm not going to relate to patients as a disimpacting finger. You've got to get into seeing them as whole humans."

Biotto had a following, of sorts, in the person of one Jason Adams, a medical student, who also came from California, and apparently understood whatever it was Biotto was saying. Jason would murmur "I can relate to that" to almost everything Biotto said. It was driving Iggy and Ryan crazy. Jason followed Biotto around devotedly.

Instead of going directly to make his phone calls after morning rounds, Biotto went to the conference room for coffee with the nurses. But Biotto needed some time for himself. He needed to reestablish his own space, to get in touch with himself after an hour of concentrating on other people's bowel habits and backaches.

"What Biotto really needs," said Iggy, "is to learn proper English."

6

July 14, Attending Rounds

Diana Hayes had taken Morning Report, instead of Maxwell Baptist. Baptist, at least, had the virtue of never listening to the case presentations. Iggy shuddered, seeing Hayes: Iggy had to present three cases Biotto had admitted and mishandled the night before. Baptist would never have noticed, but Diana Hayes caught every omission.

"Well, new interns," Diana had said, after making Iggy squirm through the presentations. She made all the residents, so recently interns themselves, squirm.

"A real pecking order," said one of the other residents, after it was all over.

"The only thing worse than a program where they watch every move you make," said Iggy, still sweating, and straightening his tie, "is one where they don't."

Iggy got back from Report by ten, replaced the charts of the new admissions back in the rack, already thinking about the next round of accountability, Attending Rounds. A few minutes later Frank Wright appeared. Frank wore crepe soles; interns could never hear him coming: they just looked up, and there he was. As chief resident, Frank was overseer of overseers.

He made Iggy very nervous.

"He's finished his residency," Iggy whispered to Ryan. "He could be doing a fellowship, or he could be out in practice. But he's still here!" Iggy's eyes grew wide. "He's prowling around in white pants and a short white coat, reading intern workups, reading my workups!"

Iggy looked over his shoulder, looking for Frank. "Going over

22

sick patients at two A.M. with wild-eyed, sleep-deprived, guilt-ridden, hate-filled interns."

Iggy's eyes shifted. "Interns only put up with him because he's up at two A.M., and he's already done his internship, and you know what that means."

"He's crazy?" said Ryan.

"Of course!" barked Iggy, hoarsely. "He's even crazier than the interns he hounds. He's downright certifiable."

Monday, Wednesday, and Friday, the ward attending arrived at 10:30 for Visit Rounds, also called Attending Rounds, also called The-What-Did-You-Neglect Show. It was one of the many reviews upon review of patient care at the Tower. Jason Adams asked Iggy about Attending Rounds. Jason wasn't sure what an attending was, much less Attending Rounds.

"Every ward patient has to be presented to the attending, the morning after he's admitted," Iggy told him. "The attending, poor sucker, has legal responsibility for whatever we do to the patients."

"But who are the attendings?"

"Two varieties," said Iggy, his hollow eyes widening. "The ones in the Brooks Brothers suits are privates: they all have private practices of their own."

"Then why do they want to do rounds with us?"

"Who said they *want* to round with us? In this world, people have to do things they may not enjoy. In the case of the privates, being a ward attending is dues-paying."

"Oh," said Jason, not understanding.

Iggy was off and running now. "The privates have been granted the inestimable privilege of admitting patients to this hospital, where the select house staff you see around you work their tails off, on the private service, taking stellar care of their patients. When you're an attending at the Tower, with four or five sick patients in the house, you don't have to rouse yourself to deal with patients, sick as stink, at four A.M."

"No?" said Jason.

"Of course not," said Iggy happily, "the house staff does it. Then, at a more humane hour, they call you and say, 'I've done

23

the blood cultures, the spinal tap, gotten the chest X ray. Thank you for the privilege of allowing me to do all this, at four in the fuckin' morning.' "

Jason Adams blinked. Iggy went on.

"In the sticks, at the community hospitals, with no house staff, guess who the nurses call?"

"The privates?" asked Jason, horrified.

"You're learning," snapped Iggy. "So the privates here are only too happy to pay their dues by attending for a month on ward, a month on the private service, which means rounds Monday, Wednesday, and Friday, and by doing clinic once a week."

"What clinic?"

"Actually," shrugged Iggy, "they're not too keen on clinics."

Ryan, who had been taking this in silently, opened his mouth, but closed it with a struggle.

"The clinics are another matter," Iggy said. "In the Department of Internal Medicine, every private has to work in either General Medical Clinic or in a subspecialty, like cardiology or endocrine. They aren't real good about showing up."

"And the other variety?"

"The full-timers," said Iggy impatiently. "No private practice. Salaried." That dispensed with the full-timers, to Iggy's mind.

"Then what do they do with their . . . ?"

"They are paid by the medical school to teach embryos, like you, and to pour out papers, no matter what happens, to fill the journals."

"Like Diana Hayes?"

"Oh, you know Dr. Hayes?" said Iggy, peering at Jason Adams.

"I have a subscription to the *New England Journal,*" said Jason, proudly.

"Very good," said Iggy, with an irony which was lost on Jason.

"And *Lancet,* the *Annals,* and—"

"Enough!"

"Anyway," said Jason, chastened, "she's always got an article, every month, in one or another of them."

"That's her job," said Iggy. "Publish, whatever. Doesn't matter what it is."

"Heavy trip," said Biotto, who up to this point had shown no sign of being conscious. He had been sitting in the chair by the telephone, staring at his belt buckle.

"In some institutions," said Iggy, "the full-timers have all the power."

"What does power mean? I mean in the long run?" said Biotto, abstractly, not to Iggy, but to the air. Iggy ignored this.

"At the Tower, it's the privates in the saddle. They fill the beds. Filled beds means bucks."

"And the full-timers?" asked Jason.

"A resource," said Iggy. "They do the assays and all the special procedures. Like Hayes, your hero: any private wants a cath or an echo or a thallium stress on a patient, has to call Dr. Hayes. So the full-timers have some leverage. But the privates bring in the bucks."

"What difference does it make?" said Biotto. "Iggy, you're so into power."

"Well," shrugged Iggy, "it means you're civil to privates. But with most of them you would be anyway."

"They're okay?" said Jason.

"Most of 'em came up through this program," said Iggy. "You can't be a klunker and get privileges at the Great White Tower. Like us, they're a select bunch. Not quite as select, of course. But they're no dummies."

"And rich," said Biotto, with no little irony.

"That, too," said Iggy happily. "Exclusiveness has its rewards. Rich and smart. They don't miss much, especially if you screw up on one of their private patients. But don't mess up on the ward patients either. Attendings have a way of smelling it. Even when they're just paying their dues on the wards, they're always watching."

Ryan was amazed how infrequently the attendings thought of any possibilities Iggy had missed. They always tried to catch the house staff, but Iggy had Ryan and Biotto a step ahead.

"And what was the serum magnesium?" the attending asked, slyly, sure the serum magnesium would never have been thought of.

"One point nine," Ryan replied, as though knowing serum

magnesium levels was routine. Ryan, of course, had never thought of magnesium deficiency in his alcoholic patient. Iggy had thought of it. Iggy had asked about it on Morning Rounds. Ryan had not ordered the test.

"Draw the blood now! Run it up to the lab yourself, as soon as we finish," Iggy had screamed. "He'll ask. You can bet your ass, he'll ask."

"How can you get into that?" Biotto asked the breathless Ryan, just returned from the dash to the chemistry lab. "That whole one-upsmanship scene," sniffed Biotto.

"Can't relate to that one-upsmanship scene," echoed Jason Adams, softly.

Ryan looked from Biotto to Jason, and didn't know where to begin.

"It's not just for the Visit," said Ryan. "I forgot the magnesium. I should have thought of it. Iggy was right . . ."

"Guilt trip," said Biotto, shaking his head sadly. "He's got you turned in on yourself. Everybody forgets. You'll know next time. Why knock yourself out running to the chem lab?"

"Self-excoriation," volunteered Jason Adams, medical student.

"Exactly," said Biotto, looking approvingly at Jason. "Hair shirt."

Maxwell Baptist strode into the Diagnostic Cardiology Suite as Diana was advancing a catheter into the aortic valve of one of Sidney Cohen's private patients. Diana was concentrating on the pressure monitor above the cath table, and Baptist watched her, arms crossed, from a corner.

"Be right with you," said Diana, never taking her eyes off the screen.

The patient looked over at Baptist. Baptist smiled reassuringly. The patient looked back at the monitor Dr. Hayes was so intent upon.

"Just wanted to say thanks for taking Morning Report for me," said Baptist. "I hate to have to miss it this time of year, with all the new—"

"No problem. No problem at all . . ." said Diana Hayes, obviously distracted. She glanced at Baptist, and asked with a smile if he would mind putting on a lead apron. She wanted to shoot some rapid-fire X rays of the valve. Baptist did as he was bid.

Diana stepped on the fluoroscopy pedal. The catheter could be seen abutting the orifice of the left main coronary artery. Diana gave the word and a technician Baptist hadn't noticed injected a few milliliters of contrast, while Diana fluoroscoped.

"Okay," she said, "roll 'em."

Baptist said, "Well, I can see you're busy . . ."

"We've got to step out for a second now, anyway," she said, guiding him out the door. The technician stepped behind the lead screen, leaving the patient looking around in the suddenly vacated room.

"Hold your breath," Diana called back into the room. She was in the hallway, with Baptist.

"It went just fine," she told him. "The residents were all thoroughly intimidated, of course. They're a good lot. Some of the interns have to be watched, though."

"That's what the residents are there for," said Baptist.

"And who watches the residents?"

"We do," said Baptist. "And the chief resident."

"They'll do fine," said Diana, disappearing back into the cath room. Baptist could hear her say "Breathe!" as the door swung closed behind her.

Baptist went back to his office, down the hall, and paged Frank Wright.

"How's it going?" he asked Frank.

Frank never knew what to do with such open-ended questions. He knew something specific had prompted it.

"It's July," said Frank.

"The interns have things under control?"

"So far."

"Keep after them, Frank," said Baptist, hanging up, raising Frank's already phenomenal anal sphincter tone another thirty millimeters of mercury.

27

7

July 14, On Call

Visit Rounds ended at noon. That gave Ryan three hours to attend to his patients, and see new admissions, on days he was admitting. Then at the stroke of three Iggy appeared again for X-ray Rounds. That took one hour, during which the radiologists went over whatever X rays patients on B-7 had that day. Iggy loved "Ray Rounds." "It's so clean," he said, straightening his spotless tie. "They never touch the patient."

After X-ray Rounds Ryan and Biotto dragged Iggy out of the air-conditioned Diagnostic Radiology Suite and back to the floor. On B-7 they sat in front of the chart rack and did Chart Rounds. They checked all the lab results, which the scribes had inked into the patients' charts during the day as the results flowed back from the various laboratories. The Manhattan Hospital hired scribes to spare the interns the onerous task of charting lab values.

"When you're at the Tower, you don't have to diddle," Iggy said.

After Chart Rounds Ryan chased after missing data and checked his patients over before he went home, if he was not on call.

On nights he was on call, it was different. The intern on call for the night takes care of all the admissions from Morning Rounds until the next morning. By six or seven the other interns sign out their problem patients to the intern on call, and by seven thirty the resident leaves; by eight the intern on call is desperately alone.

With luck Ryan got to dinner when he was on call. With a lot more luck he got to eat what was on his tray before his beeper went off with news of the next admission. It took a week for Ryan to learn to eat dessert first, not to miss it, should his beeper call him to the Emergency Room.

Throughout the evening, admissions rolled in through the Emergency Room. Each was assigned, in turn, to a separate floor, depending on whether or not the patients were private or ward. The object was to get each workup done on each admission before the next one rolled in, and before Frank Wright came by.

By midnight Ryan was finishing his note on his third admission, and hoping to get to bed. But interns do not go to bed until all the admissions are completely worked up. And no admission was completely worked up until Frank had gone over the note, the lab values, the X rays, and the physical exam with the intern. Wednesday night Ryan felt fairly secure: he had four admissions: three middle-aged men with chest pain, who were "rule out M.I.'s" (question of heart attack), and one confused, demented, diabetic old bird named Mrs. Whiting, who kept insisting that she was at the bakery, and could not understand why Ryan kept asking so many questions. Ryan had her confusion workup all in place. You name it, he had done it.

Ryan was ready. Ryan was downright eager. Frank came by and looked at the chart, while Ryan eyed him expectantly.

"What's her blood sugar?" asked Frank.

Ryan had not thought to draw a blood sugar, although now that Frank had mentioned it, the patient was on insulin, and hypoglycemia has been known to confuse old ladies on insulin.

"Hasn't come back from the lab," said Ryan.

"You'll let me know?" said Frank.

Ryan ran right in as soon as Frank left, and drew the blood sugar. Then he pushed in fifty milliliters of fifty percent glucose solution intravenously. Thirty seconds later Mrs. Whiting knew she was in a hospital and was performing like a mental giant on all the mental status tests she had earlier failed so miserably. The blood sugar came back at forty, a very low level.

Ryan was dazzled by the miracle of IV glucose, the celerity and drama of its power. He had to share the triumph of the glucose with someone, and not wanting to wake Iggy, paged Frank. As he waited for Frank to call back, Ryan felt his elation crash through a black hole twisting somewhere deep in his duodenum. He had blown it. Had it not been for Frank, Mrs. Whiting would still be a baffling goon, instead of the sweet little old dear eating her midnight meal. Ryan grabbed her chart, flipped to his list of diagnostic possibilities, and plummeted even deeper: Frank had added "hypoglycemia" to the end of the list.

Frank rang.

"Good job," he told Ryan, without a trace of reproach, "you saved her." Ryan hung up, excoriating himself. Frank had saved her. Ryan had just been there to do something any third-year medical student should have remembered. And Frank had been kind about the oversight, at twelve thirty in the morning, when anyone who had already paid his dues should have been asleep.

Ryan found himself admitting a confused renal dialysis patient at 2:00 A.M. The patient was a little delirious, and it took a nurse and an aide to hold him down for the spinal tap, but Ryan knew Frank would be around to ask about the workup, and Ryan had everything in place, except for the spinal tap. Ryan had done everything he could think of which might be in any way relevant.

By the time Frank came by, Ryan had counted the cells in the spinal fluid, gram-stained it, and was attempting to do an India ink stain, looking for a parasite called cryptococcus, which likes to live in the spinal fluid and brains of immunosuppressed patients. But India ink stains are tricky and Ryan had ruined three before Frank arrived. Ryan presented the case, and Frank asked about the India ink stain.

"I was just going to look at it," said Ryan, hoping his fourth attempt had been successful.

"This stain is worthless," said Frank, looking through the microscope.

Frank tried three times, himself, before the stain was finally right: it was negative for cryptococcus.

"When was the last case of cryptococcal meningitis at The Manhattan Hospital?" asked Ryan.

"Two years ago, I think," said Frank.

"Then why did we just spend an hour, at two A.M., looking for a bug we haven't seen for two years?"

"Because if we ever see it again it'll be in an immunosuppressed patient, like this one. And if this guy had it, it'd kill him," said Frank, leaning back in his chair and lighting a cigarette, reflecting. "It's called the pursuit of excellence."

8

Tuesday, July 18

B-7 was one of seven floors in Manhattan Hospital which constituted the "private service." Every patient on the private service had a private doctor, or "private attending," who had admitted the patient, and who hovered around while the interns and residents tried to discover what was wrong and decided what to do for him. Since it was the private who got sued if anything went wrong, or sometimes even if nothing went wrong, the privates tended to hover frantically, raising the level of anxiety on the wards, which in July was already pretty high.

The private service was slow in July. The privates knew better than to admit during that month. Ryan had only five notes to write. He would be admitting Wednesday. He wanted to get the notes done and get home early, to sleep. By six o'clock he was beginning his fifth patient. The attending, Hyman Bloomberg, had admitted a forty-year-old interior decorator with diarrhea and weight loss. The patient, Peter Brown, was a good-looking man, with eyes made more prominent by his ten-pound weight loss.

He hadn't traveled, but he said his diarrhea was the worst since a case of turista he had ten years ago in Spain.

"Have you had contact with anyone who just got back from tropical areas?"

"Well, I did make love with a young lieutenant, just back from Vietnam," he said. "But he wasn't ill."

"Oh," said Ryan, who was halfway down the hall, almost to the nursing station, when it registered:

"A *male* lieutenant?"

32

Frank was seated in front of the chart rack, reading one of Ryan's notes.

"Tell me about your patients," he said.

Ryan told him.

"What about this guy Brown?"

Ryan told him.

"What do you think he's got?"

"Could be GC proctitis, if he's homosexual."

"Bloomberg cultured for gonorrhea, already,"

"How'd you know that?"

"It's in his note," said Frank.

"I couldn't read his note: it's illegible."

"You'd better learn," said Frank. "What else could he have?"

"Can't think of much else, unless the soldier brought back a parasite."

"Bloomberg did stools for parasites."

"That in his note, too?"

"Yes."

"Well, I don't know, then."

"Try a duodenal aspirate. Sometimes you get a higher yield with that," said Frank. "Those stools for parasites usually get to the lab all dry and cold. They have to be warm and wet to be any good."

Frank handed Ryan the chart and left. Ryan felt smaller and smaller. Second-year medical students knew about duodenal aspirates. Thinking about what Frank had said, he felt himself disappearing into a dot.

Ryan had Peter Brown swallow a duodenal tube and took a specimen, warm and wet, to the micro lab. He wrote his note, putting in a line about the duodenal aspirate, and went home.

When the aspirate culture came back positive, Ryan telephoned Hyman Bloomberg with the news.

"You're a good man, Ryan," Hyman said, "to even think of doing an aspirate, even though I'd already sent stool for parasites. Gordio in the aspirate. And you took it to the lab before it cooled off and dried out. Gordio lumbus. Imagine that. A very good thought."

33

"Trouble is," said Ryan, hating himself for taking all the credit, "I still don't understand where he got it."

"I've had a sneaking suspicion that homosexuals pass it around among themselves," said Hyman. "But I've never seen a venereal transmission documented in the literature."

"Venereal Gordio?"

"All things are possible. I've had seven Gordio cases over the last two or three years, all in homosexuals," said Hyman. "Why don't we do a paper on it?"

"Wouldn't know how."

"Just call up medical records and ask them to pull every case with a discharge diagnosis of Gordio. Then go to Parasitology and have them show you the logs for every positive Gordio, and pull those charts. Most of them should overlap. Then check the charts, see how many are homosexual. If the chart doesn't say, call them in."

That all sounded like a lot of work, and Hyman remembered he was talking to an intern, still trying to keep his head above water.

"Look, Ryan, I'll call Records and Parasitology and have them pull the charts, in your name. You just go down twice a week and go through a few, keep tabs, and we'll write it up."

"Well, maybe when I get back from Whipple."

"When are you going to Whipple?"

"August," said Ryan. "I'll be there until October."

"What luck!" thundered Bloomberg, "I'll be attending over there in August. What floor you on?"

"Eight."

"My floor!" Bloomberg had gotten so loud Ryan had to hold the phone away from his ear.

"See you at Whipple. We'll talk all about it," said Bloomberg, and hung up.

34

9

July 21

Ryan was thinking about the splendid air conditioning in his study as he slogged homeward in the paralyzing July heat. He had the night off.

He got home at 7:00 P.M. He felt soiled. Arch's attaché case was in the hall, still open, as when Ryan left that morning. Ryan was bothered by the attaché case. He went down to Arch's rooms. Arch was alone in bed.

The light hurt his eyes: he buried his flushed, wet face in the pillow. The sheets were soaked. Arch's eyes looked hollow, and his pulse was racing.

"Worse damn diarrhea, nausea, and vomiting. Fever's got me so weak."

"At least you give a good history," said Ryan, who took Arch's blood pressure sitting and lying. Ryan disappeared, but was back in minutes with a plastic IV bag.

"I don't need all that shit," groaned Arch, too weak to put up serious resistance. Within five minutes Ryan had D5W with potassium, magnesium, and vitamins running into Arch's vein. Ryan pushed some Compazine into the IV, and ten minutes later Arch could swallow aspirin without vomiting. Within an hour Arch was feeling like living.

"I think I can even sleep," he said.

When he awoke, Ryan made him swallow Compazine, aspirin, Lomotil, and chicken soup. He got Arch out of bed and changed the sheets. He pulled the IV out after a liter had run in. By 4:00 A.M. Arch had broken fever. When he awoke at seven, there was a note from Ryan:

"Stay in bed. Drink six quarts of water before I get back tonight. Finish the three cans of soup on the kitchen table. Take Compazine and two aspirin every six hours. I called Jane." Jane was Arch's chronic disease.

She was there when Ryan got home that evening.

"It was all I could do to keep him in bed. But he says he's okay. He's just so weak. What'd he have?"

"Nothing fatal," said Ryan. "Just a virus."

"He keeps saying how you cured him in an hour."

"Wonders of modern medicine: Compazine and aspirin."

"You may not think much of them," said Arch, coming into the room, "but I was dying. After a few pills and the IV, I was back among the living."

"You still look out of it," said Ryan.

"He looks like a dehydrated bear," said Jane.

"I weighed myself when I got up. I was down ten pounds. I've gained back four since this morning, just drinking."

"You keep drinking until you get back the other six."

"Hell no; that's the quickest diet I ever had."

"Until you can stand up without getting dizzy, do what I tell you."

"How'd you know I was dizzy?"

Ryan knew because he was a great doc. Arch told everybody that. Ryan, of course, knew better.

During four years at The Manhattan Hospital's university medical school Ryan came to believe the prevailing gospel that The Manhattan Hospital was, in fact, the Pinnacle, everywhere else being "Elsewhere General," otherwise known as the "minor leagues."

The great Boston hospitals, of course, were well known to The Manhattan Hospital house staff, but they were in *Boston,* two hundred miles from the Big Apple, a fact which spoke for itself.

Manhattan Hospital was a prestigious internship, which should have been Ryan's clue to avoid it: the medical school was prestigious too, which was about all it had to offer. But Ryan listed the Tower first on his computerized matching form, and got it.

36

Besides, staying at the Tower meant he could stay in the town house with Arch. And when he wasn't at the hospital, or in his study at the town house, he could go watch women at Bloomie's. The town house was exceptional. He got the top two floors, Arch the bottom two, and they shared the middle, which had the kitchen and dining room.

Ryan had spent the twenty days between medical school graduation and internship getting organized, which amazed Arch, who thought Ryan was already distressingly organized: Ryan's socks were folded neatly in the top dresser drawer, arranged by color (blacks to browns to grays to white). His closet was worse: shirts were blue to white. Arch got nauseated just looking at the drawer or opening the closet. Ryan became acutely disoriented, and somewhat light-headed, if the order was disrupted.

Arch celebrated Ryan's internship selection with a big party for all their friends. A lot of lawyers from Arch's firm came. That was fine with Ryan, who had few friends of his own. Ryan liked Arch's friends because they talked about nothing but law firms. Ryan loved law firms: they were so tribal. Arch's friends saved their best stories for Ryan.

As far as Arch was concerned, his best hours were spent reading on the couch in Ryan's study, with Ryan at his own station, behind his desk.

About two days after his virus Arch was sipping lemonade on the couch, with his *Wall Street Journal.* Ryan was reading about experiments with eye-patching in kittens, in which one eye was patched, subsequently uncovered, and found to be blind.

"Then they patched *both* eyes of each kitten, and unpatched them, and what do you suppose they found?" asked Ryan.

"How should I know?"

"Well, if one eye patched went blind, what should two patched eyes do?"

"Well, I don't understand why patching the one eye blinded it in the first place; unless they pressed too hard or something."

"Arch, sometimes you amaze me. Because you are profoundly ignorant of medical thinking, you cannot be sucked in; you are not impeded by a set of shared assumptions. Thus, you're capable of formulating precisely the right question."

Arch wasn't sure whether he had been complimented or insulted. But Ryan was standing on his chair, looking as though he might take flight any moment, so Arch kept listening.

"I assumed the patched eye went blind because the brain segment which receives that eye's signals had been unstimulated for so long: atrophy."

"So why *did* it go blind?"

"The solution is in what happened to the two patched eyes: neither went blind!" shrieked Ryan, barely able to contain himself, dropping back into the seat.

"It wasn't atrophy at all! What emerged was the concept of the dominant cerebral hemisphere: the mechanism for the blindness in one eye had to do with one part of the brain gaining dominance over the other."

Ryan's fingers were tapping wildly on his desk blotter, his eyes wide and dilated.

Arch considered how many great thoughts had been stimulated by cruelty to animals.

Arch actually welcomed Ryan's spasms of medical enthusiasm: apart from an occasional deep sigh, they were the only indication Ryan was still awake, and when Arch read his *Wall Street Journal,* he wanted Ryan awake. He liked to bounce ideas off Ryan, who had absolutely no interest in finance.

"Think I should buy some Textron?"

"Why not?" said Ryan, without looking up from the *New England Journal of Medicine.* Arch got some of his best advice like that. It was a productive place, Ryan's study. And it was comfortable, the only place under Ryan's control unafflicted by his unbearable order.

"It's the only place that isn't at all like the rest of Ryan," Arch said.

And it was where Ryan spent the most time, sitting at his desk, listening to Brahms or Joe Cocker, tying knots in surgical silk, and reading eclectically.

10

July 25

Every Tuesday afternoon Ryan paid for his weekly sins in a special form of purgatory, called "General Medicine Clinic." Except when rotating on the Intensive Care Unit rotations, or in the Emergency Room, every house officer had to see hostile patients, once a week, in the GMC.

It wouldn't have been so bad, except for the undermanning. The clinics had a full complement of doctors scheduled each day: six house officers and six private attending physicians. Trouble was, the attendings often didn't show, or if they did, they came late enough to exhaust the endurance of the patients, who had long since stomped out.

Ryan was looking over the list of his six patients when the clinic nurse, Myra, handed him a second list, with six more names.

"You'll have to take Dr. Monelli's patients today. He can't make it."

"Can't make it?"

"He's tied up at his office."

"These patients are his problem," said Ryan. "Don't make them mine."

Myra looked defeated.

"His secretary called five minutes ago. They scheduled patients for him in his office, for this afternoon, by mistake. He can't come."

"His mistake, my problem."

"Sorry."

"No, Myra," said Ryan, *"I'm* sorry. I can't keep my patients waiting because Monelli made a mistake. I've got my resident upstairs covering for me, trying to keep the lid on things until I get back, and now you're telling me I'm going to be here twice as long."

"When you're not in the clinic someone covers for you."

Myra had been dealt a bad hand, and was trying to play anyway.

"When I'm going to be out, you'll know months in advance. Patients aren't scheduled for me."

"Someone's got to see these patients."

"Don't give me Monelli's problem."

"Why don't you call Monelli, Mr. Hard-ass?"

"I just work here," said Ryan.

"Then do what you're told."

"What's Monelli's number?"

Myra gave it to Ryan, who went to the phone. Myra was sick of this fight. She had it five times a week. But Ryan had the reputation of a warrior, and this time she might see some action.

Ryan began to dial, then heard Arch's voice, "Low profile. Silence is golden."

Ryan's hand was poised over the phone. He could feel all eyes in the conference room fixed on him: Myra dared him with her eyes; Biotto and his shadow, Jason Adams, were studying him too.

"I'm right, aren't I?" said Ryan to Biotto.

"Anger is self-destructive," said Biotto. "Lay back a little. Just go with the flow."

"There's a waiting room full of patients out there," said Ryan. "They're the ones who're really getting screwed."

"You can see six more patients," said Biotto.

"Not in less than two more hours."

Biotto's eyes grew wide. "Six patients?" Biotto laughed. "Fifteen minutes." Jason Adams smiled benignly.

"What?" laughed Ryan, not understanding.

"Biotto's got extra patients today too," said Myra.

"How're you gonna take six histories, do six physicals, order tests, make reappointments, in fifteen minutes?" Ryan shouted.

"Who does all that?" shrugged Biotto.

"Who does less?"

"Hell," said Biotto, voice of experience, laying it on the line to callow youth, "none of these patients is sick, not like what we've got on the wards. What they need is someone to relate to their problems, to listen to them."

"You don't examine them?"

"Most of 'em don't need it."

"What do you do, then?"

"I listen," said Biotto. "I relate."

"For two and a half minutes a patient?"

"You have to set limits," shrugged Biotto.

"I don't know about your patients," said Ryan, "but I find a lot who need more than hand-holding."

"Hey, don't get hostile."

"I'm not hostile," roared Ryan, "I'm pissed."

He grabbed the phone and dialed page. He had Frank Wright on the line in three minutes.

"Ryan," said Frank impatiently, "what is it this time?"

"Dr. Monelli didn't show for clinic. Three other attendings didn't show. This place is a mess. We need some attendings."

"Did you talk to the PCM?"

"Frank, in four years of medical school here, doing clinic every week since the clinical years, I haven't yet seen the PCM."

"If you went to medical school here," said Frank, "then you know the chain of command: problem in the clinic, call the PCM."

"The PCM is never around," said Ryan.

"Then go to the next link in the chain."

"I did: I called you."

Frank laughed. "Thanks for the promotion, big boy, but the next guy to call is Baptist."

He hung up.

"What'd he say?" said Biotto.

"I should call the PCM."

"Good idea," said Biotto, who loved the PCM, or primary care man, even though Biotto had never seen the PCM in clinic

41

either. The PCM had given Grand Rounds the first week of internship, and Biotto had related.

"I really got off on what he had to say," Biotto reminisced. "I really have to hand it to Baptist for attracting a guy like that to The Manhattan Hospital."

Baptist was aware of the mess in clinics. He had handled it, in his own fashion. He had hired someone else to worry about it. The clinic director had billed himself as a "primary care man." Ryan had once asked him what that meant, and received a rambling, jargon-filled response, from which he understood that the primary care man decried the cutting up of patients into various organ systems by subspecialists. The primary care man wanted to see the patient as a whole human. His eyes filled with hot tears over technology elbowing its obstructive, dehumanizing way into medicine. He apologized to Ryan, and almost everyone who would listen, for medical hardware, and the trappings of medical professionalism. He wore a turtleneck sweater under his lab coat.

Nobody had ever seen him in clinic. The primary care man had spent the time since his arrival organizing studies which revealed: 1. Patients hate clinic. 2. Doctors hate clinic. 3. Patients want prescriptions from doctors. 4. Patients do not mind filling out questionnaires.

The primary care man presented these findings at Grand Rounds, and disappeared. He hated being faced with clinic patients. It was excruciating, sitting in the office with them, listening to their incomprehensible stories, absorbing their fears and hostilities, trying to think of them as whole human beings, when, in fact, it was easier thinking of them as problems.

The clinic was a pit.

"You gonna call the PCM?" asked Myra.

"Where is he?"

"Haven't seen him in weeks."

"Guess not, then."

"So, now what?" she pressed.

"So I can call Baptist, or see the patients."

"So?" asked Myra. "Which will it be?"

So instead of six angry, hostile patients, burning with resentment and smoldering with fear, he had to see twelve even angrier, more hostile patients, who resented the even longer wait, and who would have to miss buses home, and travel after dark, and who would hate Ryan for it.

11

July 27

Ryan had to spend his night off preparing a case presentation for Professor's Rounds, with St. John. Maxwell Baptist, chairman of the Department of Medicine, was called "St. John," of course.

Ryan had to present to St. John, and he wanted to do it right. Not that he thought St. John would know the difference: nobody thought St. John was much of a clinician.

He had been an immunologist, puttering around some lab at Columbia, mixing antibodies and antigens, when Manhattan Hospital was looking for a chairman for its Department of Medicine. Government money was going to research in those days; it was hoped that St. John could attract some of it. And he had stumbled across some abnormal immune profiles for a kidney disease which turned out to be quite common. The disease was named for him, "Baptist nephritis." So he had credentials.

Ryan had to present because he had admitted a patient with "Baptist nephritis." Once a month some luckless intern had to present to Baptist. The cases were presented as unknowns, and the professor was supposed to make the diagnosis. The residents chose Ryan's case because they thought it was the only case Baptist had any hope of recognizing: if there was one diagnosis Baptist ought to be able to make, it had to be Baptist nephritis. Besides, it reassured the chairman that the house staff had not forgotten his disease. And it would give Baptist an opportunity to say "When I invented nephritis."

It was a chance to kiss ass.

But something had happened to Ryan's capacity to kiss ass. It had been happening since medical school, and it had something to do with all those glowing expectations from high school onward. He had attained what everyone thought him most likely to attain—success, but it had a slightly rancid smell. Ryan had an inkling that his little outbursts of rectitude had something to do with all those sullied expectations. Ryan felt as though he had been kissing ass his entire postpubescent life, and he was beginning to wonder why. Anyway, Ryan thought Baptist's was the wrong ass to kiss: some committee made the decision on who got cut or kept on. St. John didn't know anyone's name anyway. He always had to look at the name tags. How could it matter what he thought of you, if he didn't know who you were? That's why Ryan never wore his name tag.

Name tags were worn on the white jackets, and there was a rule that white jackets be worn whenever St. John was on the floor, or in the immediate vicinity. The jackets were hot, and a bother. But he wasn't around that much, so it wasn't much of a problem.

He hid in his office, guarded by a secretary. If you wanted to see him, you needed an appointment. The secretary placed your folder on his desk, so Baptist would know to whom he was talking. Nobody really wanted to talk to St. John.

The only time most house officers saw him was at these case presentations once a month, at the Christmas party, and at Grand Rounds. And of course, at the end of the year, around December, if you didn't make the cut, you got called to see St. John.

St. John was a striking-looking man. Ryan thought that he looked more like a general than a doctor; he never seemed to want to hear what anyone was saying. He appeared to be listening for good news but forever hearing only bad. Infrequently, he would hear what he wanted to hear, and raise his hand, stop the speaker, and repeat the good words.

But mostly he looked disturbed, and hunted. He was tall and broad shouldered, with graying temples and prominent cheekbones, and an imperious nose. He had gotten more striking with age, with weathered skin adding to his becoming gauntness.

45

Ryan read his biography in the catalog: St. John was in his early fifties, which meant that he was made chairman as a youngster, in his early forties. The house staff said that he had passed his prime before he was made chairman. If that were true, then he had peaked young. Conventional wisdom was that he was just awaiting emeritus-ship and senility. His "productive life" was over, Ryan heard, which meant that Baptist had stopped publishing.

That all seemed a little narrow-minded to Ryan, who supposed there must be something left to a chairman's life, once the thrill of publishing had burned out: like running a good department.

Baptist had chosen talented lieutenants, so he really didn't have to do anything but hide in his office. The department moved without him. He had brought good people with him from Columbia, so many, in fact, that the attendings at Manhattan grumbled that The Manhattan Hospital was becoming nothing more than a "Columbia East." Not that that would have been a bad thing, but there was a traditional rivalry between Columbia Presbyterian and The Manhattan Hospital; the influx was viewed with suspicion.

The invasion from the West Side had brought mainly good people, though; the only really weak division left was Cardiology, where a mediocre chief was entrenched and unremovable. Even there, Baptist had managed to bring over Diana Hayes to be head of Diagnostic Cardiology, effectively undermining the chief of Cardiology, and assuring first-rate diagnostics.

So if he had done nothing else, which is about what he had done, he had organized a solid core of talented people, and built an admirable department. Some said it was the best in the city.

Whatever credit Ryan gave Baptist for Baptist's earlier accomplishments, Ryan was not happy about having to spend a night off preparing a case to present him. And as Ryan worked over the patient's chart, he became somewhat disquieted; he was even moved to go to the library and read.

46

He read Baptist's original article on Baptist nephritis. He read more recent reviews. He read until he could no longer resist the idea: the patient did not have Baptist nephritis at all. The patient had run-of-the-mill nephritis. The patient met only two of eight diagnostic criteria for Baptist nephritis: a compatible biopsy, and a high level of a nonspecific antibody.

Chairman's Rounds, July 28

The next day the assembled residents, interns, medical students, and nurses filed into the solarium to hear Dr. Baptist's wisdom. He arrived with a retinue of assistant chief residents, Frank, assorted sycophants, and some visiting professor from Greece who spoke little English but who had come to spend time in the master's presence.

Ryan handed the chart to Dr. Baptist, and presented the case. Baptist listened, more attentively than usual, scrutinizing. Ryan watched the initial interest in Baptist's face fade by the time Ryan got to talking about the lab results.

The patient was wheeled in, grateful to have been chosen as a case for the chairman. He was examined and dismissed. They looked at the X rays, and at the biopsy. Baptist pronounced it a case of Baptist nephritis, and monotoned his standard lecture, which bored even him, but never said, "When I invented nephritis," which was the only thing anyone wanted to hear.

Then came question period. Ryan sat there, squirming against his own verbal urges. He twisted as another intern kissed Baptist up. Finally, Ryan raised his hand. He recited the eight criteria from Baptist's paper, pointed out, his voice wavering only a little, that this patient met only two, and politely asked why the diagnosis had been made.

Anxiety was palpable among the house staff. Frank Wright was suppressing a smile. Ryan was shaking, but delighted with himself. Baptist handled it with a sniff.

"Some criteria are more important than others. If checking off criteria on lists was all there was to clinical judgment, then we could leave patient care to medical students and interns."

The assemblage laughed and clapped, much relieved.

Ryan's elation was still cresting at lunch, when Frank sought him out in the cafeteria.

"Ryan, the answer to your question is, 'There's no business like show business.' "

Ryan laughed, but Frank cut him off.

"Just remember, there's still a pyramid at the Tower, and Maxwell Baptist has a composite photo of the interns in his office. Every month he puts a black mark on somebody's picture."

"No guts, no glory," said Ryan.

Frank smiled. "Make it to junior resident first, big boy."

12

July 31

As Ryan's resident, it was Iggy Bart's job to inspire, protect, instruct and keep Ryan from killing his patients during his first month of internship. Iggy's first announcement was his intention to go into radiology just as soon as he finished his internal medicine residency.

"Rads are good money and nice hours, but you'll miss the patient contact," Ryan told him sagely.

"That's the best part of it," said Iggy.

Iggy sounded serious enough to shock Ryan; Iggy, after all, was a proven seer.

"How can you say that?" demanded Ryan.

"You'll say it too by the time your internship's over," said Iggy. "I know: you think the real reward is the grateful patient. You picture yourself walking down the street with your black bag, people saying 'There goes good ol' Doc Ryan,' " said Iggy, his eyes growing shrewd. "Well, what they're really saying is, 'There goes Doc Ryan: my husband's heart attack paid for his new sports car.' "

Ryan shut out Iggy's words angrily. But then there was Room 220. Room 220 had four hateful patients, and all belonged to Ryan. If ever there were four patients capable of proving Iggy right, they were in 220.

There was Mrs. White, a black woman with chest pain, recovering from a heart attack; Mrs. Cushing, with asthma; Mrs. Harvey, with alcoholism and bleeding; and Miss Osler, with disseminated gonorrhea. Ryan dreaded crossing that threshold.

Mrs. White maintained, at length, that her myocardial infarc-

49

tion was the fault of her private doctor. She had phoned him, complaining of chest pain, the morning of her attack, and he told her to see him that afternoon. By that afternoon she infarcted. What she neglected to say was that she had called him every third day for three months, just as she had called her two previous doctors, before they refused to see her again.

None of them cared about her. The people in the Cardiac Care Unit alternately ignored her or came close to killing her with their bumbling. Ryan avoided her. Her face was set and hard, and she never listened to a thing he said. Every morning at 2:00 A.M. she got chest pain. Ryan was summoned, groggy, to her bed. She was sweating, terrified, not at all sorry for Ryan, and sure that she was about to die. And every morning at 2:00 A.M. Ryan felt sorry for her, and did an EKG, examined her, and assured her that everything was normal, which she vehemently denied. She always demanded that a resident be called. What did Ryan know? He was only an intern, awake at 2:00 A.M., trying to be civil and sympathetic. She was pathetic, but a pain.

"She just gets uptight in this nonhuman plastic environment," said Biotto. "You just have to get into her head. I mean you have to think of her as vulnerable."

"Iggy can't stand her either," said Ryan, absently.

"Iggy has a button-down mind."

Mrs. Cushing, with asthma, was as compliant as Mrs. White was hostile. She was the only ward patient on the private floor, admitted there because Ryan had followed her in clinic, ever since medical school. She was the only patient for whom Ryan was solely responsible. She had recurrent asthmatic attacks, despite the welter of medications Ryan tried. One treatment after another went down to defeat, despite Ryan's enthusiastic predictions for success with each new regimen. Mrs. Cushing would smile knowingly and come back the next week, still wheezing. She took each new prescription with a tolerant smile. A week later she'd be back, asthma worse than ever, she was pleased to say. Ryan finally had her on such outlandish amounts of medication that her blood pressure skyrocketed, and he had to admit her for it. As he tapered the drugs, she started wheezing again.

"I knew this would happen," she gasped. Then she got phlebitis and had to be anticoagulated, which made her bleed into her bladder. Ryan doubted he would ever get her out of the hospital. She was pleased with each setback, patiently waiting for Ryan to fail, and forgiving him, needing him more and more as she fell before the complications of his therapy.

"Sorry about all these problems," he said.

"You try," she'd say sweetly.

Ryan was touched, but Miss Osler told him that Mrs. Cushing was not so forgiving when Ryan was out of the room.

Frank was reading charts at the nursing station when Ryan ran in to write some orders.

"Nice job you did on Mrs. Cushing."

"Yeah, she's breathing better today."

"I meant in clinic: she could have stroked out from all that stuff you pumped into her."

Ryan tried to say something, but so many explanations hit his tongue, it just stayed there, unable to move.

"St. John is coming by to review charts on this floor today. You'd better hide this one."

The thought of Baptist reviewing Mrs. Cushing's chart precipitated an immediate migraine in Ryan's left eye.

Miss Osler was Ryan's greatest supporter in Room 220, she was eager to point out. Ryan was initially mildly in love with her. She was a call girl, who had noticed a vaginal discharge about a week before her admission. Then her right hand began to ache whenever she tried to grip. Her right knee swelled and hurt. She shook with fever and chills and erupted with a red rash. She was convinced she was dying, the day Ryan admitted her.

Her blood culture grew out *Neisseria* gonorrhea, so Ryan started her on penicillin. She refused to believe that she had gonorrhea and, once convinced, refused to believe it could be cured. Within a day she was feeling much improved. She gave all the credit to Ryan. But every morning, just before Ryan was due for Attending Rounds, she'd start crying. Her illness overwhelmed her. Ryan would sit with her until he got paged to rounds.

"I know I'm such a baby."

"No, you're just not used to being sick."

"You really know where I'm coming from. . . ." Her voice trailed off.

But more and more Ryan was called to her bedside. She even learned how to page him from her bedside phone: her IV had infiltrated, and she wouldn't let anyone but Ryan change it. She could hardly bear the nights he wasn't on call, and she was left to the care of less sensitive healers. Ryan tried to avoid her.

"Bill"—she called him Bill—"I just want to know if it's something I've done or said," she asked tearfully.

"What?"

"You just seem to be avoiding me."

"It's just that my new admissions have been so sick. I've been pressed for time."

She became an ever-expanding demand, and he an exhaustible resource. Ryan began to count the days until her penicillin was done and she could be discharged. He put her off more and more, and she became hurt and surly.

Maxwell Baptist and Frank were on the ward, unannounced, and Ryan was coming out of a patient's room, wearing his tunic without his white coat. He almost ran into them.

"Good morning," he said.

"Morning," said Baptist, tightly.

"Bill!"

Baptist and Frank turned. Ryan could see past them: it was Miss Osler, in her hot pink nightgown, pulling her IV pole along the floor, its wheels creaking.

"Bill!" she wailed. "My IV's hurting my hand again."

"Be right with you, Miss Osler," said Ryan, emphasizing the *Miss*.

She went back to her room.

"Do all your patients call you by your first name?" asked Baptist.

It was one of those no-win questions.

"She read it on my name tag," said Ryan, pointing to the WILLIAM RYAN, M.D. on his tunic.

"Ryan," said Baptist.

"Yes, sir?"

"Why don't you put on your coat before going to attend to her."

Ryan looked from Baptist to Frank, and back again.

"Of course," said Ryan.

And then there was Mrs. Harvey. Mrs. Harvey was a chronic alcoholic with cirrhosis, who came in every few weeks, bleeding to death, narrowly saved by frantic interns through harrowing nights, only to go out and drink again. The cirrhosis caused increased resistance to blood flow through the liver; the gut blood trying to return to the heart gets diverted through esophageal veins, which swell and occasionally burst, gushing out liters in minutes.

She had that friendly, smiling, alcoholic personality which was thoroughly impenetrable. Ryan had a very long, serious talk with her before he discharged her the last time, and she vowed to abstain forever. But Ryan knew the chances of that. Her friends, all reeking of alcohol at midday, sat around her bed during visiting hours, talking about nothing but drinking. They knew each other by what they drank: Mrs. Harvey drank Gilbey's gin by the gallon.

She had come in a week before, stinking of gin, vomiting up foul-smelling, partially digested blood, before she really opened up and spewed forth the fresh blood from ruptured esophageal varices.

Fortunately, Iggy was on call covering Ryan that night.

"She looks like a ghost," Ryan told Iggy, "like she has one foot in the grave, the other here, in a pool of blood."

"Don't panic," said Iggy, smoothing his Pierre Cardin shirt.

"She's going to do it this time," said Ryan. "She's gonna go right down the tubes, and they're gonna ask me why at Death Rounds."

"Ryan," said Iggy, from the depths of his scrawny larynx, "sit down; repeat after me: 'I did not give this lady her disease.'"

Fifteen units of blood transfusions, and a Pitressin drip, began to turn the tide. Blood rushed out both ends: it washed over her chin and chest and out her rectum, so that she sat in a stagnant red pool. The blood from below was semi-stool, and the smell could knock even an intern senseless.

53

Ryan called the blood bank every four minutes to harass the poor technician, who was trying to type and cross the blood. The barrage of phone calls made the tech so nervous it took her twice as long. Ryan knew full well that even if the tech managed to keep up with Mrs. Harvey's varices this time, Mrs. Harvey would go right out and drink again, and bleed again, until she did it just a little too far from the hospital, where she'd finally drown in her own bleeding, or exsanguinate. But for her to go down the tubes right under Ryan's eyes, in a Manhattan Hospital bed, with Ryan's name on the chart, and with Baptist taking Morning Report the next morning, was unthinkable. Naturally it was all Ryan could think about.

No patient had bled out from a G.I. bleed at The Manhattan Hospital in five years, and Ryan was determined that no patient of his would break that record. So the tech got called every four minutes, and fifteen units poured into Mrs. Harvey, along with the Pitressin.

Ryan paused by a window and looked at the sun coming up over the East River in a pink blaze: it was a beautiful sunrise, a lovely morning. Mrs. Harvey would live to see it, through no effort of her own. She had cost Ryan one of life's greatest pleasures: a night's sleep.

Ryan looked over his four charges in Room 220, and could not truthfully say that he cared what any of them thought of him. But he did care about their care, their charts. He took pride in their management, whether or not it did them any good. Still, it wasn't what he had expected.

Mrs. Harvey looked at her bruised arms, heavy with tape and IV lines, and she complained about the bruises, and the pain, never mentioning how nice it was that her blood pressure line had never dipped below ninety, that her chart showed every unit of blood, every drop of Pitressin she had received. She was not at all impressed that Ryan had already interpreted her EKG, looked at her urine and clotting factors, and arranged for a barium swallow. If she permitted herself to realize that Ryan had saved her life once again, she wasn't thanking him.

13

August 1

In the short space of four and one half weeks, internship had taken Ryan from his normal state of mild mania to a very solid and overt depression. By the end of his third week on the private service, he had dispensed with compound sentences and just monotoned monosyllables.

Fortunately, Ryan had Arch. Someone had to know what he was going through. Biotto knew, but was little consolation. Ryan felt like whining, until he talked to Biotto.

"This internship," Biotto would say, "it's destroying the caring part of me." Biotto would cast a somber look through his yellow-tinted glasses, which somehow destroyed the effect, and drone, "I mean you have to deaden yourself to make it through the day. It just has to make you so insensitive."

Commiserating with Biotto was out.

Arch decided Ryan needed a break from the hospital, and its people, and told Ryan they were going to a local spa, away from the hospital and all that crowd. Ryan was sitting inert at his desk, in his jogging shorts and an old sweat shirt.

"Naw," said Ryan, "I'd have to change."

Arch dragged him out the door and over to Belinda's Place.

Nancy Damiani and Diana Hayes paused in the doorway of Gleason's Bar. It was dark inside, and their eyes needed to adjust.

"Oh," said Diana, when she regained her vision, "the place is crawling with house staff."

"I see a table," said Nancy, catching Diana's arm, and pulling her to the table.

"I feel as though I'm being visually undressed," said Diana.

"It *is* wonderful here," said Nancy.

"Well, I guess I'm out with the girls," said Diana. "Haven't done this in a while." She ordered a Manhattan.

"Well, you're out with me, I guess that qualifies. Haven't been out with the girls myself in ages. Vowed I'd never be caught in a bar with another woman after college. I spent my entire college career in bars with women."

"Where was that?" asked Diana, distractedly.

"Vassar nunnery."

"When were you there?"

"Class of '69."

"Oh, you are a youngster. And you spent your time in bars? I thought everyone spent the sixties in the streets, demonstrating."

"Well, I was a premed. Premeds went to the library and to bars. The FBI didn't mind if you went to bars. It wasn't un-American, and wouldn't be held against you when you applied to med school."

"You thought the FBI was on the admissions committee?"

"Hey, I was a premed, as in paranoia. Weren't you a premed?"

"Not until my senior year," said Diana, taking an ice cube into her mouth. "And those were gentler times, apparently."

"Where was that?" asked Nancy, as long as the door had been left partly open. Something about Diana kept Nancy from really pressing questions.

"Vassar."

"No kidding. I never knew," said Nancy, surprised Diana had not volunteered it. "What were you before you turned premed?"

"Chem major."

"Going to be a Ph.D.?"

"No danger of that. Chem labs seemed a dreadfully dull and cloistered place to spend one's life. Got to senior year and decided it was either a trip around the world, or something practical, like medical school."

"What decided you?" asked Nancy, hoping it was a man.

"A man," said Diana. "My father, actually. Said he wouldn't mind paying for an apartment on the Hudson if I wanted to go to Columbia, but he'd be damned if he'd have me galavanting around Paris."

"So you took him up on his offer?"

"New York seemed every bit as wonderful as Paris," said Diana, lighting a cigarette. "It was swell."

"You worked with Winthrop at Columbia?"

"Yes. Let me do all kinds of things to cats and rats."

"So you got into hearts in med school? You were a precocious thing."

"Girl wonder, child bride."

"You got married in medical school?"

"As a fellow."

"You met him puttering around the lab?"

"Alan? Heavens no. He has nothing to do with labs or medicine. He's an economist. Taught at Columbia; met him at one of those deadly faculty sherry hours you get dragged to."

"I resolved never to marry another doctor," said Nancy.

"Stick to it," said Diana. "Alan and I have an indestructible marriage; it's based on the firmest of all bases—we've absolutely nothing in common."

"Sounds like you must have hit it off immediately."

"Well, he kind of grew on me."

"Did you live in the city then?"

"Oh, yes. Didn't move to Nyack until last autumn. We kept my old apartment on the Hudson. I've been a kept woman: two men, one apartment."

"I guess I'd love any man who'd pay for an apartment on the Hudson," said Nancy.

"Oh, it was a great place. Had a dormer window. Used to sit in it for hours and watch the river flow."

"Your father didn't worry about you, alone on the dangerous West Side?"

"He's not like that. Always wanted me to experience life. Always asked if I had any hot affairs going, even in college. He said he wanted to read my memoirs someday, and not be bored.

Bores easily, my father. Of course, he put three locks on the door and bolted every window."

"Great."

"Not at all conventional. Conventions are for the conventional."

"He did send you to Vassar."

"My misfortune. Clatches of old hens. Got mad if you dated their boyfriends. Clucked if you didn't come home from a date until the next morning."

"Sounds bad."

"Guess things were different by the time you got to college. But a woman's school for me was a gross error. Never really liked the company of women, after that. Present company excepted, of course."

"I'm honored."

"Say, they are just leering at us from that corner table," said Diana. "Don't look. Do you know a place that isn't so thick with hospital people?"

"Belinda's is around the corner, and a block uptown."

Ryan was urinating his first three beers down the toilet when Nancy and Diana Hayes came in and sat down two tables from Arch. Ryan had been worse than no company; in fact, he had said nothing but "No shit?" since they arrived. So Arch moved over next to Nancy and introduced himself. Nancy turned a shade of deep red and started to choke, but Diana kicked her sharply in the shin, under the table. Nancy perked up, rising to the occasion.

"I'm Doc—I'm Nancy, and this is Diana."

Diana smiled.

"I'm Arch, but more important, this is Ryan, who's awfully depressed," said Arch, gesturing toward the empty chair which had held Ryan.

"Lovely face. A little transparent, though," said Diana.

Arch looked at her, not understanding at first, then caught her meaning and decided he didn't like her, even though she was a very good-looking woman. Nancy had her leg hard by his.

58

"Oh, he's in the bathroom," said Arch. "You'll know him when he comes out: he has a little black cloud over his head."

"Why's he so down?" asked Nancy.

"Hates his job."

"Why doesn't he quit?"

"He hates it too much to quit."

"Oh."

"He may though, after last night."

Ryan came out of the bathroom and went to the now empty table he had shared with Arch. He just stared at the tabletop, playing with his beer mug.

"There he is now," said Arch.

Nancy looked over and recognized Ryan immediately. Just before meeting Diana, she had been looking at his internship photo. She looked to Diana, who registered no recognition. She was looking at him the way a woman in a bar looks at a man, and Nancy coughed to get her attention. She could not be distracted.

Arch waved Ryan over. Ryan seemed a little cheerier, sitting by Diana, who was still looking him over. He began returning the appraisal, much to Arch's relief and delight. Nancy, on the other hand, was getting squirmy.

"You always so cheerful?" Diana was saying.

"This is good, for me," said Ryan.

"Your friend says you need a new job."

"Great discernment, my friend."

"What depresses you about your work?"

"Awfully quixotic."

Nancy blinked. There didn't seem to be any discreet way of alerting Diana without blowing their cover. She had strict instructions from Diana not to reveal their profession. They were just a couple of girls out for drinks.

"Quixotic?"

Arch laughed a little drunkenly at that.

"Tree pruner," said Ryan.

Both Arch and Nancy started, but this was lost on Diana, who was now completely absorbed with Ryan's eyes. They were both oblivious to the others. Diana was crunching ice from her now empty Manhattan. Nancy still could not be certain whether or not Diana realized Ryan was an intern.

"Tree pruner?"

"Yeah, I trim the trees in Central Park. You know, like a very tall gardener."

"Yes, yes, I understand," said Diana, touching his arm. "But how is that a quixotic line of work?"

"They keep growing back."

"But isn't that the idea?"

"Whose idea?"

"I mean the idea of pruning the trees in the first place, so they'll grow right."

Arch signaled the waitress for refills on the drinks, and Nancy touched his arm to object, but he buried her hand with his. Nancy whispered in Arch's ear, more for the effect of putting her lips near his ear than to register her objection.

"He's no tree pruner."

Arch whispered back, twice as close, sending a major chill through Nancy's back, and deciding her in a flash that she was spending the night with Arch, no matter what happened.

"Don't tell anyone; this is the happiest I've seen him in weeks. Your friend is therapeutic."

"If you only knew," Nancy whispered back.

Arch decided it was time to divide and conquer, so he invited Nancy to the Pong game in the corner. Diana hardly noticed them get up. They played the machine for a while, then Arch edged Nancy out the door. She looked back, wanting to warn Diana, but Arch kept her going.

"How did you get into this line of work?"

"Luck. And placement. Worked for the Parks Department, Raccoon Service, when the pruning job opened up."

"Raccoons?"

"Terrible problem."

"In Central Park?"

"Odious creatures."

"Never seen a raccoon in Central Park."

"Nocturnal animals. Ever been in the park, after dark?"

60

"But they're such clean little darlings. Why do you call them names?"

"Caddish, ill-bred little brutes."

"Wash their hands before they eat, don't they?"

"Regular little Lady Macbeths."

"Wash their food, don't they?"

"Raccoons make rude noises," said Ryan, "like snorting."

"Clean, though."

"Undeserved reputation," said Ryan. "Usually they go around caked with mud. Hands are the cleanest things about them."

"Oh," laughed Diana suddenly, "you are the most absurd man I've ever met."

"What do you do?" Ryan asked.

"Dabble. I just dabble."

Ryan had been on call the night before, gotten almost no sleep, and was fading fast. He was working hard not to yawn.

"I think you're fading fast," said Diana.

"I'm dying to stay and hear you tell me even less about yourself," said Ryan. "But . . ."

"But you have to be up for rounds in the morning, is that it?"

"You didn't believe a word I said."

"Not a word."

"No gullibility left in this city," said Ryan, and they went home separately, Ryan still wondering who she was.

BOOK II

Whipple

1

August 4

Ryan was having lunch in the hospital cafeteria. It was a pleasant lunch: he had joined Iggy, who was eating with a nice-looking nurse from the wards. Ryan squinted at her name tag: BRIGID SULLIVAN, HEAD NURSE. She was friendly enough, even for a head nurse. Ryan was talking about cutting out early so he could run across the street to Whipple to write his on-service notes. It was Friday, and Arch had fixed him up with a date. Ryan didn't mention this, with Brigid sitting there, but he wanted to have his notes written by seven, and be free and clear for the weekend.

"Whipple?" said Brigid. "Poor boy. You'd better take your vitamins and Elavil every day for the next two months. Interns coming back from there never look too great."

"Cancer City," said Iggy.

Ryan's beeper went off, and he had to leave Brigid to Iggy. It was Arch.

"Be home by eight, buddy," said Arch. "This woman's a work of art." Arch always said that about Jane's friends.

"I'll go over and write my on-service notes at Whipple, and be home by seven."

Arch had no idea what on-service notes were, but he was happy. He hung up.

Whipple was red brick, small windows, six-bedded rooms with fecal smells. Two months at Whipple. Get it over with. Then the rest of the year safe within the walls of The Manhattan Hospital.

Only fifteen patients.

Goldstein, the intern Ryan was replacing, had the Blue Team, imaginatively named for the color of the looseleaf notebook which held the order sheets on each patient. Each patient also had a chart, marked with blue tape, and kept in the aluminum chart rack.

Ryan called Arch with the encouraging word, "Be outta here earlier than we thought, just fifteen patients."

A resident grabbed a chart from Ryan. Residents were usually more friendly at Manhattan Hospital. The resident was not impressed that Ryan was in early to pick up his service; nor did he think it was a good idea. Ryan took another chart, but a nurse demanded it: her time was important, she said.

Ryan piled the blue charts in front of him. The clerk gathered the charts up and started putting them back in the rack. Ryan watched her in silent rage and with a certain amount of incredulity.

I know I'm not invisible. But she's giving me doubt.

"I was using those."

"All these at once?"

"Well, one at a time, but all of them."

"Well, I gotta chart the temps. I don't know what you gotta come in here today for. I'm going off at three thirty, and I gotta chart now. Come back at four."

"Why don't I use them after you put in the temps?"

"Just don't get in the way. You take the charts I give you."

"I just want the Blue Team."

The clerk's face softened.

"Are you taking over for Dr. Goldstein?"

"Yeah."

"He's a doll. We got along," said the clerk, looking at Ryan appraisingly. "Too bad he's leaving."

Only fifteen patients, but each had thirty problems. Joan Green, age thirty-four, was a happy homemaker in Bethesda, Maryland, who played tennis and was having a nice life, when she developed a little ache, then a steady pain in her left leg: osteogenic sarcoma.

Her doctor in Maryland referred her to Whipple, sent her all the way to New York, to the most famous cancer hospital in the world. Whipple was not only the most famous, but also the best, according to Mrs. Green's doctor.

At Whipple she had been treated with a drug which was suppose to kill the tumor, but wrecked her kidneys instead, making her retain metabolic wastes and fluid. The fluid backed up into her lungs, sending her into congestive heart failure. But her latest problems began when they tried to wash out the metabolic wastes.

The washouts, peritoneal dialysis, involved slushing sterile solutions into the sterile abdominal cavity, which is supposed to stay sterile. Unfortunately, sterile technique is sometimes less than perfect, and the cavity and its organs got infected.

The same drug that had wrecked the kidneys also wiped out most of the white blood cells needed to thwart infections. The drug made her vomit, throwing her out of electrolyte balance, which was already in no great shape because of the metabolic wastes and the unthwarted infection.

She was not a happy woman. As far as she and her kidneys were concerned, Mrs. Green ought never have set foot in Whipple.

Her tumor, on the other hand, was not at all intimidated by the drug which had played havoc with her kidneys and white cells: she had new lesions, metastases, sprouting daily, on her chest X rays. Her lungs were more than half replaced by tumor, and she had fluid weeping out of the injured lung, pleural effusions. She was short of breath, which, considering what showed on her X rays, was understandable.

Ryan recognized the names of about half her medications, and knew the toxicities of none. He looked them up one by one. Finally, tired of reading, he went to see the patient.

She was still a lovely lady, minus one leg, amputated with the original tumor. She talked about her home in Maryland and her husband.

"I told him I'd never let them cut off my leg; ruin my tennis, I said. That was when they first told me. Now they're talking about my life: the leg doesn't seem like so much anymore."

She started to pink and cry. Ryan gave her a Kleenex. And a

67

pat on the shoulder. Cancer is the disease of nice people. Heart disease gets the bastards, but cancer is the disease of nice people. Iggy Bart had told Ryan that.

By seven Ryan had done two on-service notes. By midnight he had done four and had received several indignant phone calls from Arch and the women. There was Mrs. Green; and Mrs. Christensen, with acute myelocytic leukemia and a recently pregnant, unmarried daughter.

Mrs. Christensen had fungus growing in her lungs, among other places. She commended that concern to Ryan.

"My fungus is your problem. My daughter is mine. I think you've got the better end of the deal."

Ryan agreed silently. He was more daunted than she.

Jon Littleman was another leuk, Whipple's longest surviving AML.

"Three years on the brink," he said. "I used to wonder about life after death. Now I'm wondering if there's life after birth." Ryan caught his strange and steady look, and gave him an A for composure.

And there was Mrs. Ritalovich, with cancer of the pancreas, which was wasting her away. She had saved up for a Caribbean cruise and, five miles out on a calm sea, started vomiting. It wasn't seasickness. She just couldn't stop. The disease had badly obstructed her small bowel.

At 2:00 A.M. Ryan began his fifth chart. Mr. Schwartz, a fifty-four-year-old white, male Auschwitz survivor, had a tattoo he didn't get on Forty-second Street, and a liver full of colonic carcinoma. The lights were out in his six-bedded room. Everyone was asleep or unconscious except the patient next to Mr. Schwartz, Vince Cotti. Cotti was vomiting into a brimming emesis basin. Cotti had eaten curried something for dinner, and the smell impregnated the sticky ward air. Ryan went to Schwartz's bedside.

Mr. Schwartz was covered with a light brown rash: it darkened his face and arms but spared his chest, which was under the sheets. Its most curious feature was that it wiped off. It was a light sprinkling of Vince Cotti's vomit.

68

Some people have all the luck. Auschwitz, now a bed next to Cotti in this little cave of a room at the best cancer hospital in the world. At least he's been to famous places.

Ryan reeled into the hall and drew a breath. A nurse held out a sputum jar.

"Will you look at that?"

"What is it?"

"That's what I'd like to know," she said. "It's from Mr. Sullivan. I know he's not your patient, but you're around, and I don't want to wake the intern."

Ryan peered into the jar.

"Looks like sputum."

"No, that." She pointed to a gray, spongy chunk floating in the bloody slime.

"A piece of lung," said Ryan.

He went to the bathroom and vomited, then walked home in a sweat. The city air smelled positively sweet. Ryan's arms and legs moved with unremembered power. The racy New York night shot through his nerves.

August 5

The next morning Ryan stayed in bed, trying to think of a reason to go back to Whipple. People had quit internships before they began, but what happened to them? They probably wound up doing insurance physicals, or worse, selling insurance. Besides, Ryan had already invested one month and one night, and written five Whipple notes; now he had to finish. He dragged himself back, whipped off a note on Jack Peoples, who had melanoma everywhere. There were two other melanomas on the blue team: Vince Cotti, who had it almost everywhere, and Willie Williams, who had no known spread of disease.

Vince Cotti told Ryan a classic Whipple story: Vince had melanoma fungating messily all over his right arm and chest. The tumor was breaking down in spots, and the pussy nodules smelled as bad as they looked. Dressings just slid off and collected on the floor at bedside. The arm was swollen with lymphedema to twice the normal size.

Willie Williams had just had a small melanoma removed from the back of his left hand. Willie could not understand why his doctor had made such a fuss over a little black-and-brown mole that bled. But the doctor badgered Willie into the hospital, and the nurses assigned him the bed next to Vince Cotti.

Willie asked Cotti what he had.

"Melanoma," Cotti replied, throwing some pussy dressings on the floor.

"Well, as soon as I said it, and saw his expression, I knew what he had. 'Melanoma!' he says. 'I thought melanoma was just a little black mole!" Nothing I could say after that helped. 'Well, they probably got yours early,' I says. He didn't say nothin' for three solid days. Can you believe putting him in the bed right next to me?"

Ryan believed. The nurses had been late and in a hurry; a psych conference had run over. They had been in a sensitivity session with the shrink.

Ryan told Arch that story. Arch was more appalled by Ryan's phrasing than by the substance.

"What do you mean, 'He's a melanoma'? You mean he's a human being afflicted with melanoma."

Ryan played with his dinner.

"Arch, right now, he's a melanoma. Monday, when I've got all the notes written, he might become Vince Cotti, human being, with melanoma. But until then, he's Vince Cotti, melanoma, pericardial effusion, lung mets, liver mets."

"Mets?"

"The little seedlings from the tumor: metastases. He had the original on his neck: now he's got its mets all over the place. There's a line about that, though: 'Whipple Hospital: The only place where the Mets always win.' I think Iggy Bart came up with that."

Arch didn't laugh. Ryan was laughing too hard to notice.

Back at Whipple, Ryan had finished Cotti's note when he

70

noticed a mole on his own arm, growing. Ryan struggled to continue writing, but his eyes kept drifting back to the mole, which was getting bigger all the time. It itched. It was about to bleed. The mole destroyed his concentration.

Ryan went out for a walk, envying the people on the street, who didn't have melanoma. Bypassers looked worried, or absorbed in thought. They were patently foolish: whatever their concerns, all paled next to Ryan's melanoma.

He found himself near The Manhattan Hospital Emergency Room, and ran in. They cut off the mole, and Ryan went back to Whipple.

Ryan never got to put his note on Cotti into the chart: Cotti was dead by Monday, transferred to the Eternal Care Unit. In fact, of the fifteen notes Ryan finally finished by midnight Sunday, only ten ever got into the charts on Monday. Ryan came in with his stack to discover the Grim Reaper had made weekend rounds on the Blue Team. Mr. Schwartz, Jack Peoples, Cotti, and two others were gone. There was a lesson in that: sooner or later the Grim Reaper made rounds on everybody; at Whipple it was always sooner.

2

August 7

It was 7:00 A.M., and Diana Hayes had already made her bed in her little room, across from the hospital. She straightened her books and put the piles of EKG's in neat stacks. Shrugging on her white lab coat, she took up a stack of echos and walked over to have breakfast in the hospital cafeteria.

The East Side was stirring on this still cool summer morning. Dr. Hayes hurried in the chill. Gray faces nodded, and she nodded back. Manhattan Hospital was a small town: all the house staff, and most of the attendings, lived within three blocks of the Tower, so everyone saw each other every day, for better or for worse.

Diana kept a room across the street, which she used when she had an early cath case. But she had a life apart.

Nancy Damiani was already drinking coffee over a composite photograph of the new internship class. Diana sat down beside her.

"Hate these early cases," said Diana to the top of Nancy's head.

"It is a beastly hour," said Nancy. "Last I saw you, you were talking with a fragile-faced tree pruner."

"Oh, he was just a punchy intern."

"I'm glad you found out," she said, pointing to Ryan's picture on the composite.

Diana glanced at the photo and shuffled through her papers.

"Did you think I was in danger?"

"Well," said Nancy, trying to decide whether to be honest or tactful, "he had such marvelous eyes . . ." But seeing Diana's arched brow: "No."

"Of course not," said Diana. "I may be playful, but I am certainly not careless."

They were joined by Hyman Bloomberg.

"Looking over the new interns?" he asked Nancy, and he bit into a muffin.

"I never get to meet the interns," said Nancy. "I just see their handiwork."

"At autopsy you mean?" asked Bloomberg, laughing. "Pathologists have the most ghastly sense of humor." Bloomberg devoured a bagel. "July must be a busy month for you."

"Not as bad as one might think."

"Well, I hate July and August," said Bloomberg. "And this year they've even got me attending over at Whipple for August. Ward attending. No air conditioning. I've got patients in the Tower, and they've got me schlepping over to the Annex to be a ward attending."

"You're not alone," said Diana. "I'm attending for Cardiology at Whipple for August."

"We can suffer together," said Bloomberg, gulping coffee. "But Cardiology's a consult service. All you have to see is the consults. I have to hear every last case admitted to the eighth floor."

"That is a blessing," said Diana. "I only have to hear the heart problems, and do a conference once a week. Those wards are foul and nasty."

"And they're not air conditioned," added Bloomberg.

"Yes," said Diana, getting up and gathering her echos," I know."

"I always feel like I've offended her," said Bloomberg, looking after her. "She's a bit of an ice princess, isn't she?"

"Come again?"

"I've been here twenty years. She's been here, what? Five? And I've been on committees, at conferences with her. I don't feel as though I know her any better now than I did five years ago, when she first arrived," said Bloomberg, with his dolphin smile.

"Oh, I don't know," said Nancy.

"Well, maybe you know her better. I'm just an old fart. And she's a big honcho now. What's she got to say to me?"

"Oh, everyone adores you. Stop feeling sorry for yourself. Diana's just . . ."

Bloomberg waited for her to finish her sentence, but she never did.

3

August 14

August ground into a routine.

Mornings began with blood-drawing: the interns arrived at seven thirty to poke and stick the bruised and squirming arms of their sleepy, terrified patients. Most arms had veins which had long since clotted off, or gone into hiding under the daily assault. The patients hated it, and sensed that the whole ordeal benefited them little, a feeling Ryan shared, since these patients all had fatal disease, which meant all the blood tests were good for was to document the expected decline. But these patients were getting therapy, and once blood counts dropped too low, therapy had to be held. So the blood had to be drawn and the patients tormented a little.

By eight the bloods were drawn, and the resident arrived to do rounds with the three interns on each patient.

Biotto had rotated over from the Main House, and Ryan waited with him and another intern, Wilson, for their resident, Fick. Compared with Iggy's brisk rounds, Fick's were meandering, and the ward was sodden and stained after the gleaming halls of B-7. Biotto was talking less since coming to Whipple, and nobody smiled. There were no medical students on Morning Rounds at Whipple because there were no medical students assigned to learn medicine at Whipple. "You don't send new recruits to the Siberian Front," Iggy had said, by way of explaining the absence of medical students. So Morning Rounds were done with just the interns and the resident. They didn't even rate a nurse.

It seemed very far away from the layer upon layer of review, the tight control of The Manhattan Hospital. It all seemed so fragmented. Even the territoriality of the Tower was shattered: at the Tower one team of three interns took care of all the patients on one ward of forty patients. But at Whipple there were just too many patients—sixty of them stuffed into a ward —for any one team to manage. Each Whipple patient had more problems than three patients at the Tower. So two teams of three interns and a resident divided the patients on the ward.

Ryan had trouble remembering which patients in a room belonged to his team and were his responsibility. They did Morning Rounds so the interns could learn and visually recognize all the patients, even those belonging to the other two interns. But cancer rendered the patients such look-alikes.

Before the first patient could be seen, a nurse confronted the group and asked Ryan whether or not he had written an order for rectal temperatures on one of his leukemic patients. She seemed annoyed. Ryan knew nurses hated rectal temps; it was easier to take them orally. But if he had learned one thing in medical school, it was that oral temps were unreliable, the mouth being artificially cooler than core body temperature in patients who breathed through their mouths.

"Fick," said the nurse, to Ryan's resident, ignoring Ryan, "do we have to put up with this?"

"Oral temps," said Fick.

The nurse went off.

"Why?" asked Ryan, red-faced.

"Rectal temps are a no-no in leukemics, turkey."

"Why?" asked Ryan.

"Ryan," said Fick, impatiently, "what are white blood cells for?"

Ryan stood there, taunted, unsure what the trick was, then answered unambiguously.

"They fight infection, among other things."

"Correct. Now, Mr. Pipps, on whom you wanted rectal temps, has about one thousand white blood cells per cubic millimeter. The normal being?"

"Seven thousand."

"Correct again, star," said Fick. "So if you stick a thermometer in his WBC-deprived ass, what happens? He gets a rectal abscess, seeds his bloodstream with who-knows-what gut flora, gets septic, and crumps."

"Oh," said Ryan, realizing they had neglected some details in medical school.

They worked their way down the ward, going bed to bed. Only a third of the beds were filled with patients belonging to Ryan, and he tended to drift off while Biotto or Wilson examined and questioned their patients. Fick endeavored to prevent these lapses by firing questions at Ryan.

"Ryan, why do you think we all do rounds together?"

"So we can all get to know every patient on the team."

"Good man. So pay attention, so when you're on call tomorrow night, and get called to see one of Biotto's patients, you'll know what the hell is going on."

They came to Mr. Pipps, whose leukemic rectum Ryan had almost invaded with silver-tipped glass. Outside the room, Fick stopped.

"Mr. Pipps has acute myelocytic leukemia," said Fick. "What is the one, key feature of AML?"

Ryan stared blankly at Fick, whose questions always sounded so simple, but left Ryan absolutely speechless.

"I give up," said Ryan at last. At least neither Biotto nor Wilson knew.

"AML is totally incurable. It kills every last patient who has it," said Fick with satisfaction.

Ryan conceded, silently, that that must be the salient feature of the disease.

"And what is the one, key feature of our treatment of this patient, with AML?"

Again, none of the three interns knew.

"The key feature is that we keep patients with AML alive, more or less. When their peripheral blood smears show nothing but ugly, leukemic blasts instead of mature, functional white blood cells, we hit 'em with chemotherapy, henceforth referred to as 'poisons.' And when the poisons wipe out their bone marrows, and they're ripe for infections, we hit 'em with antibiotics."

Fick looked at his interns.

"Now, Ryan, when Mr. Pipps gets febrile and crazy tonight, or tomorrow night, and his respiratory rate triples, what will you think is happening?"

"He might be septic?"

"You asking me or telling me?"

"He's definitely septic," said Ryan.

"Better. Remember, you're a doctor now. Even when you're not sure, you know. You have no doubt."

"And what if I don't know?"

"Act like you *do* know."

Fick looked at Ryan, smiling.

"Now, Ryan, what is good therapy for a hot leuk?"

"Don't know," said Ryan.

Fick laughed. "What is this? Elsewhere General? We are in the big time now."

"Penicillin?"

"No! What bugs does penicillin cover? We're talking about bugs that live in the bowel, stain gram negative, and kill leuks. Penicillin is for kids with strep throats."

Ryan didn't know. Biotto took a wild guess and threw out "gentamicin." Wilson looked as though he might start crying.

"K and G. Keflin and gentamicin. Remember: culture, K and G, and call nobody, especially your resident, especially after midnight."

By the end of rounds Ryan had amassed a two-page list of tests to order, things to check for each of his patients, and Fick disappeared.

By four that afternoon Ryan had gotten almost to the end of page one when Fick reappeared to go over charts and find out the results of the tests he had asked Ryan to check on that morning.

"What was Green's liver scan?" Fick asked Ryan. Green's liver scan was on page two.

"Didn't have a chance to check on it."

"Didn't have a chance?" smirked Fick. "You went to lunch didn't you?"

"Yes," admitted Ryan, guilty as hell.

"You took time to take a shit today, didn't you?"

"Yes," said Ryan, even more contrite.

"Then don't tell me you didn't have time. Go tell Mrs. Green you just didn't have time to check to see if her liver is full of crab when we see her on Morning Rounds tomorrow."

Ryan called the scan room after Chart Rounds, but they had closed for the night.

4

August 16

If Ryan was on call Monday night, then he was kept awake into the early hours of Tuesday morning. That meant that for most of Tuesday he had a numbing headache and low-grade nausea. When he got home Tuesday evening, he went straight to bed. But Wednesday he would get to work at seven in the morning and get home by seven that evening, awake and with the whole night beckoning, before having to admit the next day.

That third night was scheduled for resolute sensuality. If Ryan wound up sleeping alone, life had passed him by, on the one night he had to engage life.

Engaging life meant pressing himself against warm, undiseased flesh, squirming between clean, unbloody sheets, heart pounding, free of chest pain.

The women were a comfort, but consistently disappointing. The excitement was fleeting. Ryan yearned for the enduring fantasy. There were two kinds of women in the world, but he was meeting only one.

With his bedmates, the action ended in bed: natural impulses had been happily discharged. But he didn't dream about it. At least, it wasn't the light of his life.

Where were the Gloria Steinems, the Sylvia Plaths and Joan Didions, whose heads buzzed with little worlds of derision and passion? Wherever they were, he wasn't. For Ryan's women, passion amounted to little more than panting.

During medical school he had resolutely refused to lower his estimable standards. But that degenerated into celibacy. In New York nobody pined away if Ryan played hard to get. It wasn't that they didn't care. They never noticed. No envies were aroused if Ryan sat home and communed with mad housewives through their diaries. New York was filled with working women.

Working women were uninspired by the momentous principles which inflamed Ryan. Angry young men, dirty old men, men who buttoned their shirts up to the collar, were of no interest.

If they wanted to know anything about Ryan, it was where he was likely to take them to dinner, and how often. They didn't hear Ryan, they saw him.

The women did look good: they were a delight to Ryan's hungry eyes. He had never seen creatures like the women who floated through Bloomingdale's, catching their own images in the mirrored walls with sidelong glances. They were gorgeous. But all they could talk about was how they got that way.

Ryan asked a woman out for what she was not. If she was not fat, loud, or demanding, she was in the running. If she was, in addition, willing, she had a date.

It wasn't exactly joyless fucking. Ryan really liked the feel of soft, nontumorous skin. But he generally wanted them gone as soon as possible in the morning. The greatest decency was to leave without saying a word. For those who didn't simply dress and leave, breakfast was permitted.

Ryan would go off to rounds, leaving Arch to contend with the latest guest in the kitchen, who had been left drinking coffee and searching for silverware.

"Jesus, at least if it were the same two or three, I could learn their names. But it's never the same one twice."

"Can't ask them to wear name tags," said Ryan, munching toast.

"At the rate you're going," said Arch, "numbers would seem more appropriate."

"Consider it."

"Sounds like a great way to relate to women."

"Not related to any of them."

Arch let that go.

"Whatever happened to the Right Woman?"

"Hasn't happened yet," said Ryan morosely. "All that's happened is Whipple."

Arch considered this. The remark had symmetry. A lot of Ryan's remarks lately had symmetry. Lately, Ryan had been stronger on symmetry than meaning.

"It's Whipple's fault?"

"Just an opinion."

Arch started reading *The Wall Street Journal.*

Ryan looked at him.

"I'm engaging life," said Ryan, "love in the ruins, affirming life among the dying, salvation in screwing." Ryan's voice was rising up through the octaves.

Arch looked up from the paper.

"Okay, chief."

"Arch," said Ryan, "right now, it just feels good."

Of course, Ryan was occasionally presented with the Perfect Woman, supplying him with the opportunity to transform his ennui into angst. Iggy sat down to watch Ryan eat dinner in the cafeteria, and absently dropped the bomb that Faith Stern had been seen hanging around the hospital cafeteria.

Ryan was in love with female feminist editors as a class, and Faith Stern in particular. Faith's mother, a patient of Hyman Bloomberg's, had been admitted to The Manhattan Hospital. Ryan didn't hear the rest of Iggy's monologue about feminists, female editors, food at The Manhattan Hospital cafeteria. Ryan was thinking about his affair with Faith Stern. He had seen her on late-night talk shows, read her, fallen in love with her—from afar, which made it more piquant.

"I wouldn't have minded getting Faith Stern's mother."

"Yes, you would have."

"Why?"

"She came in at two A.M."

"But she's Faith Stern's mother."

"You're interested?"

"Of course."

"Ryan, repeat after me: 'After midnight there is no such thing as an interesting admission.' "

He haunted the cafeteria on every night off, stretching dinner into three-hour vigils. Abandoning his fifth vigil, he slumped empty-handed toward the cafeteria exit, when she walked by him.

Ryan wasn't prepared for her walking by. He was going to be sitting, drinking coffee, when she sat down. He would have moved his cup over to her table and said something unaggressive, intriguing, and light.

Ryan could never quite hear the opening lines, but the sequence after the introduction was well worked out.

"I read your piece on Marilyn Monroe a dozen times, and liked it better each time," Ryan would say.

"I'm so glad," she would say. "No one ever seems to appreciate that article."

Ryan watched her move to the food line. She was thinner than she looked in photos, and had gray streaks in her hair. But the most attractive thing about her was that she was alone. Ryan looked around to see if there was someone at a table, waiting for her. She was bravely, conspicuously, and invitingly alone. Ryan was in love.

She went through the line alone, with Ryan sliding his tray along the steel rails, behind her. She stopped at the hot food section, which meant Ryan could not avoid overtaking her. He stood frozen, by the salads, several feet from her, unable to draw any closer.

She got her stew and moved toward the register, Ryan now in hot pursuit. She forgot her iced tea, and turned to retrieve it, bumping into Ryan.

"So sorry," she said. "Forgot my tea."

Ryan opened his mouth, but nothing issued forth. He fled the line in disarray. Days passed. Ryan's fevered mind produced a thousand witty, open-ended, inviting rejoinders to "I forgot my tea."

"The tea here's entirely forgettable."

Anything would have done, but now she was lost forever, leaving Ryan with a lifetime to regret her loss.

5

August 21

At two thirty in the morning the eighth floor at Whipple is a black hole. The rooms and halls are dark, the only lights coming from the nursing station and the flashlight of the night nurse, moving in and out of the rooms. There's a window at the end of the hall, but on a cloudy night it admits no light. Ryan was finishing his last admission note, the last of five since 9:00 P.M., when he became aware of a presence behind him, in the nursing station. He swiveled in the chair just enough to catch sight of someone sitting silently behind him, and flinched.

"Jesus, you scared hell out of me!"

Even looking at her, he wasn't sure she was real: she was wearing a nurse's uniform, sitting behind Ryan, on the workbench, lovely legs crossed, smiling, holding an unlit cigarette. She was Oriental. Ryan supposed she was one of those incomprehensible, minimal English night nurses, who would find things to keep him awake all night. She was a delicate-looking creature, and annoyingly amused.

"You speak English?" he asked, not totally convinced she was really there.

"Like a native," she smiled, without a trace of accent.

"Oh," said Ryan, flustered, "I thought you might be the night nurse. She doesn't, at least not too well."

"You see, I was educated in your country, at U.C.L.A.," she said.

"I'm sorry," said Ryan, bleary, wiping his eyes, still trying to decide if she was real. He had to go to the bathroom, but he didn't want to come back and find her gone. She had a high-cheekboned, finely etched face, vaguely Eurasian, and long dark hair, falling straight.

"That's okay," she said. "It is night, and I am a nurse." She smiled. She wore a large gold cross, which dangled off the end of the rise in her uniform, over her breasts.

"I usually don't get to see the night nurses," said Ryan, watching her recross her lovely legs. "They just call me in the on-call room. And I didn't recognize your voice."

"Probably because I haven't been on nights when you've been on call," she said dryly, blowing smoke. "I'm a special on Mrs. Christensen."

"You just take care of one patient?"

"I'm a spy for Maxwell Baptist on the side."

"Did you really go to U.C.L.A.?"

"Barnard, actually."

"And Cornell nursing," said Ryan, looking at her pin.

She lit her cigarette and blew the smoke up her nostrils. Ryan couldn't smell it.

"Do I get a good report card, for Baptist?"

"Highest marks."

"Everything by the book," said Ryan.

"Oh, of course," she laughed, with white teeth. "You even write your own book, from what I've heard."

"I beg your pardon," said Ryan, disturbed.

"Oh, yes. You've gotten a reputation: went down to the president about old Miss Ratched over at B-seven locking up your syringes. And you didn't buy the death certificate rules either. Oh, I've heard. You've got your principles."

Ryan began to believe she really was an agent from the department office.

"So you've got the scoop on me, and I don't even know your name."

"Hope." She looked at him, amused, taking a drag, and said, "You don't like Whipple much, do you?"

"Not at all."

"Kinda grim, isn't it?" she agreed, twisting her cross around its chain.

"Oh, it's the best cancer hospital in the world; didn't you know?"

"You don't say?" said Hope.

"No, I don't."

"What do you say?"

"It's a disgrace."

"Not up to your standards?"

"It's a pit. People shouldn't have to die in a pit like this."

"There you go again, making rules."

"What's wrong with that?"

"Who's that woman, at the end of the hall, with osteogenic sarcoma?"

"Joan Green."

"Yes, Mrs. Green. I read your note on her. Very nice, even legible. At any rate, there she was, happy homemaker in Bethesda, Maryland, and for no reason, having broken no rules, boom: sarcoma."

"That is disturbing, isn't it?" said Ryan, glumly.

"Well," laughed Hope, "maybe she did something nasty to deserve it, something we don't know about: beats her kids, cheats on her husband, something deserving."

"Nobody deserves that," said Ryan, getting really depressed.

"Well," said Hope, inhaling her cigarette, "maybe the good die young."

"They do around here," said Ryan.

"They do everywhere," laughed Hope.

6

Late August. The temperature had topped ninety-five degrees every day, with humidity to match. Arch had nightmares about the air conditioners failing, and slipped out of the town house at dawn daily, seeking out the cool places on the early Wall Street expresses. The heat panicked him.

Ryan, on the other hand, sat in his study with the window open, under a mosquito net, in khaki shorts and shirt, sweating dreamily in the steamy heat. Ryan hated extremes of temperature even more than Arch did, but when he was reading about Pygmies, Ryan felt compelled to swelter. He read late into the night, lathering in the leather desk chair, tying knots without looking, reading about the Congo, the forest, and the Pygmies.

Arch got home after dark, a little light-headed from the downtown bar, and worked his way upstairs, turning on air conditioners. He swung into Ryan's steaming study and was immediately paralyzed by the heat. There was Ryan, under the nets, soaked khakis, at his desk only bodily, spirit in deepest Congo.

Had Arch not lived with Ryan for several mind-expanding years, he would have thought that Whipple had finally broken Ryan's fragile grip on sanity. But during medical school, Arch had seen these rituals, and had faith that no matter how bizarre Ryan was in his study, he would return to apparent normality by daybreak.

" 'One's real life is so often the life one does not lead.' " Ryan was fond of quoting Oscar Wilde.

Now it was Pygmies, the Congo, and mosquito nets.

"You okay?" asked Arch, closing the door behind him, to keep the heat confined to Ryan's asylum.

Ryan looked up, startled.

"Hi." He smiled from under the nets.

"Thought you might have died in the heat."

"Naw."

"How are the little people?"

"They're okay."

"Why not turn on the air conditioner?"

"It's okay," said Ryan, holding up his Pygmy book. Arch knew that meant one does not read about the Congo sitting comfortably in air conditioning.

Arch went downstairs to his air conditioning, thinking about weekending in the cooler Hamptons. Arch traveled two hours to escape. Ryan could escape anytime by just opening a book or closing his eyes. The Pygmies, if Turnbull was to be believed, escaped from village life into a forest dream world, running along clear streams, under a leafy canopy. Ryan would like to play that game with Whipple, investing as little of himself as possible, retreating to a dream world. The trouble was, he had no forest. His study was as close as he got to a world apart. His study, Bloomie's, and occasionally Central Park.

If he could ever overcome his fear of parasites, Ryan would visit the Congo, follow Stanley and Turnbull and seek out the Pygmies. But Ryan knew he'd just get malaria, leprosy, or trypanosomiasis, and die soon after arriving, as Byron did in Greece.

So, as second best, he turned off the air conditioner, opened the window, put on his jungle shorts, wrapped himself up in the mosquito net, and immersed himself in his books. Someday he'd go to exotic places where English was spoken, safe from parasites, like Scotland, and have real adventures.

August 23

Ryan was on the night Mrs. Christensen died.

It had been a night jinxed by one of the day nurses, who had commented breezily as she was leaving, at 4:00 P.M., that it would probably be a quiet night.

"Don't say that!" gasped Ryan, hysterically. "Don't ever say that!"

"Say what?"

"That it'll be slow"—his voice flying up octaves. "Bite your tongue."

"You're really nuts. You know that?"

"Whenever anybody says it'll be quiet, all hell breaks loose," stammered Ryan.

It was true. It worked like that. Ryan had been an intern only two months and had discovered the ironclad clinical truth: optimism begets disaster.

"Take it back," Ryan said.

"No admissions," squealed the day nurse, vanishing into the elevator. "It'll be slow tonight."

He had just admitted Ira Landau, who had considered himself a normal twenty-year-old student earlier that day. Ira had gone out to play softball, but sometime in the second inning he discovered that his right eye was blind. His local doctor looked in and saw blood, did a blood count. It was full of blasts: Ira had leukemia, probably the AML variety.

Anyway, Mrs. Christensen's pregnant daughter was getting married that weekend, and Mrs. Christensen would not be denied. She was going to be there if it was the last thing she ever did, which, of course, it was. She signed all the "Against Medical Advice" forms, listened stonily as her private attending warned and Ryan pleaded. She was in no shape to go anywhere, but she was going to the wedding.

Ryan slipped a subclavian IV under her collarbone, into the large, immobile subclavian vein. She needed an IV that wasn't likely to come out. Of course, if it did, she didn't have any platelets and would exsanguinate. Ryan sewed it in like a rock.

Ryan showed her husband how to adjust the IV, and Sally, the nurse, made up some bags with gentamicin. Ryan ran in a unit of fresh frozen plasma and ten units of platelets. And she was off.

Ryan admonished her to be back by eleven or he'd call out the National Guard. He also reminded her that the night shift would appreciate some wedding cake.

At midnight she hadn't shown up, and Ryan was worried. She rolled in (*literally*—she went to the wedding in a wheelchair) about 1:00 A.M., in high spirits. She brought the cake, and some punch. They got her back to bed and checked her out.

Her vital signs were better than when she left. She had gotten her IV's just as directed. But she vomited at 4:00 A.M.

"Just those fishy hors d'oeuvres," she said.

It was worse than that. Her blood pressure plummeted, her respirations doubled, and she poured blood out of every orifice. Every puncture site ran red.

Nothing Ryan did worked. Plasmonate, blood, Levophed, dopamine, ringer's, all went in, but her blood pressure was sinking like a rock.

"I feel like I'm dying," she said, searching Ryan's face for an answer. "Am I dying?"

Ryan was conscious of someone standing behind him, but he concentrated on Mrs. Christensen and her question.

"I can't be sure," said Ryan.

"Yes, you can," she said, tears streaming.

Ryan was amazed that a lady as hypotensive as Mrs. Christensen could carry on so: most people with blood pressures like hers just lapse into unconsciousness and don't ask questions.

"You want to know? Yes, I think you are dying."

"God."

She began to breathe in deep, sighing heaves, and her eyes rolled back up into her head. She arrested.

90

Ryan thumped on her chest and shouted for a nurse. He need not have shouted. Hope had been behind him all along. There was little to be done: every chest compression broke another rib, and with her clotting mechanism shot, her chest just filled with blood.

Ryan went to wash up. Hope watched him from a corner of the room.

"Well, if it isn't the spy," said Ryan, still angry about Mrs. Christensen going down the tubes. "How did I do this time?"

"Disgracefully," seethed Hope.

"Not up to your standards?"

"Not hardly."

"What's your problem?" asked Ryan.

"It's hardly my problem."

"Well, then, what's my problem?"

"You're a sanctimonious, self-righteous ass."

"Well, that narrows it down."

"How could you tell her she was dying?"

"She asked, as I recall."

"You couldn't comfort her, in her last few minutes? You had to tell her. Why, for chrissake?"

"Because it's the truth."

"Oh, another one of your little rules?"

"One of my bigger rules: I tell the truth."

"Which truth?"

"The truth that she was dying."

"At the moment, she was also living, and needed some help."

"What would you have me do? Tell her she's doing just fine, as I'm pumping on her chest?"

"Tell her she'd live to see her grandchild, and hold her hand. What good did it do to have her leave this world even more distraught? And why in God's name pump on her? Why not let her go unpummeled? What you did, you did for yourself, not for her."

"Just a fucking minute," said Ryan, but Hope was disappearing out the door. "Doctors are supposed to tell the truth, even when it hurts."

7

Weekend of August 25

Ryan dreaded the day ahead; it was an eighty-two-hour day. He was on call for the weekend. Unlike the Tower, where a different intern was on call each weekend day, at Whipple one intern was on from Friday night to Monday. Ryan arrived to draw bloods at 7:00 A.M. Friday, and would not go home until after Chart Rounds, Monday, around 7:00 P.M.

The first bad sign was the day nurses talking about how calm things had been the last two days.

He got his first admission during Attending Rounds. He was not supposed to miss rounds; words of wisdom from the ward attending were only handed down three times a week. If Ryan cared about this, the patient waiting to be admitted clearly did not. The patient demonstrated his indifference by arresting, despite rounds. Ryan and the nurses resuscitated, and rounds went on without them.

The second admission arrived during the resuscitation: a colonic CA with a liver full of mets, yellow, vomiting, and talking incessantly about the color of his stools. The third came in about noon, an AML for another shot at chemotherapy after a six-month remission, during which he believed himself cured. Now he talked about suicide.

By the time the fourth admission rolled in, Ryan was doubting the wisdom of the admitting system. After four admissions Ryan's eyes ached, his feet hurt, his hemorrhoids throbbed, and he had developed the low-grade nausea that usually began around midnight the nights he was on.

He couldn't even drink the malted shakes: the malteds were

high-calorie, high-protein concoctions the dieticians made for the cachectic patients who were nauseated by their chemotherapy, and chewed up by their highly metabolic tumors. When a patient died, his malteds kept coming until Mrs. Sachem, the clerk, notified the kitchen. But Mrs. Sachem refused to notify the kitchen of a patient's death if it occurred after noon. She notified in the mornings; she charted temps in the afternoon, and went home at 3:30. This endeared her to the house staff, who dearly loved the malteds.

But Ryan was too nauseated to drink his by 5:00 P.M. After Chart Rounds the intern on the seventh floor signed out and went home, and five minutes later seven got an admission. Fick told Ryan to go work it up.

"Why can't the resident on seven do it? It's his floor, not mine. I saw him in the kitchen, stealing our malteds, just three seconds ago."

The resident refused. The path of least resistance was to make the intern do it. The resident had paid his dues, he said. Nobody wants to do intern's work as a resident. Working up unexpected admissions is intern's work.

Ryan gave up, and went to see the patient. He had five admissions with workups in various stages of completion, three more empty beds on his own floor, a blinding headache, and now this.

The admission turned out to be a glioma who herniated her brain stem ten minutes into Ryan's exam. Ryan, by that time, was interested in her, and watched transfixed as one pupil got larger and larger. The patient stopped breathing and turned gray, but Ryan could not tear himself away from that ever-expanding pupil. Finally he shook himself into action. He pumped on her chest and screamed wildly for stat mannitol; nurses flew around, but to no avail.

The death note took only ten minutes. An admission note would have taken an hour. Ryan was profoundly grateful: the patient had the graciousness to die with a sense of timing. During the postarrest lull Ryan suffered acute guilt at having considered the passing of a life as one less note to write, but was saved by a stat page to his own floor.

93

It was hard for him to dwell on his guilt running the twenty stairs from seven to eight. The nurses were semihysterical about Mrs. Garcia. Mrs. Garcia was fifty, with metastatic breast growing out in her lung, bones, and skull. She spoke no English, but had mastered what the shrinks called nonverbal communication. She was sitting next to the window, looking down longingly at the sidewalk, eight stories below.

Her intentions were confirmed by a Spanish-speaking aide. Ryan called the psychiatric hospital across the street. That is, he tried to call. He discovered that the psychiatrist was not available after 4:00 P.M.; that the psychiatrist would not have come to Whipple anyway (since policy required all patients to be sent to the psychiatric hospital for consults); that the psychiatric hospital did not want patients sent from Whipple (they depressed the psychiatrists); that all psychiatric consults had to be referred to the psychiatric hospital, which didn't want to see them; and, the coup de grâce, that there was only one Spanish-speaking psychiatric resident anyway, and he was not doing consults this month.

That was enough for Ryan. He presented the problem to his resident, Fick, who was home watching the Mets (the baseball team) on TV. Fick cursed Mrs. Garcia, for Ryan's benefit. Fick did not speak Spanish, and the outcome of the game was in doubt, which was more than could be said for Mrs. Garcia's outcome, given her widespread disease. It was just a question of when and how.

"Just put her on suicide precautions."

"I tried that. Turns out that means a nurse has to watch her twenty-four hours a day. We have only one nurse for her side of the floor tonight, and you know what that means."

That meant one nurse to pass out all the meds and check all the patients, and that Mrs. Garcia was a bigger problem than anyone was prepared to handle.

Ryan wound up calling her husband, who didn't understand much more English than Mrs. Garcia, but who did come to the hospital, thinking she had died, only to discover that Ryan had assigned him the task of vigil, by default. The husband wanted to leave after an hour.

94

Ryan was working up another admission. It was 9:00 P.M. He told the husband that he would have to stay until Mrs. Garcia promised not to jump. The husband told Ryan that the nurse should stay with his wife. Ryan said that was impossible. The husband replied, through the interpreter, that that was Ryan's problem, and left. Ryan underwent an acute guilt reaction for considering pushing Mrs. Garcia, or at least goading her into it. Then he went back to his admission.

The admission (number six) was a twenty-two-year-old white female who had just graduated with a B.A. in archaeology, from Wellesley, and had a diagnosis of Hodgkin's disease. Her name was Caroline Smith. She was excavating some colonial relic in the Village when she developed a fever. She wrote it off to the August heat, but became so limp she could hardly wield a pick. She was articulate, wry, and just the kind of girl Ryan had not been meeting in New York. She was far more interesting than her fever or her detestable disease. But Ryan felt compelled to ask some pertinent questions.

She had done well on her chemotherapy, her lymph nodes having regressed, until the fever, which was worrisome, appeared. Fever can signify infection, which is an unpleasant prospect in anyone who has a bone marrow wiped clean of white cells by chemotherapy.

She was pale, alternatingly animated and listless, and her chills shook the bed violently. Ryan started the IV with a big Medicut, and lashed it down with half a roll of tape.

"I feel as though I've been lashed to the mast," she said, looking at her arm.

Ryan was determined to avoid torturing her with a lot of restarts. That IV was in for the duration. He drew blood cultures, made her cough up sputum, looked at her chest X rays, and turned on her radio.

"Trying to set the mood, or are you just trying to drown out anticipated screams?" she said as Ryan fiddled with the radio.

"Looking for mood music."

"For what?"

"You need a spinal tap."

95

"Uh-oh," she groaned. She had had several in her brief life.

"I don't suppose this is a matter that could be negotiated. I don't have a choice, huh?"

"You get to choose the music."

She chose KTU, which was in the middle of a mellow hour, with Rod Stewart's quieter stuff.

She curled up into the fetal position for the tap, like a pro.

"How I got my spine tapped to Rod Stewart," she trilled. "Somewhat suggestive, a little indecent. I'll write it up and send it in to *Cosmo.*"

"Spine-tingling," observed Ryan.

She groaned. Ryan looked up, startled. He had just entered the outer layers of the cord coverings with his needle.

"Hurt?"

"Not the tap, which is going quite nicely, incidentally. But that awful pun. You must be tired. 'Spine-tingling.' Unmerciful."

Her nimble face dissolved into earnestness.

"Look, you've really just got to get me better, and quick. I've got to get right back. I didn't tell them about the Hodgkin's until after they hired me, and they were so nice about it all. And I've only worked a month. And we've just got things in pieces till I get back." She looked at Ryan, and her face changed back to imp. "You look exhausted, and here I'm demanding things. Why don't you just get some sleep and cure me in the morning?"

Ryan liked the last idea. As for the rest, he wished he could promise her recovery. Anything else, and he would have granted it: something possible, something money could buy. But she wanted what most sick people want from doctors.

He had worked up the fevers, seen the vomiters and the chest pains, and patted Mrs. Garcia's brow by 1:00 A.M. Then he sneaked off upstairs to the on-call room. He sat on the bed and the phone rang: it was the night nurse. She was Oriental; her English was mainly unintelligible.

"Patient in loom nine-two-four got pain."

"Who? What patient?" Ryan heard the click.

One EKG later Ryan was climbing back to the tenth floor,

extracting from himself the solemn promise that he would go into dermatology right after internship. He dived for the bed. The phone rang.

Forty minutes later he was back. He started toward the bed, but hesitated. Getting into bed was an act of optimism. If Ryan got into bed, even considered the likelihood of his getting some sleep, it couldn't possibly happen.

If I get in, if I touch that bed, the phone will ring.

He sat in the chair and the phone did not ring. But every time he nodded off, a sharp pain in his neck woke him. He sat on the bed. The phone rang. Caroline was vomiting.

"We've got to stop meeting like this," she said, looking up sheepishly from her emesis basin, which she steadfastedly called a vomit bowl.

Ryan went over her.

"I think it's the antibiotics upsetting your stomach," he said hopefully.

He feared worse: increased pressure within her skull, from a meningitis, was also a possibility. Ryan could have missed a meningitis. Tonight he could have missed a meningitis if it had walked up and shaken his hand. Even rested, he did not feel confident looking at spinal fluid. Hers looked clear, but he could never be sure he hadn't washed all the spinal fluid off the slide trying to gram-stain it. And his India ink stains were totally unreadable. So he could have missed it. He checked her neck again. He checked the book on antibiotics again. The antibiotics he had chosen for her should work for meningitis.

Ryan fell into bed, waiting wide-eyed for the phone to ring, thinking about the two empty beds still left, open and ripe for two more admissions.

The phone didn't ring until seven. Someone had been found dead in bed. She was NTBR (not to be resuscitated) so it was okay. Ryan had to go downstairs and pronounce her dead, call the family, fill out the death certificate, and try to get permission for the autopsy once the family showed up.

The dead patient's husband arrived with his brother. The patient was in a single room and the door was closed. The nurses intercepted the husband at the desk and detoured him to the conference room to meet Ryan.

The husband stared at the closed door of his wife's room from the conference room. Mrs. Cole had been Biotto's patient; Ryan had seen her on rounds, knew she was an ovarian CA, and NTBR, and not much more. Looking at the husband's earnest face, Ryan had the sudden, swelling urge not to tell him. Ryan wanted to lie. What could he say? You probably wondered why I called you here; your wife asked me to explain that she can't see visitors for the next century.

He told the truth, more or less.

"Mr. Cole, I was called to see your wife this morning. As you know, she has been very ill. Very ill. This morning, I could see she didn't have much time left. We did all we could for her. She did not have any pain. But I'm afraid that she has died." Ryan considered dropping to the floor, for effect. His legs were limp.

The brother-in-law said:

"Oh, God."

The husband said:

"May I talk with her?"

The brother-in-law gaped at the husband, his brother, stupefied.

Ryan said:

"I meant to say that your wife is dead."

"I just want to talk with her. I won't stay long. I know she needs rest."

The brother-in-law put his hand on the husband's shoulder.

"Ernie, she's dead. She can't hear you."

The husband looked at his brother. The message penetrated. The husband sobbed, face in hands. He was a big man, and he shook the chair with his sobs. Ryan handed him a Kleenex.

"May I see her?"

Ryan took them in. The wife must once have been a lovely woman. Now she was yellow, totally bald from the chemotherapy, and wasted down to cavernous cheekbones, hollowed temples and eye sockets, a remnant.

The husband stood in the doorway, the brother-in-law behind

him. Ryan stood by the bed. Escape through the door was blocked by at least four hundred pounds of related manhood. The husband gasped, and bit his fist, to cut short his own cry.

"Look what they've done to you," he sobbed. He buried his head in her sheets. His brother stayed at the door, but finally walked over and patted his shoulder. Ryan looked at what they had done to her.

She was not good advertising for the wonders of chemotherapy. Ryan edged toward the door, not wanting to take responsibility for the failures of Cytoxan and adriamycin.

But the brothers did not feel that way. They emerged from the room, the husband now composed.

"I want to thank you for all you've done," he said, shaking Ryan's sweaty hand with both of his. "I know how hard you've all tried." He walked to the elevator ahead of Ryan and the brother-in-law.

"Just six months ago, they were hiking in the Rockies, would you believe? She was so beautiful then."

Ryan looked at him blankly.

"I guess that's hard for you to imagine," said the brother-in-law.

Ryan did not push his luck by asking for an autopsy. The elevator arrived, and they shook his hand and thanked him again.

"What'd they thank you for?" asked one of the nurses coming on morning shift.

"I don't know. All I did was pronounce her dead."

"Oh."

"That makes sense to you?" Ryan said.

"You ended their suffering."

Ryan thought about the woman in the bed. *Now I've got three empty beds.*

8

He made rounds with Fick in the morning, and got his first admission at noon. Alice Smithy, an AML, with fever. He was done with her quickly, and there was time to catch up on scut work: hematocrits, stool guaiacs, pushing chemotherapy into veins (known as "pushing poisons"), starting and restarting IV's.

He even got two hours' sleep before the bottom fell out. Mrs. Green turned blue, got short of breath, gasped, in fact dropped her blood pressure, and looked as though she was about to die.

None of this was lost on her husband, who was visiting at the time, and watched from the visitors' area as Ryan hustled around with blood gases, ordering X rays, lung scans, oxygen, and heparin.

"She's had a blood clot in her lung, I think. But she may have bled into tumor in her lung," Ryan told Mr. Green.

"What tumor in her lung?" said Mr. Green, pugnaciously. "She's got bone tumor."

Ryan realized the awful truth: nobody had told the husband about the lung mets.

"Didn't Dr. Thompson tell you that your wife's tumor had spread to her lung?"

"Never," said Mr. Green, beads of sweat popping out on his ashen forehead. "You don't know what you're talking about. She's had leg tumor."

Ryan took him to the conference room and showed him his wife's X rays. He searched around for a normal X ray, which on that floor was a rare commodity. He put the normal up next to

Mrs. Green's X ray: it didn't take four years of medical school to see the difference.

"Problem is that her symptoms could be caused by a blood clot or by bleeding into the tumor in the lung, which happens spontaneously sometimes."

The husband followed Ryan intently.

"The treatment for a clot is heparin, which would worsen bleeding into a tumor."

"How do you make the distinction?"

"With a lung scan. I'm sending her down with heparin hanging. If it's positive for a clot, we'll start the heparin right there."

"And if it's tumor bleeding?"

"We'll call a surgeon, and observe her."

Mr. Green did not ask what the surgeon could possibly do, or what observing her meant, for which Ryan was glad. Mr. Green had heard enough bad news for the time being. He cursed the private attending for not telling him about the lung mets. He was going to sue that lout for not telling him.

It was clearly clot by the ventilation-perfusion scan.

Ryan was hurrying to see one of Biotto's patients, who was bleeding from her vagina, when Mr. Green caught his arm. Ryan flinched.

"Just wanted to say thanks for explaining things earlier," said Mr. Green. "I can handle things if I have some idea of what's happening, what the problems are."

Ryan wasn't sure that he could be as confident as Mr. Green. Even if Ryan knew the problems, he wasn't sure he could handle them.

Mr. Green's face turned ugly.

"But I'm going to sue that bastard Thompson for not telling me, if I don't punch him out first."

Ryan thought it politic to refrain from pointing out that Dr. Thompson did not give Mrs. Green the lung mets. Although Thompson was a coward for not delivering the bad news himself, and deserved to be punched out.

Biotto's patient needed platelets. Caroline was vomiting again. Her abdomen was a little tense, and Ryan was thinking

101

about calling a surgeon. Then Mrs. Ritalovich and her pancreatic carcinoma died. Ryan liked to think of the tumor twitching and agonizing in its own death struggle after it had killed the patient. She was a No Code (NTBR), and so all Ryan had to do was inform the family and ask for an autopsy. Her family was visiting, which simplified things. Ryan was grateful for that. He could never say the right thing over the phone, and usually just asked the family to come in because the patient had "taken a turn for the worse."

Jon Littleman ended his reign as the longest surviving leukemic. He arrested just as Ryan finally got to the toilet. He arrested before visiting hours ended, so the crowd had to be herded from the room while the team scurried around. Jon was not helped by the effort, but the visitors were impressed.

The visitors were always impressed by arrests. Lots of equipment and frenetic nurses, just like on TV. They forgave Ryan for not saving Jon. They could see he had tried.

During the arrest an admission arrived. Ryan was struck by his unequal pupils. He looked into the eyes with an ophthalmoscope. The optic nerve, coming directly from the brain, is the portal to the brain. Ryan could see he had another brain stem herniation on his hands, and called for the mannitol.

Betty, the nurse, told him.

"No mannitol."

"What do you mean, 'No mannitol'? You mean, 'No, we're fresh out of mannitol,' or, 'No, we got it,' but you're not getting it for me?"

"I mean, this patient gets no mannitol. He's a do nothing, admitted to die," Betty said. "His wife just couldn't take him dying at home."

He did look pretty dead. No reflexes, no withdrawal from painful stimuli. Every once in a long while he'd take a deep breath. He must have been comatose awhile. He was covered with decubitus ulcers.

Caroline got febrile that night, and her abdomen was still a little tense, but her belly X rays were normal. Ryan decided to spare her the worry of a surgeon's visit.

Ryan had all the fevers worked up by midnight and slumped

off to bed. So far he had known what to do for everything. But he was beginning to dread the next round, the next call to action. The heavy legs, tight, buzzing head, contributed. He knew he didn't have the stamina for another admission or arrest, or even to get out of bed. But it was more than that. He felt alone. He hadn't seen another doctor since morning. The evening nurses were mostly minimal-English types. And what if something happened and he couldn't figure out what to do. Or worse yet, if he figured wrong? He'd have to call Fick, who didn't want to be bothered, and probably wouldn't come in anyway. That was the way Fick dealt with his own fear of inadequacy.

What if Caroline went sour with a surgical abdomen he hadn't called the surgeon for, or if Biotto's patient started bleeding again, or if Mrs. Green got short of breath and turned blue again? Most nights he could hope that they all held on and lasted until morning, when the rest of the house staff arrived. But the next sunrise brought Sunday, and more admissions. Ryan usually warmed to his admissions once he actually walked in and met the patient, but until that moment admissions were the bane of his anxious life, regarded with a mixture of fear, hostility, loathing, and paranoia. Fortunately, there were only two beds left open for admissions, unless somebody died. Interns had been known to go to heroic efforts to keep bodies breathing, and beds occupied by nominally living patients, until an admitting day was over.

Sunday was a gift. The admissions rolled in early: two electives for routine chemotherapy. Except for their cancer, they weren't sick at all; no acute problems.

Sunday night Ryan headed to the on-call room at twelve thirty. Convinced by now of the futility of trying to sleep, he put the phone on the bed and turned on TV. Channel Eleven had a telethon: people were fighting cancer with a checkup and a check. Ryan reflected that if every member of the viewing audience sent in just five dollars, cancer would kill just as many people as it did last year. But maybe they'd all get to die in a two-bedded room. Death with dignity was dying in a two-bedded room.

Ryan watched the screen, luminous in the dark room: the

telethon was pulling in money to win the war, to maim, humble, and intimidate the great crab-god cancer. Somehow, Ryan couldn't imagine the nodules on Mrs. Green's films being much intimidated. They just kept rolling along. Someone was singing: it was a bond rally in the war against cancer.

Iggy Bart had said that more people live off cancer than die from it: cancer research was a major industry. Maybe some gray-skinned laboratory gnome would notice some little mold in the wrong place on some lab dish, publish the observation in some gray journal, where scores of equally gray minds would churn it over and out of it all would come a penicillin or a methotrexate for choriocarcinoma.

Everyone pointed to choriocarcinoma, once invariably fatal, now entirely curable, *le sale espoir* of the cancer crusades. Ryan dropped off to sleep as another dancer jigged across the screen, but the phone rang, and he awoke.

"Sorry to bother you, honey, but that guy you admitted to die yesterday. Either he's done it, or he's just set a new world's record for breath holding," said Lucy.

Lucy was on. What a pleasure, a night nurse who spoke English. Ryan went to the room and looked at the patient with Lucy.

"He looked so dead when I admitted him, it's hard to say there's much difference now," said Ryan. "Besides, every time I press on him for deep pain, he seems to move a little."

"Ryan," said Lucy giddily. "Press the pillow."

Ryan pressed the pillow. It moved a little. The patient was on a water bed for his decubitus ulcers. Lucy began to laugh. She was crazy when they made her work nights.

"Either you pronounce him dead, or the pillow alive." She was laughing louder.

"Quiet," said Ryan, thinking of the relatives in the hallway. "They'll hear you."

Ryan wheeled in an EKG machine and settled the issue. The wife came in to view the body.

"Is he really dead?" she asked. Her back was to Lucy, who had buried her face in one hand. Ryan bit his cheek.

"Yes, ma'am. He is."

After that, Lucy kept the floor under control, and Ryan got a solid seven hours' sleep. Watching the sun rise over the East River, sky red, Monday morning, Ryan rejoiced. Reinforcements were on the way. He had lasted until Monday. He wasn't admitting. All he had to do was Morning Rounds, X ray Rounds, scut on his own patients, Chart Rounds, and then he could go home.

9

August 28

Ryan met Hope coming out of the hospital as he was heading home from Whipple.

She was alone, and wearing a light summer dress, which was blown snug around her contours by a summer breeze.

"Well, if it isn't Dr. Ryan, of the Great Moral Imperative."

Ryan's smile collapsed. He struggled past his chagrin to say something. "You always such a warrior?"

"A strange question, coming from the man who set up the great seige of the hospital president's office."

"If you're not in a hurry, would you have a drink with me?"

Hope was unprepared for such civility; disarmed, she accompanied Ryan a block down the street, to Gleason's.

"You know, if I enjoyed adversary relationships, I would have been a lawyer," said Ryan.

Hope fiddled with her martini.

"Are you asking me to lay off?"

"No, but you're no less of a crusader than I am."

Hope's face flushed. "You see nothing but life according to St. Ryan, with your little truths and mandates and sense of justice. But patients don't give a shit about your abstractions. You force it all on them, like some priest with his certainties."

Ryan lowered his voice to answer her. "What makes you think telling them what they want to hear really makes them feel better?"

Hope looked at Ryan's earnest face, and her anger drained away.

"You're right, of course. We shouldn't be fighting. But you

106

shouldn't make the patients your adversaries, either. They shouldn't have to suffer for your principles."

"Look, don't you think I see the truth in what you say? Don't you think I had to admit you were right the other night? But I'm getting better. Hey, you can't know everything the first day."

Hope's face softened, and she ordered another martini.

The drinks were washing over them in soothing tides.

"Whipple isn't easy," Hope said. "But I was just sick of your principles."

"Okay," said Ryan, taking her hand.

"Maybe I expected more of you."

"Why?"

"Your notes. When I read them I see more than just numbers and facts. Your notes seemed almost human."

"No foolin'? Biotto tells me I'm turning into a machine, crushing out my own humanity."

"Biotto?" laughed Hope, with a bitterness that surprised Ryan. "He's one to talk." Hope caught his look. "He's all sensitivity, until he has to get out of bed at three A.M."

"Don't imagine I'm much better, at that hour."

"But you are," said Hope, khaki eyes glowing. "And you care. . . . Why don't you ask me back to your apartment?"

Ryan wasn't sure why she stunned him so. Was it the words, the drinks, the fatigue, or everything combined? But he was sure he couldn't stand with the erection he had.

They repaired to the town house.

10

Dr. Bloomberg was Ryan's attending on the eighth floor at Whipple for the month of August. Ward attendings served a month; they had to hear every case admitted to the ward and help the house staff manage the patients. Bloomberg was an outstanding attending. But he drove Ryan crazy. Until the Halsted conversation.

Bloomberg was a big, round man. He was a gastroenterologist, and appropriately enough, loved to eat.

Apparently, he made a point of searching out the best restaurant in each town he ever passed through.

He knew Blue Point Oyster in Providence, and The Black Pearl in Newport, so Ryan believed he knew what he was talking about. He was quite animated when he was talking about restaurants.

But then again, he was never anything but animated. And cheerful. He was too happy to be at Whipple. He was unflappable, and persistently, even tenaciously, cheerful. Ryan thought cheer entirely inappropriate to Whipple. Ryan was depressed. So was Fick, and so were all the nurses and patients. It was comforting, being miserable in good company.

But Bloomberg refused to be miserable. Ryan presented case after heartbreaking case, tales of suffering humanity, lives humming along with little joys and setbacks, when suddenly, or gradually, an ache in the leg, a little coughed-up blood, turned into a major disaster. Tales of the stricken, told by Ryan, who was stricken in their behalf. And Bloomberg would shake his head. And as often as not, he would smile, or even laugh. He would say happily:

"There, but for the grace of God, go you or I."

He was sympathetic, but unphased.

One day Ryan asked Bloomberg to see Mrs. Halsted, otherwise known as "The Arm." Mrs. Halsted had metastatic breast CA, and had had it a long time before she finally summoned up the courage to see her doctor. By that time her breast was rock hard. Her chest felt like cement had been poured under the skin on the left side. The tumor had insinuated its way into the left armpit, where it obstructed all the lymphatic return, leaving her with the neoplastic equivalent of elephantiasis of the left arm.

She had to lie on her left side all day, staring at her enormous pink arm. For some reason, the skin had not hardened, as is usual, but remained soft, pillowlike, and pink. She weighed about ninety pounds, at least thirty of which was arm.

She never said more than three words at a time to Ryan, who thought it better that she just drift off and die. Ryan hated thinking about Mrs. Halsted, condemned to spend what was left of her life staring at her pink arm. He never drew any blood on her, or sent her to X ray. He just ordered morphine. And he said "hi" on Morning Rounds. Sometimes she said "hi" back.

Ryan brought Bloomberg by just to see if he could think of anything to do for her. Bloomberg elicited the irrelevant fact that she came from Salt Lake City.

"Salt Lake City? I've been there. They have a great little restaurant there, Quail Run. Know it?"

Ryan rolled his eyes. Ryan regretted asking Bloomberg to see her. The Arm didn't know where she was most of the time, much less "Quail Run."

But to Ryan's stupefaction The Arm replied, quite clearly:

"Oh, yes. Of course. It is the best. They serve liquor, did you know?"

"Do I know? That's why I went there in the first place. That's no small thing in Salt Lake," chortled Bloomberg.

They prattled on for ten or fifteen minutes, like old friends. Then Bloomberg left. Ryan was thoroughly contrite and depressed. He had never bothered trying to talk with her. He didn't think she could put together a sentence, much less converse.

Ryan stopped referring to her as "The Arm," and tried to talk with her, as much as he could bring himself to.

He stopped in one morning, to see if her morphine dose was holding her.

"I think I get enough morphine," she said. "But I worry about getting hooked on it, you know."

Ryan was speechless. There she lay, unable to do anything but defecate and stare at her arm, blood calcium climbing daily, every medical regimen useless, waiting for the end, and worried about becoming addicted.

"Well, I—I wouldn't worry about that, Mrs. Halsted; I mean, you need the morphine, in your condition."

"Well, yes, but I don't want to need it forever, for all my life."

Ryan couldn't think of a single thing to say, and left. But the next day she had apparently done some thinking.

"You're not worried about my becoming an addict, are you?"

"No, I'm not."

"Is that because you think that getting hooked would be the least of my problems?"

"Well, I think you shouldn't worry about getting hooked. You need the drug."

"I need the drug because there's nothing more to be done for me, is that it?"

"Yes, I'm afraid so."

"I see," said Mrs. Halsted.

Ryan looked at her bedside table. There was a clipping from the *National Enquirer* about the latest cancer cure.

When she died, two days later, Ryan told Bloomberg. But Bloomberg didn't seem to remember who she was.

11

Wednesday, August 30

Nancy sat down next to Diana in the cafeteria.

"Freezing in the cafeteria," said Nancy. "Such a delight to come in from that steambath out there. What an ugly month." Diana had not looked up from her papers. "That for the Whipple conference?" asked Nancy.

"Yes. It's today, again. Rounds are just so deadly. They asked me to discuss some guy getting adriamycin, and they want to present some cases I haven't even heard about yet. It should be a disaster."

"Whipple is so depressing."

"What's really annoying is that I had to stay in the city last night to look up all the studies we did on this patient. And probably nobody will even show up for these dismal proceedings. And I've got all this data: EKG's, echos, thallium stress. I had to call Alan and tell him he was being denied his conjugal rights again, for the sake of medical science."

"Couldn't you have taken the stuff home?"

"Oh, it was easier to just do it all here. Had to pull the stuff from six different files."

"I take it Alan was not pleased about your staying in the city."

"Not particularly. He has a passive-aggressive way of registering his displeasure. 'Well, dear, do what you think best.' That kind of thing."

By eleven that morning Diana Hayes was in an elevator at Whipple, concentrating on the overhead lights, which showed the numbers of the floors passing, trying to ignore the two interns who stood behind her. She was sure they were inspecting her, visually undressing her, and being quietly lewd.

She got off at twelve. Her page beeper went off. Her new fellow had paged her three times a morning since July first. He couldn't seem to do anything by himself. He kept bugging Diana. Diana hated clinging.

Why couldn't men be men? Why did they not simply know when she wanted to be intruded upon and when she did not? If she wanted to be with a man, or to hear from him, she'd let him know. If not, why bother, as if whimpering could change her heart?

And why could this new fellow not make any decisions himself? He'd page her, present all the relevant data, assembled competently enough to lead to an inevitable decision, then ask her what to do.

"Well, what do you think you should do?" Diana would ask incredulously, having heard him come right to the point of obvious conclusion.

"Well, I just wanted to check it with you," the fellow would say.

Diana found some men very difficult to take.

Wednesday had potential for being another bad day. Things had been relatively calm Monday and Tuesday. Now Ryan was admitting again. Mrs. Green arrested while Ryan was examining her, on Morning Rounds. She came back to life, with just a little chest thumping, but had to go to the ICU. Ryan wanted to call her husband, but Fick wouldn't let him, until they finished rounds.

Then an admission rolled in, looking very gray. Loaded with sarcoma. Fick was bitching about Ryan's missing rounds to see the admission, when the admission arrested. And died. Ryan had to fill out the death certificate, which made Fick even more unhappy, because Ryan missed even more rounds. But there was a rule that the death certificate had to be in the secretary's office downstairs within fifteen minutes of a death. The secretary would page Ryan every five minutes until he answered, or until

112

the death certificate showed up. And Ryan was tired of fighting about death certificates.

To add insult to injury, Ryan had to go to the Cardiology conference, which he usually managed to avoid. He was presenting a case. There would be three cases. Ryan would present the third; Biotto had the second, and the attending would discuss the first. Ryan had heard about the first case. It was typical Whipple: Adriamycin cardiomyopathy; the drug killed the tumor, but also destroyed most of the heart. Ryan considered it a decent trade. The heart was a casualty of friendly fire.

The lights were off when Ryan arrived; an attending was going over slides at the screen in the front of the room. Ryan made his way to the sandwiches in the back. The attending was a woman with a nice voice.

Ryan knew that voice from somewhere, and squinted at the attending, seeing her only by the light of the projector. Her presentation was crisp and sure. Usually he switched to another channel after the first few sentences. He had worked his way to the back of the room to get to the sandwiches, but now he squirmed up closer to the front, toward Diana Hayes.

She was showing the echo slide. Ryan couldn't see her well, but he was sure it was her. The lights came on and he blinked. She started to summarize the findings.

"A big heart, decreased ejection fraction, deteriorating systolic ejection intervals," she said, looking at her audience. Diana had good eye contact with her audience. Then she came to Ryan, staring wide-eyed back at her. She finished the rest of her presentation looking directly at him, without a flicker of fluster.

"Consistent with a diffuse cardiomyopathy, gross failure, and decompensation."

She asked for questions. There were none.

"Let's hear the cases, then."

Biotto got up to present the first case. Ryan, of course, couldn't take his eyes off her. Her attention eventually drifted back to him, and she returned his stare with an impenetrable blue-eyed haze. She was almost smiling, and looking directly at him, but not at all uncomfortable, at least not outwardly. Ryan was roiling.

Biotto started all wrong.

"This is a lady with breast CA, and very negative feelings about her own body image, who comes in now as a rule out M.I., which is why she's being presented at Heart Rounds, but her main problem is coping with her disease, really."

"Coping?"

"Getting in touch with her feelings about her cancer."

"It's customary to identify the patient by sex, age, and occupation, if relevant," said Diana. "Then a chief complaint. Helps everyone get oriented if we all speak the same language."

There were three JAR's and six interns. They could all feel the chill.

"How old is this patient with chest pain?" asked Diana. "She does have chest pain, Dr. Biotto?"

"Yes, chest pain. Three hours of substernal pressure. She was sent to Whipple from The Manhattan Hospital E.R. because she was here before, for her breast CA."

"How old is the patient?"

"Sixty-one."

"Prior history? Risk factors?"

"Not really."

"Not really?" asked Diana evenly.

Ryan began to squirm. There was nothing he could do to help.

"What are the risk factors for myocardial infarction, specifically, this patient did 'not really' have?"

It was a medical-student-level question, and it hurt.

Biotto limped through the case.

Diana obviously was not liking what she was hearing, but finally stopped interrupting, terminating the agony. Everyone but Diana was drenched with sweat.

Ryan was next. He met her glacial eyes.

"This is a sixty-seven-year-old white male, retired house painter, with a long history of chronic obstructive pulmonary disease, who usually runs blood gases with a PO_2 in the sixties

114

and with CO_2's in the forties, with a three-pack-a-day habit, who presents with increasing chest pain, shortness of breath, and fever."

Ryan waited to be interrupted. Diana Hayes just looked at him, raised an eyebrow, amused.

"On physical exam, he showed a blood pressure of one sixty over ninety, a pulse of one hundred, and regular rhythm, and a respiratory rate of thirty with a rectal temp of thirty-nine degrees centigrade. His physical was remarkable for muffled heart sounds, an absent P.M.I., and a positive Kusmaul's."

Ryan paused again, but Diana Hayes just stared at him.

"Would you like to say something about his lab?"

Ryan rattled through the lab, the summary and formulation, and she never said a word, except "thank you" at the end.

Ryan looked at Biotto, all crimson and sweating. *This ain't the minor leagues, boy. Maybe next time, you'll be ready.*

Ryan watched her listen to questions about pericardial effusions. She was whirring, humming inside. Her hair was too blond, her nose a shade too long and thin, but basically, she was perfect.

12

September 4

Ryan had the night off, and got home at 7:00 P.M. Then his beeper went off. He had a firm policy of not answering his beeper once he got home, but the number the page operator called out indicated an outside call, and he thought it might be Hope, who might want to sneak over for a shower. (Hope loved screwing in the shower, despite having to stand up, and all the imaginable inconveniences wrought by tile and glass.) It wasn't Hope. It was Hyman Bloomberg.

"Ryan, I've been paging you and those *meshugeneh* operators kept paging me the wrong intern. Well, anyway. I had all the charts pulled, but the record room ladies tell me you haven't come in to go over them. There turned out to be a hundred and fifty."

The thought of spending his nights off working through a hundred and fifty charts of patients with Gordio in their feces, trying to figure out whether or not they were all homosexuals and whether or not they were passing it back and forth, seemed distinctly unappetizing just when he was thinking of exercising his most heterosexual urges on Hope.

"Dr. Bloomberg, I've been pretty swamped. I just don't know that I'll have time for all this."

"Nonsense, you can do five charts a night; before you know it, you'll be done. It'll be a huge success."

"But even if we prove all these positive Gordios belong to homosexuals, that doesn't prove your theory. Maybe they all use the same john in some gay bar. It doesn't prove it's venereal, even if they're all queer."

"Quite right. Quite right. You're a good man. But I'll bet the only link will be their sexual preference. They'll be from all five boroughs. If Gordio is a venereal disease, or just a disease of homos, it'll be important to know. Think of all the gays with diarrhea and belly pain, and nobody even thinks of Gordio."

Considering all the homosexuals in New York with belly pain and diarrhea was even less appealing than going through a hundred and fifty charts.

"Dr. Bloomberg, I'll think it over. Whipple's really got me tied up."

"You'll be missing a good thing," said Bloomberg, and he hung up.

Ryan's phone rang. It was Hope. She'd be over later. Ryan couldn't say he was really looking forward to seeing her now. Bloomberg's call had depressed him.

He had gotten himself into this whole thing for the wrong reasons. Disease didn't fascinate him. Gordio didn't intrigue him. Disease depressed him. It depressed him just reading about it in medical school, where he thought he had everything he read about.

And if pathology depressed him, clinical medicine induced catatonia, especially when it meant death certificates. Claude Bernard had said it; now Ryan understood: "Medicine is the noblest of professions, the most depressing of trades." Only Hyman Bloomberg could like any of it.

There was more to the problem of Hope. Hope was a way out. But lately Ryan had the feeling he was getting *in,* and faster than he could control. She was at the town house more and more. She wouldn't let Ryan just crawl off. Her very presence was a demand. And Ryan had all the demands he could handle right now. He loved her skin, her smells, and her wonderful khaki eyes. But she was getting *involved.* Everyone wanted Ryan to get involved: patients, Bloomberg, now Hope. Ryan wanted a shell, a place to hide.

13

September 5

When Caroline was feeling well, she was a delight. It was hard to believe she was really a patient, with a potentially lethal disease. Once her fever dropped, she felt stronger, and once her white blood cells regenerated, she could walk around the ward. She bounced back quickly, changed her hospital gown for a Villager sundress, and took her archaeology books down to the window at the end of the hall, where she read in the sun.

The head nurse wouldn't let her drink coffee in the nursing station, so Ryan had his coffee at the window, with Caroline and Sally, her favorite nurse. It was the only pleasant part of the morning. Caroline looked so normal when she was feeling well. She hadn't lost her hair or turned yellow or wasted away. Except for the dark bruises over her veins, she didn't even look like a patient.

Ryan went to see her that evening after Chart Rounds. She was eating dinner and Ryan had the night off. He had a date with Hope, who would come over to his apartment and want to take a shower. But he thought he'd take Caroline outside for a walk, down the avenue, like a normal person, just for a few minutes.

"It'd be therapeutic, Caroline."

"I'm not allowed," said Caroline. "Dr. Woods gave me my chemotherapy today and said I'd better stay in bed tonight."

"You feel bad now?" asked Ryan, noticing a subtle, sudden change of shade in Caroline's face.

"No," she said, sitting up suddenly; she grabbed an emesis basin and filled it with vomit.

"I just get so sick," she said, "and you can never tell when it'll come over me."

"See you tomorrow," said Ryan, and he went home to Hope.

Ten minutes later Ryan was walking home, along Sixty-eighth Street, past the concrete playground with the stony geometric figures even city kids could not destroy. He usually hurried home after signing out, but tonight Hope would be there, talking with Arch in the kitchen. Ryan would have to go with them to Gleason's, or somewhere like that, for an hour. All he really wanted was to sleep.

Ryan had called Hope two days before, from Whipple, when he was feeling his hormones surge. But now, unpredictably, he came home wanting just to be alone, to minister to no one's needs but his own. But he had a date with Hope, and would have to talk and listen and react. He just wanted to get in the bath with a glass of wine, read *Sports Illustrated,* and go to bed. He wanted to lie between cool, clean sheets. But Hope would be there, undemanding, compliant, ready for action.

Ryan's list of great pleasures had been reordered over the last two months. First, by a wide margin, was a long, uninterrupted, dream-filled sleep. Then friendly, uncomplicated sex. A distant third came food, fresh air, and movies. At least that's how it was for this month, at Whipple.

Hope was in the kitchen with Arch when Ryan arrived.

"You look beat," she said.

"Just staggered by my awesome responsibilities."

"You look rotten."

"He's okay," said Arch. "He always looks like that when he gets home from Whipple."

"But your eyes," said Hope. "Look at his eyes. They're colorless. You look like you've been bled."

"Staggered is all."

"I think you need a bath and to bed," said Hope.

"We'll go for a beer," said Ryan, dutifully.

"Gleason's," said Arch.

"To bed," said Hope. "This is my date."

119

Ryan had his bath. Nothing heals like suds and water. Showers can be almost as good, but the soaking, steaming of every pore in hot bathwater is unmatched.

Ryan stepped out, feeling like a new man. He wrapped himself in his white terry cloth robe.

Hope had made his bed with new sheets and was waiting there, between them. She had Blood, Sweat and Tears on the stereo.

Ryan threw the bathrobe on the floor and rolled under the sheets, falling asleep instantly.

Hope understood. She didn't get angry so much anymore.

14

September 6

Ryan had come over from Whipple to eat in the cafeteria and to check up on some X-ray results. The X-ray reading rooms were all in the Main House, and Ryan needed little excuse to desert Whipple, jog across the avenue, and feel a part of the world of the living again.

Ryan was in the elevator, on his way to X Ray, reading the notes on his clipboard. Throughout the day he wrote himself notes on his patients. Check Smith's upper G.I. series, check the lung scan on Jones. His face was buried in the notes when Diana Hayes got on, carrying a pile of EKG's almost up to her nose. She was talking to another cardiologist, and her voice penetrated Ryan's preoccupation.

Ryan was standing behind her, and he knew she hadn't noticed him. He continued to stare at his clipboard, but his full attention was now on her. His floor came and went, and he stayed fastened to his clipboard.

She had a nice voice, and great assurance. Diana and the cardiologist got off together, and Ryan studied her slim ankles and thin but shapely legs. When the doors shut out his view, he pushed the OPEN button and followed her.

Ryan tore himself away from her office door. It said DIANA HAYES, M.D., DIRECTOR OF DIAGNOSTICS, DIVISION OF CARDIOLOGY. He went to X Ray and looked at the films distractedly. He went to the department office. He got a medical catalog and looked up Diana Hayes: Vassar College, P&S, Associate Professor. Ryan read it over and over, trying to extract new information with each reading. He went down to the library and took out the *Index*

Medicus, authors' list, and looked her up. She had published about six articles a year for the past six years. Ryan got the journals from the stacks and made copies until he ran out of dimes for the Xerox machine.

Retiring to his study, Ryan turned the pages of Diana's articles tremulously. Her words danced across the photocopied stage, and Ryan felt smaller and less significant with each paragraph. There she was, on display and dazzling. Ryan read her crisp discussions. She made it sound so easy. Ryan wondered if she knew how good she was. He looked up from the pages and visualized her walking down the hallway to her office. He thought of her at Belinda's. She knew. She was alluring, and conscious of her own effect. But it was her sheer indifference to her own allure that overwhelmed Ryan and made him feel small by comparison. She had work she cared about, and it freed her from the need for others.

Hope called around midnight; she was getting off the evening shift at the Tower and was angling for an invitation to Ryan's shower.

"I called you around dinner, but no answer," she said.

"I was in the library, looking up some stuff."

"You reading now? This is getting serious. I'll have to come over and take your temp."

"I'm afebrile."

"You alone?"

"Just me and Diana Hayes."

"Oh," said Hope, tightly.

"She's the author of the article, turkey. Come on over."

"Very funny."

Hope and Ryan sat in bed drinking wine and listening to Rod Stewart on the stereo. Hope hadn't worked at Whipple for several weeks.

"You'd be so proud of my progress," Ryan said. "The eighth floor is totally divorced from reality. You'd really approve."

"Do you lie?"

122

"All the time."

"Oh, delightful, tell me some lies."

"I've transcended confabulation with a certain Mr. Kelley: with him, truth, reality, psychosis all blend. It's wonderful."

"Kelley? Must be new."

"He is. He's a retired Navy captain, with a pain in his back, protein in his urine, and, you guessed it, myeloma in his bone marrow."

"Bad news."

"And a calcium which almost, but not quite, set a new eighth-floor record, which, added to his underlying senility, was the final insult to an already precarious mental status. He's convinced it's 1943, told me that on rounds the other day. You should have seen the nurses when he said that: the nurses just couldn't take another crazy, after Mrs. Christensen."

"I can imagine."

"Well, I asked Captain Kelley where he was, a little time-place orientation, and he fires back a set of coordinates, which I presumed put us all in the middle of the Atlantic. Everyone just groaned. But did I groan? Did I say, 'I cannot tell a lie'? No. I said, 'Yes, sir.' And I asked if he had any special orders, which he did, of course. Ordered himself a commode and bathroom privileges."

"Good for you. Good for the Captain."

"Oh, it was terrific. Everyone really got to like the Captain. The nurses started saying 'Aye-Aye,' till it drove me crazy, and it really got out of hand. Sally says 'Blow me down' or 'Avast' to everything Kelley says, that kind of thing, and the head nurse got pretty worked up about the patient's dignity."

"She's such an old fogey."

"But you know, the Captain got better: he got out of bed, which made his calcium one hell of a lot easier to control. Jesus, I started wishing he'd slow down: he marched up and down the halls, like he's striding the decks."

"Sounds wonderful," said Hope.

"Yeah, it was," said Ryan, taking a sip of wine.

"Was?"

"He arrested this morning. A true disaster. Sally found him just blue and bloated not ten minutes after Morning Rounds. We had just gone over him. And the code was terrible: he didn't come back at all; his bowels emptied . . ."

"Oh, shit," said Hope, absently. "I hate that."

"Most indelicate. Doesn't do wonders for sterile technique. We were all covered with it by the time we finally gave up. We would have stopped sooner, but Sally wanted us to keep trying. The Captain went down without his ship."

"That's too bad for Sally."

"Yeah, she really liked the old guy. She was all teary-eyed. She said she felt like we should wrap him up in a flag, carry him down to the East River, and drop him in."

"You should have."

"I thought it was indicated, but the head nurse was standing there, and I think she thought we might really try it, so she wrapped the body herself and had it down to the morgue before we had finished washing up."

"No foolin'?"

"I kid you not."

"That must be the first body she's wrapped in twenty years."

"I'm sure."

"Well, at least Captain Kelley went out with his boots on, for all he knew," said Hope.

15

September 7

Whipple was something you just had to get used to: the smells, the dying, the heat. It took a month for Ryan to numb sufficiently to ignore it, and learn not to care about being called at night to see patients for whom he could think of little to do, or for whom the only thing to be done was to fill out a death certificate. In black ink. As he began to expect things to go wrong in every imaginable way, he found things less uncomfortable, more predictable, easier to handle.

Most of Whipple was beyond human, or technological, control. But some order could be invoked. When things seemed to quiet down, Ryan could say, "This is the calm before the storm." When the number of scheduled admissions was low, he could say, "We're gonna get clobbered with emergency admits tonight, for sure." When some patient Ryan couldn't stand see suffer any more finally passed on to the Eternal Care Unit, he could say, "There's another empty bed to fill with a new admission." And when, against all probability, a patient at Whipple actually improved, he could say, "She'll find a way to crash, probably after midnight, some night I'm on call with ten admissions." It helped. It really did. If it happened, he had the satisfaction of having predicted it. If not, he was still ahead.

Ryan was glad to have August behind him. Of course, September had ended Diana Hayes's tenure as Cardiology attending at Whipple. To glimpse her, Ryan had to cross the avenue separating Whipple and the Tower. And Bloomberg was no longer the ward attending on Ryan's floor. Ryan missed Bloomberg's dolphin face, his irritating cheerfulness, his maddening irrepressibility.

Ryan had Hope at night. During the day he was stuck with Biotto. And Fick. Mostly Biotto. Fick disappeared as often as possible, confining his supervision to Morning Rounds and afternoon Chart Rounds.

The days quickly solidified into a routine of arrival, rounds, problem after problem, X-ray review, Chart Rounds, and trying to finish up and get home as quickly as possible after Chart Rounds.

The guilt was wearing off. Ryan no longer cringed at the news he had decimated another bone marrow with some chemotherapy pushed into some invaded vein—it was expected. So what? So what if a calcium set new records in the bloodstream of some patient, while Ryan unsuspectingly continued to pour more calcium in through an IV line? It happened to the best of them.

The problems just happened. Nobody wore hair shirts. You just shrugged and thought about the big picture. Ryan could lean back in a chair now and imagine as many disasters as possible for a given patient, and then watch, with some imperturbability, as each disaster actually happened, despite all efforts to avoid it. The routine was the important thing. Write the orders in the morning, think of all the little things that could foul up the plans those orders outlined, and then watch things disintegrate. The routine was the thing. It got you through the day.

Morning Rounds were dragging by. Ryan had been on the night before, and all he could think about was sitting down in the nursing station with a cup of coffee and his list of things to do for his patients, and getting the telephoning out of the way. But Fick stood between Ryan and all those calls to chemistry, scan, and hematology. He kept doing rectal exams on every leuk. Once a week Fick stuck his finger into every leukemic rectum, looking for unsuspected abscesses. Leuks were dying with sepsis, meningitis, cerebral abscesses, and peritonitis, but Fick would be damned if he let a single rectal abscess go undetected.

"Rectal abscesses are the one thing we can do something

126

about," said Fick. "We can call the blades, and get them drained. I just get sick thinking how bad it would be having a rectal abscess, not being able to take a crap or even fart without excruciating pain."

So they were doing Rectal Rounds.

"Does that hurt?" Fick asked one of Ryan's leukemics.

"Not a bit," said the leukemic, whose head was held a good four inches off the bed, without benefit of pillow. Ryan noticed the head-holding, hoping Fick was too fixated on the rectum to notice himself. No such luck. Fick tried to flex the patient's neck. It was stiff as a board.

"He needs a tap, a blood count, some cultures, and a neuro consult," Fick told Ryan.

Ryan looked at his list and realized a lumbar puncture would set him back at least half an hour.

"His white count was less than a hundred yesterday; he's on every antibiotic known to man," said Ryan. "What good would a tap do him?"

"Antibiotics? Any of 'em good for fungus, for cryptococcus?"

"Come on," said Ryan, angrily. "Suppose I find fungus in his spinal fluid? Then what? Amphotericin for this guy? I'd rather croak than get amphotericin dripped in my spinal fluid."

"Would you?" said Fick, ironically.

"Yeah," said Ryan.

"How do you know?" said Fick.

Ryan stared at Fick in disbelief. Fick was as cynical as anyone else, was he not?

"These leuks didn't come here for us to give up on them. They came here because we offer them something; even if it's pretty awful, it's better than the big zero they're facing. You know how they died before chemotherapy?"

"In blastic crises or sepsis, I guess," said Ryan. "Same way they die now."

"I beg to differ," said Fick. "They died with everyone standing around their bedside wringing their hands, saying nothing can be done. Neither way is too pleasant, but I'll take the aggressive way out any day."

Ryan stared at Fick in disbelief; Fick, who absented himself and wrapped himself in the cloak of therapeutic nihilism, had moments of doubt.

Ryan recalled Iggy's words the night Mrs. Harvey almost bled out and Ryan thought they were going to be up all night and still lose her. "Doing something is better than doing nothing," Iggy had said.

"For whom?" asked Ryan. "She'll tube, no matter what we do."

"I didn't say it's better for her. It *might* be better for her. Nobody can know that. For us. It's better for us."

"If it doesn't help her, it sure isn't gonna make me feel any better to lose a night's sleep pumping blood into her."

"Try going to bed, with her bleeding," said Iggy. "See how you feel when you get up in the morning."

"She'll just go out and drink again, if we get her by this time."

"Then go to bed," said Iggy, with his wise, sunken eyes.

"What would you tell Baptist?"

"That we just couldn't save her. That she arrested," smiled Iggy. "Don't tell me you'd stay up just because you'd be afraid Baptist might review the chart. Don't blame Baptist for this one."

"You'd really let her go?"

"If you want to."

Of course Ryan had stayed up, and saved her.

16

September 11

Even at Whipple, some mistakes were best avoided. Ryan was called to see Mrs. Green, Monday morning, just as Morning Rounds were beginning. Ryan had learned to ignore Fick's grumblings about missing rounds, and about priorities, and he hurried to see Mrs. Green, arriving just in time to see her heart monitor show her going into complete heart block.

Ryan tried getting an IV into each arm, without success, and watched Mrs. Green become hypotensive before his eyes. Her blood pressure was falling—not what one likes to see when the electrical activity of the heart has just gone on the blink. She needed atropine injected into a vein, and maybe a pacemaker, which is put through a vein. Ryan decided to get access to a large vein, and slammed a CVP line into the vein under the right collarbone. In his haste he sheared off the polyethylene part of the CVP with the metal needle, and the polyethylene tube floated free, downstream, to the right side of the heart.

Not easily daunted, Ryan got his IV line in the other side, under the other collarbone, pushed atropine through it, clearing the heart block.

That left the problem of the polyethylene tube in Mrs. Green's right ventricle.

Ryan dragged Fick away from Morning Rounds. Fick was not pleased.

"You're sure you sheared it off?"

"Positive."

They got an X ray. The tube was coiled in the right ventricle, all right. Mrs. Green kept asking what the problem was.

Ryan looked at the X ray and felt tears well up.

"She'll have to have her chest cut open to get that thing out," he said.

"There might be another way," said Fick. "I heard Dr. Hayes give a talk about fishing those things out with a net device. She put it in through a vein."

"What?"

"She puts it in through the right arm, floats it to the heart, over the same path your tube followed."

Ryan hated the sound of "your tube."

"It works sort of like a tampon coming out of the cardboard tube," Fick was saying. "It has a sheath; you pull back, and out pops this little net. You snare the offending polyethylene tube, pull everything back into the sheath, and get out."

"Let's call her," said Ryan, overjoyed.

Fick called her, and she told him to bring Mrs. Green over in an hour. When they got to the cath lab, she was already gowned and ready to go.

Diana was very nice to Mrs. Green. She was less nice to Ryan.

"To whom does she owe this little tube?" asked Diana, holding Mrs. Green's X rays up to the light, peering at the offending tube, which was looking bigger and more menacing as Ryan looked at it.

"To me."

"Didn't they ever tell you not to pull back once you had the needle engaged with those CVP's?"

"I was in a hurry."

"Evidently."

Diana went back into the lab where Mrs. Green was lying on the procedure table. She handed a lead apron to Fick and one to Ryan, and went to work.

Ryan couldn't believe how fast and sure she was. She had the catheter in the clutches of the net within five minutes. They watched on the fluoroscope as she pulled the tube and net back into the sheath.

"It's like TV," said Mrs. Green, who could see the monitor above her head.

"Live, but not in color," said Diana.

Mrs. Green laughed.

Diana pulled it out, tube in tow.

"Feel anything?" Diana asked Mrs. Green.

"No."

"Good."

Diana held up the polyethylene tube for Fick and Ryan to see.

"Nice haul!" roared Fick.

Ryan felt himself breathe again.

"Thanks," he said.

"Anytime," said Diana. "Just don't make a habit of it."

They wheeled Mrs. Green back to Whipple, through the tunnel.

"She's very nice," said Mrs. Green. "Really a lovely person."

17

September 12

Ryan was haunted by that CVP in Mrs. Green's right ventricle for a solid twenty-four hours, which is about as long as he stayed haunted by any one item for any reason, at Whipple. She had not suffered any real discomfort, and in fact Ryan had saved her life again, a fact which Mrs. Green had taken into account, but which consoled Ryan only a little. Of course, had she been lost to all efforts, the CVP line would have seemed a small bungle, and disturbed Ryan not at all. He could have excoriated himself for bigger things.

But as it was, Ryan plunged into a twenty-four-hour depression over the CVP line. He had screwed up; had to be bailed out. And everyone knew. Diana knew. Fick knew. And by now half the house staff was probably chuckling about it over coffee and cafeteria doughnuts.

Ryan knew he would have laughed had it happened to someone else. Had Biotto sheared off that catheter and had to drag his patient off to Diana Hayes for rescue, Ryan would have entered it into his file on Biotto. Laid-back, spaced-out, sloppy Biotto. Now it was part of Ryan's file, entered into the mental registers all the interns and residents kept on each other.

They did watch each other. Not at all maliciously: curiously, they watched. Ryan watched his residents and attendings, as a child watches his mother doing the most commonplace things, watching with rapt, unshakable attention. He learned how things were done that way.

And they talked about each other. Residents discussed interns, and interns dissected the talents and deficits of just about everyone. And Ryan knew that CVP line would not be entered in his own plus column. It wasn't a big screw-up, but it smarted.

The big black marks were for the unthinking and the uncompulsive: house officers who didn't notice a low serum potassium, or didn't think to check the serum potassium at all, or, worse yet, who noticed but didn't bother to ponder its significance. There was a book on everyone. The book was more than reputation, it was a compendium of stories and cases about each attending, resident, anyone who had been around long enough to be remembered.

There was a book on Iggy, and Fick, and Bloomberg, and Maxwell Baptist. And it mattered to each of them. For the residents it mattered because a good book meant people listened, asked your opinion. Interns who had never worked with you did what you told them, and worked hard for you, because they knew the book on you. For the attendings a good book with the house staff and other attendings meant referrals.

Fick summed up the book on anyone with the slightest provocation. Fick was a walking synopsis. He knew Ryan had worked with Iggy for a few weeks before coming to Whipple, and he wanted to be sure Ryan had come away with the proper impression.

"Iggy may be a scrawn-ball Yiddle from the Lower East Side, but he's one of the smartest men to ever stick his ears between a stethoscope," said Fick.

"He's a maniac," said Biotto. "He doesn't relate to patients."

Ryan, through sheer force of will, managed to remain silent, although he developed a remarkably sudden headache over his left eye.

"Oh, that's just his second-generation imitation of the WASP establishment doc," said Fick.

Ryan started listening, despite his determination to ignore whatever either one of them had to say about Iggy.

"He was the first Queens College boy to get into the pristine halls of the university medical college at The Manhattan Hospital," said Fick, who had been rejected from the same institution before matching with the Tower for his internship. Fick had to settle for Hopkins for medical school, but finally made it to The Manhattan Hospital for house-staff training. Iggy, however, was a "full blood," meaning medical school and house-staff training all at the Tower.

Throughout medical school Ryan had followed the progress of several upperclassmen as they moved along ahead of him from preclinical to clinical training to graduation and to internship. Snatches of conversation in elevators documented the growth: talk of grades and exams gave way to bilirubins, sed rates, and arrests. Ryan knew few upperclassmen well enough to talk to but he had followed a half dozen silently. Some of these had stayed on to do their internships and residencies at The Manhattan Hospital, and Ryan continued to watch them pass their milestones. Iggy, of course, was a curiosity, and had been watched, with his cadaverous face, redheaded coloring, and his wise, starved eyes.

Fick was still talking about Iggy.

"The Manhattan Hospital's medical school did not admit people from places like Queens College. But Iggy got in somehow. And where did he finish?" Fick was looking at Ryan for the answer. Ryan had no idea. Ryan was thinking that there had been five people from Queens College in his class, one year behind Iggy, at The Manhattan Hospital's university medical school.

"I give up," said Ryan.

"Numero uno," said Fick, with conviction. "Don't let the designer shirts and ties fool you," Fick told Biotto, who was rolling his eyes. "Iggy knows a shitload of medicine, and he doesn't miss a thing."

"Ever heard his gomer-orientation lecture?" asked Biotto.

"Ever hear about Marjory Sweeney?" replied Fick.

"Who?"

"Little old constipated lady came to the E.R. one night, when Iggy was a medical student, doing an E.R. elective. Lady's crazy as a gomer can be. Disoriented, wild. Iggy knows old ladies can get like that when they need to be catheterized. He caths her, and thinks the urine's pretty dark. The resident says 'Sure it's dark, Iggy. It's concentrated urine.' Iggy doesn't buy that. He talks to the family, finds out the lady's gone bonkers every time she's taken her tranquilizer. Tranquilizer turns out to be pheno-barbital. Iggy fights to get her admitted. Iggy thinks she has porphyria. The resident laughs, sends her home. But Iggy makes her an appointment for his own clinic. The long and short of it is that he got a delta levulinic acid on her, and it was positive. The only case of porphyria to be discovered at The Manhattan Hospital in ten years. Iggy Bart."

Biotto shrugged. "Anyone ever test Iggy's urine?" he said. "He's got to have something to make him as crazy as he gets."

Ryan sniffed at Biotto. He had heard the book on Iggy and the book was good.

18

September 13

Hope called just as Ryan was getting past the second lock. He got the phone on the sixth ring. Ryan wasn't on call, a night off, and it was 6:30 P.M. She said she'd be over that night for dinner, Walter Cronkite, and a long, steamy shower. Ryan looked at his watch.

He put a chicken in the oven, cleaned up, not thinking about Hope. He had Diana Hayes on the brain. Why did she dangle before him so invitingly?

Hope got there in time to save the chicken, whisking it out of the oven and shaking salt and paprika around. She threw a little brown bag into the refrigerator and started washing dishes, which Arch and Ryan had let collect.

"Jesus, a lucky thing for you they don't send health inspectors to nonproprietary establishments. This kitchen'd be closed in a minute."

"Yeah," said Ryan, reading inertly at the kitchen table. He was reading an article by Diana Hayes, on nuclear imaging after myocardial infarction.

Ryan went to the refrigerator for a root beer and discovered the brown bag.

"What's this?" he said, looking in.

"Hey, leave that alone," said Hope, trying to grab it away. "Those are mine."

"Mycostatin suppositories? I didn't suppose they belonged to Arch."

"Jesus," said Hope.

"Why do we rate a supply of our own?"

"Because I'm over here at least two nights a week, and I keep missing them, so I need a supply here."

"Why don't you stick 'em in with the foam in the bathroom?"

"Because," said Hope, swiping at the bag Ryan dangled just out of her reach, "they have to be kept refrigerated. Great doctor you are. Don't even know about Mycostatin."

"Never had to use it, or knew anyone who did."

"Christ, you can be a pill."

The chicken was edible, although Ryan hardly noticed. He sat reading Diana Hayes, while Hope ate and talked to the top of his head.

"I've got next Tuesday off," she said. "Want to eat some real Chinese chicken down at Mott and Pell?"

"Sure," said Ryan. But she wasn't sure he had really heard.

"Sure was awful about that explosion over at the Tower," said Hope. "Blew off half the west wing."

"Yeah," said Ryan, reading.

"Call me when you get your reading done," said Hope, getting up and storming out of the kitchen.

The slamming door jarred Ryan, who got up slowly, listening for the outer door. It never slammed. So he sat back down and finished the article. Hope slid back into the room.

"Sorry I blew up."

"That's okay," said Ryan.

"You've just gotten more dedicated lately."

"What d'ya mean?"

"Dunno, you just read more, I guess. I shouldn't complain. But sometimes I feel like I might as well not be here."

"Hey, don't be ridiculous. Who would I take showers with?"

19

September 14

It was a Thursday evening, and Ryan got out of the hospital at seven thirty.

There was still enough sunlight left after rounds to get to the park. Ryan rushed home, threw on a raincoat to conceal his whites, and headed west.

He broke his pace, entering the park. He walked along the road to the Bethesda fountain and down past the rowboat lake, on toward the sailboat pond.

A few kids were zooming around the pond's encircling sidewalk, and Ryan sat on a bench near the Hans Christian Andersen statue. He followed a woman with his eyes, watching her from his bench as she approached. She was looking at the water. It was Diana.

Why was she dangled before him? Every time she receded a little, he was reexposed to her. Well, this time he was going to ignore her.

On the other hand, it had to be fate. Ryan watched her walk by. He started to get up, but realized he had nothing to say. He didn't deserve her. Some greasy, aggressive bartender, with his shirt unbuttoned to his navel, and a gold necklace on his hairy neck, deserved her: the greaseball at least would have the balls to approach her.

Ryan thrust his hands into his pockets and paced home, seething with self-contempt.

September 15

"These doctors will rob us all blind. All they care about is making a buck," said Arch, walking down Second Avenue with Ryan. "We ought to have all their decisions reviewed by a panel of lawyers, every Friday."

"Yeah, right," said Ryan, absently.

Arch cursed under his breath. The trouble with Ryan was his absences. Arch had lived with Ryan for more than four years and figured that Ryan had been conscious maybe a year of it. The only times Arch got Ryan out of the house was for a trip to Bloomie's, where Ryan was really unreachable, watching women; or when they went to the movies.

"Whipple got you down again?"

"Nothing that serious. Just women," said Ryan.

"You're not exactly hurting for female companionship. How many times a week do I hear the shower going for two hours at a stretch? I don't know about you and Hope, but since you two got thick and fast, there's never enough hot water to wash the dishes."

"Trouble with Hope is she's bright, perceptive, and in love with me."

"A major error."

"Obviously."

"Hope's not going to be easy to top."

"Remember that time we went to Belinda's?"

"Do I remember? How many times has something like that happened to me?"

"Well, that blonde I was talking to is a doctor at the Tower."

"No foolin'? The blonde with the cheekbones?"

"She's a big honcho in fact."

"She was also not bad-looking. What happened with you two that night?"

"Less than might be expected. But I've seen her since. She's really something special."

"Did you ever follow up?"

"Follow up?"

"Did you ask her out?"

"Ask her out?"

"Yeah, you know, 'Would you like to have dinner with me?' That kind of thing."

"Arch, you just can't do that with this kind of woman."

"You were loose enough with her that night at Belinda's."

"That was before I knew who she was."

"You still don't know."

"I think she's married."

"Nobody's perfect."

"I just don't have the balls."

"You ran through enough women a while back."

"That was different: if I got shot down I didn't really care. No real risk."

"Hey, you're starting at zero. You've nowhere to go but up."

"I just wish I could talk to her."

20

September 18

Monday should not have been a bad day. Ryan wasn't admitting. His patients were as stable as patients ever are at Whipple, and the September mugginess had abated a little.

The chief resident stopped by with an unsolicited encouraging word.

"Ryan, you bitch too much, but your write-ups are the best we've seen around here in a while."

Then Sally told Ryan that he had better go see Caroline. When Sally said things like that, Ryan knew he'd better go see. All the patients looked so sick all the time, and Ryan hadn't developed a sense for who was going sour. Sally had it; most of the good Whipple nurses had it. They spent more time at the bedside, while the interns were writing prize-winning notes, or off at rounds. The nurses read the patients. It was remarkable how they sensed a patient beginning to slide down the tubes.

Ryan hustled in to see Caroline. She looked about the same as she had on Morning Rounds, which meant Sally had been right: nobody at Whipple looked stable unless they were about to die. She wasn't as bright and quick as usual, and when she sat up, her blood pressure dropped twenty points.

Her physical exam was unremarkable, except for the blood pressure. But she was limp as a rag doll. No fever, no stiff neck. But those signs were often absent in patients on steroids. Seeing her lying there, so pale, Ryan forgave her for spoiling the one opportunity he had all week to catch up on his paperwork. Still she was creating a problem, with her hypotension and her limpness.

He got out a spinal-tap tray. The spinal fluid was yellow, and thick. It was loaded with pus. Ryan started her on Chloramphenicol. He would rather have used safe, reliable penicillin. But someone had told Caroline once that she was allergic to penicillin. Now Ryan couldn't use it. Chloramphenicol was risky. It occasionally did nasty things to white blood cells, and Caroline had few enough of those. But Ryan used it.

He went back to write a note in Caroline's chart. He thought about calling a Neurology consult, or maybe Infectious Disease. Or just Fick. But he decided not to panic. He'd see how she did. If her fever was down in a few hours, he'd hold steady. Ryan had learned to have the courage of his mistakes with everyone but Caroline. He tried to be strong. He tried to think and rethink, to miss nothing.

The trouble was, he couldn't concentrate. Before he'd even finished the note on Caroline, he was being pulled off to do a blood culture on one of Biotto's febrile patients. The nurses wanted the culture stat, meaning now. And Biotto was busy admitting. Ryan tried to turn his attention to the new problem, the blood culture lady. He was always doing that at Whipple. There was just never any time to think.

The patient was sitting in a pile of her own feces.

"Do you always go in bed?"

The patient smiled pleasantly.

"No, just lately."

"Can you stop it, if you try; or do you just give up waiting for the bedpan?"

"It just comes out," she said, still smiling incongruously.

Ryan looked at her chart. She had metastatic breast. He went back over her. Her rectal sphincter was flaccid. Her toes fanned out when he stroked the soles of her feet. He called Biotto.

Biotto disagreed with the physical findings before he even saw the patient. He didn't want to believe there was anything wrong. He was admitting today, and he didn't have time for a problem.

"Don't do me favors like this," he snapped.

Ryan went back to his own problem, Caroline. She looked better, having gotten some IV fluid. She also felt better.

"You cured my headache with that tap," she told Ryan.

"You denied having a headache," said Ryan.

"Did I?" Caroline looked concerned.

Biotto came by later to tell Ryan that the lady in the feces had been seen by a neurologist, who ordered a myelographic study of her spinal cord: a large metastatic tumor mass was compressing her cord. She had gone to surgery.

Ryan was glad he hadn't rubbed it in when he arrived the next morning and heard about Biotto's bad night: a patient had told Biotto that he was sick to death of having his blood drawn. If Biotto stuck him one more time, the patient said, he'd kill himself. Biotto had heard that before, and drew the blood culture. The patient waited for Biotto to leave, smashed his IV bottle, slashed both wrists with a piece of broken glass, and exsanguinated before anybody knew what had happened.

21

September 19

With just two weeks left to endure at Whipple, Ryan allowed himself to emerge from the one-day-at-a-time mentality the place demanded. He drifted over to the Tower, more and more, and even let himself daydream about the possibility of his impending escape.

Each morning he found it noticeably easier to get out of bed. He began to fear that, this year, something would happen to delay October.

He still found himself somnambulant during Morning Rounds, trying to remember whether or not he had gone home the night before. The headache was the giveaway. If he had one, he had been on call. If not, he must have been home, asleep, the night before.

On nights when he wasn't on call, his head began to clear by the end of dinner. Then Hope came over, and he realized he was actually home.

But now the fog in which he spent his days was breaking up. He drifted back across the great divide of First Avenue, to The Manhattan Hospital. He allowed its faces and sounds and smells to insinuate themselves back into his limbic system. He was emerging from the underworld.

The possibilities in the living world called out. Diana Hayes passed him in a hallway, smiled, and disappeared around a corner.

Now Ryan was no longer content with chance sightings. Unexpected encounters caught him off guard, unable to closely observe her. Ryan discovered that she went to the medical library every morning, so he stationed himself there. He hid behind a *Times,* which he never read, and waited. She breezed in, every morning, at ten thirty, sometimes earlier, and used the *Index Medicus.* She would smile, just once, in Ryan's direction, his morning dole, stirring him wildly.

Every morning it was the same silent frenzy, Ryan running through scenario after dreary scenario, despondently, and ultimately being paged back across the street, to Whipple. Whatever he might say, she had obviously heard better.

She was married: Iggy had confirmed that. Her husband was older, a professor of something nonmedical. They lived in Nyack, or someplace outside Manhattan. She had a room in one of the residences.

Iggy didn't think she fooled around. Iggy said that if she did, he would certainly like to know. Iggy thought she had the world's most enticing legs, especially for a woman her age. Ryan stopped listening. She was definitely out of the question, out of his sweaty, hysterical reach.

Ryan's floor was having an easy day admitting. They had a lady with breast cancer whose main problem was a heart murmur. She was suppose to have a cardiac catheterization. Ryan was overjoyed. For starters, she took up a bed and very little time. For another thing, every cath patient got seen by Diana Hayes. She wrote a note in every cath chart, which Ryan could read in silent agony.

Ryan did not have to wait for the note. Diana strolled into the patient's room just as Ryan was finishing his physical exam.

"Well, what do you think?" she asked Ryan, pulling him out into the hall. Ryan stood blinking, overwhelmed. She was obviously delighted with the disarray her sneak attack had wrought.

"What do I think?" repeated Ryan, numbly.

"I already asked you that," said Diana. "What do you think is making that racket in Mrs. Costello's heart?"

"Oh," said Ryan, feeling truly moronic, "a lot of aortic stenosis." He was noticing her straight, white teeth. He had never noticed how straight and white they were before.

"Think she should go to the blades?"

"Guess that'll depend on the cath," said Ryan.

"Find out tomorrow," said Diana, turning on her heels and disappearing down the hall, leaving Ryan with a heart rate of one hundred and sixty.

"She just came by today, out of the blue," Ryan told Arch. He was jumping from one foot to the other. "I mean, I think it was some kind of feeler."

"Oh, she's settled on you," said Arch, puffing on his pipe reflectively. "It all comes down to timing. She's on the line, don't jerk her off it."

"This is going to be the Main Woman, if I'm lucky."

"That's Ryan," laughed Arch. "Always looking for that consuming passion. Waiting but never ready."

Ryan went to the Diagnostic Lab the next morning. Diana was finishing up the case.

"Hi, Bill," she said in her thrilling, low voice. "Come with me to the darkroom." She put the cinefilm, a videotape, on the projector. "Catch the lights for me," she said, turning on the projector. Ryan flicked off the lights, leaving them alone together in the dark. Diana put her hand on the projector but didn't turn it on for a long moment, during which Ryan clung to the light switch, heart pounding, hoping she was making her way across the pitch black room to rip off all his clothes. Diana flipped on the machine.

Ryan watched her face in the flicker of the projector light. Her perfume was White Shoulders, intoxicating from yards away.

She went over all the findings with facile clarity. Ryan could have understood easily, if he were listening. But he wasn't even attempting to disguise his inattention. He was studying her face.

"You can never know about someone's heart, until you look," she was saying.

Ryan couldn't think of a thing to say.

"The low-risk methods of evaluation all share that one common failing, all the knowledge gained is by indirection, and much has to be inferred."

"In short, you can be fooled," said Ryan.

"Even high-risk methods can leave you fooled," said Diana, flatly. "But not as often."

"Why don't I take Mrs. Costello back to the floor?" asked Ryan, who had decided that the best tactic at this point was to retreat and regroup.

Diana looked at him for a few seconds. She let the projector run down, and flipped on the lights.

Ryan rolled Mrs. Costello back to Whipple. Diana leaned, arms crossed, against the hallway wall, looking after them.

She typed the report up later, and in the space for "Requesting Physician," she started to type the usual "House Staff," but hesitated. She typed "William Ryan" instead.

She hoped that nobody but Ryan would notice, and tried to think of what she could say if anyone commented.

"Oh, what the hell," she said aloud, pulling the report from the typewriter. "I'm a citizen above suspicion."

Ryan ran home that night to have Arch analyze the day's events.

"She was speaking on two levels, I'm sure," Ryan said. " 'You never know what you're going to find in a heart, until you look.' Jesus, she couldn't have been talking about cardiac catheterization."

"Doesn't sound like it," said Arch.

"But she cooled off. It just dropped. I mean, she didn't say anything, and nothing happened."

"Ryan, you have to make something happen. You are a hopeless adherent to the romantic rescue theory of life. One dazzling woman will come and sweep you away. But you've got to do something to make it happen."

"She's just so unfathomable," Ryan was saying, hearing nothing of what Arch was saying. "But I don't think she's really made up her mind yet. She's not ready to make her move."

"Why does she have to make the move?"

"How can I?"

"Grab her. Ask her out and grab her."

"Hey, she's Diana Hayes."

"She's unattainable, of course," laughed Arch.

"That's how I know she is the one," said Ryan. "Nothing worth having is within reason."

22

September 20

Ryan's beeper went off. It was Hyman Bloomberg. Ryan hadn't seen him since August.

"How's Whipple?" boomed Hyman.

"Great. A million laughs."

"You're a great clinician. How many interns would pick up a Gordio I missed?"

"Thanks."

"You'll never guess what happened."

"You're right," said Ryan, determined not to guess or ask more about it.

"Peter Brown sent in a 'friend' last week, a *faygeleh,* of course." Bloomberg paused.

"So what?" asked Ryan, despite himself.

"So, this guy's got the same symptoms Brown had: belly pain, diarrhea," roared Bloomberg. "And what do you think his duodenal aspirate showed?"

"How many guesses do I get?"

"Gordio!" roared Bloomberg, so loud Ryan had to hold the phone away from his ear.

"No shit?"

"No, duodenal aspirate," said Bloomberg. "What d'ya say? Interested? This could be a paper, not to mention a great discovery. 'Gordio: Another Cause of the Gay Bowel Syndrome.' I can see it now: *Gastroenterology.* No, wait: the *New England Journal of Medicine.* They'll snap it up. It'll be great."

Ryan thought about his total indifference to Gordio, venereal disease, and homosexuals. It was a gigantic indifference. He decided he ought to do it, to spite his indifference. And because Bloomberg was, after all, a great and kind physician.

"Okay, Dr. Bloomberg. I'm on. I'll go over the charts."

"Call me Hyman, Ryan."

"Okay, Hyman. I'll go over this afternoon, and start reading through them."

"And keep a table of the results!"

"And I'll keep a table of the results."

"Keep me posted!" shouted Bloomberg, and he hung up.

If Bloomberg was so interested, why didn't he do it himself? Of course, Hyman Bloomberg had one of the busiest G.I. practices in New York and didn't have time to go poking through a hundred and fifty charts. But neither did Ryan. But Bloomberg *was* interested in the problem. He just wasn't interested in writing papers: that was just the bait he thought might lure Ryan to do the legwork. Ryan wasn't interested in papers either. But he had committed himself.

Ryan went over to The Manhattan Hospital Record Room that night, after Chart Rounds were finished at Whipple. He was tired, and in no mood to look at more charts. Iggy was in the Record Room.

"What brings you here?"

"Going over some charts for Hyman Bloomberg."

"Bloomberg? August company. A great and good man, Hyman."

"Not to mention persuasive."

"Hey, he's a good man to have on your side when they make the cuts. Besides, he'll teach you more medicine in an hour than—"

"Maxwell Baptist will teach you in a year," Ryan finished for Iggy.

Ryan made a table with the patients' names, telephone numbers, symptoms, travel history, and sexual preference. His sexual preference column began to look pretty sparse.

Ryan was just getting around to resenting Hyman Bloomberg for dispatching him to the Record Room to squander another night of his young life when he flipped past a note by Diana Hayes.

Diana Hayes had been in this chart, writing on it with her firm, white hands, thinking over this very chart. She had written Ryan a note. Not a personal note. Not for Ryan alone. But for anyone who might want to know about this patient's heart. This patient, with Gordio in his stool, pain in his belly, homosexuality in his limbic system, had a murmur in his heart, which Diana Hayes was quite sure was coming from a bicuspid aortic valve. She knew that because she was director of Cardiac Diagnostics, and nobody could know any better. And she knew because she had done an echo on said homosexual, Gordio-infested, belly-aching patient and seen the bicuspid aortic valve in the blurry fuzz of ultrasonic sound waves. Waves her little transducer somehow converted to light, fuzzy blurograms on the echo paper, and which she could somehow confidently decipher. Diana Hayes was sheer magic. Ryan read her note, and looked at her incomprehensible echo, and decided to call it a night.

23

September 23

The only source of hope was her age, and maybe the fact that she was married. She had to be at least thirty-six, ten years older than Ryan. Thirty-six-year-old married women have been known to be quietly restive. Ryan had read *Fear of Flying.* She had to be flattered. She'd probably laugh.

Another hopeless Saturday morning. Ryan began his weekend off with his library vigil. It was oppressively hot. Dr. Hayes had the weekend off too. She flashed by in shorts, a pink Lacoste T-shirt, and Top-Siders. Her smile was in place.

Ryan considered a flying tackle.

"No guts, no glory."

He gravitated to the *Index.*

"Your lab coat does your legs a great injustice," Ryan blurted out at her back, regretting the words as soon as he let them fly.

Diana Hayes turned and, seeing it was Ryan, laughed.

"I can't say that the *Times* does much for your face, either," she said.

Ryan missed the next few words. His brain had become transiently ischemic. When he came back to full consciousness, she was saying, "I guess I am pretty casual for The Staid Manhattan Hospital. But I figured it was hot enough to be forgiven."

I forgive you.

"Besides, if I kept my lab coat on, I'd wind up seeing patients all day."

She could be trying to tell me something.

"It's great beach weather," she said, looking past Ryan, out the window.

She is trying to tell me something.

"I'm going to the beach," said Ryan, surprising himself. She looked at him, smiling, wordless.

"Today," added Ryan forlornly. She still said nothing, throwing him into total confusion.

"Would you like to come?" Ryan finally croaked out.

"Sounds lovely," she said. "I'll get my suit. It's in my office. I was going by myself."

Does that mean, we'll be alone?

They were alone. She was on her own for the weekend.

She had him meet her at her car. They weren't to be seen walking together on the street.

"Try to look inconspicuous," she told Ryan. "I don't want the word out that I give interns rides to the beach."

"I'm sure people would be interested to know."

"Really?" said Diana, delighted. "And I maintain such a low profile."

"There's lots of prurient interest among the house staff."

"Shouldn't surprise me," said Diana. "They *are* a select group." She laughed. "Of course interns and residents have prurient interests in almost anyone."

"It's focused on you, really."

"Oh, I do like Manhattan Hospital. I may stay forever."

The exit to Jones Beach was backed up to the Long Island Expressway.

"This will never do," said Diana. "We'll go on to the Hamptons. I have a place."

Ninety minutes later they were on Main Beach, East Hampton. The sun drove them into the water. Diana went in first. Ryan watched, uninvited, from the beach. He ambled down to the surging water, trying not to tag along like a younger brother.

She surfaced, blowing out air, like any sea mammal, then disappeared. Ryan worked on getting in up to his waist, then plunged. She slid behind him, wrapping her legs around his. Astonished, he twisted free to face her as she wrapped her warm arms around him. She pushed off his chest, running her hand along it, then glided out of his adoring grasp. He looked around, and she was gone. He wanted to do that again, to feel her sun-baked arms in all that cold Atlantic surf.

But she was running back to the towels, the sun shining through the space between her legs. She pulled her bikini bottom over the exposed underlip of her buttocks.

They cooked hamburgers and corn and drank wine on the deck overlooking Three Mile Harbor. The night was cloudless. A full moon lighted the deck.

They huddled together under a blanket. She sat close, touching him with her hip.

"Never realized there were so many stars until I went sailing," she said. "Alan couldn't believe I'd never seen the constellations."

Her husband, I presume. Alan.

"You like sailing?" asked Ryan, determined to avoid the obvious question about Alan.

"My husband does. I can take small doses."

Strike two, and I've already struck out.

"You know, I can't screw you tonight," she said. Ryan laughed, not knowing what else to do. He decided against a "Whatever-do-you-mean?" laugh. It was the laugh of an accomplice.

"Well, that's a beginning," he said.

"That remains to be seen," she said.

Ryan looked at her, but it was like looking at a picture.

"Let's go downstairs," she said.

They went downstairs, to the bedroom with the window wall which faced the bay. But the bay didn't interest Ryan that night. He was too busy watching her sleep. He was exhausted in the morning.

"Well, I've still got my clothes on," she said. "You've passed the first test. I suppose I can trust you. Some."

They drove back to Manhattan, Ryan in a turmoil, Diana chatting about the sky and the great Hampton houses. At least she omitted Alan. Ryan listened to parts. Mostly he thought about the night.

154

24

September 27

Wednesday mornings, Ryan drew blood on Joan Green. He liked Joan Green. He looked forward to seeing her, even if it was to puncture her. They were friends. He ordered bloods on her only for Monday, Wednesday, and Friday, sparing her the other days. She appreciated this little gift.

"What's a nice lady like you doing in a place like this?" Ryan asked her.

"Oh, is it *Wednesday,* again?" she said, dropping the *Times,* pulling the cover over her head. From under the cover a bruised arm flopped out.

"Now, Mrs. Green . . ."

She sat up. The cover fell from her pretty, anemic face.

"You really don't hurt me with your needle," she said, averting her eyes. "Well, only a little."

She winced as Ryan tightened the tourniquet and wiped her clotted veins with an alcohol prep.

"And I was having such a good time with Vincent Canby. Know what I really hate about blood drawing?"

"No."

"That awful alcohol smell."

"It goes away quickly."

Ryan did his duty swiftly.

"Dr. Ryan," Mrs. Green asked as he started off, "I wonder if you might have the time to stop by later. I have something I want to ask."

"Sure," said Ryan, with a distinct premonition about the question.

He tried to avoid walking by her door the whole morning, but finally got frustrated taking stairways and long detours, and went to see her.

"I've never asked you about—about my chances," she started, "about my outlook, so to speak." Ryan thought about Mrs. Christensen, and Hope. "I guess, in a way, I really don't want to know, not everything you know. That is, I want to know, and I don't want to know too much."

"It's hard to tell only part of the truth," said Ryan.

"Well," said Mrs. Green, turning red, and starting to cry, "I'm asking about what to expect, if there's any hope at all."

"There's always hope. As far as what to expect: more tests, more scans, one today, one on Friday . . ."

"Oh, I don't mean that. Where is the tumor now? Why do they keep giving me chest X rays and lung scans? Is it in my lungs, for God's sake, is it everywhere?"

"It's not everywhere. It is in your lungs," said Ryan.

"My God," Mrs. Green sighed. Her face turned red again. "It is in my lungs. I hadn't let myself believe it. It's gone from my legs to my lungs. Where else? Where next?"

"As far as we know, just the lungs."

"As far as you know?"

"I can only tell you what I know."

"But you imply it could be anywhere!"

"Could be isn't meaningful. I could have tumor, too. But if we can't find it, we assume it's not there."

"But there's a lot of difference in our cases. You don't have to feel every little ache and think: 'Is it tumor, or just an ache?' Have you ever thought what it's like? I mean, what would it mean to you, to know that you are dying?"

Ryan had never had the question put quite that way, from quite as compelling a source. He sat down, hoping Mrs. Green would calm down if he could shift the focus a little. She did.

"What would it mean? I guess I'd regret never having really lived. I mean, I've been in preparation, in school, all my life. Not like you. You have kids."

"And a husband," said Mrs. Green. "John is trying to be brave, but he's so transparently sad."

Ryan gave her a Kleenex. She held his hand a moment.

"I'm not ready to leave them," she said. "Will I ever be ready?"

Ryan thought about the bald, yellow lady, and about Mr. Schwartz: they were so dead by the time they died, they must have been ready.

"Yes, you'll be ready. When the time comes."

25

The day after Mrs. Green stopped Ryan cold with her questions, Fick stopped Ryan after Morning Rounds and told him to get Caroline's chart in order to do a discharge review that night at Chart Rounds.

Caroline had been looking better and better. Which made Ryan more and more nervous about her.

Fick and Ryan went over her chart page by page at Chart Rounds. Ryan had collected all the data, white blood cell count, temperature charts, lymph node sizes—everything was back to normal.

"She's ready to roll," said Fick. "Call her private, and set her up for discharge in the A.M."

"Let's get her out of here before something goes wrong," said Ryan.

Her private doctor agreed. Ryan wrote the order, then went to tell her.

"How're you doing?" asked Ryan.

"Never felt better. Wish I could convince you guys of that."

"Oh, we've been noting."

"Yeah, well note this: I'd like to know when you turkeys are going to spring me. This place is okay for an overnight, but weeks do drag by."

"Tomorrow."

"I mean, my white count is back to normal; you told me. What's a girl got to do . . . What did you say?"

"I said 'tomorrow.' You're out of here, in the A.M."

"Hallelujah!" Caroline threw her arms around Ryan's neck,

and hugged, laughing, crying, and making Ryan regret she wouldn't be around anymore.

"Holy Jesus, I've got to call my mother and have her pick me up, and call my job, and this is just . . ." She looked at Ryan. "Hey, you'll come down to the Village and see my excavation, won't you?"

"Sure."

"Here's my address," she said, scribbling madly on one of her little white cards. "And here's my phone number, and my excavation address. Actually, it's just a hole in the ground, but the buildings next door have addresses."

She handed the card to Ryan.

"We'll go to Sweet Basil and all. We always go there after a day's digging. It's dark and jazzy. You'd love it, if you can stay awake."

Ryan thought about wandering by some weekend off, and taking Caroline to Sweet Basil. They'd probably stay out till all hours. She'd have to get her sleep, and Ryan would have to take her home. No relapses from sheer exhaustion allowed. He'd take her home. She'd get a chill in the cab, and a red-hot fever by the time they got to her place. She'd vomit, and he'd have to call another cab, and take her back to Whipple.

You know you're in trouble when your dreams start turning out like real life. Ryan decided to avoid the Village, once Caroline was discharged.

26

It was bad enough that Caroline had gone home, but Diana Hayes had disappeared, too. She didn't show up on her usual morning library rounds. Ryan felt sure that her absence was calculated.

There weren't that many people in his life Ryan really looked forward to seeing, and Diana was a lot of them.

Diana had no plans to fade quietly from Ryan's life, however. She let most of the week go by, and then she paged, and Ryan almost didn't answer. It was five o'clock, actually five minutes past, and Ryan didn't answer pages after five on his nights off. Besides, he was depressed that Diana had disappeared. But the call was coming from outside the hospital, so he took a chance. She said that she had an early cath case the next morning. Would he like to drop by?

Ryan knew better than to hope this might be what it sounded like. She had already said yes in the library, and no at the Hamptons. She was one of those women who need to have men hanging around, adoring them. Ryan adored her.

She probably would have paged earlier, if she could have remembered his name.

He had to play it cool: distance, control, were the keys to handling good-looking women. It threw them off balance.

She was hardly distant when he arrived. She had her hair down, and wore nothing but a man's shirt. She removed Ryan's white jacket with her usual cool-eyed look.

"We will have to be most discreet," she said.

"I know."

The shirt came off, and she pulled him to the Persian carpet. *"Most* discreet," she added with a sudden inrush of air.

Her skin was moleless, and her hair smooth and silky; hands could run through it from every direction and never catch or snarl.

He was not allowed to stay the night. Someone might see him leaving at an unseemly hour, and Manhattan Hospital was a small town.

Ryan sneaked out of her room that night thinking that if the world ended the next day he could not feel cheated.

27

Thursday, September 28

Ryan was off for the night, and before signing out he checked Joan Green's blood results. Her clotting mechanism was normalizing. Ryan had her on Coumadin after the blood clot hit her lung, but with her chemotherapy wiping out her platelets, he was worried she might bleed out some night. She was off her Coumadin a week now, and her clotting was almost back to normal, despite the chemotherapy. Ryan was happy. She'd be okay for the weekend, and her husband was coming up from Maryland, starting the weekend early.

September 29

Friday morning, when Ryan bounced in, Joan Green's bed was empty. Ryan turned, head thundering, and bumped into Biotto, who had been on the weekend, and looked like it.

"Bad night," said Biotto. "I mean, it was just morgue city around here. I'm still trying to get my head together, know what I mean?"

Biotto went over to draw bloods on the patient in the bed next to Joan Green's bed. He nodded at the empty bed.

"Your lady Green bought it last night." Ryan fought the urge to smash Biotto's mouth.

"Big P.E., looked like. She had one once before, didn't she?" Biotto continued abstractly.

"Yeah," said Ryan, eyes drifting over to the bed.

"Why'd you take her off the Coumadin?"

"I was afraid she'd bleed out." *No Coumadin, and Joan Green throws a big clot to her lung and dies.*

"It's a bad trip, either way. I can relate to that. Take her off, and she crumps from a clot; keep her on, and she bleeds into her head, or somewhere else, and crumps. Well, she just sat up in bed, her face as blue as your eyes, foaming blood at the mouth. Big right shift on her gram. Gases were black, just black. I mean, I'm sure it was arterial blood, but they were just black, no oxygen."

"You called her husband?"

"Didn't have to, he was here. Oh, by the way, he was pretty pissed at you all weekend."

"Why?" asked Ryan, shocked.

"I don't know. Well, maybe it was because you told her she was going to die. Or maybe you told her she had mets in her lungs. I didn't think you'd lay a death notice on the lady. I mean, I told him that. You might have told her about the mets. But anyway, whatever you said, she was really just decompensated when he got here Friday night. I just couldn't relate to the anger. He kept asking if you were going to come in this weekend. But he dropped that after she died. I mean he was just unable to cope, you know? He just sat there sobbing. They must have had a tight thing going, you know?"

"Yeah, I know," said Ryan.

"Hey, I got the post, would you believe it? I mean, my first one, and it wasn't even my patient. He just about asked me if we would do one."

"Great," said Ryan, despondently.

"They're doing it this morning, if you want to check out the lungs."

"Yeah, thanks," said Ryan, who had no intention of going near the room where they were slicing up Joan Green.

Her last weekend with her husband, and she was despondent because Ryan had to adhere to his truths. Her husband had flown in to cheer her up, and would be taking her home in a casket. What had Joan Green done to deserve a jolt like that? And what could her husband have done to merit that kind of Thursday night?

Ryan could just hear Hope now.

"Congratulations, hero. You win the prize for honesty and truth under fire. The Whipple Trophy for moral rectitude. Take it home and put it on your mantel." That's what Hope would say. And she'd be right.

Ryan wanted desperately to go home. But he had to round. There were twenty-two other patients waiting, and even before Fick arrived, the nurses were dragging Ryan to see Mrs. Babcock.

Mrs. Babcock had dropped her blood pressure and was clammy. She had a fungus called mucormycosis chewing up the cartilage in her nose. She made ugly noises when she breathed. Ryan hung some plasmonate, ordered a chest X ray, drew some blood gases and a blood count, ordered some oxygen, and thought about how it must have been for Joan Green, trying to suck air through a lung full of clot. She would have been better off exsanguinating. The only blessing was that Ryan wasn't on at the time. And fortunately for Ryan, Mrs. Babcock was going rapidly down the tubes. So he wouldn't have time to dwell on Joan Green.

Ryan was lying on the couch, in his study, waiting for the phone to ring. He was willing it to ring. He wanted to hear from Joan Green.

The phone rang. It was Jane, calling Arch. Ryan looked at the clock: it was ten o'clock. Arch was already asleep, downstairs. Jane was stuck at her office, trying to get some work done. She wanted a break, so she chatted at Ryan.

"Whatcha doing, Doc?"

"Just lying here, on my couch."

"Ain't that the life?"

"Sure."

"And you're always bitching about internship. Here I am, late at night, still absorbed with the concerns of my clients. It's a rough life."

"Jane," said Ryan, "what's the difference between a lawyer and a rooster?"

"Dunno."

"The rooster clucks defiance."

28

Monday, October 2

Ryan had the weekend to get over Joan Green, but Monday dawned and most of it passed and Ryan remained catatonic. He went to work, came home, sat on the toilet, ate little, lost weight, and was a one-man pall for days. Arch finally succeeded in dragging him over to the Intensive Care Bar & Grill, where Ryan sat motionlessly behind a beer for an hour as Arch appraised the local beauties, said kind things about Joan Green, and finally lapsed into a gloomy silence of his own, drinking beer after beer.

After about an hour Brigid Sullivan came in with some nurses. Seeing Ryan, she split off and sat down at the dreary table.

"Can I join the party?"

Ryan started, looked up, and seeing Brigid, almost smiled. Arch, seizing the lifeline, said, "Boy, am I glad to see you." Arch had never met Brigid. "Joan Green died. This is Ryan's idea of a wake."

"I'm so sorry," said Brigid, not knowing who Joan Green was, but guessing accurately. "She was a patient of yours?"

"At Whipple. Osteogenic sarcoma."

Brigid asked about her, and about Ryan's friendship with her, in her smooth, sympathetic way, guiding Ryan effortlessly to the brink of tears, and back to smiling. Arch watched, amazed, as Brigid got Ryan to talk, for the first time in complete sentences, with obvious catharsis.

Finally, near midnight, Arch took Ryan home.

"She's a great woman. A very great and kind lady," said Arch, referring to Brigid.

"She's a decent person," said Ryan.

"The amazing thing," said Arch, "is that you're both so young."

BOOK III

The Great White Tower

1

October 4

It was October, and still hot. They finally let Ryan out of Whipple. He could go back across the street to the Tower, to its white, crystalline walls, its green courtyards and gothic windows and arches.

Ryan stood on the Whipple side of the avenue and looked across, lovingly, at the Tower. House staff in crisp, white uniforms, and nurses in surgical scrub blue, moved in and out of its orifices.

He looked at the adjacent residences, dorms, and labs, all made of the same white brick. And he glanced over his shoulder, at the squat, red-brick Whipple. He bounded across the street, past the flower beds, past the sculpted hedges, and unable to embrace the edifice, he simply ran inside.

Back in the Great White Tower again. The corridors glistened, the nurses spoke English, and the patients survived. Ryan went days without a death, and then it was an eighty-seven-year-old whose emphysematous lungs finally dissolved after seventy years of tobacco assault. No more Joan Greens to break his heart.

No more leuks, no more neutropenic rectums, and only an occasional misplaced melanoma: now it was G.I. bleeders, congestive heart failures, acidotic diabetics, pulmonary edemas, who were quickly cured and profoundly grateful—they all got plugged into the big white machine, and got better.

Sometimes a patient would shove a personal check into Ryan's hand, a certificate of appreciation for a night spent pushing blood by the bedside. Ryan refused with humble flourish. He modestly insisted that he was only the most visible part of an enormous, magnificent, benevolent life-saving system. For each person the patient saw at his bedside, Ryan told them, there were twenty behind the scenes, a figure he made up, but which wasn't too far from the truth.

Things worked properly here. Order prevailed. E.R. residents drew the initial blood tests, got the X rays. The escort service trundled the patients to the floor; clerks sent off the lab slips and blood gases to labs, lab techs called results back to the floor and cross-matched blood; surgical consults arrived; senior medical residents doing subspecialty electives swarmed, examining, endoscoping, writing long notes, full of references nobody had time to read, getting excited and exciting Ryan, reassuring him that he was learning medicine. And if he had to stay up all night to learn it, it was an honor.

"Some honor," said Biotto, who had gotten "back from Death City," as he called it, a week before Ryan.

"Compared to Whipple," said Ryan.

"Don't talk about Whipple," said Biotto. "Whipple was one bad trip."

Biotto had been reunited with Jason Adams, who was finishing his clerkship in Medicine on the floor to which Biotto and Ryan had been assigned. Iggy was their resident again, a true blessing. "He's no blessing," said Biotto.

"Compared to Fick?"

"Fick wasn't a bad dude," said Biotto. "He just couldn't get his head together. Didn't *integrate* the whole time we were there. Half the time he was in retreat, the other half he got off on some ego trip. Couldn't handle the authority role."

"Iggy runs a good ward."

"He really gets into the authority thing too much."

They were delighted to be back among the living.

"The whole Whipple scene is just there to make the Tower look good," Biotto said. The Tower seemed almost festive now.

Fridays ended with Liver Rounds, the ceremonial, illegally alcoholic fraternity party for the house staff. They laughed together, talked about nurses they hadn't screwed, told stories about patients, and lambasted absent attendings. The lucky ones, with the weekend off, continued things across the street, at the local favorite, the ICB&G.

With the possible exception of Biotto, they all spoke the same language now. Everything got abbreviated: it was the tribe's language, the alphabet soup. Outsiders could listen, but not comprehend.

"She was all worked up: EKG, IV, all the ROMI stuff, but the JAR wanted an echo and everything but a CAVB before morning."

And even Biotto slipped into the dialect whenever he talked about patients. Hard as he tried, Biotto could not resist the gravitational pull toward the classic intern way of seeing things.

"No admission after midnight is an interesting admission," Ryan heard Biotto say. It was one of Iggy's favorite rules.

"Biotto," asked Ryan, amazed, "what if the admission is a whole human?"

"Everyone has to respect each other's space," said Biotto. "A patient comes in after midnight, and I feel positively *violated.*"

Arch insisted that Ryan spend one evening a week with his lawyer friends, speaking complete words. But Ryan had his own friends now and found it increasingly difficult to be with anyone outside the fraternity.

Lawyers didn't appreciate the stories or see the humor between the bones. They shot strange, intolerant looks at Ryan when a reference to "some old gomer" slipped past his guarded lips. Lawyers couldn't be admitted backstage—except Arch. But even Arch could be trying. He kept interrupting for explanations.

"EEG?"

"Electroencephalogram."

"Oh," blankly.

"Arch, you know: the brain wave machine."

"Oh! Right."

Ryan was less amused now by anemic lawyer stories. They couldn't compare with Tower Tales. He felt comfortable at the hospital. He was a cog in the great white wheel, and loving it.

Everyone knew his part, and usually could be counted upon. When things went wrong, it was the exception, unlike Whipple, where it was the norm. And when there was a screw-up, everyone knew who was at fault. There were rules, and amazingly, they even made sense.

There were bad floors, but most were well run. Horror shows were somehow mystically concentrated on one pathetic floor, B-2, which acted as the latrine, relieving the other wards of execrable problems.

The floors got patients from the Emergency Room in rotation, by the luck of the draw. But somehow it was B-2 that always drew the gomers: the ninety-year-old, aphasic, stroked-out diabetic, with a urinary tract infection and bilateral pneumonia. The tired, the poor, the aged masses yearning to pee, they washed up on B-2, or B-Zoo, as it was affectionately known.

Iggy Bart claimed that he could be blindfolded and led all around Manhattan Hospital and when he was led onto B-2 he would know it from the smell alone. There was something distinctly fecal in the air on B-2, made more pungent by the incessant attempts to spray it away with Lysol.

Nobody could figure out where it came from. Even when the patient census was low, it lingered. After a few hours on the floor you could hardly notice it, but go to lunch and return and it was there waiting, insinuating itself through the nasal passages and settling in the stomach.

The big problem on B-2 was the curse that drew these unfortunate, uninspiring patients to the floor. The second problem was the clerk. She was worse than useless.

The clerk runs the floor. If the clerk is a turkey, it doesn't matter how good the nurses, doctors, or patients are—the floor doesn't work. The clerk gets the blood tubes set up for the morning drawing, sends them to the various labs after they are filled, schedules patients for the tests doctors order, sets up X rays, gets escort service to take patients to tests, and does anything the nurses don't have time for or don't want to do.

B-2 had a disaster for a clerk. Ryan was convinced that the only reason they didn't get rid of her was that she made all the other clerks look so good. The other interns tolerated her. Ryan warred with her. Another crusade: she was a great wrong to be righted. Ryan was back at Camelot now, and crusades were back in style.

It all culminated in the Great Wheelchair Bust. Ryan had a patient, Mr. Hirshsprung, who had been waiting five days for his barium enema. It was the last part of his workup, and the only thing between him and discharge to a nursing home.

The nursing-home bed would only be held seven days. After that, Mr. Hirshsprung's lamentable name would go to the bottom of the waiting list.

But B-2, or more precisely, its clerk, could not seem to get the barium enema done. Actually, it wasn't entirely her fault. One night Mr. Hirshsprung was insufficiently prepped, the next time his escort got lost, and when he finally arrived, X Ray refused to do him; the next night, Mr. Hirshsprung refused his third consecutive castor oil clean-out, and nobody called the intern, so Mr. Hirshsprung was again insufficiently prepped.

Iggy was giving Ryan lectures about the cost of prolonged hospitalization, cost containment, and Ryan was frustrated beyond words.

Finally, the deed was scheduled for Friday morning, 10:00 A.M. But at eleven Ryan noticed that Mr. Hirshsprung was still sitting in his bed. Ryan confronted the clerk, who was studiously charting temps, determinedly ignoring him.

"I couldn't help notice Mr. Hirshsprung, sitting in bed, not getting his barium enema."

The clerk had no comment.

"Why isn't Mr. Hirshsprung down for his B.E.?"

The clerk never raised her eyes from the charts.

"Oh, there aren't any chairs to send him down in," she said.

"Wait a minute. I can't believe what I just heard."

The clerk didn't answer.

"I'm talking to you," said Ryan, indignation swelling murderously.

"What do you want from me?"

"I want Hirshsprung down for his B.E."

"I told you, there aren't any wheelchairs."

"Let me get this straight. You're telling me this patient can't go down for his B.E., and will have to stay the weekend, and lose his bed at the nursing home, because there aren't any wheelchairs in all of Manhattan Hospital?"

That was the problem. The clerk didn't care about tight beds, or cost containment, or nursing-home waiting lists. She went on her break at eleven if she could get the temps charted. What she really now cared about was that Ryan was keeping her from her charting.

"I cannot believe that in all of The Manhattan Hospital there is not one, single unused wheelchair."

"Believe it."

Ryan disappeared, and returned with two wheelchairs. Two minutes later three more wheelchairs were deposited in the hall in front of the clerk's desk. Within fifteen minutes fifteen wheelchairs were clogging the hallway. Every telephone line to B-2 was lighting up. Clerks from other floors were calling. A doctor from B-2 had taken their wheelchairs.

Ryan sat down casually next to the clerk, who was frantically trying to answer the phones.

"Think you might be able to find a chair to get Mr. Hirshsprung to his B.E.?"

The clerk stormed off to find her supervisor. Ryan wound up taking Mr. Hirshsprung down. But the clerk had to return all the chairs.

Iggy laughed, but pulled Ryan aside later.

"William Ryan, M.D., humiliating a minimum-wage clerk is not the way to win friends and influence people."

"I wasn't trying to win friends. I was trying to shame and intimidate," sniffed Ryan.

Iggy laughed. Iggy laughed at everything Ryan said.

"Very democratic of you," said Iggy.

"Iggy, that's just it: this place can't be run as a democracy. There's got to be a hierarchy, or nothing happens."

"You sound like a surgeon," laughed Iggy. "And this from the man who fought the Death Certificate Battle, and sat in at the president's office. You're going establishment on me."

"When it comes to establishment," Biotto said to Jason Adams, "Iggy should know." Biotto and Jason had been taking this exchange in from their chairs in the nurses station.

Ryan truly loved Iggy, despite the fact that Iggy had to be the kindest man on earth. Iggy didn't care about *who* wasn't doing his job, even if he had to do more work himself. Iggy stayed up all night with gomers his interns had given up on. Iggy felt sorry for the interns, having to stay up all night, and he felt sorry for the gomers, so he stayed up himself and let the interns go to bed. Of course, he never had to do this when Ryan was his intern. It was a point of honor with Ryan never to go to bed before his junior resident.

Coming from Iggy, that humiliation remark made Ryan twist. The clerk was a turkey, but Ryan apologized to her. He did it for Iggy.

Biotto couldn't understand Ryan's devotion to Iggy. Biotto thought Iggy was a decompensated psychotic ever since Iggy's comments about gomers in the first weeks of internship. And Iggy had added fuel to the fire as the year went by. It was true that Iggy was one of the world's few anoretic nervosa males, but that didn't make him crazy. Sick, yes. Strange, yes. But not necessarily decompensated. Iggy was just concerned about his self-image. Iggy was six three and weighed one hundred and twenty pounds.

Iggy agonized about being that fat. He ate almost nothing. Occasionally, he would gorge on a bagel with coffee after Morning Rounds, then feel guilty, run into the john, stick a finger down his throat, and vomit up the offending bagel.

But Iggy ran B-2 about as well as B-2 could ever be run. Patients did eventually get their tests, and some even got diagnoses, despite the massive indifference of the nurses and aides and clerks.

Basically, though, B-2 was the proverbial exception that proved the rule. The Tower worked, and Ryan thrived. He had the one quality most essential to be a good intern: he was unreasonably compulsive. His notes filled patients' charts with cramped details. This did not go unnoticed. Diana heard Iggy present Ryan's cases every morning at Morning Report.

Each night's admissions were presented at Morning Report. While the interns were back on the floors, doing scut work, the residents were sweating it out with Diana in the department office. Every detail was scrutinized, errors of omission, commission, and supposition were excoriated. There was the case of lactic acidosis which had kept Ryan up all night. The survival rate was five percent, Ryan had been thrilled to read.

He had drawn blood gases and pushed bicarbonate through the IV all night, and by dawn's early light, after twenty-eight units of bicarb, he knew he had beaten the odds and won another star for the Tower.

A neat little flowchart plotted the patient's gratifying response, with acid-base measurements, pulse, respirations, blood pressure, all forming happy little curves along a time line.

Iggy presented, and Diana absorbed herself in Ryan's meticulous flowchart.

Frank Wright leaned over and looked at the chart as Diana studied it.

"Ryan did a nice job," he said.

"It's such a pretty little flowchart," said Diana.

Every morning, after Morning Rounds, the interns would sit down at the telephones, calling for lab results or ordering tests for their patients, while Iggy disappeared off to Morning Report with the charts on the previous night's admissions under a thin, winglike arm.

"What goes on there?" Ryan pressed Iggy.

"Oh, we just present the admissions to the attending, while he looks over the chart and bitches at all the little things you forgot to do the night before, and at us for not having supervised you guys better."

"Sounds pleasant," said Ryan.

"Well, it depends on the attending. Some are okay."

"Who was it today?"

"Diana Hayes."

Ryan's pulse became transiently irregular. To think she had been looking at his write-ups just fifteen minutes ago.

"Well, how was she? I mean, is she a hard-ass?"

"Oh," said Iggy distractedly, looking at a bagel. "She only cuts off one ball at a time."

"She's tough?" said Ryan.

"She's reasonable, but she doesn't let anything get by."

"What'd she say about my workups?"

"Well, you didn't have a guaiac in the chart on Kopek, and you didn't write down the interpretation on Browning's chest X ray."

"Jesus, Kopek was in for a rule out M.I., and Browning had a G.I. bleed. I could see if I didn't have the chest X ray on Kopek and forgot the stool guaiac on a gut bleed . . ."

"That's why I never say anything about what's said at Morning Report. They have to find something wrong with every workup, or they feel they've failed. They're gonna challenge everything you do. They think house staff needs a surrogate conscience. The game is guilt."

Biotto by now was listening.

"Well, if they're into laying guilt trips on, I can be spared the report on Morning Report."

"Did she say anything else?" asked Ryan, eagerly.

"Hey, what do you care what she said?" said Biotto, waving a bagel at Ryan, tantalizing Iggy, whose red-rimmed, blue eyes followed every movement of the bagel. "Don't get into what other people say about you," continued Biotto, munching. "It's a bum trip. Listen to your own inner sounds." Biotto had not forgiven Diana for that conference at Whipple.

Ryan ignored him. "What else did she say?"

"Nothing. Oh, wait. Yeah. She said you went to Isordil awfully quick on Kopek; she would have used Nitropaste."

"Anything else?" asked Ryan, depressed.

"She likes your handwriting. She said it reflects an anal-compulsive personality, and what's more, it's legible."

"What!"

"Told you she didn't say much of interest," said Iggy, finally giving in totally to temptation and devouring a bagel, heavy with cream cheese.

Ryan poured himself a coffee, wondering what she meant by that, and wondering whether she meant for it to get back to him. He was about to ask Iggy about that, but Iggy had disappeared into the bathroom.

2

Thursday, October 5

Ryan spent most of Grand Rounds watching Diana shift in her front-row seat. He sat in the back of the amphitheater, with the rest of the interns, whose beepers went off distractingly like erratically bursting bubbles. She had her golden hair up, in a shining twist. The subject was the metabolic consequences of diabetic hyperglycemia, and Diana looked decorously bored. She kept glancing at her watch, surreptitiously. Ryan smiled at that. He was behind her, about twenty rows above her, and to her left. The amphitheater was dark, but she sat close enough to the screen to be caught by the light. Even from twenty rows away she was exquisite.

Ryan had to speak with her. Any pretext would do. She had given him one with the remark at Morning Report about his anal-compulsiveness. It was a veritable invitation.

The speaker finally stopped; lights came on; polite applause. Ryan zipped out the door in the back of the amphitheater and ran down the hall and up the two flights of stairs to Diana's office in the Cardiac Diagnostics suite.

He rushed past her secretary, who started to say something, but stopped. There was a man in Diana's office. He was standing with his back to Ryan, writing at Diana's desk. When he turned around, Ryan knew instantly he was not a drug salesman: he did not have the standard three-piece, double-knit drug salesman suit. Ryan was immediately impressed, and depressed that any man like this vied for Diana's attention. He wore a heather-colored crew neck sweater under a rich brown Harris tweed jacket, which matched, in a planned, casual way, his brown hair.

He was graying at the temples and had a robust, leathery face accented by light blue eyes. He looked to Ryan with an expression which asked Ryan his business. Ryan, of course, was in uniform and, if anything, looked more appropriate to the setting of this medical office. But he felt he had to explain his presence.

"Oh," said Ryan, "I was looking for Dr. Hayes."

"So was I," said the tweedy man. Ryan noticed his white teeth, very perfect looking for a rugged face, and high cheekbones. "But she's not back from Grand Rounds." The tweed had a rich, resonant voice, the sort of voice Ryan wished for himself. If Ryan had a voice like that, he thought, people might not treat him like a kid.

Ryan turned to go.

"Don't go," said the tweed. "Her secretary said she'd be back any minute." There was quiet command in the voice, and in his presence. He was only a little taller than Ryan but much broader and deeper chested. Ryan was lean as an adolescent. This man was solid and thick as an oak. Ryan felt boyish in his presence.

Before Ryan could answer, the tweed swept out, past Ryan, past the secretary, and strode off down the corridor, pulling a pipe from a pocket and lighting it as he walked. He disappeared around a corner.

Ryan sat down at the chair in front of Diana's desk, then popped up to read the note he had left.

> *Thought you might be free for lunch, if G.R. finished early.*
> *No such luck. Will take the 6ᵀᵘ. A.*

Ryan heard the secretary say "There's a young doctor waiting . . ." and flew back to his chair.

Diana swept in, closed the door, and moved to her chair, behind her desk.

"Hi," she said, and was cut off by the buzz from her intercom.

It was the secretary. "Your husband stopped by," she said over the electric box.

"I see his note," said Diana, taking it up and glancing at it with no special expression.

Ryan was at the door.

"Well, leaving so soon, and only just arrived?" said Diana.

"I can feel my beeper about to go off."

"You must have met Alan, then."

"Not formally."

"Oh, he's not a formal sort."

"Oh."

Diana crossed her arms and stared at Ryan with just a flicker of a smile.

"Well?"

Ryan stared back, dumbly.

"What did you think of each other?" she said finally.

"He thought I was charming," said Ryan, straight-faced. "But a bit young."

Diana laughed and flopped into her chair.

"You are a wit," she said, shaking her head.

Ryan noticed that he was sweating profusely, and felt his face turn hot and red.

"And what did you think of him?"

"Nice tan," said Ryan. And he slipped out the door.

3

October 6

"Hey, remember me?"

It was Hope. Ryan hadn't seen her for weeks. He had received three messages from Arch that she had called, and just never got around to calling her. He was too busy thinking about Diana. Now Hope had paged. It came over his beeper as an outside call, and Ryan thought it might be Diana, so he answered.

"Well, how've you . . . Well, where you been, stranger?"

"I was going to ask you that very question," said Hope.

"Well, just saving lives and leading the clean life."

"Want to break the habit tonight?"

"Saving lives?"

"The clean life."

"You mean, no shower?" said Ryan.

"Whatever."

"Well, I've got to go back over to the hospital," said Ryan, thinking that Diana might yet call. "It might be pretty late."

"Okay," said Hope, "I get the message."

"Aw, Hope, I can't help getting consults."

"Well, either patients have gotten a lot sicker, or you've suddenly become the only doc on call over there; I haven't been able to see you for weeks."

"I don't know, Hope," said Ryan. "I've just been really busy."

"Things don't always turn out, I guess," said Hope. And she hung up. Ryan started to call her back, but decided to wait for Diana to call. She never did.

4

Wednesday, October 11

Ryan scanned his list of patients for General Medical Clinic. Mrs. Cushing with her incessant asthma was first. That was no surprise. Ryan had heard her wheezing the moment he stepped into the waiting area, and she caught sight of him and waved with a happy wheeze. It was going to be Ol' Home Afternoon for the infamous Room 220. Miss Osler was due, and Mrs. Harvey, the alcoholic. The only one missing was Mrs. White, the black woman with heart pain. Ryan had refused to take her into his clinic, even when her private doc refused to see her because she was suing him, and she called Ryan to ask sweetly if he had a practice. His clinic was his practice, but Ryan told her no, he did not see patients unless they were hospitalized. He felt a small pang of guilt as he hung up, but reassured himself that she would probably wind up finding a way to hate and sue him in no time. Besides, there were lots of docs in New York.

Mrs. Cushing came wheezing into Ryan's office.

"How are you today?" Ryan asked.

"Not so good," wheezed Mrs. Cushing. "Can't seem to catch my breath."

"Is it worse today than usual?"

"Worse than usual?"

"Better than you are at home."

"Oh, I never wheeze at home," she said blandly.

"I can't believe you never wheeze at home."

"Never do," she said. "No wool at home."

"What?"

"I'm allergic to wool. All the chairs in the waiting room are wool covered."

"You mean, you only wheeze in clinic?" Ryan asked incredulously. "I can't believe you never mentioned this."

"You never asked."

"You mean I've been writing prescriptions for you for drugs you only really need when you come to clinic and wheeze on our wool chairs, to which you are allergic?"

"Well, you write the prescriptions. You say I need them."

"But they're for wheezing. And you only wheeze here."

"Well, I suppose if you look at it that way."

"Mrs. Cushing, I had to hospitalize you once, you were wheezing so bad. You're telling me you only wheeze here, in clinic."

"Well, mostly only here. At home, a little, once in a while, but much worse here."

Ryan decided not to kill Mrs. Cushing, to have mercy. He took her off all her medications and sent her away.

Miss Osler was in for her monthly gonorrhea culture. She always came in right before she menstruated. She looked smashing.

"You look smashing," said Ryan. "You really do."

She was wearing a violet, V-cut cashmere sweater, which set off her newly blond hair attractively, and a gray, tight, wool skirt. It was a little too tight for Ryan's comfort, and he was afraid he might not be able to stand up to do her pelvic exam.

"Oh, thanks ever so," she said, grabbing his hand and squeezing. "What would I ever do without you to cheer me up?"

"Have you needed cheering?"

"Doesn't every girl?"

Ryan thought she sounded quaintly dated. "Don't your boyfriends cheer you up?"

"Well, they're not really boyfriends, you know," she winked. "But I might be kinda settling down."

"Really?"

"Yes." She beamed. "He's a doctor, too. A gynecologist. Got a wife, but he's awful nice to me. Got a new apartment with a brick wall. He pays for most of it."

186

"Sounds like you're doing well."

"Oh, yeah," said Miss Osler, taking off her skirt and panties, with an enticing modesty, and sitting on Ryan's examining table for her pelvic.

"I'll have to get a nurse," said Ryan, wondering how he was going to get up with the erection he had. All she had on was that sweater, with no bra underneath.

"Do you have to?"

"It's a law."

"Oh, I won't say you raped me," laughed Miss Osler. "Who'd believe a girl like me, anyway?"

"Why wouldn't anyone believe you?"

"Well"—she flicked her hair from her face—"you know."

"You sell yourself short."

"Think so?"

Ryan managed to get a nurse and do Miss Osler's pelvic, hoping neither one noticed the bulge in his pants.

Mrs. Harvey didn't show. Her chart didn't make it either, so Ryan felt better. He hated seeing patients without their charts. The secretary called the Record Room for it. Ryan got a call about it.

"You wanted that chart on Harvey?"

"Well, she didn't keep her appointment."

"Not surprising, Doc," said the clerk in the record room. "We found out who had her chart. The Autopsy Room. She died a week ago."

After clinic Ryan went by to see the chart, to find out if Mrs. Harvey had bled out at home or what. Ryan had never gotten used to the smell of the Autopsy Room. The pathology resident dug the chart out of a pile.

"She bled out in a bar. She was DOA in the E.R."

"Oh," said Ryan.

"She a patient of yours?"

"Once."

"Well, her liver was shot, and the varices blew."

Ryan walked back to the floor, thinking about Room 220, and about internship. Each day and each patient had seemed unconnected, an isolated event. It was hard to imagine that people had lives that continued after their discharge.

When he got back to the floor, the clinic clerk paged him to say that one of the attendings couldn't make clinic and to ask Ryan to see his patients.

"Sorry," said Ryan. "Did you want Dr. Ryan? Dr. Bill Ryan?"

"Yeah," said the clerk, confused. "Isn't that you?"

"Damn page operators," said Ryan. "No, this is Dr. Reagan. Ryan's gone home. Sick."

5

Monday, October 16

The stone benches by the river, in front of the hospital, were filled with white-uniformed bodies at lunchtime. The sun was warm, and a bracing breeze along the river made it the place to be. Iggy was sitting next to Biotto. Iggy had his shirt off and balanced an aluminum reflector on his scaphoid abdomen, soaking up the tanning rays. For a redhead, Iggy managed to nurture a pretty good tan; and it was still glowing in early October. Iggy was ignoring Biotto's feeding sounds. Biotto hated eating lunch with Iggy, who never let Biotto out of his sight during the day. Iggy feared Biotto would decide to follow his inner sounds to Central Park for the afternoon, and miss rounds. Biotto also hated eating lunch with Iggy because Iggy never ate, but just followed Biotto to the delicatessen, watched him order and eat, watched him with those big red-rimmed eyes, and never ate a bite. It was like trying to eat in front of one of those support-a-starving-Korean-kid posters. So they sat on the bench by the river, and ignored each other.

Hope came and sat between them. She was in uniform, working on Surgery for the day.

"Who's watching the store?" she asked.

"Your compulsive friend," said Biotto. "He's really getting into this organizational mentality. If they made white uniforms in gray flannel, he'd wear one."

"He's on the floor?"

"You bet," said Biotto. "Going over charts, calling the labs, collecting all the numbers on his patients. He's really getting into numbers now."

189

"He's getting to be a decent intern," observed Iggy, in his dry tone.

"Not like me," said Biotto. "But you've got to be a human, first."

"Ryan tells me you're getting a little more compulsive yourself," said Hope. "On the rare occasions he talks to me."

"Does he?" said Biotto, turning to beam at Hope. "When did he say that?"

"Last week," said Hope. "He always refers to you as Spaceship, but last week he called you Rocketman, from the Elton John song."

"Rocketman," said Biotto, rolling the word around in his mouth.

"I like Spaceship better," said Iggy. "You're improving, but you still can't remember anyone's electrolytes. When you know the numbers, I'll call you Rocketman."

"Ryan said that about me?" Biotto went on. "I thought he just buzzed around, thinking about lab values, reading the *New England Journal*. Never figured he'd notice me."

"He said you presented three cases at Attending Rounds and didn't have to read your notes."

"Ryan is a prince," said Biotto.

"He's always watching," said Iggy.

"You two into something heavy?" Biotto asked Hope.

"Really, Biotto," said Hope. "You've got to learn the dialect."

"You know what I mean."

"We hang out together," said Hope. "More or less. Lately, mostly less."

"Why lately?"

"Hell if I know," said Hope, looking keenly at Biotto, then scrutinizing Iggy briefly. "Lately he's been all intern."

"We noticed," said Biotto.

"Internship only lasts a year," said Iggy. "He's savoring it."

"He can have mine," said Biotto.

"Well, at least it's not me going crazy," said Hope.

"Ryan's relentless," said Iggy. "One of his more admirable qualities."

"His insight is his most admirable quality," said Biotto.

Iggy looked at his watch. He dragged Biotto to his feet. Iggy put his shirt on and folded up his reflector.

"You'll have to excuse Spaceman and me. Time to gather numbers and save lives."

Iggy hustled Biotto back across the walkover spanning the FDR Drive below.

"We were being sleuthed, you realized," said Iggy.

"She likes the guy," said Biotto.

"Too much, perhaps," said Iggy, with his wise smile.

6

Wednesday, October 18

Ryan was in his study that evening, drinking anisette from a coffee cup, with his feet propped up on his desk, looking at the ceiling. He heard the doorbell ring downstairs and heard the heavy thuds of Arch's steps going to the door.

Ryan was thinking about Diana. In a curious way the sighting of her husband had been liberating. Seeing him face to face, Ryan realized how hopeless his little fantasies really were. It had brought reality crashing. Given the choice, Ryan would have taken Alan over himself. The tweed was a solid citizen, an authentic item, as Biotto would say.

Ryan was a wispy boy-man, good for an older woman's ego, but not a serious future commodity. The crazy thing was that he had allowed himself to spin off endless scenarios, fitting Diana into all of his secret little pipe dreams. They would sail off to Scotland and start a clinic. They would travel trains in Europe, living from lectures or vagabond medical practice in socialized systems. The details had not been worked out.

Arch escorted Hope into the room.

"Surprise, sport," said Hope, bouncing over and throwing her arms around Ryan's neck. "Can I buy you a beer?"

Arch took a beer can from his pocket and snapped open the pop-top. He stood there drinking and watching the two of them as if they were on TV.

"Beer?" said Ryan.

"You know," said Hope. "Arch is drinking some right now. Show him the can, Arch."

"Where?"

"The ICB&G," said Hope. "Or wherever."

Ryan took his feet down from the desk. He was still in his whites.

"Have to change."

"We'll wait," said Hope, plopping down on his couch with Arch.

The phone rang. Ryan answered it at his desk.

"Hi," said Diana, with her dulcet voice.

"Oh," said Ryan, looking at Hope and Arch, who were both looking at him. "Hi." He sounded even more stiff than he looked.

"You have company . . ." said Diana, with satisfied irony.

"Never a dull moment," said Ryan. "What can I do for you?"

"Oh, you *do* have company," said Diana. "Well, I can tell this is not a good time."

"We were just going out for a beer."

Hope and Arch stopped looking, but were still listening.

"I'll talk to you later," said Diana and hung up.

"Okay," said Ryan into the empty receiver, "that sounds just fine. I'll see you tomorrow at rounds."

Ryan went to his closet in the bedroom and changed into jeans for the ICB&G. The three of them drank a few in the dark bar, but talked little. Ryan was too distracted to follow the conversation very well.

Hope spent the night. Ryan spent his night wondering whether Diana had stayed in the city or had gone home to Alan.

7

Thursday, October 19

Grand Rounds were held in a large amphitheater. The entrances were at the top rows, and from them you could overlook the audience. Diana stood by one entrance. She was looking for Ryan. He came in with Iggy and Biotto and fell asleep almost immediately upon sinking into the soft chair.

For thirty years the seating in the amphitheater had been hard wooden benches, purposefully uncomfortable, so the interns would stay awake during Grand Rounds. Over a year ago the attendings had finally voted to replace them with soft theater chairs. The interns could sleep, for all the attendings cared. The attendings were rump-weary.

So Ryan fell asleep. He was awakened by his beeper, and had to find a seat in the back, having lost his seat while he was on the phone. Diana stood in an aisle behind him, studying the back of his head, and what she could see of his face.

Had he known he was being studied by Diana Hayes, Ryan could not have dozed off. But he didn't know, and quickly succumbed to the soporific effects of Grand Rounds. It was a challenge to stay awake, even without a sleep deficit, during the Thursday morning gathering. For one thing, every speaker felt inexpicably compelled to dim the lights in the auditorium, and to show the maximal number of slides in the shortest amount of time. The total effect was like a succession of headlights on a long, numbing night drive.

Beyond the audiovisual effects, the speakers were uniformly dull. Part of the problem was that they were all physicians and had little or no regard for their audience. And such language.

Anything was tolerated, if the speaker was an authority. This particular morning the speaker began with "If I may wax poetic for just a few prefatory remarks of introduction," at which point he turned off the lights on the first slide and Ryan fell asleep, in mute protest.

Mercifully, Ryan was able to sleep through until the lights came on and everyone applauded. Ryan awoke with a start and looked up to see Hyman Bloomberg standing above him. Hyman sat down next to Ryan. Diana, standing behind them, turned and left. Bloomberg looked after her.

"Hey, boy, what can you tell me?"

"About what?" asked Ryan.

"About Gordio! What else about?"

"I've gotten through about fifty charts. We're going to have to call in most of the patients: there's usually no note about whether or not they're homosexuals."

"How many?"

"About twenty-four charts. No mention of sexual prefer-ence."

"How many of those have private docs?"

"Almost all."

"No problem: we'll just call their private docs. It'll be easier than trying to get the information from the patients."

"I didn't keep a record of who the private doc was for each patient. I just have a column for ward or private, yes or no."

"Well, it's only twenty-four charts," said Hyman, punching Ryan on the shoulder.

Ryan recalled all twenty-four charts and made two new col-umns on his table for "Private Doctor" and "Phone Number of Private Doctor."

By the third week in October he had his table filled out on eighty patients, seventy of whom turned out to be homosexual. Five were nonhomosexuals who had traveled to places known to have lots of Gordio. Hyman Bloomberg was no dummy.

"We still haven't proved this is a venereal disease," said Ryan.

"Keep going: eighty down, seventy to go," said Bloomberg, rubbing his hands.

8

Saturday, October 21

The operator woke Ryan in the on-call room at 4:00 A.M., Saturday.

"Dr. Ryan?"

"Who else, at this hour?"

"This is the operator."

"The who?"

"The telephone operator."

Ryan struggled to arouse his mind enough to understand why
it was not a nurse.

"Did you approve a call to Jedda, Saudi Arabia?"

"If this is a joke, I'm not laughing."

"I'm serious."

"I'm lost," said Ryan. "I don't know anyone in Saudi Arabia.
I'm not even sure anyone lives there, really."

"I'm sorry, but there's a man on the line from the nurses
station on B-2, trying to call Saudi Arabia. You are the intern for
B-2, right?"

Ryan went down to B-2. There were no nurses in the nurses
station, but Mr. Toth was there, stark naked, with his CVP line
dangling from one arm, dripping blood from the right side of
his heart into a puddle on the floor.

"Mr. Toth, what are you doing, stark naked, in the nurses
station, on the phone, at four A.M.?"

"I'm trying to call the Prince. They won't let me dial from my
phone. It's a damned nuisance, I admit."

"Saudi Arabia's a toll call, Mr. Toth," remarked Ryan.

"I asked the operator to put it on my card, but she was no help at all," said Mr. Toth, unable to fathom her lack of cooperation. He continued. "I can't get any goddamn service around here. The Prince'll put me up at his place in London. Best damn hospital in the world. Color TV's and saunas in every room."

Mr. Toth was a self-made man. He was also, at this moment, clearly out of his head, either from his steroids, or his infections, or his hypercalcemia, or his multiple myeloma, or a combination. He had built a financial empire from a travel agency, and really did number princes and other luminaries among his personal friends.

At the moment, however, he was cut off. Despite his naked lunacy, he perceived that Ryan was the man with the power to help him swing his deal now. Ryan marveled at how ingrained patterns asserted themselves in the expression of craziness when people flipped. Mr. Toth would continue to be pleasantly manipulative, to wheel and deal, to extol Ryan as the last reasonable man left in the world, the only man who would be a human being and help, help Mr. Toth call Saudi Arabia at 4:00 A.M.

"Well, it's not four A.M. in Jedda. This is the perfect time to call," said Toth.

Ryan could not refute that, and if Mr. Toth was not sitting there, stark naked, dripping his heart's blood over the floor, Ryan might have been persuaded. But as it was, he put Mr. Toth to bed with assurances that he would see to the call first thing in the morning.

"Right after breakfast?" asked Toth.

"Sure thing, right after breakfast," said Ryan.

Ryan had no sooner put head to pillow than his beeper went off.

"Six-eight-four-oh," said the page operator. It was the number for a call coming from outside the hospital. An outside call at 4:00 A.M.?

"Did I wake you?" asked Diana.

"No," said Ryan, "I've been getting all kinds of calls tonight."

"I saw you were on call and figured you might be up."

"Makes more sense than *your* being up at this hour."

"Couldn't sleep."

"Where are you?"

"Across the street."

"Oh."

"I miss you," she said, sending a serious chill jolting through Ryan.

"I didn't know you were staying in the city tonight."

"Would you have been interested?"

"I'm on call," said Ryan. "So I guess I'd be interested, but unable to do much about it."

"You're still interested?"

"You called to ask that?"

"Is that so strange?"

"It is, if that's what kept you up."

"I'd lose more than sleep if I lost you."

"What brought this on?"

"You haven't been exactly forthcoming since you ran into Alan."

"I guess I saw the future in his eyes. And it didn't include me."

"I wish I could see the future," said Diana. "I'm so mixed up. I'm dying to find out how it's going to turn out."

"I think I know."

"Neither of us knows," said Diana hoarsely. "Bill, let's meet for lunch."

"I need time to think."

Ryan's beeper went off. It was the floor paging.

"Got to go."

"Lunch?"

"Okay."

It was Mr. Toth again, out of bed. He was coaxed back with little difficulty.

By Morning Rounds Mr. Toth had forgotten completely, and vigorously denied, ever having been out of bed.

Ryan finished his calls, went to Attending Rounds, and paged Diana at noon. They met in her office. She locked the door, pulled down the window shades, and came around the desk to Ryan. She had his tunic off and belt unbuckled before her lips left his. His pants were off by the time they settled onto her Persian rug.

Her skirt was up around her waist, and her panties off.

"Don't mess up my skirt," she breathed.

"Take it off."

"No time for delicacies," she said.

9

October 28

Late October, and summer showed no signs of abating, except it rained more.

Ryan had the weekend off. There was a cooling rain, dissipating the heat. Ryan walked down Second Avenue, with his raincoat open, letting the water seep into his Top-Siders, and watching the avenue flow.

He was down to Eighteenth Street before he knew it and, reaching into his pocket, found a little white card. There was a pay phone a block off. He called from there.

"Hello?" said Caroline.

"Don't you dig in the rain?"

"Who is this?"

"Dr. Ryan, at your service."

"Well, hello, stranger. No, I take good care of my body, and do not dig in the rain. Besides, nobody else would dig with me, and I can't do it all alone. Where are you? Sounds like you're in a parking lot."

"Close. Seventeenth and Second Avenue."

"You're only seven blocks away," she said happily. "Come in out of the rain."

Ryan liked her place. High ceilings, enormous floor-to-ceiling windows.

"Staying out of trouble," she told him, answering his first nervous question. "Staying away from doctors and out of hospitals," she laughed.

"You're not keeping your appointments?" asked Ryan, a little alarmed.

"Stop sounding like a doctor," laughed Caroline. "I am positively a model patient."

"You'll be fine," said Ryan.

"I know: I have a potentially curable . . ." said Caroline. "Sit down, for chrissake. Give me that thing. What are you? Playing Columbo?" She took his beat-up raincoat, and got a pair of wineglasses.

"You're not going to get hysterical if I have some wine with you?"

"You're allowed, aren't you?"

"Used to make my lymph nodes hurt, the wine, you know."

"No, I didn't."

"Does that to some people with Hodgkin's."

"Sure."

"Enough talk of disease."

"You will keep your appointments?"

"Of course, muttonhead. Have one with Woods in a couple of weeks."

"Then you're not out of the woods yet."

"No, he's still my doc . . . Oh! What a dreadful pun! Unmerciful," Caroline laughed. "Positively unmerciful." She sipped her wine, looking at Ryan over the rim of the glass.

"We're almost done with the hole I was working on when I had my little setback last August. Got three new prospects. Colonial excavation is all the rage now, lucky for me. Now you've heard all about me. Tell me about you."

"Well, I'm back at Manhattan Hospital, the main place."

"You never liked Whipple much, did you?"

"I like the Tower better."

"Better social life over there? Nurses were pretty cowlike at Whipple. Except Sally, of course. How is she?"

"Don't see her much."

"She's such a good egg," said Caroline, eyeing Ryan. "Ever take her out?"

"Sally? No."

"Got a girl?"

"Well, sort of."

201

"Sort of?" laughed Caroline. "Sort of? Sort of's like being a little bit pregnant, or having a little Hodgkin's."

"Well, I am seeing a nurse. Hope Lo. She specialed at Whipple sometimes. Mostly nights."

"Didn't get to know many of the night people," said Caroline, a little flatly. "Usually had the pillow over my head trying to hear and see no evil. Nights were bad there. You sound kind of tentative about this Hope Lo." She eyed Ryan, who was looking at his shoe tops.

"Well, she's very nice."

"Well, that's a relief. Don't have to worry about sort-of-Hope-Lo. Damned with faint praise, if ever I've heard it."

"You never have to worry."

"I don't worry. I'll get all well, then come claim you. But I want to know my competition."

"Sometimes," laughed Ryan, "you're positively witchlike."

They shared a laugh.

"Well, I have been seeing a doctor."

"You mean a psychiatrist?"

"No, a woman doctor."

"Oh, I thought you meant a shrink. Whenever one of my friends in the Village says he's been seeing a doctor, he means a shrink."

"No, no, I mean I've been . . . dating one; a woman who is also a doctor, a cardiologist."

"Intern?"

"Attending."

"An *older* woman cardiologist doctor." Caroline could make "older" sound very pregnant. "You like her more than Hope-sort-of-Lo. I can tell that much."

"She's intriguing."

"Married?"

"Of course."

"Scratch her."

"I really should."

"Nobody ever takes sound advice," said Caroline, looking sourly at her empty glass.

"Well, I can't just stop seeing her. I'm doing an elective with her next month."

"An elective?"

"A month off ward duty. I get to spend a month learning cardiology."

"Sounds just ducky."

Ryan steered things toward safer talk. About a half an hour later Caroline helped him on with his coat.

"Hodgkin's isn't catching, is it?"

"Don't think so," said Ryan, who had decided ten minutes earlier to kiss her on the cheek, if the occasion arose.

He did. She smiled unhappily.

"Have a nice elective," she said.

They said good-bye. Ryan walked to the subway at Fourteenth Street in the rain.

10

Monday, November 6

November swept away the last traces of summer, and everything came alive. For Ryan the most exciting thing about November was that he was on elective for the entire month. No nights on call, nine-to-five working days. A month's vacation, relatively speaking. A month with Diana Hayes.

Diana was actually the only reason any intern in his right mind would spend his elective month doing cardiology. The division was called "Hopeless Hearts." But the elective was popular enough; most of it was spent with Diana in the cath lab. Any Swan-Ganz catheterizations on the Cardiac Care Unit were done by the intern on the cath elective, so there was a fair share of clinical action. Ryan didn't care. He'd seen enough action for a lifetime. He wanted to see Diana.

Diana usually limited the elective to two interns. This month she allowed only one: Ryan.

"Don't you think that's a little obvious?" asked Ryan. "Manhattan Hospital is a small town."

"Don't be such an old woman," said Diana. "Anyhow, the prevailing illusion is that I'm a faithful wife." She arched an eyebrow. "And we won't do anything to dispel that."

"Of course not."

"We will," she said, "remain discreet."

Ryan arrived at eight in the morning, every morning, and was with her all day, and when she had the excuse of an early cath case the next morning, he was with her all night. She always warned Alan two days in advance of the night she had to stay in town for an early case.

"He gets disoriented so easily," she said.

She was a careful technician. Everything under control. Even her cutdowns were bloodless. She made a small nick and then blunt-dissected quickly to the artery and vein. Ryan was amazed how easy she made it look. He was amazed because he had tried lots of cutdowns, and he knew it wasn't that easy.

The diagnostic lab was her ship, and she was totally in command. Whether it was an echo, a stress test, a scan, or a cath, she could do it all. Patients were rolled in as questions and she delivered answers, methodically, smoothly, and without waste.

Ryan pondered her. With each day he pondered her more and everything else less. The more he learned her techniques and insights, the less use he had for his own. Things he had done routinely, he now discovered he had been doing wrong, from cutdowns to his written reports.

"You write too much," she said. "Who are you trying to impress? The idea is to instruct, communicate, not display."

He knew she was right. She had to prove nothing. Her reports were for the benefit of the reader. And they were worth reading.

She could absorb herself so totally in the cath lab. It must be wonderful to be able to care about something like that, Ryan thought.

Next to Diana, Ryan felt self-absorbed and petty. "She gets off on putting other people down," Biotto maintained. "She *needs* people who don't know as much as she does, to feed her own power trip."

Ryan knew Biotto was typically wrong about Diana. Biotto was stung. She did not tolerate people like Biotto. She had standards, and force. And she needed no one. She was self-sufficient. When people got in trouble, they called her, not the other way around.

Diana was useful, important even. And she knew it. And she had made it through the internship gauntlet, which Ryan wasn't sure he was strong enough to endure. These were tough people Ryan emulated. He wanted to earn their respect: Diana, Iggy, Frank Wright, even Fick. They had their defenses, some more than others. But they each hung in there, and if they couldn't prevail, at least they were there the next time, trying. Fick disappeared too much. At Whipple, it was forgivable. Desertion is the first temptation. They told everyone that as medical students starting on the wards.

"The first thing you're going to want to do when you arrive on the wards is leave. Don't. Just hang in there; even if all you can do is watch, just watch. Don't leave."

Fick was a JAR, and still deserting. But he managed to drag himself back every morning to rejoin the regiment. Iggy of course never left. And Diana not only stayed, but led.

11

November 12

For appearances, Ryan feigned interest in cardiology for the month of November. He even bestirred himself to attend the weekly conference given by Holcumb, the chief of the Division of Cardiology. Unfortunately, Holcumb's conferences were as dismal as the rest of the division's exercises. But Ryan convinced himself he'd better attend or it would be evident the only reason he took the elective was Diana.

Not that Holcumb was really that bad. He had once published some sufficiently obscure work on myocardial contractility to make him the logical choice for chief. It was the kind of basic incomprehensible science, without obvious applicability, that everyone felt must be important, and made everyone feel intensely guilty. Everyone felt guilty because nobody could understand the first thing about any of it. Holcumb had presented his insights at conferences each of the ten years he had been chief, filling blackboards with chalky curves and equations. At the end of those ten years nobody was any closer to understanding them than they ever had been. But everyone felt a lot more guilty. On the strength of that, and by virtue of a hail-fellow-well-met personality, he had been made, and kept on as, chief of the Division of Cardiology.

But his conferences were soporific. Ryan stopped going. He had more important things to think about: Diana. She filled his day. She filled his mind. He loathed the nights she packed her big attaché case and took the train home to Nyack, and to Alan.

Ryan tried to visualize her getting into a cab for Grand Central, getting on the train for Nyack, and getting off at the other end. Did Alan meet her at the station, or just wait at home in his slippers?

No, it was hard to imagine that vigorous-looking preppie-tweed not meeting her at the station. It would have been such a comfort had he been flaccid and pink, the sort Ryan could imagine having dinner with Diana at separate ends of a long table, the sort who would sleep in a separate bed. But no such luck. Ryan could imagine them eating dinner alone, together, and he could imagine much more.

"We usually eat with friends," Diana told him. "Alan has lots of good friends. Most of them seem to like to eat dinner with us. There's always someone over."

"But don't you just go off alone, to some rustic little roadside inn, and have dinner for two by candlelight?"

Ryan could imagine that tweed doing this with Diana. He could see Alan's hair in the candlelight. It was Alan's hair that ultimately bothered Ryan the most. Ryan could emulate the voice, and had been trying to lower his own since meeting Alan. But that hair was unbeatable. Ryan's hair was fine, and unmanageable in high humidity. But Alan had a thick mane, and the gray temples and streaks were totally out of Ryan's league.

Friday, November 17

"Don't look so moribund," she said as Ryan watched her pack. "You know I have to go home to Alan."

"Why?"

"He's my husband, among other things."

"What other things?"

"Oh, he just couldn't manage in that big house. He'd stay in his study reading, and forget to come out and go to work."

"How can you stand the"—Ryan searched for the word—"the dependency?"

"Oh, Alan couldn't be different. He's just too good. He can't help it if he adores me, and I can't stop him."

"Yes, you could."

"You mean by hurting him enough? I'm not sure. Sometimes people love you more if you hurt them. Love is so close to hate. Besides, it'd be so cruel. He just adores me. If I hurt him, he'd just blame himself, and try to change what he can't change."

"But he won't let you out of his grip."

"You can't blame a baby for clinging. And he sees so little of me. He just overcompensates sometimes. He can't help being possessive occasionally. Not like you. You can be strong and let me be free."

"Well, I hardly have a claim where you're concerned."

"Of course, that's what's so charming. You make no claim. Nobody should have rights to another person. But Alan has, bless his heart, through no fault of his own."

"Only because you let him."

"You don't know Alan," sighed Diana.

It bothered Ryan more than a little that Alan had turned out to be so different from Ryan's mental image of what he would be. Diana had depicted a cuddly otherworldly professor, a passive older man, of slight physical presence. Either the years had blinded her to the man's obvious force, or she was not being totally honest with Ryan about her life and feelings.

Friday Evening

Hope called.

Ryan hadn't seen her since the middle of October. He had gotten phone messages from Arch, but Ryan had been too busy thinking about Diana to call Hope. Finally, in early November, he had gotten a postcard.

> *I've given up on the phone. You're never home at a decent hour. In fact, I've tried indecent hours, and you're not home, or not answering. Out here looking for a job. Don't know about the job, but the skiing looks great. Love, Hope.*

209

The card was from Salt Lake City.

Now it was Friday evening, and Ryan pounced on the phone, hoping it would be Diana, who never called on Friday evenings. Friday evenings she had her big attaché case with her, and sped out of Ryan's life, and back to Alan. Ryan was not easily discouraged. So on this Friday evening when Hope returned to New York, Ryan had been sitting by the phone, waiting for Diana to surprise him.

"Hi, buddy," said Hope.

"Hey, when'd you get back?" Ryan tried to sound enthusiastic, but he was worried that if Diana called she would get a busy signal, and might decide to go home to Nyack.

"Yesterday."

"How's Salt Lake?"

"Well, do I have to tell you about it over the phone?"

She came over about an hour later. Diana still hadn't called. Hope was taking the job.

"You'll be a ski bum in six weeks," said Ryan, encouragingly.

"That *would* be delightful," said Hope, trying to smile. "You'll come out and visit this Christmas?"

"Sure," said Ryan.

Hope started to cry.

"Hey, what's the matter?" said Ryan, really surprised.

"You're not exactly begging me to stay."

"I just want what's best for you."

12

Saturday, November 18

Hope had given up on Ryan and New York, not necessarily in that order.

Ryan thought about it the next day, suffered a moment of true regret, and almost called, but hung up at the last moment. She might really stay. He needed room. Friends, former bedmates, called. Any voice but Diana's disappointed. By mid-November Ryan was even getting on Arch's nerves.

Arch tried to avoid him: but Ryan knew where to find Arch. Arch had to use the kitchen.

If Ryan had been errant before coming into orbit around Diana, then Arch was drifting in space. And the error of his ways began at the table, with his high-cholesterol breakfast.

"Four eggs every morning, then you go to some ulcerogenic conference at work, then a low-fiber, high-calorie, sugar-sweetened lunch. The only exercise you get is opening pop-tops, watching football on the tube," snorted Ryan. "You're cruising for an M.I., just around the corner."

Arch looked from Ryan to Jane for help. But Jane looked back as though she were looking at a dead man. Ryan stormed out of the kitchen.

Arch looked after him.

"He was never like this before he started screwing that bitch."

"It's not him I'm worried about," said Jane, tremulously.

Arched chewed his mouthful of egg.

"Well, what am I suppose to do?" he said, evading Jane's eyes.

"Skip the rest of breakfast. Go out and jog."

211

"This is New York, honey. People get raped for less in New York."

Jane started to cry.

"We're talking about changing my life-style," said Arch.

"Perceptive of you," bawled Jane.

"But I like my life-style. I consider myself fortunate to have been born into it."

"And you'll die out of it."

"All my friends are ganging up on me." Arch pushed the table away from him. "Ryan started all this. He's not himself. He's all turned around by that bitch at the hospital. Her highness don't approve of egg."

13

Tuesday, November 21

When Diana wasn't in Nyack, she was with Ryan.

"We're becoming 'a thing,' you know," said Ryan, happily.

"No, I did not know. What could be more innocent? You are on my elective, are you not?"

"But Manhattan Hospital is all eyes and ears."

"Idle speculation."

"They're always watching," said Ryan, happily.

The thought of being unwatched depressed Diana. But she was depressed less since Ryan had become her satellite. By Manhattan Hospital standards they were stars. Ryan was famous for his crusades, and she was the local ravishing enigma.

"The cynosure role becomes me," she said more than just half seriously. "I'm tired of just producing silently all day, stuck away in the cath lab."

She dragged Ryan to Gleason's for lunch and for after-work drinks.

"Isn't this scandalous?" she'd laugh. "We've been here twice in one day."

Bob Dylan's voice rasped from the jukebox.

> *Don't put on any airs when you're down on*
> *Rue Morgue Avenue,*

"You love it," said Ryan.

> *They got some hungry women there, and*
> *they really make a mess out of you.*

Diana looked at Ryan.

"Within limits. I love it, within limits," she said, smiling at two residents coming into Gleason's.

Ryan sipped his beer. Biotto came in, flashed a raffish smile at Ryan, and moved to the bar for some serious womanizing.

"Look at Biotto," said Diana. "He's wondering whether I'm screwing you. But then, he thinks, if we were doing it we wouldn't be seen together at Gleason's. But then, what are we doing at Gleason's?"

"Biotto isn't that convoluted," said Ryan. "He thought, 'I hope Ryan's getting into her pants,' and then concentrated on that redhead at the bar."

"Absolutely absurd," said Diana, looking annoyed. She knew Biotto was thinking about getting into her pants himself; the redhead was only a foil.

> *Sweet Melinda, the peasants call her*
> *the goddess of gloom.*
> *She speaks good English and she invites*
> *you up into her room.*
> *And you're so kind and careful not*
> *to go to her too soon.*
> *And she takes your voice and leaves*
> *you howling at the moon.*

"Let's get out of here," said Diana. "We've thrilled the crowd enough for one night." Diana walked straight for the door, eyes straight ahead, oblivious to the glances from the residents scattered among the barroom tables.

"Exits are so important," she told Ryan when they got outside.

They got back to her room by separate routes.

He knocked at her door.

"Who is it?"

"The invisible man."

She let him in.

"What was that suppose to mean?"

"I guess I'm just tiring of being a nonperson."

"You sound like a psychiatric social worker."

"Forget it," said Ryan, humiliated.

Diana lit a cigarette, and blew the smoke ceilingward.

"Listen," she said. "Just trust me. You'll get what you want."

"What I want?"

"What we both want," smiling now. "And don't look so sad: love should be fun."

"I just feel like I'm twisting in the wind."

"And you want to be firmly rooted?"

Ryan nodded.

"Take it from me, from personal experience. That doesn't help any."

Wednesday Morning

Maxwell Baptist dropped down to the cath lab the next day. He glanced at Ryan and spoke to Diana.

"I see you have a devotee for your elective this month."

"He'd better be," said Diana. "He's going to be one of the Cardiology fellows in a few years."

If St. John was surprised, Ryan was stupefied. St. John spoke: "Well, we'll see."

Ryan shrieked at Diana as soon as St. John was safely gone. "Why? Why did you say that?"

"Why shouldn't I?"

"Because it isn't true, for starters. Jesus, he's out for me as it is. I haven't even thought about fellowships, much less getting one here, and in Cardiology."

"Well, then, it's time you did. I can't think of a better fellowship. It's the best part of Internal Medicine."

"But I haven't even talked to Holcumb."

"What does he know? He's just division chief. He'll take you if I tell him to."

Diana had to go to an executive meeting; she left Ryan palpitating in the lab. Baptist caught her at the end of the meeting.

"Were you serious about considering Ryan for a fellowship?"

"Yes, quite."

"I'm only keeping him for junior residency because Hyman Bloomberg insisted. They're doing some kind of project together. I wouldn't count on his making senior resident. And we usually pick our fellows from the senior residents."

"Well, then," said Diana, "we'll have to see, won't we?"

14

November 29

Ryan sat in the clinic Wednesday morning, contemplating the elements which coalesced to create his current angst. There was his obsession with Diana, which mauled his powers of concentration and rendered his attempts at patient care desultory. This, in turn, swept him with guilt. The guilt translated into a massive indifference toward everything, especially work. The indifference, combined with the massive disorganization in the Medical Clinic, rendered all caring for patients an exercise in theater of the absurd. Beyond the clinic there was the greater edifice of lay hospital administrators, who thwarted some of Ryan's best efforts on behalf of his patients.

Ryan decided that he had to pare down his efforts and concerns. He would stop thinking about the dissolution of the clinic system, of systems in general, and worry about one patient at a time. He would conspire on behalf of one patient and see if, despite the clinic, he could do some good.

He looked at the next patient's chart. Mr. Jefferson was a forty-three-year-old black who had been working fifteen years for Manhattan Hospital as a mail-room clerk. He had his first myocardial infarction a year ago. Since then he had severe angina.

With relatively little exertion Mr. Jefferson's heart became profoundly ischemic. The arteries supplying his heart muscle were so narrowed they just couldn't carry the big volume of blood required by a heart at work.

He laughed when Ryan asked whether or not he still had chest pain, despite all the medication.

"I take three Isordil four times a day, two propanolol three times a day. I take nitroglycerin before I walk up the subway steps, and three times on the way to the hospital. With all those pills, you'd think I wouldn't have time to notice the pain. But it's still there."

On bad days, when he was having a lot of pain even before leaving his home in Queens, Mr. Jefferson drove to work. But he usually got angina looking for parking around the hospital and running out to feed the meters.

"Why don't you get an assigned parking space?" asked Ryan, ingenuously.

"I'm a mail-room clerk, Doc. Parking spaces are for doctors."

"You have worked here for fifteen years," said Ryan, trying to restrain himself. Here was a man who accepted outrage with equanimity. It was probably better for his heart that he did. "You could work another fifteen, if you could get to work without angina."

"Hey, I'd like to work another twenty. But that won't get me the permit."

Ryan needed a minute to collect his thoughts. He stepped into the clinic conference room, where Biotto was writing a three-line note on a patient. Ryan told Biotto about Jefferson.

"He's right, of course," said Biotto. "No way he's gonna get the permit."

"I'll write a letter," sputtered Ryan. "Why force this hard-working guy with a bum heart out of his job and onto welfare, when a parking space could save him?"

"In the first place," said Biotto, "who you gonna send it to? Nobody wants to admit having anything to do with parking. You'll just get the runaround. If they give Jefferson a space, every hypertensive aide, every arthritic clerk, will be beating down the doors, demanding parking."

Ryan made a few calls and kept getting referred elsewhere, being told each time that mail-room clerks were not entitled to parking, by people who claimed to know nothing about parking. Ryan sent Jefferson back to the mail room.

Then he went to his car, and delicately removed the parking

218

decal from his front window, intact. He called Jefferson, in the mail room, and told him to drive his car to Parking Lot B. Jefferson drove up in his battered VW.

Ryan stuck the decal on Jefferson's windshield. Jefferson got out and looked at the decal.

"Never underestimate the power of positive thinking," said Ryan.

Jefferson thanked Ryan, Jesus, The Manhattan Hospital, and drove into the lot. The guard looked at the decal and waved him into a space. Jefferson hurried to call his wife.

"You can tell your wife," said Ryan, "but not another soul. Don't offer anyone a ride, if it means letting on about the space. Nobody is to know."

Ryan moved his car to the street. Then he went to the garage across from the town house, where they let him have a space for eighty dollars a month, exactly twice the hospital parking rate.

Ryan told Arch:

"Five months at the Tower, and the best thing I do for a patient is give away my parking space."

15

Thursday, December 7

At the end of Ryan's elective month a true disaster befell the CCU. Brigid Sullivan's father was admitted with a severe M.I. Brigid was one of Ryan's favorite people. Two weeks earlier Ryan had been given the afternoon off and had been paid to walk through Central Park with Brigid. Now her father was doing poorly, and Brigid had come to grief.

Head nurses at The Manhattan Hospital were a separate species, and Brigid was the progenitor, in a manner of speaking, of that order. There were three ward medicine floors, a Cardiac Care Unit, and a neurology floor. Five floors, five head nurses for ward medicine. Three of the other head nurses had been groomed and honed by Brigid. To Ryan these women always seemed a shade too dedicated and forbidding, although they were a young and relatively attractive lot. Any one of them could have played around with any number of residents, and some did, until they became head nurses. Then nobody asked them out, at least nobody from the hospital.

Brigid Sullivan's father had a big M.I. His blood pressure was kept up only by the grace of Levophed. He looked bad. Brigid took a week's leave to be with him. She didn't want to leave the bedside, which, of course, made it tough on the nurses, who couldn't bring themselves to order her out, but couldn't do the things Mr. Sullivan needed with Brigid hovering around.

The CCU nurses knew Brigid liked Ryan, and cornered him. He had to do something about her. Two weeks earlier, when Medical Nursing was putting together a recruiting pamphlet, Brigid had been picked to be in the photos. Hi, you'd love working at Manhattan Hospital. See how happy I look here on the ward, in the cafeteria, and wandering through Central Park, with this gorgeous resident, one of many. Ryan never knew whether Brigid or someone in Medical Nursing picked him for the Central Park pictures, but it meant the afternoon off.

They stopped off for drinks at the Palm Court, and she invited Ryan back to her apartment. It was a crisp fall day, and they walked along the park, up Fifth Avenue. They were both pleasantly high from the Palm Court drinks and the autumn weather. Brigid talked about college football games on fall afternoons in Ohio, and Ryan forgot she was a head nurse, the most famous head nurse. He began to notice how blue her eyes were, and how dark her lashes.

Her apartment was in hospital housing. It was an efficiency, with travel posters from Greece and Spain vacations. (She went alone.) She had an aquarium with goldfish and an oxygen pump. Ryan inspected the books in her bookcase while she made coffee: there was Vonnegut, Wodehouse, Lessing, Wouk, Wambaugh, and Katherine Anne Porter.

They talked about the park, and somehow got onto gynecologists. Brigid had a love-hate relationship with hers.

"He's so thorough and caring, but he treats me like such a baby. He called me back for a repeat pelvic last month, but was so maddeningly evasive about why that I could have screamed. Turned out I had a Class II Pap. Why couldn't he have just told me that?"

"He's older?"

"Yes, of course. He's very old-school. The ultimate in paternalism. He doesn't want me worrying my pretty little head about anything. He wants me to leave myself in his hands."

She lit a cigarette and blew the smoke into the air.

"That's one thing I like about your approach, Bill. You let the patients in on what's happening."

They chatted about less medical things, but drifted back to one of Ryan's least favorite patients, an alcoholic with a penchant for 2:00 A.M. admissions.

"He drinks himself into acute pancreatitis, every third night, like clockwork," said Ryan. "Doesn't even have the decency to do it during daylight hours. I've always got to come in at two A.M. and stay up all night with him."

"Oh, he's such a pitiful thing. He can't help it."

"He knows better. This isn't pediatrics. He disregards everything I tell him. He says, 'Sure, Doc,' then goes out and does just what he pleases."

"But that's human frailty. You have to accept frailty, if you're going to treat suffering," said Brigid, a little perturbed. "It's called compassion."

"I call it abuse. I wish that alcoholic had some compassion for me. Maybe he'd let me sleep through a night."

"Ryan," laughed Brigid, blowing smoke in his face, "you're such a hard-ass. But a hard-ass is still an ass."

Ryan respected Brigid. For some reason he felt sorry for her, sitting in her efficiency apartment with her goldfish, her books, and her important job, husbandless and kidless at nearly thirty. He had the feeling she was lonely, and maybe even unfulfilled.

Ryan told Caroline about Brigid, and Caroline howled at him for being a chauvinist. Brigid was probably quite fulfilled, and happy, despite the fact Ryan wasn't screwing her, or nobody else Ryan knew was screwing her. Maybe she had men outside the hospital. Or maybe she was happy without them.

Now, two weeks later, Ryan went to Brigid's father's room, on the CCU, and put his arm around her.

"Brigid, remember Mrs. Spivak?"

"Mrs. Spivak?" said Brigid, distractedly, as Ryan walked her out of her father's room. "Oh, yes, Mrs. Spivak." She almost laughed. "The Gypsies. She was Mrs. Spivak last month. Gypsies change their names so fast I can't keep up. They camped out in the solarium."

"They wanted to camp out in the room, but you convinced them they'd do more harm than good, hovering by the bedside, getting in the nurses' way."

Brigid stayed in the visitors' room after that. The nurses on the unit were happy for that. Brigid stayed in the visitors' area night and day, for five days, just leaving to shower and eat. Then her father arrested and died.

222

The room is usually quickly deserted once an arrest has ended. The doctor running the arrest ends it with a "Thank you, everybody," and they all leave, except the nurse who has to wrap the body. But this time nobody wanted to walk out. They knew Brigid would see from her post in the visitors' area.

So Ryan went out alone and took Brigid into the conference room. He came out a little later for coffee. Then about half an hour later they came out together, Ryan looking ten years older, but Brigid looking quite composed.

One of the nurses was given the night off to go home with Brigid, home to her aquarium, across the street.

16

December 14

The nurses had decorated the conference room with Christmas things, and everyone collected there for coffee. The medical students, nurses, and interns sat on ledges and desk tops and relaxed for a few minutes in the warm room. Outside, a surprise snow flurry whitened the gray day. It was ten thirty in the morning, and Iggy was back from Morning Report. Biotto and Ryan waited with him for the attending to show up for Visit Rounds. Two nurses drank coffee in the corner while Biotto studied their legs. Ryan watched the snow.

Biotto looked at Ryan.

"Nice to be on the inside this time of year," said Biotto.

Ryan looked at him for meaning.

"*We* are on the inside," said Biotto; then to Iggy, "Bet Jim Cross and Bob Walker don't feel real full of Christmas cheer right now."

Iggy shook his head.

Cross and Walker were interns. Ryan didn't know them well. They were at the other end of the rotation schedule. Ryan had never worked with either. He usually arrived on service as they were leaving.

"What's he talking about?" Ryan asked Iggy.

"They got cut," said Iggy.

"They got cut," said Biotto. "Baptist called them in last Monday."

"Jesus," said Ryan.

"Nice Christmas present," said Biotto. "Running around looking for residency positions in Podunk and Oshkosh."

"Why them?"

"Cross ran afoul of the wrong man," said Iggy. "Mortimer Stearns."

"Mortimer Stearns? That gomer? He must be a hundred years old."

"Practiced at The Manhattan Hospital for forty of them. Grand Master, American College of Physicians. Member, Board of Trustees. And a direct line to Maxwell Baptist," said Iggy.

"What did Cross ever do to Mortimer?"

"Last August, Mort got a call from one of his patients—actually, from the guy's wife. She tells Mort her husband's real sick. It's about midnight, and Mort tells her to just take her husband to the Great White Tower, where the boys will take good care of him. Mort will see him in the morning. Now, Mort doesn't want this guy hassled, so he calls the E.R. resident and says to admit the guy directly to the private service. No evaluation, you understand. Mort doesn't want a delay.

"The patient rolls in around two A.M. Cross has to get out of bed to see this guy, who turns out to be dead drunk, combative. Vomits all over Cross. Refuses to be examined. Cross works the guy up the best he can, then calls Mortimer at three A.M. Wakes up Mortimer to tell him there's nothing wrong with his patient, except that he's drunk. Cross let Mort have it at three A.M."

"Mortimer never even examined the guy? Never had the guy evaluated in the E.R.? Just admitted him?" asked Ryan.

"Yup."

"He deserved a call at three A.M."

"Cross is out on his ass."

"Jesus."

"Mortimer has a lot of moneyed patients. One of them donated the bucks to overhaul the CCU last spring."

"I still think Mort's a turkey."

"Nolo contendere."

"What about Walker?"

"Dunno."

Ryan didn't hear much of what was said at Attending Rounds that morning. He kept thinking about the death certificates, the

225

syringes, the Great Wheelchair Bust, and Frank Wright reminding him about the pyramid after Baptist's conference.

Someone had saved Ryan's ass. Maybe Frank. Maybe Diana.

Ryan caught Iggy after rounds.

"Who evaluates us?"

"Everybody."

"Who's everybody?"

"The attending who makes Visit Rounds. The head nurses on the floors you're assigned to. The residents you work with. And any attending who wants to write a note to Baptist."

"Then anybody can get you."

"Some hurt more than others," said Iggy. "Don't go getting paranoid." Iggy punched Ryan's arm. "You made it."

"Until the next cut."

"Senior residency is a long way off, boy," said Iggy.

17

December 22

Ryan was hurrying across the avenue in front of the Tower Friday evening, trying to get home for Diana's surprise phone call, the one he was certain would eventually come some Friday evening. He was narrowly missed by a taxi. The cabdriver was not gracious about it, but the passenger turned around as it sped off, and waved. It was Diana.

Homeward bound. Diana would not break tradition that night. Ryan watched the taxi disappear, with his hands jammed deep in his pockets. He shuffled home.

The crowd in the ICB&G was raising the usual Friday afternoon roar. Ryan peered in the window. It was all bodies, lots of white uniforms, with eager Friday-afternoon scent following.

He walked on, but heard rapid footsteps and whirled to meet his pursuer.

"Been ages."

"Hope!"

"Saw you looking in the window," said Hope, laughing. "You looked like a little boy left out of the fun."

Ryan met her eyes, unable to think of anything clever to say.

"Don't you say hi to your friends anymore?"

"Sure."

"I waved to you through the window," said Hope. "You just stared at me and turned away."

"Couldn't pick you out. It was such a mob."

"You're forgiven."

"You're all heart."

Hope walked with Ryan along the street. She lit a cigarette.

"Haven't heard from you," she finally said.

Ryan was afraid of what was coming.

He didn't say anything.

"Didn't you care whether or not I went out to Salt Lake?"

"You'd never go to Utah."

"True."

They crossed First Avenue, heading toward the town house.

"But you didn't have to rub it in," said Hope.

"Rub it in?"

"You could have called," she said, laughing artificially. "Collect. It's only twenty blocks."

Ryan tried to laugh appreciatively.

"Sorry."

"That *was* kind of adolescent," said Hope. "Trying to pull a bluff with Utah. I should've figured you'd never bite."

"I was worried," said Ryan. It was a well-motivated lie. He didn't want Hope to think he didn't really care whether she stayed or left. At that very moment, in fact, he wanted her to stay with him, to continue on to his bed.

"I'll bet," laughed Hope. This time the laugh was quite natural. "I'll bet you worried a whole ten minutes."

They reached Ryan's block.

"This is where I get off," said Hope. It had gotten dark.

"Come have some anisette," said Ryan.

"Call me sometime," said Hope. "Nothing formal. But premeditate it." She walked off down the avenue.

Ryan went home and poured himself some anisette. Hope was right, of course. He could get very hot and bothered in her presence, but he was too preoccupied with Diana most of the time to think of Hope very often. But Hope seemed so much more important tonight, with the vision of Diana disappearing off in that cab fresh in his mind.

Ryan dialed.

"Hello?"

"Care for some anisette?"

"Ryan!" laughed Hope. "Wait a few days, then call me."

"I've just followed instructions: you said premeditate."

228

"So you premeditated for all of twenty minutes."

"You didn't say for how long."

"You miss the spirit, not the letter . . ."

"Come on."

"Your Friday night juices are flowing, that's all."

"That's plenty."

Hope was a woman of less reason and will than she seemed. She gave in, and came over an hour later.

18

The day after Christmas, Ryan went down to the Village to see Caroline. He gave her a Rod Stewart album, and she gave him a photo of Central Park. She asked about the hospital, meaning Manhattan Hospital of course. They never talked about Whipple anymore.

"The tough thing about the Tower is that it looks so damn impressive," Ryan said.

"I thought it was designed by Walt Disney," said Caroline. "But they tell me it was copied from some palace."

"Whatever, it's a veritable beacon of hope. I mean, we admitted this eighteen-year-old girl a month ago. She had blood in her urine, pain in her joints, and a lupus rash on her skin. Her mother walked her all the way from East Harlem to bring her to the Tower. She died yesterday.

"The mother was there with about twelve relatives. They had all been there before, at one time or another, impressed by the machinery, the IV's, the white uniforms, the wonder drugs. All the magic made believers of them. They couldn't believe we couldn't save her daughter. But she died.

"And of what? She didn't have leukemia, or anything they'd heard of," said Ryan, not noticing the jolt that went through Caroline, "and I had to tell them."

"A singular privilege," said Caroline quietly.

"I had the nurses bring them in, one at a time, Mrs. Diaz first. She lunged for the window as soon as I told her. The window was behind me, fortunately, so I stopped her with a tackle. A pretty decent tackle, if I do say so. Ruth Hines, one of the nurses, got some IM Valium. We held her down, all thrashing and screaming and sobbing, and socked her full of Valium. Same scene with the older brother. And one by one, we brought each relative in, and each reacted like it was a total shock, despite the fact that they could see all their relatives lying around narcotized. I mean, wouldn't you be able to guess? Well, as soon as they were all told, the less narcotized helped the worse ones home, all of them staggering away."

"Ryan, promise me something," said Caroline, without smiling.

"Anything."

"You'll be the one to tell my parents, if anything should happen to me."

Ryan sickened.

"Hey, don't be morose. You're over it. You just can't believe the good news: you're doing fine."

"Wish it were true, good doctor. Dr. Woods did a bone marrow on me last Wednesday. I'm being admitted in three weeks."

19

December 31

The Department of Medicine New Year's Eve party was never much fun, but Arch and Jane came to connect faces with all the names they had come to know. Everyone was talking medicine, which bored Ryan and fascinated Arch and Jane. Ryan spent the night looking for Diana, who had not shown.

"Who's that regal beast?" asked Jane, tugging at Ryan's sleeve and pointing out St. John.

"St. John the Baptist."

"Oh, my. He is gorgeous. He's a dissipated Gregory Peck. I expected him to be much older. You made him sound like such a fogey."

Ryan could never understand what made men attractive to women.

Hope arrived and stood by Ryan and Arch and Jane. They all drank vodka. Attendings and wives and nurses and house staff dressed up and stood around drinking cocktails from paper cups, poured by medical students behind makeshift card-table bars.

Hope was behaving herself, not trying to hold Ryan's hand, just standing there casually, playing it cool.

Ryan kept scanning the room for Diana. He looked for Brigid, too. That at least was a relief. He wasn't sure how he felt about Brigid, but with Hope there, he was just as happy Brigid wasn't.

Baptist was a stiffening presence. He was there with his wife, a dowdy woman with intelligent eyes.

"She's a novelist," said Hope. "Melinda Hansen."

Ryan looked at Hope dumbly.

"Ryan," said Hope, *"The Woman in the Window. The Enduring Lie.* Gads, you're illiterate."

"That's her? Baptist's wife?"

"Didn't you know?"

It was hard associating that pleasant-looking woman with those desperate female novels—or associating either with Baptist—but there she was.

"I *knew* I recognized her," said Jane. "I've seen her on *A.M. America.*"

Ryan drifted off into his usual, distracted state, scanning the room for Diana. Hope was stunning tonight. He wanted Diana to see. And he wanted to see her husband. He had run several scenarios through his mind about tonight, but none of them included Diana's not showing.

Arch and Jane walked back to the town house with Ryan and Hope. They drank some anisette, Ryan wondering where Diana was. Then Ryan and Hope went upstairs.

20

January 2

"Does Bill Ryan live here?"

Arch knew her from Belinda's, that elegant, in-bred look, nervous energy moving sleek lines.

"Yes, but he's not home yet."

"Perhaps I can wait in his room?"

Arch could not think of a single clever reply, and so showed her to Ryan's study. He lumbered ahead of her, crushing a beer can in his hand, wearing his old Brown football jersey.

Diana sank into the leather wingback, from which she surveyed the room.

"What on earth are those?" she asked, pointing to the brass lamp. Strands of knotted surgical silk and catgut, seven inches long, dangled from the lamp. She ran them through practiced fingers.

"Ryan's knots," said Arch.

"His what?"

"Knots."

"What does he do with . . . ?"

"He ties knots. He likes tying knots. Actually, what he really likes is untying knots, but he has to tie them first."

"How peculiar."

"Oh, Ryan's peculiar, if nothing else," said Arch, assuming his barrister posture.

Diana was looking at Ryan's bookcase. The discernible order struck her. Several shelves of biographies struck her.

"He has a taste for important people."

"Yes, he knows all about medical history, and people long since dead."

"Disapprove?"

"I make it a point not to disapprove of taste," said Arch, disliking her.

"But you disapprove of people."

"Not as a general category."

"How reassuring."

"I didn't really mean it to be," said Arch. He left.

Diana investigated the study. She went back to the knots. She looked at the books. She put Joe Cocker on the stereo and began untying the knots. Then Ryan flew in.

"Waiting long?"

"Time flies when you're having a good time."

"How was your weekend?" asked Ryan. Diana was unbuttoning his shirt while Ryan worked on slipping off her panties.

"A smashing success. We both finished the *Times*. And Alan let me read 'The Week in Review' first."

"Who could ask for more?" asked Ryan, pulling her on top of him.

"It's like getting my head out from under a pillow, just taking the train in from Nyack, knowing I'm going to ravage you after work," said Diana, moving into him.

"This sounds like it's getting serious."

"Heaven forbid."

Ryan stopped.

"Don't stop."

"Why 'heaven forbid'?" asked Ryan, stopping.

"We're too important to get serious about," laughed Diana. "Don't stop."

Ryan looked gray.

"Be happy with what we've got," she said.

"What have we got?"

"Passion, didn't you know?"

"That's all?"

"That's plenty. Passion wins, in the end. Hadn't you heard?"

"No."

"Trust me. Would I lie to you?"

"Truth?"

"Of course, but there are more important things."

"What could be more important than truth?"

"That you don't stop, until I do."

Ryan was lying on his stomach, and Diana was running her fingers over his back.

"Poor baby," she said. "You've got heat rash." She disappeared into the bathroom and returned with a plastic container.

"What's that?"

"Stay put," Diana commanded. "You're all broken out."

"What's that?"

"Baby powder."

"Baby powder? For chrissake, I've heard of going out with older women, but this is ridiculous."

"Hush up," said Diana, patting powder, "I've got to take care of this. You'd never do it yourself."

"To get to Ryan," Arch always said, "you've got to get him where he lives."

Diana appreciated that fact, although she had never heard Arch say it.

She planned with Ryan for their clinic in Scotland.

"The American Clinic in Scotland," Ryan said, visions dancing before his eyes, "on Princes Street, of course."

Diana liked the idea, but insisted on an annex in London, for alternate months, with dormer windows, working fireplaces, and a tasteful location. South Kensington would do, and the Brompton Hospital for Chest Diseases of course. They could ski in Scotland and vacation in Spain. They'd only come back to America for the American Heart meetings, to present a few papers and to scandalize old friends.

"Britain's dreary in the winter," said Diana. "We'll need some diversion."

"An expedition to New Guinea, perhaps."

"No, I'd need a few short, well-spaced vacations. Spain and Italy. You can't be an American woman of consequence, finding herself, without a vacation shucking American inhibitions and the Protestant Work Ethic. I'll go where women are women and men are men."

"Rome's humid. I'd rather swelter in New Guinea," said Ryan.

"I can see I'll have to go alone. All the better. Can't be liberated in company."

"Separate vacations?"

"Don't look so glum. You can join me after a week or so, on the Riviera."

"Sounds terrific."

"Come on now," laughed Diana.

"But I hate vacationing alone."

"Oh, all right. We go to Spain together. But I zip off for a week in Rome."

"Hey, don't do me favors."

"Maybe I should leave you in Scotland. Someone has to run the clinic."

21

Monday, January 8

Ryan did not let himself think past the next day on call or the next night with Diana. But it was the time of year more senior or more perspicacious house officers reached a frenzy, pursuing fellowships or subspecialty residencies. Interns and residents would call Ryan to switch on-call nights or coverage in order to free themselves for interview trips. It was all vaguely disquieting to Ryan, who did not want to stir himself.

He was at the pinnacle, after all. Why would he want to think of going elsewhere?

"Internship isn't forever," Arch reminded him.

"But then there's residency," Ryan said. "It's all so far off."

"Then why do you keep getting calls from guys interviewing elsewhere?"

"Beats me. They're here already. They're at the Great White Tower."

"Bastion of East Side Establishment," echoed Arch.

"Damn straight," said Ryan. "White-Anglo-Saxon-Not-Just-Protestant-But-Episcopalian, East Side wealth. This is where every immigrant wave since 1890 has wanted to send its children to learn doctoring."

"The last hospital in New York to admit Jews to the attending staff," added Arch.

"No one would ever accuse the Tower of being trendy," said Ryan. "We've even got some black docs now."

"What will they think of next?" asked Arch.

"What I can't figure out," said Ryan, "is why all these guys are thinking about doing fellowships elsewhere."

"Can't imagine."

"Even Iggy's leaving," said Ryan.

"What!"

"He's determined to go into radiology as soon as he's done with internal medicine."

"The eternal resident," said Arch.

"He's happy as a resident," said Ryan. "He has enough money to buy his designer clothes; they house him, feed him in the hospital cafeteria, tell him when to work and when to go on vacation. He wasn't on rounds this morning. Someone covered for him. He was interviewing for a radiology residency at Yale, I heard."

"Iggy wouldn't be happy out of New York," said Arch. "Can he wear his Gucci shoes in New Haven?"

They washed the dishes and went out for a beer. Ryan was less wrecked at nights now. He could be on the night before and not crash when he came home. They spotted Iggy as soon as they walked into Gleason's.

He was holding court at one of the big round tables in the corner. He was wearing his blue three-piece Yves Saint-Laurent suit.

"New Haven's a pit," he said. "The hospital's no great shakes, either, architecturally speaking. It was built around 1800, and is currently being held together by a layer of Scotch tape applied in 1945."

His words were being gravely absorbed by three interns and two residents. They held steins of beer firmly in grasp, pounding them on the table to urge Iggy on.

"The program's a real hot one. The chairman interviewed me for an hour, and he's one sharp cookie. There's lots of smart people at Yale."

"Think you'll go there?" asked Ryan.

"Not likely."

"Why not?"

"Because," said Iggy, "it's just not the Tower."

General acclaim for the Tower.

239

"I mean," said Iggy, warming up now that he had an audience in hand, "the house staff is smart—there are smart people all over—but it's just so *casual.*" Iggy made *casual* sound very obscene. " 'Laid back,' as Biotto would say. They wander around in corduroy pants with stethoscopes draped 'round their necks, carrying knapsacks and wearing work shoes."

A muttering went round the table.

"Kid's stuff."

"And New Haven is such a pit," said Iggy mournfully. "It's just not the East Side."

General approval for the East Side.

"No river."

"No East River?"

"Just a port, with gas refineries."

Raucous disapproval of gas refineries.

"I've been up and down the East Coast in search of a better place. I've been to Mass General—looks like a cheap imitation of the Tower from the outside, and on the inside the best and the brightest are falling all over each other trying to one-up."

Massive disapproval.

"The General has no *esprit,*" said Iggy. "Not like the Tower."

Calls for more beer went up amidst a roar of approval.

Iggy started to talk faster.

"I've been to Hopkins. It's an armed camp in the Baltimore ghetto. Hostile black natives. More like a fort than a hospital."

"Screw Hopkins."

"I've looked North, and I've looked South. Positively everywhere."

"Duke?"

"I've been to Duke. Now, there's a place that's almost the match of the Tower, aesthetically speaking."

"No!"

"Yes," said Iggy, wagging his head. "In all honesty the place is impressive. Manicured lawns, inspired architecture—not as inspiring as the Tower, but nice—and outstanding people. The department is dynamite, full of young, smart people. But," said Iggy, pausing for effect, holding everyone riveted, "it's in Durham, North Carolina!"

"Nowhere!"

"It's cloistered!" shouted Iggy. "Positively cloistered."

"Screw Duke!"

"I mean, in Manhattan you've got the world's most beautiful women roaming around free on the streets. Of course, you never meet 'em, and you're too tired to go out at night, but you know they're out there."

"Right."

"At Yale, everyone's married. At the General, everyone's too hyper to get it up. At Duke, you're a monk!"

"So where'll you do your Rays?"

"The Tower!" came the cry from six throats. "The Tower!" before Iggy could reply. "The Tower!"

22

January 11

Ryan was presenting the last of his three admissions from the night before when his beeper went off. He asked Biotto to take the call for him, and continued the case presentation for the attending. Biotto came back and listened to the rest of the discussion. Ryan had gotten three hours' sleep, and badly wanted a shower. When rounds ended at noon, all the admissions having been seen and discussed, Ryan told Iggy he was going to the on-call room for a shower. Biotto and Jason were hustling off the floor for lunch.

"Did you take care of that page for me?" Ryan asked Biotto, catching his arm.

"Oh, man. Clean forgot," said Biotto. "Some girl named Caroline, says she's at Whipple, and you'd know."

"Okay."

Ryan started down the stairs for Whipple, then decided he needed a shower, and why be grubby for Caroline? He'd see her after evening Chart Rounds, after he signed out and was off for the night. He could visit at his leisure, after he got off. He went to shower and shave.

Biotto was admitting, but at two o'clock he paged Ryan from the E.R. Biotto had slumped off the hall ten minutes earlier to pick up his admission, enveloped in the gloom with which he greeted any admission. But his voice sounded buoyant now, over the phone.

"Guess who we're getting?" asked Biotto, not waiting for Ryan to answer. "Mrs. Cushing, that asthmatic of yours." Ryan would have to work her up, even though he wasn't admitting, and Biotto would get credit for the admission. But she was Ryan's clinic patient, so he had to work her up, in the name of continuity of care. She was wheezing tightly.

"I thought you only wheezed in clinic, on the wool chairs?" Ryan asked her in the E.R.

Biotto was looking at her chart.

"You took her off all her asthma meds?"

"She said she only wheezed in clinic."

Mrs. Cushing was wheezing too much to say more than "It's the wool."

Ryan wheeled her upstairs, shoved an IV into her arm, gave her aminophylline and oxygen, got respiratory therapy to give her their special magic oxygen and bronchodilators, and by the time he had her more comfortable, it was time for Chart Rounds. After Chart Rounds he signed out to Biotto and went back to check on Mrs. Cushing.

She looked blue. Ryan did a set of blood gases. He was going to find Biotto, to tell him to check the blood gases after he left, when Mrs. Cushing stopped breathing altogether.

Ryan thumped her, pumped her, but she just got more and more dead. Iggy flew in and did an EKG.

"She always have this big right shift on her gram?" Iggy asked.

"It's new," said Ryan, feeling sick, looking at that ugly EKG. It pretty well made the diagnosis.

"Pulmonary embolus. Big P.E.," said Iggy.

They intubated her anyway, but she was in electromechanical dissociation. Her heart had electrical activity, but no muscular pumping response. There was nothing to do but pronounce her dead.

Ryan slumped off the floor and headed home. He needed to soak in a bath. He got to the door of the town house when his beeper went off. It was six o'clock, but it was an outside call, maybe Diana, so he fumbled through the locks and answered the page at the foyer phone.

"Hi, stranger," said Caroline.

It was only on hearing her voice that Ryan remembered. But he just couldn't face Whipple tonight.

243

"You sound great," he said, trying to sound happy to hear from her.

"I wish I could say the same for you," said Caroline. "I wake you up at six o'clock?"

"Just got home. Long day."

"I guess you're not coming tonight?"

"I'm kind of wiped out," said Ryan, hearing the silence at the other end. "Can I stop by before rounds tomorrow?"

"When do you mean?"

"Seven."

"In the *morning?*"

Ryan felt ridiculous. She sounded hurt.

"Let me shower. I'll be by tonight."

Ryan showered slowly, and began to revive in the steaming stream. He just did not want to be in Whipple tonight. He considered calling Caroline and asking her to meet him in Gleason's. It would never do. The phone rang.

"Surprise," said Diana, in her breathy voice.

"Hi."

"Someone there?"

"No, I'm alone, just dripping wet."

"Can I see you tonight?"

"Of course."

"I'll be over in a half an hour."

"I've got to go over to Whipple first."

"Well, I can tell when I'm intruding."

"You're never an intrusion."

"What time then?"

"What time is it now?"

"Seven."

"Eight, then."

Ryan hung up and jumped around trying to dress in record time. He had an hour to see Caroline and get back to the town house. If he was late, Diana would leave in a huff. She wasn't going to hang around his door stoop, waiting.

Caroline's favorite aunt was visiting when Ryan arrived at 7:20. He had met her before, when Caroline was in Whipple

244

during the summer, and she was always introduced that way, "my favorite aunt," and no other. Actually she was Caroline's only aunt. Ryan thought she might provide the perfect excuse for just saying hello and leaving. But Auntie wanted to know all about Ryan, where he went to school, where he grew up, and where he wanted to practice. It was twenty to eight when Ryan stood up to edge toward the door, which he figured would take another five minutes to gracefully negotiate. Auntie had heard about Ryan and was not about to let him off the hook so easily.

"Now, don't you go. Caroline can see me anytime. I'm on my way." Auntie got up, gathering her things.

"I really do have to be home by eight," said Ryan. "I've got company."

"I can imagine," said Caroline, only half kidding.

"Well, I'll leave you two," said Auntie, kissing Caroline good-bye.

It was fifteen minutes until eight. It took that to make the town house walking, seven and a half minutes on the run.

"Oh, don't go yet," said Caroline. "I'll be alone."

"I wish she hadn't left," said Ryan. "I really can't be late. They'll be waiting outside."

"Bill," said Caroline, "I'm terrified."

"Why?"

"Dr. Woods said he had to do a bone marrow. He's afraid it may have spread there."

"He said that?"

"Why else would he be doing one?"

"Your white count probably dropped, from your chemotherapy."

"Haven't had any. But the count is down."

"Sometimes the effect is delayed. When was your last dose?"

"September sometime. I don't want this disease anymore," said Caroline, starting to cry and shaking her head. It was ten to eight.

Ryan put his arm around her.

"You'll be okay," he said. "Just hang in there. I've got to shove off."

"I won't cry. Please stay."

"I'll visit you tomorrow, at lunch. Caroline, if I could have called this thing off tonight, I would have."

"Is it your cardiologist friend?"

"It's Arch's girl friend and one of her friends." Ryan saw the look of disbelief. "Arch isn't home yet. Won't be for another hour. They'll be standing out there."

"She doesn't have a key? I thought they more or less lived together."

"We had new locks put on. Arch had his stuff stolen at the gym."

"See you tomorrow," said Caroline, reaching up and kissing Ryan on the lips.

Ryan flew down the stairs, six flights, and reached the street at five minutes to eight. He raced home and reached his block by two minutes after. He never liked running on city streets. And in January, at eight o'clock, it had been dark for three hours. He could see a woman's figure walking away from the town house, or at least past it, at the other end of the block. He couldn't be sure it was Diana. But he raced after her anyway. She picked up her pace, hearing him charge. Then she looked around and crossed to the other side of the street, and he could see it was not Diana.

Breathless, he walked back to the town house. Lights were on. Arch was home.

"You have company," Arch said, pointing up to Ryan's study.

"When did you get home?"

"Fifteen minutes ago. She got here about three minutes ago."

Ryan ascended the stairs in great leaps.

23

January 22

They kept Caroline in Whipple for a liver scan and a bone scan.
They also succeeded in making her febrile. The fever required
a workup—blood, urine, and spinal-fluid cultures—all negative.
Finally they realized it was a drug fever, induced by her sleeping
pill. By that time she had a gallium scan, to rule out the possibility of an intra-abdominal abscess causing the fever their sleeping
pill had wrought.

Each new test raised a new possibility to worry about, and by
the end of three weeks Caroline's nerves were badly frazzled.
Ryan stopped by with less and less frequency. Caroline was
becoming more of a patient and less of a friend. She was asking
questions he didn't know the answers to, and she wasn't hearing
what answers he did have.

"I'm getting worn down," she said one afternoon. "I'm getting on everyone's nerves."

"After three weeks in this place, you'd be crazy not to be
crazy."

"But you put up with me," said Caroline. "Though I do drive
you away sometimes."

"No you don't."

"Sure I do. But you keep coming back. You're a solid citizen,
Bill. I met another member of your fan club, couple of nights
ago."

"Oh?"

"I was down at the nurses station trying to bum a sleeping pill,
and there was this nurse, Hope Lo. Beautiful girl. Why is she
Hope-sort-of-Lo?"

247

"So you two got together and compared notes on Billy Ryan?"

"Sure as hell did."

"Great."

"Don't worry," said Caroline, laughing, "I didn't give away any state secrets."

"What secrets?"

"Your cardiologist."

"Jesus, don't blow that one."

"Hey," laughed Caroline, "you can trust me. Lips are sealed."

Ryan looked at her, trying not to look worried. Manhattan Hospital really was a small town.

"She really thinks the world of you, this Hope Lo," Caroline said. "She thinks you have character."

"No, she thinks I am a character. There's a difference."

"I agree with her," said Caroline. "You're okay."

Ryan went home, worrying about how much Caroline might have told Hope. He finally broke down and called Hope.

"I hear you've been fraternizing with my patients," said Ryan.

"She's a nice person," said Hope. "I was hoping you'd call. Been thinking about you since Caroline and I spent the night extolling your virtues."

Diana had gone home to Alan. Ryan looked at his watch.

"Why don't you come over and tell me about it?"

"Okay," said Hope. "I never did know when to give up."

24

Friday, February 2

By February Ryan hated the Record Room. Every time he handed in ten charts, he requested ten more from Hyman Bloomberg's list. Then he'd have to sit down and try to read the illegible inkings of interns, hoping each time there would be some mention of homosexuality in the "Social History" section of the admission write-up. The interns all recorded "Foreign travel: Without" or "With," as the case might be, but mention of sexual preference was hit or miss. The private docs usually knew, but that meant calling each one, explaining about the whole project each time, assuring confidentiality, stressing Hyman Bloomberg's name, and finally entering it all in the table. But at the end of that month Ryan looked at his list and his six-page table and realized he had only ten more charts to do. He ran down to the Record Room, pulled the ten, and got lucky on eight. They had some reference to the patients' homosexuality. The other two had private docs. Ryan turned the charts back in with a grin. He kissed the old lady who took the charts and ran all the way home.

It only took a week to call in the twenty patients who were still "unknowns" from the standpoint of homosexuality. Some were so flagrant Ryan didn't have to ask. Others looked as straight as Ryan but turned out to be homosexual. Ryan had trouble asking the question straight out. He had gotten them to come in on the pretext of following up on their Gordio infections.

"We've, uh, been trying, uh, to figure out how people get this Gordio parasite you had. We've discovered that in some cases it appears to be related to, uh, sexual practices."

"Are you asking me if I'm gay?"

"Yes, are you gay?"

"Yes. Why didn't you just come out and ask?"

Ryan made a Xerox copy of his chart and took it over to Hyman Bloomberg's office. He had never seen a private attending's office. Bloomberg's office had a Park Avenue address. There was a sign on the door: RING FOR ADMITTANCE. Ryan rang. The secretary peered through an inner door and buzzed the lock on the street door, letting Ryan in.

The waiting room was cramped, made smaller by the crowd of patients packed together and by the secretary's desk. The phone never stopped ringing.

"I wanted to leave this for Dr. Bloomberg."

"Who, may I say?"

"Dr. Ryan."

"Dr. *William* Ryan?"

"Yes."

"Just a moment."

The secretary disappeared, leaving Ryan with the patients. They inspected him, none too discreetly. Bloomberg came charging out.

"It's done?"

"All present and accounted for."

"Congratulations!" shouted Bloomberg, startling the herd in the waiting room.

"Oh, congratulations!" echoed the secretary, standing behind her desk, extending her hand to shake Ryan's hand. The three of them went back to Bloomberg's office while one or two patients nodded and smiled their congratulations.

"The champagne! I've been saving it for this occasion," roared Bloomberg.

The secretary came in with the bottle on cue. The cork popped, Dixie cups were filled, and Bloomberg sent the bottle out to the patients in the waiting room.

Bloomberg sat down with the final table Ryan had brought. He had seen the preliminaries, but this was the final table. Bloomberg handled the pages like gold.

"Good man, good man," he kept muttering. "You hung in there and finished it."

He stood up and shook Ryan's hand.

"Splendid job," he said, smiling like a proud father. "I'll write it up, and send it in. But the table's the thing. The paper is really the table. Looks good to me."

Ryan walked home, wondering whether or not he could ever get that excited about proving something like the venereal transmission of Gordio lumbus. Not even proving it—providing circumstantial evidence and making a good case for it. Bloomberg was crazy. Ryan was glad to be done with the Record Room.

25

Monday, February 12

Morning Rounds were just finishing when Ryan got paged to call the E.R.

"Nine A.M., and it begins already," said Ryan, who was admitting.

The E.R. resident said the magic words: "Ryan, I'm going to give you this admission out of order. You're not next up—"

"What!" shouted Ryan.

"Before you go calling the chief res, just listen."

"I'm listening," said Ryan. "But I'm not smiling."

"Well, I can give her away, but this patient says she knows you."

"Who?"

"A nurse," said the resident, with an inflection which bespoke his assessment of her. "Hope Lo."

"I'll be right down," said Ryan. "What's the problem?"

"Don't really know," said the resident. "That's why I'm admitting her. Couldn't get the neurons to see her for another hour. Her eyes are stuck."

"What?"

"She can't look down. They're stuck."

"What are you trying to say?"

Ryan ran downstairs to the E.R.

"Hope," he said, relieved to see she looked good.

She was staring at the ceiling.

"Damnedest thing," she said, sounding scared. "I can't get 'em down, Bill. Am I having a stroke?"

"She's not on birth control pills," added the resident, standing behind Ryan.

"Hope," said Ryan, calmly, smiling, taking her hand, "have you felt okay lately?"

"Had the flu," said Hope, impatiently. "This whole weekend."

"What do you mean by the flu?"

"*Ryan!*" said Hope, tears running down her cheeks. "It was a flu. Nausea, vomiting, diarrhea."

"Did you take anything for it?" asked Ryan, smiling more broadly now, his voice quavering with anticipation.

"Compazine, aspirin . . ."

"Compazine!" shouted Ryan, turning to the resident behind him, who looked blankly at him. Ryan swept past him. He was back in seconds with some IV Benadryl.

He pulled a tourniquet around Hope's arm and found a vein.

"Bill," said Hope, trying to look at him.

"You'll be okay in a second."

He drew back, to be sure he was in a vein, then pushed the Benadryl in.

Hope's eyes fluttered down.

"Better!" she said.

"When was your last Compazine?"

"About an hour ago."

"That was it."

"The Compazine?"

"You had a hypersensitive reaction to it," said Ryan, "an oculogyric crisis."

"Thanks," said Hope, kissing his cheek.

"Good pickup," said the resident.

"I'll never make fun of your reading about blindfolded kittens or any of that neurology again," said Hope, gathering her things. "Can I go home?"

"Sure," said Ryan.

"I was so terrified of being admitted," said Hope, as Ryan walked her to the E.R. door. "I just panicked. It was better when I heard you'd be my intern. But it was still scary."

"Nobody wants to be a patient."

"It's irrational, I know," said Hope. "I was scared of what was happening to me, that's rational. But I was even more scared of

253

having to get admitted, putting that plastic patient I.D. bracelet on my wrist, being wheeled upstairs."

"You're okay now."

"I would never have come to the E.R. Just would have walked home. But I couldn't see anything but sky. Couldn't have found my block."

"It's over."

"Could you love a gomer? If I had been stroking out, would you have taken care of me?"

"Some of my best friends are gomers."

26

Tuesday, February 20

Social Service Rounds were about to begin in the conference room. Today it was Mr. Hirshsprung, of the Hirshsprung Memorial Revolving Bed. He was back again, having been bounced from the nursing home with a urinary-tract infection, fever, and abdominal pain. By a cruel twist of fate he had managed to avoid B-2, and by sheer luck of the draw was assigned to Ryan on one of Ryan's most infamous admitting days. Now began the heroic effort to arrange a return ride to Gracious Manor Nursing Home and Care Center.

He had only been on B-5 for two weeks, and had at least a week of antibiotic therapy to complete, but Ryan wanted him ready to meet the transport ambulance on the same day his antibiotics were finished. Ryan had already issued emphatic verbal orders that under no circumstances was any nurse allowed to approach within two feet of Mr. Hirshsprung with a thermometer. No temperature taking, no fever. A simple but often neglected principle in the management of recidivists like Mr. Hirshsprung.

Miss Gotz was there, from Social Service. And Brigid. And Ryan. They went over a few of Ryan's cases, patients who were about to be discharged and would need a visiting nurse or a housekeeper for a few weeks until they could get back to full activity.

"Marvelous," Ryan kept saying, "really is amazing how the city can pay for someone to care for these people after they're out of here. You'd think the city would never think of it."

"Better to spend the money on homemakers and visiting

nurses than on readmissions," said Miss Gotz, perceiving an irony in Ryan's tone, which, for once, wasn't there. Miss Gotz didn't know Ryan well. Many of the interns knew Miss Gotz quite well. She originally thought she might marry a doctor, but had decided against it after only her tenth intern. She had the most inviting, bouncy breasts, but a lonely heart. The interns were only interested in her breasts.

"Now about Mr. Hirshsprung," said Ryan, seeing the cloud pass over Miss Gotz's face. "Can you reserve a bed at Gracious for him?"

Ryan saw Miss Gotz's firm breasts heave.

"I can do it," she sighed, "but he really has to be guaranteed discharge on the day he's due."

"I guarantee."

"Nobody can guarantee Mr. Hirshsprung."

"Then how can we ever reserve a bed for him?" asked Ryan.

"You're beginning to understand," smiled Miss Gotz, shifting in her seat, her breasts bouncing.

"He'll be delivered as promised," said Ryan.

"Every time I reserve a bed for him, he gets sick. The ambulance arrives, and the appointed hour, and he can't go. Then I have to reapply and do all the work all over again."

"He's stable now."

"He's still got an IV?"

"Yes, but only for antibiotics."

"Antibiotics?"

"Just a sprinkling," pleaded Ryan. "He hardly needs them."

"Let me know when he's okay off antibiotics," said Miss Gotz. "I'll apply."

"He's off them," said Ryan. "I just decided."

"Ryan," said Miss Gotz, "if you send him out too soon, he'll come right back."

"Maybe on someone else's admitting day," smiled Ryan.

27

Wednesday, March 7

Hope was getting out of Ryan's shower when he got home at seven. Arch had let her into the town house.

"You couldn't wait?" asked Ryan, taking her wet body into his arms. "I was looking forward to a mutual lather the whole way home."

"You got a call," said Hope, sullenly. "From some woman who wouldn't leave her name."

"Is that why you're so huffy?" asked Ryan, trying to conceal his panic. It had to be Diana. And Hope had answered the phone.

"I'm not huffy," said Hope. "I'm pissed. Serves me right for answering your phone. But I thought it would be you."

"No message?"

"No explicit message," said Hope, unbuttoning Ryan's shirt as he dried her with a big white towel. "But she was obviously not happy to hear another woman's voice on your phone."

Ryan kissed her, to fill the vacuum which had enveloped his mind. When she kissed back, he started whirring. He had to get her out. Diana was probably staying in the city, and who knew if she would ever speak to him again?

"And here I thought you were a pretty straight arrow," said Hope. "Maybe hesitant to let a woman in your life, but not a runaround."

"Hardly think I qualify," said Ryan, as she pulled him on top of her. Hope had no intention of leaving Ryan that night. He never got a chance to sneak off and call Diana.

28

Thursday, March 15

"Never allow yourself to feel sorry for an intern," the admitting resident was telling Ryan, by way of introduction to the admission he was sending up from the E.R. "It affects your judgment and doesn't make the intern feel any better."

Ryan was getting a sinking feeling, listening, pressing the phone to his ear.

"But in this case," said the resident, the din of the E.R. almost drowning out his voice, "I have to admit I feel sorry for you."

"What is it?"

"Not 'what,' Ryan; the question is 'who.' 'What' is not so bad. It's a rule out M.I. It's the 'who' that makes it hurt. It's Mrs. White again."

"No," gasped Ryan. "Tell me you're lying. I'll forgive you."

"And don't bother calling the CCU. I already tried. Burns came down here, found out it was Mrs. White, and turned her down. Her story is good. Four hours of crushing chest pain, nausea, vomiting, diaphoresis. But her EKG is unchanged. Burns has two empty beds left. He could have taken her. He said no way."

Burns was the resident who controlled admissions to the Cardiac Care Unit. Ryan went down to fetch Mrs. White. It was 11:00 A.M. when he got the call. He ambled down to the E.R., hoping against hope that Mrs. White would have miraculously recovered by the time he arrived. She was there.

"I'm having a heart attack, and they keep me waiting in the Emergency Room." These were her words of greeting to the intern whom she would wake at four every morning for the next

258

week. She didn't recognize Ryan from her previous admission. She had enough problems without having to learn her doctors' faces.

"I'm having trouble breathing," she said. Ryan rolled her up to the elevator and rode up with her to B-5. By the time she arrived, she had, mercifully, stopped talking. Ryan was so happy for her silence, he didn't pause to consider its significance.

The nurses were waiting to help transfer her from the stretcher to the bed. Ryan could see they wouldn't have time. She was frothing at the mouth, breathing at two or three times the normal rate, looking pale, and her eyes were rolling up.

He listened to her lungs.

"She's in pulmonary edema," he said, incredulous. He looked up to find Brigid, who always seemed to materialize just in the nick of time.

"Sit her up," said Brigid. The nurses adjusted the stretcher so Mrs. White was bolt upright. The nurses slapped on the tourniquets. Three tightened, one limb allowed to have circulation. Oxygen appeared.

Some nurse, unseen, slapped a syringe with a hundred milligrams of Lasix in Ryan's hand. She had an IV from the E.R., into which Ryan shot the Lasix. A nurse catheterized her bladder. No urine. Brigid ran off an EKG. Ryan looked at it as it came off the machine.

"She's really doing it this time," muttered Ryan, looking at the hyperacute changes, and hating Burns for closing the door to the CCU.

"Talk about judgment. Call Dr. Burns, at the CCU. That turkey!"

"We already did," said Brigid. "He's on his way."

Brigid was a fortress.

Mrs. White was having an acute funeral for part of her heart, the anterior wall, and the blood trying to get out of the lungs was not moving. She was in big trouble.

"She's still not peeing," said Brigid, looking worried. Burns still had not arrived.

"Do we have any phlebotomy jars?" asked Ryan.

"What kind of jars?" asked Brigid as one of her nurses called out Mrs. White's dwindling blood pressure readings.

"They might be on the crash cart."

One of the nurses hauled out two large glass jars, still sealed. "These them?"

"Are they vacuum jars?" asked Ryan. Ryan had never actually seen a phlebotomy jar, but Frank Wright had given a lecture about pulmonary edema and mentioned the possibility of using the jars if all else failed. Fortunately, the jars came with three sentences of boldly printed instructions.

Ryan detached a polyethylene catheter with a needle on either end and plunged one end into Mrs. White's weak femoral pulse, entering the artery. The blood, looking dark for arterial blood, but pumping like arterial blood, pulsed through the tube.

"Stick that end in the jar," shouted Ryan.

Brigid jammed the needle on the other end through the rubber seal on the jar top. To everyone's joyful stupefaction the jar filled from bottom to top in fifteen seconds, filled with blood from Mrs. White. The blood got brighter and brighter as she oxygenated better.

"Ah," sighed Mrs. White, "better."

Burns arrived, slapped Ryan on the back, saying, "You win. We're stuck with her," and trundled her off to the CCU. It was a good day for the book on Ryan.

29

Saturday, March 24

"I can't get used to the idea of sharing you," Diana said.

She had let a suitably agonizing number of days pass after calling Ryan and finding Hope at the other end of the phone. Ryan had managed not to call her. She was the one who had to call.

"You're not," said Ryan.

"Who was the lady?" asked Diana. "You have no sisters and you never mentioned a maid."

Ryan had to smile. She was sitting across from him, on his sofa, in the study, legs crossed, one bobbing up and down impatiently. He had never seen her ruffled before.

"I'm surprised," said Ryan. "If I'd known I'd see such concern, I'd have hired one to answer all my calls."

"What did you expect?" asked Diana.

"Cool," said Ryan. "Amusement, even. You actually sound concerned."

" 'Concerned' is putting it rather mildly."

Ryan was quite disarmed. Diana, ice princess, was letting a little passion show. It was having the desired effect. Ryan was breathless. She really cared about him after all.

"She was just a friend," said Ryan. "Arch let her in."

Diana looked at Ryan appraisingly.

"I'm overwhelmed," said Ryan, moving across the Persian rug. He sat on the arm of the sofa, his arm around her.

She stroked the inside of his thigh.

"Silly ninny," she said. "You know I'm wild about you."

"You've been most careful about not showing it."

"I have to be careful, Bill," she said, riveting him with a blue-eyed look. "You know that."

"You disappear a lot."

"Don't let's go over old ground," said Diana. "You know what you do to me."

"It just seems foolish sometimes."

"I know," she sighed. "But we'll have the clinic someday. We'll look back from Edinburgh."

"Yes," said Ryan. "With separate vacations?"

"Of course." She smiled. "It appears that you will require some time away from me, to satisfy your appetites."

"Now that's the Diana I know."

30

Friday, April 13

It was time for Chart Rounds on B-5. The medical students, interns, and Iggy gathered at the nurses station. They rolled the chart rack down to the conference room, off the solarium. The conference room, unlike the nurses station, had windows, which Ryan threw open.

Velvety April breezes moved through the room. Iggy seated himself directly in front of the chart rack, loosened his green Yves Saint-Laurent tie, and undid the first few buttons of his khaki Bloomingdale's shirt. Biotto made noises about getting a natural high from spring, and Ryan said something about stirring dull roots with spring rain.

"How can you talk about rain on a day like this?" said Biotto.

"I was talking about spring," said Ryan.

Nobody had the heart to open the first chart. The chart in the upper left-hand corner of the rack, where they always began, belonged to one of Ryan's patients.

"I don't want to think about this," said Ryan, appealing to Iggy. "It's going to be sunny tomorrow, and I'm off. I want to think about Saturday in Central Park, about playing rugby."

"Ryan," said Iggy, "for three more months, spring, summer, all the natural pleasures are irrelevant to your life. Tell me why."

"Because," said Ryan, "internship lasts a year."

That was it. Internship lasted a year. Stamina was the key. From irrelevant, meaningless, pain-in-the-ass college courses like organic chemistry, which required few smarts but lots of stamina, to pain-in-the-ass medical-school courses which required even less intelligence but even more stamina, to internship, which required nothing but stamina.

"We're coming down the home stretch," said Iggy. "Don't fail now. This is the part that counts." Iggy looked at them through his hollow eyes. "In Thoroughbreds, it's called heart."

They went through the charts. Biotto signed out to Ryan, and Ryan started thinking about his Saturday. Ryan had to make it through Friday night on call, but he wasn't worried. Even if he got bombed with admissions, even if he had a G.I. bleeder and had to stay up all night, he was going to Central Park the next morning, right after Morning Rounds.

Getting bombed with admissions didn't bother Ryan anymore. Nothing bothered him anymore, as far as new admissions went. G.I. bleeders, pulmonary edemas, heart attacks, organs failing singly and in combination. He'd seen them all, *ad nauseam.* He knew what to do now. He knew when he'd done all that could be done. That was the main thing. Nine months ago, in his early gestation, he didn't have a feel for where the medicine had to end and God took over. He sat there palpitating, or depressed, sometimes both, certain that the patient going down the tubes before his eyes could be saved, if only he knew more. Now he knew more. And the most important thing he knew was that there isn't all that much to do. All the biochemistry and anatomy he never learned didn't matter. When it came down to practice, there just wasn't that much to do.

After dinner he got just two more admissions. A lunger, whom Ryan cupped and coughed and treated with oxygen and antibiotics. And a diabetic in ketoacidosis, who responded nicely to IV fluids and a sprinkling of insulin.

Iggy didn't even come in to see the patients until Morning Rounds. Ryan called him and Iggy asked a few questions about blood gases and about what Ryan intended to do, and said, "See you in the morning." It was an expression of confidence. Iggy trusted Ryan to go it alone. Of course, Ryan had handled a score of similar cases with Iggy, and Iggy should have known Ryan knew what to do. But it still gave Ryan a fillip to hear Iggy say "See you in the morning." Other residents had let Ryan go it alone, but Iggy, for all his cavalier pretensions, was the most relentless anal-compulsive when it came to patients.

Iggy always came in for Biotto's new admissions. He pulled on his Calvin Klein slacks and walked across the avenue at 2:00 A.M., whenever Biotto got an admission. Of course, most of the other residents still came in for Ryan's admissions. But Iggy stayed in bed. Ryan would ask around, and see if Iggy had done that for anyone else.

Saturday Morning

They went over the new admissions together, fifteen minutes before Morning Rounds, and Iggy said, "Nice job." That was a nice way to put it. Ryan left before Iggy got back from Morning Report.

He walked home in the bright morning light, its brilliance magnified by the white hospital granite. Ryan felt fine. He hadn't been afraid, or disgusted, or angry all night. It was morning. He had gotten four hours' sleep, and he didn't even have a headache.

He hadn't thought about Diana all night. That was important too. Of course, he hadn't thought about Brigid Sullivan either, and he had a date with her for the rugby game. But it was more important that he had gone through the night absorbed in his tasks, undistracted.

Ryan got home at ten o'clock. Arch and Jane were ready to go. Brigid was there too. She looked so bright-eyed. Diana was home for the weekend of course. Brigid and Ryan went upstairs.

"Rough night?"

"No," said Ryan, as she watched him shave.

"Just two admissions after dinner."

"Sick?"

"Not very."

They went downstairs.

"A new man," said Jane. "You look one hundred percent better!"

They walked down Sixty-eighth Street to the park. Arch and

Ryan carried their rugby shoes and shirts, and Jane carried the food. Brigid had the wine.

It was one of the first real spring weekend days, and the streets were full of smiles.

"I'd rather be here than anywhere in the spring," said Jane.

Fifth Avenue was impassable. Mobs of cars carrying people from New Jersey to the park snarled the mobs of taxis, which were already snarled by the mobs of walkers. It wasn't an angry snarl. It was too nice a day.

The rugby game was in the Sheep Meadow. The medical school had a rugby team, and all alumni, house staff, relatives, hospital employees, relatives of employees, and passersby were pressed into action. As Ryan's roommate, Arch naturally felt an inescapable obligation to play on the medical-school rugby team. The medical school had the worst rugby team in New York City, which says something, considering some of the teams. Arch was a most welcome ringer.

Of course they always lost miserably. Arch occasionally succeeded in dragging Ryan into the lineup, and both of them would go into congestive heart failure by the second half. Jane came to watch Arch and Ryan get mauled. Like most women, Jane could not fathom the primal magnetism violent sports hold for some men. Ryan explained primitive combative urges and the origin of the aggressive instinct. But Jane rejected all that. She knew that men do not have to prove themselves with displays of viciousness. She was at every game.

At any rate, Arch always got so drunk during the postgame party that he couldn't even sing the obscene party songs.

During the postgame party this day, Arch discovered that some of the medical students practiced the arcane sport of rappelling. The students had recently rappelled off their dormitory walls, and were hauled off by the police, who were not amused to see students bouncing down walls hanging onto ropes. The dean had to get them out. Arch was thoroughly captivated by the story. He demanded to be part of their next target.

"We were thinking about doing the Tower before we graduated," said one student.

266

"The Tower!" Arch's drunken eyes were saucers, spinning with delight.

Jane pulled at Arch's sleeve.

"Calm down, tiger, you've only just begun to drink."

"Of course!" roared Arch. "The Tower! The Great White Tower! What else?"

Arch dragged them off to get the equipment.

Ryan didn't hear any of this, but Jane was almost incomprehensible from fear when she finally found him, getting his knee wrapped lovingly by Brigid.

"He's going to rappel off the Tower!" she shrieked.

"Do what?"

"Rappel. With ropes and things. You bounce down the side of a building, hanging on to a rope."

"Sure, Jane."

"He is, he is!" she sobbed. "He just dragged off some students to get the rope."

"Don't be ridiculous," said Ryan. "The Tower is twenty-four stories."

Ryan panicked, hearing his own words, realizing in a flash that Arch would be satisfied with nothing less.

They raced over to the hospital, Ryan still in his rugby shorts, and pounded on the door of the elevator that ran to the top of the Tower. The operator opened it.

"What? Jesus! Another one." He slammed the door shut. Jane pounded.

"Open this door. It's life or death!"

The door opened. The elevator man said he had just taken a howling mob of rugby players, with ropes, up to the roof, and he wasn't going to do that again. Ryan threatened to kill him. So he took them up.

When they arrived there were two bodies draped over the wall. But no Arch. The two bodies were looking over the side. The rope was firmly anchored to the wall.

"Where's Arch?" screamed Ryan. Jane sat down, in a near faint.

267

"We don't know!" shouted Jason Adams, one of the bodies draped over the wall.

"You don't know?" shouted Ryan, grabbing Jason murderously.

"He was doing fine. Then he seemed to disappear into the wall."

Ryan looked over the wall. There was no body on the ground, just an empty rope, swinging in the breeze.

Suddenly, from the wall, out popped Arch's head.

"Where's my rope?" he asked, looking up eight stories at Ryan and the others.

"Arch, don't move!" shouted Ryan.

"Where the hell is he?" asked the student.

"He must have gone through a window."

He had indeed gone through a window, the picture window of the hospital president's apartment on the sixteenth floor. Ryan didn't know that anyone had a private apartment in the Tower. Not many people did. The Tower was a hospital, not a high-rise apartment. It was a well-kept secret. So was the woman in the president's apartment, who was sitting on the couch when Arch smashed through the picture window.

Arch had crashed through the window, found himself standing in the president's living room, in front of the president's guest, who was sitting on the couch.

"James, there's a man in the living room!" the woman shouted.

"Don't be ridiculous," the president called back from the shower.

"Where's my rope?" Arch asked the woman, drunkenly.

Ryan, Jane, and Brigid arrived shortly, and pounded frantically on the president's door. Hospital security guards, summoned by the elevator operator, arrived. The president just wanted to get rid of everyone. His woman friend had disappeared into the bathroom.

"Sorry about the window," said Ryan.

Security took everyone's names and let them go. They dragged Arch to the E.R., where Ryan sewed up Arch's lacerations.

Ryan was standing in the Cut Room, in his muddy rugby shirt, sewing Arch's forehead together, when Maxwell Baptist walked by the Cut Room door. Baptist strode into the room.

"May I ask?" he said.

Ryan looked up and turned a shade grayer than Arch.

"My roommate," said Ryan. "Sir."

Baptist looked Ryan over, head to toe.

"We've been playing rugby."

"The surgeons generally do the suturing in the E.R.," said Baptist. "Their sterile technique tends to be better than that of the medical house staff," he said, looking at muddy Ryan, whose sterile rubber gloves looked like an afterthought.

"I want Ryan to do it," bawled Arch, raising his bloody head from the suture table.

"He's my roommate, Dr. Baptist."

Baptist looked around, noticing Jane and Brigid for the first time.

He smiled. "Hello, Miss Sullivan," he said, unstiffening. "You taking care of these rowdies?"

"Yes, Dr. Baptist," said Brigid, smiling brightly. "I've got them under control."

"If anyone could, it would be you," said Baptist, wasting no more time on Ryan.

"He's a pussycat," said Brigid, when he had gone.

31

April 16

Ryan got paged Monday morning. He shuddered, hearing the number coming across his beeper.

"Dr. Ryan: seven-oh-seven-oh, seven-oh-seven-oh."

It was the chairman's office.

"Dr. Baptist would like you to come down, *now,*" said Ginny, Baptist's secretary.

Ryan squirmed in the black chair directly across from Ginny. It had The Manhattan Hospital emblem on its back.

Ginny's intercom went off with a buzz.

"Send him in," said Baptist. Even over the intercom Ryan could tell he wasn't happy.

"Have a seat," said Baptist, gesturing to the chair on the right side of his desk. Ryan had never been in this office. He imagined that Cross and Walker must have sat just where he was sitting now, last December, staring at the same pictures of Baptist's daughters on the bookshelves behind his desk. The daughters smiled brightly at Ryan.

The office had a blue oriental rug richly embellishing the hardwood floor, and a little sitting area with two couches and a coffee table.

Baptist stood behind his great mahogany desk.

"I believe you told me, Saturday, that your roommate had received his injuries playing rugby," said Baptist, grimly.

Ryan's mind went cold. Then blood began to circulate again.

"I said we had been playing rugby," said Ryan. "The injuries were glass cuts, suffered later."

"Then why did you mention rugby?"

"I presumed you were concerned about my being in the Cut Room, suturing, out of uniform . . ."

Baptist glared at Ryan, a cold, steady, controlled glare.

"Did you think I wouldn't find out what really happened?"

"I think you know everything that happens."

Baptist seemed satisfied with that, at least.

"Did you threaten an elevator operator?"

"No, sir."

"He says the group he took up threatened his life," said Baptist. "Did you get to the twenty-fourth floor by the stairs?"

"No, sir," said Ryan, evenly now. "I took the elevator"—Baptist's eye was glinting—"after I heard that the students and my roommate were headed to the roof." Baptist drew in a breath. "I was trying to stop them."

"You realize your roommate could have been killed?"

"Yes, sir."

"He could have injured Mr. Kennedy, had Mr. Kennedy been near that window when your roommate came crashing through."

"Yes, sir."

Baptist sat down behind his desk and contemplated Ryan over his arched fingertips.

"You went up there to stop it?"

"Yes, sir."

"Miss Sullivan, fortunately, confirms the substantive parts of your story."

Ryan began to breathe again.

"I would hope, though, that in the future you can keep your roommate off the premises."

Baptist left it there, and Ryan staggered back to the floor, to find Brigid.

32

Friday, April 20

"Jesus, does it feel great to be home again," Caroline said.

Ryan cradled the phone between his chin and shoulder.

"Sorry I couldn't get by to say good-bye."

"The occasion was joyful, even in your absence," said Caroline. "Though I had hoped you'd get by. Hope tells me they've been running you ragged."

"It's been busy. But I'm changing services this Monday."

"What now?"

"Neurology."

"Oh, the brain scan people."

"No, that's Nuclear Medicine. The neurologists are medical docs."

"I *know*, Dr. Ryan," laughed Caroline. "I've had lots of neurologists go over my nervous system in my time. Every time they tell me I'm getting seen by a neuron I wind up getting a brain scan. They go over you inch by inch, then wind up ordering the brain scan anyway. I could do my own neurology consults. I'd just fill out the brain scan requisition."

"You've been seeing entirely too many doctors," said Ryan. "Try to avoid them."

Ryan hung up the phone. It rang again. He answered it on the first ring.

"Expecting someone?" said Hope.

He hadn't seen her for weeks.

"Hi."

"I don't know," continued Hope, as if he had denied all. "You have all these women calling you. Your line was just busy."

"Why don't you come over?" said Ryan. Getting to the point was the best way to handle Hope.

"Not so fast, cowboy," said Hope. "I'm just checking in. If you think of me, give me a ring. I get tired of dialing your number."

"Why don't you just whistle?" said Ryan. "You know how to whistle, don't you?"

"You don't sound at all like Lauren Bacall," laughed Hope. "Besides, I could sit here in my apartment and whistle till I was blue in the face and you'd never call."

Ryan was looking at the movie listings in the paper on his desk.

"The Seventh Seal," he said, overjoyed.

"What?"

"It's at the Carnegie."

"You know all my weak spots," said Hope. "But no soap. Come on by and see me sometime, when you think of it."

33

Monday, April 23

They were rotating Biotto and Ryan to Neurology. They would have to spend three weeks on the Neuro ward.

Ryan read neurology for pleasure; patching kittens' eyes and all those fascinating experiments were great fun, so naturally Ryan loathed his impending Neuro rotation. Whenever science got translated into patients, the fascination evaporated over the hissing coals of depressing real-life stories. And the Neuro service was distressingly well run.

Dr. Jewel ran Neurology with an iron hand. He knew what happened to every one of the forty patients on the Neurology ward. Neuro always had forty patients, one hundred percent bed occupancy. This made Administration very happy. Making Dr. Jewel happy was not so easy.

Jewel read every chart on every patient, every Monday, Wednesday, and Friday, adding truculent little notes of his own to the workups. But Tuesday was the day of maximal dread. On Tuesdays Jewel appeared at the far end of the hall, where assembled medical students, interns, residents, and the head nurse awaited his appearance with trepidation.

"I just cannot believe the tension level on this floor," muttered Biotto, who was saved from instant catatonia only by the serendipitous Student Schedule, which had placed Biotto's chief and only student fan, Jason Adams, on his floor for Neurology clerkship. Biotto had someone to lean on.

Each new case since the last Tuesday was presented by a trembling, red-faced medical student, whom Jewel called "Clinical Clerk," to emphasize the painfully obvious point that a student is not a physician. To further emphasize the point, Jewel refused to allow students to wear white pants on the Neuro ward. Students wore dark pants, interns white pants and tunics, residents white pants, shirts, and ties; Jewel knew at a glance just where you belonged in the chain of command.

Jewel listened, icy gray eyes gleaming, fixed on the student presenting the case. He allowed the student to finish the presentation, then went to the bedside, where he examined the patient, checking the student's report. Then he took the entourage back out to the hall.

There, after flaying the student for any shortcomings, Jewel turned to the intern, from whom he demanded a short summary analysis of the case.

Jason Adams quickly apprised Biotto of the Tuesday morning horror show. Jason was glad to have Biotto back.

Biotto looked green.

"Sounds like one very nasty scene," he said to Jason. "Jewel gets off on crushing people."

"It's a veritable high for the man."

There were two patients being admitted this Monday. Ryan took one and Biotto took the other. Jason, naturally, decided to work up Biotto's patient.

The patients were almost as well trained as the doctors, and arrived before noon. So Ryan had the whole afternoon to think. He got an old man with a wife who claimed he was demented. The wife claimed the old man misplaced things and then blamed her for losing them. Ryan talked to him for a while. He was really a delightful old soul, a watchmaker from Switzerland. He told Ryan all about the Alps.

"What'd you find?" asked Helen Murphy, the Neuro resident working with Ryan.

"That guy's no more demented than I am," said Ryan. "His only problem's his wife. The old bird's trying to get rid of him."

"Wouldn't be the first time," said Helen.

Helen was a willowy woman; she burned more calories thinking hard for ten minutes than Ryan used up running a mile.

The first thing Helen asked the old man to do was to draw a

275

clock, and set it to five. The old watchmaker was stumped. Ryan was appalled. Ryan became even more appalled as Helen quickly ran through a battery of Higher Integrative Function tests, none of which the old man could do. He couldn't subtract seven from one hundred, nor could he tell what "People who live in glass houses shouldn't throw stones" meant.

Biotto came to drag Helen to see his patient. Ryan followed after them. The admitting diagnosis was "brain tumor." Biotto had begun with a standard part of the neurological exam, asking the woman to name various objects. She had gotten stuck on the word *comb*.

"She tells me you comb your hair with it, but she doesn't know what to call it," Biotto told Helen, dragging her into the room.

The lady with the brain tumor couldn't name her fingers, but she could name other things quite well, and spoke fluently and with good melody.

"Well, what do you use it for?" asked Helen.

"You comb your hair with it," the woman said, taking the comb and running it through her hair.

"Then what do you call it?" asked Biotto, utterly amazed.

"Don't know," she shrugged.

Helen held up the patient's right hand.

"Whose hand is this?"

The patient stared at her own hand, held in Helen's.

"Don't know," said the patient.

"Jewel will like this one," said Helen, after she had Ryan out in the hall.

The nice thing about Neurology was that there was time to think about the patients. In fact, if it hadn't been for the general level of hysteria on the ward, Ryan might have actually enjoyed that month. But there was Helen, arriving every morning at 6:30 to teach the medical students neurology, just as Jewel commanded. And there were the students, even more amazingly, showing up to learn it out of fear. And more amazing yet, the students helped draw the bloods at 7:15, and morning rounds began at the stroke of 8:00 and ended at 9:00. Anytime Dr. Jewel looked at his watch, wherever he was, he knew what the house staff was doing on the ward.

It was fear. Fear of humiliation in a group selected for their sense of pride. Dr. Jewel did not shrink from humiliation as a teaching tool. The prior Tuesday Jason Adams could not remember a cell count on a spinal-fluid sample. Jewel ordered him to leave rounds and come back when he was properly prepared.

Certainly Jewel never failed to know such things when he was a student, in the days of the giants, and he expected no less now.

Ryan was looking over a pneumoencephalogram in the Diagnostic Radiology Suite. He was standing alone, throwing up the films on the viewing screens. He hadn't been able to find a radiologist to go over the X rays with him, and it was Monday evening. He knew Jewel would want to hear about the pneumo at Tuesday Rounds.

"Pretty study," Ryan heard Diana say. She was standing behind him.

"If you say so," said Ryan. "Of course, I have no idea what I'm looking at."

"Neither have I," said Diana. "It's not a heart, though, I can tell you that."

"Dr. Jewel says the heart exists to perfuse the brain," said Ryan. "Just pumps blood to keep the brain alive."

"He should know," said Diana. She looked at the films.

"Can I see you tonight?" she asked.

"This must be my lucky week," said Ryan.

"I just can't stay away from you," she said. "I have a thing for neurologists."

"I hardly qualify."

"And I have another early case in the morning."

"Figures."

"You'd better get a radiologist to go over these with you," she said formally. A radiology resident was approaching. "I don't know a thing about pneumoencephalograms."

34

Tuesday Morning, April 24

Biotto's brain tumor lady had just been examined by Jewel on Tuesday Morning Shrink-Flinch-and-Quail Rounds. According to Jewel's dictum, the medical student on the case had presented the history and a summary of physical findings. Jewel then led them all to the bedside. He obviously had no doubt about the diagnosis from what Jason Adams had presented. Jewel verified the findings and added a few of his own, in his effortless, intimidating way. Then he brought the group into the hallway and looked for the next man on the totem pole, the intern, Biotto, who stood weak-kneed before him. Jewel asked Biotto for an analysis.

"Parietal lobe tumor," said Biotto, sputtering. He had gone over the case with Helen. She had rehearsed Jason and Biotto. Jason had gotten by, but Biotto was blanking.

"Which particular findings lead to that conclusion?" asked Jewel, ice eyes narrowing. The format for summaries was a recitation of the relevant findings, the anatomy involved, and finally the conclusion. Biotto had just blurted out the diagnosis.

"I . . ." Biotto was stuck. "She couldn't name the comb."

"Yes?"

"I'm sorry," said Biotto, waving his hand. "I know it, it's just this stress. These rounds are such a high-tension scene."

"The nervous system is built to handle stress," Jewel intoned. "Stress is unavoidable, and nature has equipped us admirably with a nervous system capable of astounding adaptability. Stress is no excuse for poor performance."

Jewel had been stressing people since he was a young assistant

professor years before, wowing conferences with his quick diagnostic coups. He expected no less of the current generation.

Ryan flopped into his leather wingback that night. Jewel
hadn't been able to shake him. Jewel had asked for a discussion
of dementing processes, and Ryan had read Jewel's article in the
standard textbook of medicine. Ryan had impressed Jewel, he
thought. Jewel had almost smiled. Ryan was exhausted.

"I have the feeling he's watching me," Ryan told Arch.
"Watching my progress, listening to every detail and caring
about whether or not I get it right."

"Sounds horrific."

"It does, doesn't it?" said Ryan. "Then why am I enjoying it?"

35

Thursday, May 3

"I sent it in this morning," said Bloomberg jubilantly over the phone.

"What?"

"What? The paper. What else?"

Ryan had almost forgotten the Gordio paper. Bloomberg had finally written it, had his secretary type it, and had mailed it to the *New England Journal of Medicine,* where it was sure to be rejected.

"Don't be ridiculous," said Bloomberg. "It's a sure thing."

Ryan couldn't care. It was May, and he was heading to Central Park with Brigid Sullivan after dinner. They walked past the sailboat pond to the Bethesda fountain. It was a hot day, and the pond behind the fountain was full of rowboats.

"I'd like to get in a boat and just drift," said Brigid.

"Drift where? The rowboat pond in Central Park? You can drift a whole block," laughed Ryan.

"Distance doesn't matter. It's the quality of the drift," said Brigid.

"I get your drift," laughed Ryan.

"Unmerciful!" laughed Brigid.

"Why did you say that?" asked Ryan.

"Because anyone who puns like that has no mercy," said Brigid, not understanding why Ryan got so suddenly serious.

"Funny how things come back to you," said Ryan. "Caroline Smith said the same thing once, about a pun. 'Unmerciful.' Funny expression."

Ryan dropped Brigid off at her apartment and continued on to the town house. The phone rang as he came through his door.

"I called. Did you get my message?"

"I just got in."

"Your roommate doesn't approve of me."

"Arch? What makes you say that?"

"He told me you were out, and when I told him it was Dr. Hayes calling, he just had to add that you were going for a walk in the park, with a date."

"Oh, good grief. You know . . ."

"That's all right. No need to explain," said Diana. "I had wanted to know whether you wanted to come over tonight."

"Of course."

"No, I think you'd better recover from your outing. Besides, I've made other plans in the meantime."

36

Monday, May 7

Ryan was back with Iggy and Biotto on B-5. Brigid's floor. The best floor and a pretty fair team. It was the end of the day, and they were going over the patients' charts.

At the end of Chart Rounds, every day, Iggy went over the NTBR's with Biotto and Ryan.

"Who's Not To Be Resuscitated on this service?" Iggy was asking. "We haven't got a single NTBR on the floor. Somebody must be NTBR. Ryan, what about Suggs?"

"Don't think so," said Ryan.

"Oh, come on," said Biotto, who was on call and who would be called to resuscitate Suggs at some ungodly hour if Suggs were left TBR. "He's just a stroked-out old gomer, a veggie."

Ryan scanned Biotto's face. Here was the man who had held Iggy in such ill repute for months after Iggy's gomer-orientation lecture. Now Biotto called poor old Mr. Suggs a gomer and, worse, didn't want to be called if Mr. Suggs's heart went out on strike.

"Brigid says his wife's not ready for Mr. Suggs to go to the Eternal Care Unit."

"Eternal care is what he's gonna get right here on B-five if Brigid gets her way. She'd resuscitate a mummy," said Biotto. "He's aphasic, isn't he?"

"Well, he's certainly got expressive aphasia," said Ryan. "But I don't think he's got receptive aphasia. He blinked his eyes and lifted his left hand for me this morning."

"He lifted his hand to verbal command?" asked Iggy, impressed.

Biotto could see the tide shifting. "You lifted his hand," said Biotto. "I saw you. Then you said 'Lift your hand, Mr. Suggs,' and he perseverated. He didn't understand a verbal command."

"His wife just sits there by his bedside all day," said Ryan, "stroking his brow, and talking to him. Who knows how much he hears, or understands? Maybe more than we think."

"Reminds me of something Mark Twain said," said Iggy. Lately, almost everything reminded Iggy of something Mark Twain said. "He said, 'Why is it that we cry at funerals and rejoice at births? Is it because we aren't the person with the most at stake?'"

"Mark Twain said that?" asked Ryan.

"Or something close to it."

"Who are we saving this guy for?" persisted Biotto. "And for how long? His wife may never be able to accept it."

"His intern says we go the full route," said Iggy, standing up, ending the discussion. "And that's that. You know the rules." Iggy looked Biotto in the eye, then mussed Ryan's hair. "Suggs is To Be Resuscitated, until further notice."

37

May 14

Ryan raced home after rounds, just in time to catch Arch hanging up on Diana.

"Oh, here he is now," said Arch, thwarted.

"I'll be over about eight," said Diana.

She swept in and sat at Ryan's desk. He was slumped in the wingback.

"You look frazzled," said Diana.

"Bad day."

"Things should have been smoothing out by now," said Diana, pouring herself some anisette. "Only two more months."

"They are and they aren't."

Diana was sitting on the desk, legs crossed. She waited for Ryan to continue.

"Biotto just doesn't care anymore," said Ryan. "He's quit being an intern, virtually."

Diana raised her eyebrows.

"I have—had—this patient, Mr. Suggs. Seventy years old. Stroke. He couldn't talk too well, but he was a nice old guy. Wife is, too. Each is all the other had. Anyway, I've been keeping Mr. Suggs out of trouble. Last night, Mr. Suggs was having trouble breathing, urine output falling, neck veins rising.

"I'd signed him out, in detail, to Biotto, but Biotto tells the nurse that Suggs is just an old stroked-out gomer, aphasic, and we've decided to let him go."

"That wasn't the plan?"

"Not at all. Biotto knew it too. He was just too lazy to get out of bed and treat pulmonary edema." Ryan shook his head. "I mean, it made me sick to look at the bedside chart. The nurses

284

had kept it with a vengeance. He was in pulmonary edema all night. Must have been gasping for every breath."

"Pleasant."

"How could you do that to someone?"

"I couldn't," said Diana. "What is nice is that you couldn't either. What did Biotto have to say for himself?"

Ryan did not meet her eyes.

"I presume you blasted him, in your own inimitable style."

"What's the use?"

"What?"

"I'm mellowing, as Biotto would say. No waves."

"You're too young to mellow," said Diana. "You mean, you didn't annihilate him?"

"I didn't say anything. Neither did Iggy," said Ryan. "I just treated the pulmonary edema. Suggs died."

"Hearts can be quite unforgiving about being put into failure and pulmonary edema."

"Evidently," said Ryan.

"You are getting easy on your friends."

"Biotto's no friend."

"Then why the newfound restraint?"

"I'm cooling off. It's the new, laid-back, nonconfrontational Billy Ryan."

"I'm not sure I didn't like you better when you were more of a cage rattler."

"What can I do?" asked Ryan. "I'm not holding the whip. That's Iggy's job."

"Why was Iggy so silent?"

"I don't know. We've all been together so long. . . . It's hard for Iggy to remain the Prussian drillmaster. We're friends. Colleagues."

"You have to keep that distance."

"It's hard."

"Reminds me of something Hyman Bloomberg once said at an Executive Committee meeting," said Diana. "He said the biggest mistake a doctor can make is to get on a first-name basis with the people he's supposed to be supervising."

"Hyman said that?"

"He was talking about nurses and medical students, but I think the principle applies."

"Principles make life difficult."

"There's one you must never forget," said Diana. *"Qui tacet, consentire videtur."*

"Silence implies consent?"

"Never forget it, William Ryan."

38

May 17

Ryan pulled Biotto into the treatment room at the end of the hall after Morning Rounds and locked the door.

"Why you locking the door?" asked Biotto, moving to the far corner.

"Why are you cowering in the corner?"

"I'm just trying to maintain space."

"You mean avoid conflict? I, too, have been trying to avoid conflict," said Ryan. "But sometimes it's best to bring conflict out. Sometimes conflict is preferable."

"I hear you," said Biotto, trying to smile a friendly smile. It came out looking pretty sickly.

"Biotto," said Ryan, with a measured cadence, "we come from different backgrounds, and sometimes we speak different languages. But there are some things we all have to agree on, or I'm going to wind up killing you before June."

"I'm hearing you, really."

"You let Mr. Suggs go down the tubes, and it wasn't a good way to go, drowning in pulmonary edema."

Biotto looked genuinely surprised.

"That's the first unprogrammed response I've ever seen from you," observed Ryan.

"What?"

"But that's another issue."

"No, I don't think so."

"Yes, it is. You were just too fuckin' tired to get out of bed. The nurses say so, and I believe it. Everyone believes it."

"They're full of crap!" shouted Biotto, steamy-faced.

"You'll believe whatever you can live with. But the fact is you're just giving up. And everyone knows it. You had just had enough of getting up at two A.M. to save some gomer for life in a nursing home."

"Hey, if you're trying to lay on a guilt—"

Ryan cut him off.

"Can't you react without that prepackaged drivel?"

"Super-doc, tight-ass, red-hot *intern,*" sputtered Biotto.

Ryan looked at him, not unsympathetically.

"You shits: you and Iggy, and your little nursey friends. Think you're such Dukes. Well, let me tell you. There's ways of doing things other than what's been done at The Tower for eons. Not everybody gets the full route, everywhere. And when my time comes, and I'm peeing in my pants, can't talk, just drooling, just let me go, brother."

"There's ways to go and ways to go," said Ryan. "If you felt so strongly about it, why didn't you say something at Chart Rounds?"

"You would really have listened."

"Or why not get up and give the guy a shot of IV morphine? It treats pulmonary edema. Not real well. But it would at least put him out of his misery."

Biotto was silent. A tear brimmed over and ran down his face. He shuddered a little.

"Shit," was all he said.

Ryan left the room. He went back to the chart rack at the nurses station. Biotto avoided him the rest of the day. At X-ray Rounds they still weren't speaking. But after Chart Rounds Biotto stopped Ryan.

"Sorry about Suggs."

Ryan looked at him steadily.

"I'm an asshole, sometimes," said Biotto.

"Nobody's perfect."

"Shit," laughed Biotto, "I'd been thinking I was getting better."

"So did I," said Ryan. "But you have to play the game until the final buzzer."

39

Monday, May 21

It was the first time Ryan had ever seen Biotto appear actually happy about an admission. He had slumped off to the E.R., as usual, but came back towing the patient on a stretcher behind him, with a step that was positively sprightly.

It was Miss Osler.

"A real work of art," winked Biotto.

Miss Osler was obviously in pain and said nothing. She just smiled at Ryan and reached out a hand. He took it.

The nurses put her in bed while Ryan followed Biotto into the conference room. Ryan had never seen Miss Osler look so pale and sick.

"What's the story?" asked Ryan.

"You had your chance with her last time," winked Biotto. "She's mine."

"Come on."

"Came into the E.R. around six this morning with tummy pain," said Biotto. "Had some tuna casserole, with a bad batch of mayonnaise. Diarrhea."

"White count?"

"Ten-six."

"Shift?"

"No diff."

"Belly film?"

"Never got done. Surgery saw her. Not a surgical belly."

They went to see her.

"Everything hurts," she winced, as Biotto poked every quadrant of her abdomen. It seemed to hurt more when he pressed in than when he let go, which was reassuring. Her bowel sounds were high-pitched.

"Sit up for me, honey," said Biotto. "I want to listen to your back."

"Can't!"

"All right," said Biotto, "just relax."

"Why can't you sit up?" asked Ryan, holding her by the wrist, counting her racing pulse.

"I get this wicked pain, right here," said Miss Osler, pointing to her left shoulder.

Ryan's mouth dropped open. He stared at Biotto, who stared back blankly for a moment, then stepped out into the hall, pulling Ryan after him.

"You're not thinking what I'm thinking."

"You better get a stat abdominal film."

Biotto got a stat film, with Miss Osler lying on one side, since she couldn't sit up. There was free air visible along the flank.

The OB-GYN boys were there in minutes. They did a culdocentesis right in the bed, placing Miss Osler on her back, Ryan holding one leg, Biotto the other, while the GYN resident slipped a long needle on a syringe past the cervix, through the depth of the vagina, and into the cul-de-sac. The syringe filled with blood.

"What is it?" asked Miss Osler.

"Ruptured ectopic," said the GYN resident, looking at the syringe. "Nice pickup," he said to Biotto, who swelled a little.

"What!" cried Miss Osler.

Biotto and the GYN resident left. The GYN man went to schedule an operating room. Biotto went to page Iggy. Ryan stayed behind.

"You've got an ectopic pregnancy," said Ryan, taking her hand. "Instead of being in the womb, it's implanted in one of your Fallopian tubes. It grew until it burst the tube. So now you're bleeding internally."

"What're they going to do?"

"You need surgery," said Ryan. "It's no big deal, but it has to be done now."

290

"Will I be okay?"

"Sure," said Ryan, managing to think but not say: *Sterile maybe, but okay.*

"Why did this happen?"

"Just does, sometimes."

" 'Cause my tubes are scarred?"

"Maybe, in part."

"Scarred from gonorrhea?"

"Could be."

"Then I deserve it," said Miss Osler, with the most rueful look Ryan had ever seen on any face.

"Nobody deserves anything," said Ryan, holding her hand in both of his.

"You'll come with me?"

"I'll check on you, after the surgery."

"Come to the surgery."

"Can't," said Ryan, smiling. "I'd just get in the way."

Biotto came in to draw the type and cross and to start a big gauge IV. Ryan stayed with her until the orderlies came and took her away.

40

June, the Last Month of Internship

It wasn't until June that it got really hot. It was hot enough to make Ryan remember the sweltering days at the beginning of internship, last July, light years ago.

"I spent a lifetime at Manhattan Hospital one year," said Biotto.

"It's been eventful," said Ryan, looking at Iggy, who was leafing through charts. They were sitting in front of the chart rack. It was six o'clock in the evening and still bright out.

"Four more weeks," said Iggy. "And I'll be spending the rest of the summer in air conditioning."

"Can we make Chart Rounds in the Diagnostic Radiology Suite?" asked Biotto.

"You bums will be lucky if I let you in to see your own films," snorted Iggy. "The DRS is for those who've paid their dues."

"Jesus," said Biotto, "what was I doing this whole year?"

"Whatever it was," said Iggy, "it wasn't enough."

Frank Wright wandered into the conference room. He was just four weeks away from a three-piece suit and a piece of a private practice with Sidney Cohen. Frank would be an attending.

"Now here's a man who's paid his dues," said Iggy.

Frank smiled at Iggy. "Just remember, Iggy, even when you're sitting in that cool, dark suite, you're still a doctor."

Iggy shook his head, and he handed the first chart to Ryan.

"Got an office all set up, Frank?" asked Ryan, delaying the inevitable moment when he'd have to turn his attention to the chart.

"Just finished ordering the furniture. And a green carpet. Always wanted a green carpet in my office," said Frank, disappearing out the door.

"The man is sick," said Iggy. "Very sick. That's what happens when you spend four years of medical school, a year of internship, junior and senior residency, and a year of chief residency at the Tower."

"A year is enough to do it," said Biotto, shaking his head. "Quite enough."

"For what?" asked Ryan, who still hadn't opened the chart.

"To kill the best part of you," said Biotto. "They do an empathy-ectomy on you."

"Biotto, the eternal victim," said Iggy, smiling a bony smile at Biotto.

They went through the charts, meticulously, as they always did, and Ryan signed out to Biotto.

The twilight was beginning at seven as Ryan pushed through the revolving glass door and out into the street. He saw Brigid Sullivan crossing the avenue down the block. She disappeared into the hospital entrance. He crossed the avenue, thinking about being photographed in Central Park with her, and about her father.

Ryan headed toward the town house, past the ICB&G, where he had spent some good hours. He had been meeting Hope there lately. He didn't have to call in advance and commit himself. If Diana went home, Ryan could walk over to the ICB&G and have a fair chance of finding Hope. He felt guilty about how he used Hope, but Caroline had laughed at him for that. "She's using as much as used," Caroline had assured Ryan.

But Caroline couldn't help with Diana. Nobody could, not even Arch. Ryan walked faster, thinking that Diana might be calling, even now. Then he slowed his pace. Maybe it would be better to miss Diana, this one night.

BOOK IV

Land
of Milk
and Honey

1

July

July first was a Sunday. Ryan did not become an official junior assistant resident until Monday morning, July second. It was a lowly-sounding title, but it was a vast leap upward from "intern."

That weekend he piled all his white hospital tunics in a heap and ceremoniously kicked them into a corner. JAR's wore shirts and ties with their white pants and jackets. Ryan, Arch, Hope, and Jane went down to Bloomie's and bought seven shirts, one for each day of the week, and seven ties to match. Ryan knew Diana would like them. They were preppie oxford shirts, white, blue, pink. And all the ties had club patterns.

Ryan planned to show Iggy, too. Iggy was starting his radiology residency at the Tower on Monday, and would be buried in the bowels of the Diagnostic Radiology Suite forevermore. Ryan would have to make it a point to go by and show himself off, or else Iggy might miss it.

The assignments had come out Friday. Ryan pulled B-5, Brigid's floor, the best medical ward.

"I don't know if I'm going to be able to stand you now," said Brigid. "William Ryan, JAR."

Ryan put on a blue oxford cloth shirt and a tie with brown wild turkeys woven onto a blue background, and headed for the air-conditioned Diagnostic Radiology Suite.

Iggy was scanning chest films with a second-year radiology resident when Ryan stepped into the delicious cool of the radiology suite. The X-ray view boxes provided the only light in the room, like silver screens in a darkened cinema.

"Well," said Iggy, suppressing an Iggy smile, "do my eyes deceive?"

"It's me."

"William Ryan, M.D., JAR," said Iggy, extending a bony hand, and turning to the radiology resident at his elbow. "This is Billy Ryan, as fine an intern as ever came down the pike, now facing JARship with eager heart and misguided enthusiasm."

"Pleasure," nodded the other resident.

"We'll read all Ryan's films stat," said Iggy to Ryan, as though he were speaking of an absent Ryan.

"I'm on B-five," said Ryan.

"Best floor," said Iggy. "And you'll have three little interns to shepherd. Now they're gonna look to you for all the answers."

A cold pang zipped through Ryan.

"Cheer up," said Iggy, seeing all in Ryan's transparent face. "Nothing could be worse than internship. You have arrived. You have set foot in the Promised Land."

2

Tuesday, July 3

Ryan was working with Biotto on B-5. Two JAR's and three interns, one of whom was Jason Adams, freshly graduated, and happy to be back with Biotto again. He was less happy to discover that he was scheduled to admit with Ryan, which meant he was also covered at night by hard-ass Ryan.

Jason might have been disappointed, in any event, by the subtle changes evident in Biotto since the advent of JARship. For one thing, Biotto looked different. The yellow-tinted glasses were there, but his gold necklace was tucked beneath a buttoned collar and a tie. Biotto, Jason feared, was not immune to power-tripping.

It was hard to be immune.

No creature knows a sweeter metamorphosis than intern turned JAR. No more a grubby, unshaven drone, a JAR sleeps at home, beckoned only when the workup is as complete as the intern can make it. The JAR arrives for Morning Rounds, showered, shaven, to calm the interns, to console.

Ryan made Biotto swear a blood oath to make efficient rounds, that is, to run the ward as Iggy had run it.

"But Iggy was so into clock-watching," Biotto protested.

"We've got thirty patients to see before Morning Report at nine. You want to have to get in here a half hour earlier?"

That was language Biotto could understand. The JAR's could sleep later than the interns. The interns had to get in early for the onerous task of blood-drawing. By the time the JAR's arrived, nurses, students, and interns were all assembled.

The "Thundering Herd," as one of Ryan's favorite patients

called them, moved from bed to bed, the interns questioning patients, patients questioning interns. Students were at first dismayed by the rapidity of the rounds.

"The interns hardly listen to the patients," they said.

"Only fair," said Ryan. "The patients never listen to the interns."

Students presented new admissions in the stylized form demanded. Ryan listened, and corrected or praised, when either was due.

"His royal highness wants us to make lightning rounds," Jason complained to Biotto. "I can't do it. I just can't relate to my patients in thirty seconds, breezing by the beds."

"That's not what Morning Rounds are for," said Biotto, catching Jason's betrayed look. "Jason, you have to go back after Morning Rounds, when we're at Morning Report. That's when you can get into your patients' inner needs."

Jason looked searchingly at Biotto, who looked over the temperature chart for the ward.

"Be careful," Jason said. "They'll turn you into one of them."

Thirty patients seen in one hour. Complaints listened to, ignored, or investigated, bodies poked, lungs breathed, weight charts and temperature charts inspected and rejected, medical students harassed, interns consoled.

The Morning Report at the department office followed. New admissions were described, follow-ups given. Then back to the ward for Attending Rounds, where the new admissions were presented, by the interns again, to yet another attending, *ad nauseam,* and follow-ups given again, and coffee consumed. Then lunch. (Residents had time for lunch.) X-ray Rounds, conference, and finally, Chart Rounds.

· Chart Rounds were the grand finale. The lab results hit the charts about four, along with the X-ray reports. Chart Rounds were where discharge, workup, and death decisions were made. The charts were reviewed, and it was decided who would be resuscitated and who would be allowed to enter the promised land unpummeled. Chart Rounds ended, and Ryan stayed around the darkening ward, listening to interns sign out to the intern on call. Biotto always vanished posthaste.

If the routine was not exhilarating, it was, at least, efficient. Without it things got missed. When arrests or pushy attendings intruded into the deliberations, an anemia or an abnormal EKG got overlooked. The care broke down.

It was easier to be interested in medicine after a full night's sleep, and even Biotto found an occasional case intriguing. Ryan came in for Morning Rounds the night after Biotto had been on call. Biotto was so excited he couldn't wait for the interns to present their admissions from the night before. He pulled Ryan into the conference room and started jabbering about some eighteen-year-old girl whom they had gotten at eight the prior evening.

"She said she had something growing between her legs," said Biotto. "What do you think?" Not giving Ryan a chance to speak, he shouted, "It was a *penis!* I swear. Called the Endocrine mavens last night. They came right in. They think it's a Five Alpha Reductase deficiency."

"This place is such a resource," said Ryan, shaking his head at the enormity of it. "For eighteen years that guy thinks he's a girl. In one night, we make the diagnosis. Good job."

"And he'd been seen at two community hospitals. They never examined him," said Biotto. "Can you imagine what medicine must be like out there in the boonies?"

"It's nothing like the Tower."

3

July 9

As good as the Tower was, it was not without its own troubles
during JAR year. The main trouble was Soft Sam.

Soft Sam Simpson was the new chief resident, a pudgy, puffy-
eyed blond who couldn't bring himself to wield the iron fist
upon deserving interns. And the interns quickly learned what
that meant: that meant that whenever a JAR lambasted an intern
all the intern had to do was go to Soft Sam, who would forgive
all, console the bruised sensibilities of the scolded, and even
pour a brandy for himself and the intern, then sit back, smiling
benignly.

Ryan was particularly galled by Jason Adams, who had been
called by the nurses on one night shift no fewer than five times
about the same patient. When Ryan arrived in the morning, the
entire night-shift nursing staff surrounded him and demanded
Jason's head on a platter. He had refused to get out of bed until
they turned on the lights in his on-call room and screamed at
him to get up. The patient's heart was deteriorating so badly
that blood backed up into his lungs and he could hardly breathe.
Jason finally got out of bed but pretended to be busy in the lab
at the end of the hall.

Hearing the nurses' story, the first thing that crossed Ryan's
mind was *Mr. Suggs: this is another Mr. Suggs.* Ryan took Jason
aside, telling himself, *Low profile, nonconfrontation, no waves.*

"Jason, there's nothing wrong with not knowing, or not being
sure of what to do. But you've got to go see the patient. If you
don't know what to do after you've seen the patient, call your
resident. Namely me."

Jason was watching the nurses. They were all standing, arms crossed, enjoying what they couldn't hear but could richly imagine. Jason went to Soft Sam. Jason had been publicly humiliated, and he wanted Ryan reprimanded. Soft Sam took out the brandy.

The next morning, Baptist called Ryan into his office.

"I understand there's a problem between you and Dr. Adams," said Baptist.

"No problem," said Ryan.

Baptist stood up behind his desk, then sat down again.

"You know, it's part of the JAR's job to help and support his interns. If you have a personality problem, a conflict with an intern, you should bring it to the attention of the chief resident."

"There is no personality conflict," said Ryan. "The problem is one of discipline."

"Whose discipline?"

"Dr. Adams has to learn to see patients, even when he doesn't feel like it."

"And Dr. Ryan has to learn how to handle people. That's one of the bases on which I decide whom to keep for senior resident. Senior residents have to supervise, and they have to deal with people."

Baptist launched into his speech about the supportive function of the junior assistant residents, the importance of the need for sensitivity to the sensibilities of fledgling doctors, unsure of themselves, struggling for their sense of authority, the importance of not undermining the delicate authority of the intern, the difficulty of being new at anything. Then Ryan was dismissed.

Ryan dropped by to see Iggy that afternoon.

"Was I wrong? Or what?" asked Ryan.

Iggy swiveled in his chair, turning in the flat, surreal light of the view boxes in front of him. Bathed in that cool light and wearing a gray shirt with a darker gray tie, Iggy looked like a living three-dimensional television image.

"The patient was in pulmonary edema . . . all night?" Iggy raised an ironic eyebrow.

"Yes!"

Iggy swung back to face the view boxes, his back to Ryan.

"Bring me something more subtle next time, chief."

Ryan had been dismissed.

Diana came over that night.

Ryan told her about Jason and Baptist.

"He's determined to extrude me, like so much sewage," said Ryan.

"Just stay out of his way."

"Why has he got this thing for me?"

"You didn't exactly start off on the right foot, did you?" laughed Diana.

"Somehow," said Ryan, "I'd love to thwart him."

4

July 10

Caroline called Ryan to tell him she'd be at the Whipple clinic for a follow-up visit. He surprised her by suggesting they meet for lunch.

"Since when do you have time for lunch?" asked Caroline.

"Since I stopped being an intern."

"Oh! I completely forgot! July first was the magic day, wasn't it? I always try to keep my Hodgkin's under control for the month of July."

"A prudent move."

"You mean I can really have you all to myself for an hour?"

"I'll be on the electric leash."

"Oh, that beeper."

"Page me when you're through at the clinic. We'll go over to the ICB&G."

"Imagine. Little Caroline Smith going out to lunch with a resident."

"If you behave yourself, I may even be treating."

5

"You still thinking about taking on Ryan as your fellow?" Baptist asked Diana.

"He's still in the running," said Diana. "Until someone better applies."

Diana looked at Baptist. "And I thought this was going to be a social visit."

"Sorry," said Baptist. "He's just always cropping up." Baptist looked at the ceiling. "I had to call him in Tuesday. He had demolished one of the new interns. Sam told me about it."

"Who?"

"Sam, the new chief resident."

"No, I mean, whom did Ryan demolish?"

"Jason Adams," said Baptist. "Actually, it sounded like Adams had fouled up pretty badly. He was just too scared to take care of a patient."

"Sounds like Ryan was right, then."

"There's no question about that. He's always right. He just has the most irritating way of being right."

"He's young."

"Yes."

"He'll smooth out the rough edges," said Diana. "With time."

"You like him, don't you?"

"Yes," said Diana. "Or I wouldn't consider him for the fellow's spot."

"He can damage people," said Baptist. "If he's not careful."

"Can't we all? Interns are a resilient lot, though."

"They're not iron men, contrary to their own myths," said

Baptist. "It's tough enough, without someone standing over you, cracking the whip."

"How quickly we forget," said Diana.

"What?" said Baptist, coming out of his own thoughts. "What did you mean by that?"

"About Ryan," said Diana. "He didn't have an easy time, as an intern. I guess he feels if he could make the grade then, Adams can now."

"Oh," said Baptist. "I misunderstood."

6

July 13

A strange and wondrous thing was taking place. Brigid, of course, was the first to notice it. Biotto was speaking English. It had been so gradual, Ryan hardly noticed. But it began sometime after their shoot-out in the treatment room, after Biotto let Mr. Suggs go down the tubes.

All those grating, reflexive phrases—the where-it's-ats, the getting-intos, laid-backs, where-I'm-coming-froms—had gradually given way to a less manufactured language. And Biotto was spending more time with his charts, and with his patients.

"I couldn't believe I was talking to the same person," Iggy told Ryan. "It's a new person. He calls me up, asking about a reading, says: 'May I speak with the resident who interpreted the films on Mrs. Smith?' I mean, it sounded like Biotto's voice, but he's been civilized."

Brigid approved, of course, but withheld a final verdict.

"He's adapted," she said. "I'm not sure he's really changed."

"At least he's playing a new game."

"Form and content are two different things."

"Brigid," said Ryan, "you are such a hard-ass."

7

July 16

Ryan went over problem patients with the interns he covered, and went home at nine. The interns had to call him for any admission as soon as the intern had enough information to make a judgment about what was going on.

Jason Adams woke Ryan at 4:00 A.M. Diana was spending the night.

"Ghastly hour," she said as Ryan put the receiver to his ear.

"We've got a twenty-two-year-old girl with an F.U.O.," said Jason.

"Yes?" said Ryan.

"You're coming in?" said Jason.

"What's her white count?"

"Don't know yet."

"Stiff neck?"

"A little."

"Spinal fluid?"

"Haven't tapped her yet. Haven't done too many, alone."

"What have you done?"

"Blood, urine, sputum cultures. She has a pretty loud murmur."

"Anything else?"

"I think she might have a big spleen. She's got a funny rash on her face," said Jason. "She's a real nice girl."

"On my way," said Ryan. "But get that white count and the urinalysis by the time I get there. . . . Jason?"

"Yes?"

"She ever been told she had a heart murmur before?"

309

"No."

Diana was wide awake. She had heard the word *murmur*. Ryan got up, tried to be quiet in the dark, but failed miserably.

"Problem?" she asked.

"Admission with a fever, rash, and a murmur. If you can believe Jason."

"History?"

"Nothing I could pry out of Jason over the phone."

"I'm attending for Cardiology this month."

"I remember."

"Don't hesitate to call. Sounds like this could be interesting."

"After midnight," said Ryan, "there is no such thing as an interesting admission."

Diana had her phone plugged into the phone jack outside Ryan's door. If Alan tried to call her apartment in the hospital residence building, the phone rang at Ryan's bedroom door.

Jason had the blood results and urinalysis ready by the time Ryan arrived. The white count was low. The urine had some red blood cells.

"Her temp's forty degrees centigrade," said Jason.

"What'd you do for it?"

"I was afraid to give her anything," said Jason, tremulously. "How could we follow the temp?"

"Just give her one Tylenol, every four hours," said Ryan. "Round the clock. If she's got anything, she'll spike through it, but she won't go up so high. Forty is really hot. She'll be more comfortable."

They went to see her. She was a pretty girl, flushed with fever. The rash Jason mentioned was just a dark patch on her red face now. It covered her left cheek and her nose.

"How are you?" asked Ryan, feeling her pulse. "Besides tired."

"Not too swift," she said. Her name was Susan Bergmeyer. "My hands are killing me."

The joints were tender, but not swollen, except one on her thumb. Ryan thought of Miss Osler, with her fever, arthralgias, and the gonorrhea in her blood.

310

"Do a pelvic yet?" he asked Jason.

"Hadn't thought of it," said Jason, who was trying to dredge up medical school memories of gonococcal arthritis and fever.

She did, in fact, have a big spleen. And a loud heart murmur, which she had not been told about at her employment physical a month earlier. She worked for IBM. She had just graduated from Berkeley in June, and was alone in New York.

Ryan took Jason to the nurses station and went over the possibilities and the plan. They managed to find a female aide at 5:00 A.M. and went back to Susan's room.

"You're going to need a few things," said Jason, sitting down by her. She managed to smile.

"I thought you might say that."

"Your fever's coming down," said Jason, noting her drenching sweat. She had gotten the Tylenol effect.

"Feel better. What do I need?"

"A pelvic exam."

"No problem."

"And a spinal tap."

"Uh-oh. Do I get a choice?"

"You can choose which you want first. It's not an 'either or.'"

"Let's get the spinal tap over with," she said.

Jason did a decent job on the tap. The pelvic was clean. They sent off the cultures.

"Nice job," Ryan told him.

They looked at the spinal fluid, and Ryan made Jason stain it for cryptococcus. They looked at her X rays. They sat down with some coffee from the vending machine near the lab. The sun began to come up over the East River, turning all the windows in the solarium brilliant pink.

"What do you think?" asked Ryan.

"With the murmur, S.B.E. The lymphadenopathy: Hodgkin's," said Jason, pausing. "Shit, I don't want her to have Hodgkin's."

They were called by the nurse. Susan was having chest pain. She leaned forward to ease the pain. They listened to her.

"She's got a rub," said Ryan.

311

"What?"

"She's got pericarditis, whatever else she has," said Ryan. "Get an EKG and another chest X ray. Schedule an echo for the morning."

"Maybe we should call someone?"

"For what?"

"Help."

"What can anyone do? What question can we ask?"

"I don't know," said Jason.

"Don't panic."

"Maybe," Jason said, "maybe, it's just S.B.E."

"*Just* S.B.E.? Bugs on your heart valves can kill you."

"But antibiotics . . ."

"Don't wish anything on her, even the lesser of two evils." Jason looked down.

"How're you holding up?" asked Ryan.

"Long night."

"Time flies when you're having a good time," said Ryan.

8

Tuesday Morning, July 17

Ryan thought he might have time to get back to Diana before Morning Rounds. But she was gone when he arrived back at the town house at 6:45. Morning rounds began at 7:15, which meant he had time to either shower or eat. For some reason he was famished. So he skipped his shower.

He felt grubby all through Morning Walk Rounds with the interns, and irritable during Morning Report. Adding salt to his wounds, the scheduled attending, Sidney Cohen, had a sick patient in the Cardiac Care Unit and had asked Baptist to fill in for him. The admitting resident for each of the ward floors presented each admission, outlining the patients' histories, the pertinent findings on physical exam, the laboratory data, and the treatment. Baptist didn't really seem to be listening, until Ryan's turn came.

"Susan Bergmeyer is a twenty-two-year-old white female who presented with a fever, rash, heart murmur, and arthralgias," Ryan said. Ryan was the only resident who was unshaven this morning. Usually the resident who had gotten the early-morning admission looked bleary, and nobody thought anything of it. But with Baptist staring at him, Ryan felt soiled and embarrassed. Everyone else around the table looked crisp.

"What was the patient's chief complaint?" asked Baptist. "I presume she didn't walk into the E.R. in the wee hours saying 'I have a fever, rash, heart murmur, and arthralgias.' "

This drew a nervous giggle from the residents around the table. Ryan tried to smile.

It was a small point of form. Formal presentations at The

313

Manhattan Hospital began with the statement of the patient's complaint, in the patient's own words. This format was frequently abbreviated during Morning Report, but Baptist was going to see how much needling Ryan could take.

"She complained of 'feeling like a wet Raggedy Ann Doll,' as I recall," said Ryan.

Soft Sam shifted uncomfortably in his chair. Baptist did not smile. Ryan presented the rest of the story, slowly, deliberately, sticking annoyingly to the letter of the formal presentation format. The residents began to shift in their seats. Formal presentations were agonizingly tedious, information being presented according to a preformulated outline, rather than packaged and streamlined to telegraph the essential features of the case. At Morning Report the residents always presented telegraphically. That style held everyone's attention and was mercifully brief. The residents who preceded Ryan this morning had presented this way.

But Baptist had decided to play games, and had chosen the wrong game. No one could present better than Ryan. Ryan could present any case in fifteen seconds, or in fifteen minutes, whatever was demanded. It took him twenty minutes to pick his way through Susan's case. Despite the fact that she was the best case of the morning, everyone was glad when the presentation finally ended. Morning Report had run over by fifteen minutes and Ryan had two more cases to present.

But Baptist waved his hand disgustedly and dismissed them.

"Jesus," said Biotto, "he ruined Report."

"Bad vibes, huh?" said Ryan, winking.

"He doesn't like you much, does he?"

Ryan got paged as he was walking back to the floor with Biotto.

"I'm here," said Caroline. "I'll be through with clinic by noon."

Ryan went home and showered and checked back on Jason and Susan before going over to the ICB&G at noon.

Caroline looked marvelous. She was tan and lean. She ordered a turkey club and a hamburger.

"My appetite's been great," she said. "But I keep losing weight. They checked my thyroid tests this morning. If this is hyperthyroidism, I'll keep it."

Ryan was still angry from Morning Report and told Caroline about it.

"What's he got against you?"

"We started off on the wrong foot."

"Well, you've got to get along with the boss," said Caroline cheerfully. "That's basic."

Baptist was having all the chiefs for lunch at the department office. Diana Hayes was the first to arrive.

"Sidney Cohen tells me you filled in for him like a real trooper on short notice this morning," said Diana.

"I like doing it. Should find time to do it more often. Get to really see the house staff at close range and hear how they think through cases."

"Anything good this morning?"

"One that might interest you," said Baptist. "A young girl on B-five. Sounds like pericarditis. Maybe lupus. Good case. But her resident's that character Ryan."

"Did he mishandle it?"

"No," said Baptist. "He's thorough. He just presents so poorly."

9

July 18

"What did she have?" asked Diana.

"Who?"

"The woman you left me for at four in the morning."

They were in Diana's office, with the door closed.

"Looks like lupus,". said Ryan. "The antibodies came back positive as hell. She's got pericarditis, pleuritis, fever, neutropenia, athralgias."

"I'm convinced."

"Jason Adams, M.D., is not."

"Why not?"

"He doesn't want her to have anything bad."

"He'll get over that."

"He won't let anybody else change her IV."

"Pericarditis, you say?"

"Don't get any ideas," said Ryan. "She's doing fine on steroids."

"What ideas?" asked Diana, indignantly. "I was just wondering if I'd seen her echo."

"I saw it," said Ryan. "There was fluid there all right."

"When was it done?"

"Yesterday."

"Oh! *Bergmeyer!*"

"Yes."

"I remember her. It was fairly large. Have you repeated it, on therapy?"

"Today."

They went out to the echo room and found Susan's new echo.

There was more fluid than ever. The heart was encased in an inflamed pericardium, weeping fluid into a closed bag.

"Not doing all *that* well on steroids," said Diana. "How's she feel?"

"Better," said Ryan, glumly, looking at the echo. "But we'll keep an eye on her."

"How're you getting on with Jason Adams now?"

"Better," said Ryan. "Why do you ask?"

"You didn't seem to like him."

"He's not so bad," said Ryan, looking steadily at her. "He learns fast."

10

July 23

B-5 ran in its well-oiled fashion, with Brigid in command and
Ryan keeping a hawkish eye on the interns. He was the lone
resident now. Biotto had been dealt a blow by the schedule
rotation and was shipped off to Whipple for three weeks. Fortunately, things had quieted down. There were only two problem
patients: Susan, and an old alcoholic who belonged to Jason,
and whom Jason ignored. Jason was too busy thinking about
Susan to bother with some old man who had brought on his own
miseries.

"What were Gilbey's L.F.T.'s today?" Ryan asked Jason at
Chart Rounds.

"Not back yet."

"Didn't you call the lab?"

"I was busy."

"Interns are always busy," said Ryan. "Did you have time for
lunch?"

"Hey, cut the hard-ass shit," said Jason. "Come on, Billy, you
know liver functions are always bad in alcoholics."

"Jason," said Ryan evenly, "the question is how bad, and how
bad in Gilbey."

"He'll just drink himself back into a roaring hepatitis the next
time, even if we got him past this time."

"If you're not going to care for him," said Ryan, "then discharge him."

"What?"

"Discharge him."

"Okay," said Jason, writing "Discharge in A.M." in the order
book under Gilbey.

Ryan looked at him in disbelief.

"You'd really send that guy out with yellow eyes, in pre-coma, not knowing what his clotting is like?"

"You told me to."

"I said either care for him or don't: don't do a half-ass job."

"Then he's out of here."

Ryan took Gilbey's chart and ripped off the green tape, taking Gilbey off Jason's green team.

"Who will care for this unfortunate, degenerate bum?"

One of the other interns took him, without comment. He just pasted some red tape on the chart, claiming Gilbey for his own team.

Ryan noticed later that there was a strip of green tape on Gilbey's chart again: Jason had recanted.

Across the avenue the Tower's sister institution descended toward its Armageddon. Interns coming back from Whipple said there were no more Morning Rounds: each intern saw only his own patients. That meant the intern on call at night knew only one third of the patients he covered. That wasn't even the worst of it. Ryan could hardly believe the stories his fellow JAR's told as they rotated back from Whipple. Discipline had completely broken down. Interns refused to ask for autopsies and simply did not do any of the onerous but necessary tasks.

"Can you imagine?" asked Biotto, shaking his head. "I asked the intern if he had gotten permission for the post, and he said, 'No, I didn't ask.' So I said, 'Well, go back and ask.' And he just refused. He didn't want to. It made him uncomfortable. He said he 'couldn't relate' to asking for the post. He thought I ought to ask. I told him I didn't like doing it any more than he did, but it was his job. He said, 'I can't relate to it. I just can't get in touch with the whole autopsy scene.' And he didn't ask."

"Why didn't you call the chief resident?" asked Ryan, astonished.

"I did," said Biotto. "He said he didn't want to be forced to play the heavy. He didn't want to force anybody to do anything they found repugnant. So I said, 'Why don't you just excuse them all from the whole internship year? I found the entire three hundred sixty-five days repugnant.'"

319

Ryan shook his head. That was how far Whipple had fallen. He thanked his stars for being through with Whipple—he didn't have to rotate there as a JAR by the luck of scheduling.

He was safe at the Tower.

"I'll be back at the Tower in ten days," said Biotto. "I'm counting them down."

11

Tuesday, July 24

Caroline called Ryan at the town house around eight o'clock.

"What are you doing this weekend, Doc?"

"I'm off Friday, but not on Saturday."

"Oh, too bad."

"Why."

"Well," said Caroline, happily, "I've decided I'm going to survive the summer, so I went in on a house in East Hampton. And I've got a clinic visit at Whipple on Friday. So I thought we could meet and take off right after for the Hamptons."

"It still might be possible," said Ryan, wondering what Caroline had in mind for sleeping arrangements at this house. He plucked the on-call schedule from his desk, automatically, to see whom he might trade with.

"Call me and let me know," said Caroline. Then she hung up.

Ryan put down the phone and considered. If Caroline did not have Hodgkin's, there would be no question about it. But she had Hodgkin's. There was no wishing that away. She would be in and out of Whipple, and whenever she got sicker, she would get frightened, and she would eventually start looking like a patient again.

One irrational affair was enough, Ryan decided. But there was the weekend coming up, and Diana spent her weekends with Alan. Ryan picked up the phone and dialed Hope's number.

12

July 25

Ryan's beeper went off. It was a stat page to B-5. He ran upstairs from the cafeteria. Susan was having trouble breathing. Her neck veins were bulging, and Jason was about to shoot some Lasix into her IV.

"Don't!" said Ryan.

"Why not?"

"It'd make her worse. She's in tamponade. Call the cath lab and ask Dr. Hayes to get up here. Tell her to bring an alligator clamp and a long needle—she'll know what it means."

Jason raced out to the phone. Ryan stayed with Susan. He took a fourteen-gauge angiocath out of his pocket and unsheathed it. Brigid was there with the crash cart. Her nurses were clearing the other patients out of the four-bedded room. Brigid had the monitor brought down. Brigid was a rock.

"Sterile drape?" she asked Ryan.

"Yeah, right."

Diana arrived and looked around.

"Okay: monitor, crash cart, everything's set. Good job," she said to Ryan.

Brigid said nothing. Diana drew out a long, sterile needle. Brigid called out the blood pressures, which were falling fast. Diana hooked the needle up to the alligator clamp and attached the clamp to a wire which connected to the monitor. Then she plunged the needle in, heading for heart. In seconds a pattern on the monitor told her where the needle was. It was right where it should be. Brigid handed her a catheter hookup, and within seconds a hundred milliliters of pericardial fluid drained out of the sack encasing Susan's heart. Susan breathed in, and her color changed from gray to a nice pink. Brigid called out the pressures. They were almost normal.

"Better move her to the CCU for now," said Diana.

"She's better," said Jason. "She'll be okay here." If Susan were moved to the Cardiac Care Unit, she would no longer be Jason's patient.

"She'll be back," said Diana. "She needs a few days."

Diana glided out.

"She's a cool one," said Jason, looking after her.

"She knows how the scene is played," said Brigid.

They transferred Susan to the CCU.

13

July 26

Ryan was having lunch with Brigid in the cafeteria. Diana sailed over and sat down at their table.

"How did Susan Bergmeyer do?" she asked Ryan.

"Fine, she's coming back from the CCU today."

"Dr. Adams must be overjoyed."

Brigid looked at her, surprised.

"Poor Jason," said Brigid. "Is it that obvious? You were only there for a few minutes."

"Well," said Diana, speaking quickly, "he didn't want her in the CCU. Most new interns would be only too happy to ship trouble to the CCU. She is a pretty little thing."

"You're right about Jason," said Ryan. "He has to be talked to."

"You ought to know," said Brigid, getting up. "I'm late."

"Lovely eyes," said Diana, looking after Brigid.

"She's very nice."

"A little broad of hip though."

"Yes."

"You look so nice in your pink shirt."

"You like it?"

"Oh, definitely," said Diana. "Who picked the tie?"

"I did."

"By yourself?"

"With Arch and Jane."

"You're such a preppie. I love looking at you."

Ryan tried to say something equally effective, but nothing issued.

"You're really adorable when you're tongue-tied," she said.

14

Friday, July 27

Ryan was coming out through the revolving glass door in the early evening when he caught sight of Diana Hayes pulling open the door of a taxi. She was in and gone before he could overtake her. He watched her cab sail down the avenue, disappearing with a sudden jerk, heading west, into the sun. Home to Alan. Ryan hated Friday afternoons, especially now, when the warm, lingering evenings held sultry promise. Evenings now were romantic for no other reason than that they were summer evenings. But Friday evenings Diana shared only with Alan.

Ryan had learned to plan for the loneliness of Friday evenings without Diana. Before Diana he was happy to spend nights alone, behind his desk, or with Arch, swilling beer. But now to be alone was to be without Diana. Quite a lot was missing. He had to plan for the withdrawal. He called Hope midweek, and if she was working he'd plan for a night with a pal, like Brigid. But he had to have someone scheduled.

Hope was in the kitchen when Ryan got home. She was drinking daiquiris with Arch and Jane.

"Arch is taking Jane to the ballet," said Hope.

"Do you like ballet?" asked Ryan.

"Crazy man," said Hope. "All women love ballet."

"Well, let's go then."

"You have tickets?" asked Hope. Arch and Jane looked surprised.

"We can't just buy them there?"

They all laughed at Ryan and finished their daiquiris. Ryan and Hope took the subway to Chinatown.

325

"Sorry about the ballet," said Ryan. "I guess I don't plan ahead. Didn't realize about the tickets."

"Well, you've started calling days in advance," laughed Hope. "I suppose that's a sign of sorts. You're thinking about me more, no?"

Ryan looked at her smiling eyes, trying to decide if she meant it.

"Didn't I always call you in advance?"

"Matter of fact, no," she said.

They got out at Canal Street and walked upstairs to the teeming street. Hope lit a cigarette. She could look smashing.

"I feel like we're *dating* nowadays," she said, blowing smoke at him. "With all the advance notice."

"I'll never do it again," smiled Ryan.

They walked to Mott and Pell and waited in line for a seat at Bo-Hi's. Hope was wearing a navy blue knit shirt, snugly, and sheer white slacks. Ryan wondered at his own appetite for her. He was frantic, beyond reason, about Diana, but here he was excited by someone whom Diana had so thoroughly eclipsed.

"Mind your manners," said Hope.

"Pardon?"

"You've visually undressed me three times in the last ten minutes."

They were seated at a booth.

"You're lucky to be missing Whipple this year," said Hope.

"Don't let's talk about Whipple," said Ryan. "We're about to eat."

"But I see all your friends there."

"I don't have any friends at Whipple."

"Biotto."

"Is he my friend?"

"Oh, don't be so hard."

"He's okay."

"He's not much of a doc," said Hope. "But he's trying harder."

"Why isn't he much of a doc?"

"Come on," laughed Hope slyly. "You never thought he was."

"He may turn into one."

"He's changing, but he's still Biotto. Spaceship Biotto."

"What now?"

"He missed a pneumothorax on a patient the other day."

"What happened?"

"Iggy called over from X ray. Biotto had left for the day. His intern's pretty weak. Gave a lady a pneumo trying to tap her chest. Biotto told him to get a chest X ray but never checked the film himself."

Ryan sighed.

"So Iggy calls up, and there's only this squeaky-voiced intern. Iggy wound up coming up himself and getting a surgeon to put in a chest tube."

"Let's not talk about medicine."

"Okay."

The food came.

"Oh," said Hope, "I saw a patient of yours coming out of Whipple. Nearly knocked her down. She was coming out of the clinic . . ."

"Don't want to hear about it."

"Sorry. Okay."

Ryan spooned wonton soup.

"Who?"

"Caroline Smith."

Ryan looked up. He hadn't called her.

"How was she?"

"Looked thin. Lost weight. But good. She looked good."

"Damn," said Ryan. "I meant to call her."

"What's going on with you two?"

"Oh, red-hot affair."

"I believe you."

Ryan met Hope's eyes, startled.

"What's that supposed to mean?"

"That I believe you," smiled Hope. "I've had the feeling for a while. I've got competition from someone. She's a looker."

Ryan looked at Hope soberly. "And she's got Hodgkin's. Which is trouble enough for any girl."

"Ho!" laughed Hope. "Are you trouble, too?"

"The worst."

"I'll be careful," she said, winking. "Now that I've been warned."

15

August 1

Susan Bergmeyer had been back from the CCU almost a week. She was doing well on her steroids. Her fever was gone; her pericarditis resolved; her joints no longer hurt, and her lab values looked fine.

"Get her chart ready for review tonight," Ryan told Jason.

"You think she's ready?"

"Her parents are here from California, aren't they?"

"Arrived last week."

"Where'd you say they were staying?"

"At her place, on Fifty-second Street."

"Then she has someone to take care of her, and she's not going to be too far from the hospital."

They went over her chart at Chart Rounds. Jason had it completely in order. She was ready to roll.

"Call the Rheumatology group," Ryan told Jason. "If it's okay with them, she's out of here in the A.M."

The Rheumatology group, which had been following Susan, agreed. Jason was jumping around. He called her parents at Susan's apartment. They arrived at the end of Chart Rounds, forty-five minutes later.

Jason went to Susan's room with them and broke the good news.

"They want to take her now," said Jason.

"It'll empty out a bed for a midnight admission."

"I'll suffer," said Jason.

Ryan watched as Susan's father shook Jason's hand and Susan kissed Jason's cheek. He watched Jason watch them walk off the ward.

"I miss her already," said Jason.

"You haven't seen the last of her," said Ryan.

"She's doing great," said Jason. "Why do you always have to be gloom and doom?"

"You have to keep your perspective," said Ryan. "She's got a bad disease, and it's not just going to disappear."

"So what am I suppose to do?" asked Jason. "Stop liking her? Cut her off?"

Ryan met his eyes.

"Didn't you ever really like a patient?" asked Jason.

Ryan looked at Jason's glowing face. "She may do okay at that," Ryan said.

16

Brigid *was* a bit broad of hip. Diana could ruin people for Ryan with just one well-aimed slice.

Ryan would have been overjoyed to be truly swept away by someone who was not Diana, someone who could wipe his mind clear of her. But Brigid was broad of hip, more than just physically. That characterization spoke worlds of Brigid, and of Diana's intuition about people. Brigid Sullivan was just the kind of Irish Catholic girl to bring home to mother, which of course had been her undoing with many men. The world of the Tower demanded a certain degree of abandon, recklessness even, to counter the constant striving for control and the moral imperative. Brigid couldn't laugh at the Tower. She took it seriously. She took life seriously.

Ryan considered asking Brigid over to the ICB&G, getting her liquored up, and taking her back to her fishbowl apartment.

It wouldn't work. She'd get quiet. She'd think. She'd be serious, or kind, or overly considerate. She would be unbearably decent about the whole thing and not the least bit naughty or reckless. It just wouldn't be any fun at all.

17

August 6

With Susan gone, there weren't any sick patients on B-5, and Ryan was getting fidgety. He was saved by the schedule rotation. They sent him to the Emergency Room. The E.R., affectionately called "The Pits," exposed JAR's to maximal abuse from patients, families of patients, fellow house staff, and attendings. Ryan loved it.

He was abused by patients, who were sick, and sick of waiting to see a doctor. He was abused by relatives of patients who were stuffed into the waiting room to cough on each other and spread the flu.

He was abused by the interns, who begged Ryan not to admit anybody. Attendings abused him for taking so long to come to the phone. They couldn't hang up because they needed Ryan more than he needed them. They were sending him patients they wanted admitted or worked up.

He was abused by the flu, the collective gift of his patients. It made his head ache, his back ache, his nose run, his lungs wheeze, and his eyes water. He was having fun.

It was decision-making.

There was only one decision Ryan could make which interested the interns on call upstairs. The decision to admit or not to admit. Jason Adams lurked around the admissions book. He wanted to know when he was up for the next one.

"Don't you have patients to take care of upstairs?" Ryan asked him. "You're always down here looking for the next admission."

"If you were more of an iron man," said Biotto, coming through the door, "we wouldn't have to worry about getting bombed with admissions."

"When did you get back from Whipple?" asked Ryan, extending a hand.

"Yesterday," said Biotto. "Lazarus, returned from the dead."

The patients came expecting to be relieved. They often resented the thrust of Ryan's questions. They spoke of cough, and he asked whether they coughed up blood. Once he had decided to admit, just telling the patient transcended informed consent. It was theater. Sometimes he just walked in and blurted out, "You need to come into the hospital."

With others he built up slowly, talking about lab values, X rays, obscure physical findings, carrying the patient along. By the time he reached the crescendo, the patient thanked him for the bad news. At least the suspense was ended.

"You're gonna love this one," Ryan would bark into the phone to some beleaguered intern. "Come and get her."

He had only a limited arsenal of lab tests to help decide. It was really mostly "gestalt," as Iggy Bart always called it. Attendings called it "clinical acumen." Iggy called it "gestalt." Picking the dangerously ill out of all the flus, earaches, feeling dizzys, and feeling terribles who presented themselves to the E.R. door. If he missed, the patient was usually back later. But some would not make it.

The real delight was admitting an ostensible turkey who proved to be genuinely sick, like the lady with the clot in her lung. She had a few risk factors, but not much of a story. Ryan admitted her on gestalt. Jason Adams got her and sulked. But her lung scan showed a big pulmonary embolus. It was so big the nuclear medicine man didn't even hedge his report, as he almost always did.

Jason screamed at Ryan over the phone, "No way you could have made that diagnosis; no dyspnea, no hemoptysis. No way. You're holding out on me. She must have told you something."

"Omne ignotum pro magnifico," said Ryan.

Of course, Ryan had help. That was another thing he liked: the E.R. was set up to defend him. He sat in a glass-walled office, while hostility swirled around him. There were no police in The Manhattan Hospital E.R., which Ryan regretted. But there were several very tough nurses, and Mr. Perez.

Mr. Perez was the first line of defense.

He wore sunglasses, spoke Spanish and English blended incomprehensibly, and could pick out the truly sick from the merely distraught at a glance. After ten years of sitting there listening to patients, Mr. Perez could just tell.

He got their addresses, telephone numbers, and "Ever-been-to-Manhattan-Hospital-before?" If they had, he got their charts from the Record Room. Preliminaries complete, he would growl, in a voice clearly audible in every corner of the waiting room, shaking it to silence.

"What's the problem?"

The patients answered half as loud, urgently trying to give as few details as possible, which never satisfied Mr. Perez. He cared little about confidentiality, and less about demands to see the doctor forthwith.

Occasionally, a mother would refuse to talk to Mr. Perez, and stand in the middle of the waiting room, cradling her child, demanding to see the pediatrician, attesting that she had seen the movies and knew that children could die while Blue Cross numbers were being taken. Everyone stayed away from such mothers. Ryan had never seen a child die while a Blue Cross number was being taken. But he had seen mothers assault nurses. One even dropped her child while trying to swing at Mr. Perez. When she calmed down, she was led away to the pediatrician. Mothers were known to be dangerous.

Then there were the nurses. Ryan thanked benign Providence for the nurses. Stomachache for three weeks? And you came in at midnight? You can wait. You can wait for the chest pain in Room 18, who is vomiting and who had an M.I. last year. Sore throat at 3:00 A.M., and you're getting off the night shift? Don't you know we have to wake the doctor for this? Yes, this is an E.R., but the doctor does not stay up all night, except for emergencies. Maybe you had better come back in the morning. We only wake him for emergencies.

Brigid stopped by on her way home from B-5, and watched Ryan race around between examining rooms, lab, and X Ray.

"You look like you're having yourself a wonderful time."

"It's the nerve center," Ryan barked. "The veritable nerve center of the hospital." Then he ran out to see another patient.

Diana strolled through during the slack morning hours.

"I've been hearing about all the turkeys you're admitting," she smiled.

"Really?" said Ryan, visibly concerned.

"No, not really," laughed Diana. "I hear you're doing a fine job. I expected that."

"Tell Maxwell Baptist."

"He's heard."

"How do you know?"

"I told him."

Things happened in the E.R. Diabetics came in unconscious, with relatives carrying their suitcases. Ryan woke them up in minutes with some fifty percent glucose pushed into the IV and sent them home. Men arrested and were revived because there was usually a nurse right there to start resuscitation. Ryan was continuously excited, constantly dragging, and losing weight. He loved every minute of it.

18

Monday, August 13

Iggy stopped by the E.R. after dinner. Ryan was wrung out, repaying his oxygen debt after a frantic arrest. It had been an unsuccessful effort. Ryan slumped in his chair, wiping the blood from his fingernails with alcohol prep pads.

"What a bitch," said Ryan as Iggy sat silently, understanding, in front of him. He was perched on a writing ledge.

"We had this guy back three or four times with a blood pressure, sinus rhythm." Ryan shook his head. "But he crumped anyway. Damned inconsiderate of him."

"Underlying disease?" asked Iggy, in his distracted way.

"Pancreatic CA."

"Pancreatic CA?" Iggy narrowed his eyes. "Why'd you code him?"

"I called his doc when his wife dragged him in here. I could see he was going to arrest." Ryan shrugged. "And the private said full route. So we went the full route."

"How far along was he?"

"Pretty far. He must have weighed all of ninety pounds," said Ryan. "I still feel crappy about it though."

19

August 17

"Medical resident, pick up line fifty." Ryan was carrying a blood gas to the chemistry lab in back of the E.R. The P.A. found him wherever he went, even in the toilet, where he had planned to go right after he delivered the blood gas. He picked up the call from the lab.

"Hi, sweet doctor." It was Caroline.

"How are you?"

"Scared out of my skull."

"Why?" Ryan had almost said, "What now?"

"Woods wants to put me in for a liver biopsy."

"When?"

"Soon as he can get a bed. Couple of weeks."

"I'll see you when you come in. Page me as soon as you arrive." Ryan's bladder was crying out for relief.

"I see," said Caroline, hurt.

"Hey," said Ryan, "the E.R. is crazy tonight. I'll call you back. We'll have dinner."

"Okay."

Ryan hung up, really meaning to get back to her. But he never got to it that night.

20

Monday, August 20

It was Ryan's last week in the E.R. He was on nights, 6:00 P.M. to 8:00 A.M. He shuffled through the patient sheets in his "waiting" box. Two dizzys, three colds, one "feeling lousy," and a fever. The fever was Susan Bergmeyer.

Jason Adams was admitting that night. Ryan had given him the last admission, according to the inviolate Rule of the Admitting Rotation, which ensured that each intern, on each floor, got equal numbers of admissions. Jason would not be getting an admission until B-2 and B-3 each got one. But this was Susan.

Ryan went to see her. Her parents were with her. They hadn't returned to California, Ryan had the insight to observe. He took one look at her and knew she had to come in. Her temp was thirty-nine degrees centigrade, and she was taking enough steroid to keep most fevers under control. She was listless. She needed to come in. Ryan talked to her parents in the hallway. The mother cried, and the father held her, his arm around her shoulders. Ryan ordered some X rays, drew some bloods and cultures, and called Jason.

"Got some bad news for you," Ryan said.

"I just got one, not fifteen minutes ago. I could not possibly be due again," said Jason. "You mean to say B-two and B-three each got one already?"

"It's Susan Bergmeyer."

Jason was down in the E.R. almost before Ryan had hung up. He whisked Susan upstairs, stopping just long enough to say hello to her parents.

Brigid stopped by the E.R. as she was getting off the evening shift. Things had slowed, and Ryan had time to talk.

"How's Susan?"

"Looking better, by the time I left."

"Jason?"

"Frantic."

"Poor sucker."

"He's all wrung out."

"He's got to be talked to."

"Ryan," smiled Brigid, "who's going to talk to him? Biotto's his resident for tonight."

"Jason's got to be talked to, though."

"He's going through it. He's okay. You've been there before."

"I remember," said Ryan. "I got talked to."

21

Friday, August 24

Ryan hadn't been able to get Hope on the phone for two weeks. The E.R. had wrecked his sense of night and day, and he had been calling at intemperate hours. She was never home. *She's not sleeping in her bed.* The thought bothered him for a minute. It was eclipsed by an even more worrisome idea. Diana had not spent a night in his bed for almost as long as he had been in the E.R. The E.R. was stifling his grand passion.

Ryan called Diana's office.

"Where are you?" she asked, in a voice which assured him she hadn't forgotten.

"The E.R."

"Poor baby," purred Diana. She must have been alone in her office.

"I'm coming back to your turf in a few days," said Ryan happily.

"The CCU?"

"Can't come soon enough."

"I know what you mean," said Diana. "I miss you."

That was all Ryan could handle. He hung up, renewed. He'd had his fix.

He tried Hope's number later, about four in the afternoon. But there was still no answer.

22

Monday, August 27

Ryan looked forward to his rotation on the Cardiac Care Unit. He had gotten to know the nurses on the unit during his cardiology elective. He liked them. It also meant seeing a lot more of Diana.

The unit patients were always needing cardiac caths for one reason or another. Diana spent a lot of time there. The resident on the unit could trundle his patient down the hall to Diana's lab and spend time with her without causing raised eyebrows.

The unit was set up to reduce mortality from cardiac disease. The grant that helped sustain it was explicit on that point. It was supposed to be for the heart attack victim, preferably the young, salvageable patient. It was for the kind of patient who develops lethal heart rhythms suddenly, in the immediate after-shock of the heart attack. If treated immediately, this patient might be saved, gotten past the unstable period, and live for years.

The guardian of the system was the Standard Operating Procedure, the great gatekeeper, zealously enforced by the head nurse and the unit resident. Standard Operating Procedure had elsewhere acquired a bad name, especially in places where it was enforced with relish by all too willing clerks and nurses, who used it to keep people like Ryan in his place.

On the unit, however, Ryan had to concede the rules served well. This became painfully evident in the case of one of Baptist's patients, with whom Ryan had the misfortune to become involved.

As the unit resident, Ryan was in charge of deciding who would be admitted and who would not. The most venerable gray-beard cardiologist could not get a patient into the CCU unless Ryan first saw the patient, examined him, and agreed that it was likely the patient was having a heart attack. This obvious absurdity, that a mere resident could turn away a patient when a more experienced physician wanted that patient on the CCU, was most practical. Private doctors wanted their patients on the unit for the nursing care. The unit patients were constantly monitored and attended. Private docs, being private docs, and having only the interests of their own patients in mind, did not much care whether or not the patient in question had had a heart attack. All that mattered to the private doc was that the patient was sick and needed care. The Intensive Care Unit was always full, and thus impossible to get patients into. And then there was the CCU, with all those empty beds.

Left to their own impulses, the private docs would have quickly filled the twenty beds of the CCU with patients suffering from renal failure, septic shock, adrenal crisis, all of which were serious problems, but all of which could be managed on the wards. The unit was for heart attacks.

Ryan, then, was suppose to serve as the impregnable junior assistant resident. And the private docs had to go along. Actually, it didn't take much experience to tell which patients were really having heart attacks. And when there was doubt, the patient got admitted. But one Saturday morning an exception was made.

Saturday, September 1

Baptist marched onto the Cardiac Care Unit and stood by the monitor displays as Ryan and the interns were rounding. Ryan left the group and snapped to attention in front of Baptist.

"You will be getting a Mrs. Philby this afternoon," said Baptist. "The house is full, and she has angina, so I'm putting her here. She's for coronary bypass on Monday. These are her angios. She's from Connecticut. Take good care of her."

Baptist handed over the angiogram in its X-ray folder.

"Dr. Eckhardt will be in to see her."

Eckhardt was the surgeon.

It was all wrong, of course. The rules just didn't apply to Baptist. They were baby-sitting for Baptist's patient.

"Why doesn't he admit her to Surgery if she's coming in for surgery?" asked the interns.

"Baptist doesn't own Surgery. He owns Medicine," said Ryan.

Mrs. Philby arrived. She was a pleasant enough lady who had chest pain and high blood pressure. Often the pain started up and made the blood pressure get worse. She was seen by the surgical residents, and would have some new plumbing put in her heart on Monday.

The nurses kept bugging Ryan. Whenever Mrs. Philby got her chest pain, the nurses took her blood pressure, and it was astronomical. Ryan would run in and find the pressure elevated, but not nearly as high as the nurses were saying. The nurses didn't like the idea of this lady taking up a CCU bed for baby-sitting.

"They're pissed at Baptist," said Ryan to nobody in particular. "And taking it out on me."

Ryan wrote a routine workup for the hypertension, which he knew would never be done. It involved collecting urine for forty-eight hours on weekdays. And that would delay surgery.

Monday, September 3

Monday, Mrs. Philby was whisked off to the Operating Room, where she died in a hypertensive crisis. At autopsy she was found to have a tumor of her adrenal gland. This secreted the hormones, which made her blood pressure go wild. The stress of surgery had been the lighted match to the powder keg.

At the Morbidity and Mortality Rounds the surgeons were hopping mad. They blamed everything on the medical group, including Ryan, who sent them the time bomb. The pathologist read Ryan's notes from the chart to the assemblage.

"Now, Dr. Ryan," he said, "you suggested getting urines for catecholamines, did you not?"

"Yes."

"What were you thinking of?"

"Pheochromocytoma."

"You let a patient go to surgery, thinking she had a pheo?"

Ryan looked around. The surgeons were staring pure hate. The pathologists were smirking, and the people from Medicine just buried their faces in their hands. Ryan looked at Sam, the chief resident, who would carry a full report to Baptist. Baptist, of course, was busy elsewhere.

"I did not consider the diagnosis to be a likely one. Pheo is a rare tumor."

Sam smiled benignly.

"But you suggested a pretty extensive workup. Then you didn't do the workup. You were in charge of the unit?"

"I guess I wasn't calling all the shots," said Ryan.

Sam frowned.

"You were the unit resident?"

"Yes."

That's where they left it.

23

Thursday, September 6

Hyman Bloomberg called, overjoyed that the paper had been accepted for publication. Brigid invited Ryan for dinner, at her place.

"This Brigid thing getting serious?" asked Arch.

"Everything's under control," said Ryan. "I always keep everything under control." But other things *were* getting beyond his control. His time at the Tower was slipping away. He was not likely to be a high draft choice on Maxwell Baptist's list for senior residency, which meant thinking about finding a fellowship at some other hospital, maybe in some other city.

The trouble was, Ryan couldn't bring himself to think of leaving: the Tower, the streets around the hospital, the ICB&G, Arch, the town house. Why would anyone want to leave all that?

Finishing training would be bad enough, but having to finish at some other hospital was really bleak. If he could only slip past Baptist to senior residency, he would get attending privileges at the Tower almost automatically. He would set up an office a few blocks away, within sight of the Tower. And the world would be a happy place.

Ryan allowed himself to drift off on the forbidden currents of wish-it-only-were. He smiled at the thought of referring patients to Iggy for X rays, and the notes he'd get back.

Dear Dr. Ryan: Thanks for referring Mr. Jones for his chest X ray. Mr. Jones's chest is perfectly normal, as any fool can plainly see, and any internist reared by Iggy Bart should have known without an X ray, simply by using his stethoscope.

And Ryan could schmooze with Hyman Bloomberg about Gordio and homosexuals and medicine.

And of course, there would always be Diana.

Ryan did not look forward to the pivotal days ahead. He had learned to live in the present, and even if the present was just life as a hired drone, it was at the Tower. It was true, as a resident he was tied to the hospital, and to a routine, and he had to be civil to people who didn't merit civility. Still, residents led a sheltered life in many ways, free from some of the most onerous burdens of medical practice, burdens the private docs could not escape, like patients' families. Residents were largely protected from patients and their families when it came to revenge.

Mr. Sloan's family, for instance, went after Mr. Sloan's private attending with a vengeance, and ignored Ryan. Mr. Sloan was a nice man, with a nice attending, and a bad disease. The attending, Dr. Cohen, was so conscientious it was appalling: Cohen rounded on his patients at 7:00 A.M., and came back at 10:00 P.M. to check charts, consult notes, and go over cases with the house staff.

Mr. Sloan did not have much heart left. At forty-three he had already wiped out most of its underside, part of the anterior wall, and some of the back part, with three successive infarctions. The house staff said that he had a "T.M.I." (total myocardial infarction). What was left functioning sustained his life, barely.

And he knew how barely. Every walk to the bathroom left him drained and breathless. He did not have to be told how close death was. He could feel life ebbing. His wife, however, could not believe what she could not accept. He looked a little tired to her, but he could not be dying. If he was dying, it was Dr. Cohen's fault. She was possessed by a desperate fury. Bad things meant someone was to blame. She had taken her husband to Dr. Cohen, paid his prices, because he was supposed to be the best heart man in New York. But he was failing as wretchedly as her husband's heart.

Mrs. Sloan was overtly hostile to anything in white.

Ryan noticed her sitting alone in the cafeteria, staring at the interns and residents from her husband's floor as they relaxed at dinner. They were laughing, and not acting at all gloomy about her husband, who was dying upstairs. She shifted her bitter glare to Ryan. Ryan felt immediately apologetic and tried to look contrite. Mrs. Sloan did not look appeased, and Ryan remembered Iggy's admonition: "I did not give Mr. Sloan his disease."

When her husband infarcted what remained of his heart, Cohen rushed him to the Cardiac Care Unit, where Ryan tried to monitor the disaster with a Swan-Ganz device. The Swan got wedged in the wrong spot, and a small bit of lung infarcted. Several days later the heart stopped. Mrs. Sloan refused an autopsy, but she did subpoena the chart. Then she sued Cohen for killing her husband with the Swan, which of course had nothing to do with his death. But she wanted Cohen's flesh, by the pound.

"Some people just can't accept random misfortune," Cohen told Ryan. "They've just got to blame someone."

Baptist called Ryan down to his office to find out what had happened with the Swan. He had a letter from Mrs. Sloan's lawyers.

"The Swan worked fine," said Ryan. "We had no idea it had gotten out too far."

"Did you put it in, or did you have the intern do it?"

"I did it myself."

"Thank you for coming down," said Baptist, dismissing Ryan.

Ryan walked back up to the unit, wondering if he had done anything wrong.

24

Monday, September 10

Ryan had a note from Caroline when he arrived home that evening.

> *Sorry to cling like a frightened cat. Woods has me scheduled
> for admission, September 17. Love to see you.*

Ryan felt truly chagrined. He had really meant to call Caroline. He had meant to call her the night she called at the E.R. But he had forgotten. And the next time he thought of it, it was so many days later, he was embarrassed to call. So he had put it out of his mind.

And here she was apologizing for acting as anyone would.

He went upstairs to his study and dialed her number. No answer. He tried three more times. He finally got her at midnight.

"Got your note."

"Thanks for calling."

"Sorry it wasn't sooner."

"No sweat."

"How are you?"

"Fine. Scared. Just saw *The Hospital.* Ever seen it? That's where I was tonight. A busman's holiday for me."

"You'll be rid of hospitals one day."

"I just hope I'm around to enjoy it."

25

September 12

Ryan was down in the cath lab darkroom, looking at some cinefilms, when Diana Hayes slipped in. She looked at the films for a moment.

"Mrs. Morehouse," said Diana. "Notice the regurgitation on the aortic retrogrades."

"I can't believe you know these patients from the films of their hearts."

"Like looking at their faces," said Diana. "Some angiocaths are more distinctive."

"Amazing to realize I'm looking at a living, beating heart."

"Angiography *is* a modern miracle," said Diana. "Don't you forget it."

"Who had the daring to try it on people?"

"You don't know?"

"No. Some German, no doubt. They're never fazed by risk."

"Actually it was an American radiologist. An American Jewish radiologist, right here at The Manhattan Hospital."

"No foolin'?"

"Right here. He injected himself, as the first living subject. Took pictures of his own heart."

"Who?"

"You look it up," said Diana. "Medicine's never been the same since. And it all happened right here, in the land of the giants."

26

Friday, September 14

Ryan finished his rotation on the CCU on Friday and felt like celebrating. He went by the cath lab.

Diana had the big attaché case she always carried on nights she was staying over in the city.

"Just taking some work home," she said.

"Oh," said Ryan. "I thought you might be surprising me."

"Alan's meeting me at the station," she said. "Was it anything special?"

"No," said Ryan, "have a nice weekend."

Ryan walked over to B-5, where he knew Brigid was working an evening shift. He entered the floor but turned around half-way down the hall. He wanted to be with Diana. Being with Brigid would just make it worse.

Brigid came out of the supply room.

"Just can't wait to get back to B-five, can you?" she said.

"Just thought I'd say hello," said Ryan. "But I decided to wait until Monday. Hold the problems for me."

"I'm not sure they'll hold," said Brigid, pulling him into the supply room. "I'm not sure Susan Bergmeyer's going to make it until Monday."

"What?"

"They've been dialyzing her."

"She was doing so well," said Ryan, shocked.

"Her heart's okay," said Brigid. "But all her other organs are falling apart. Her kidneys went first, then she got hypertensive, so they jacked up her steroids, and then she went loony. Now they're trying to decide if it's steroid-induced psychosis or lupus on the brain."

Brigid looked at Ryan ironically. "Oh, and you know who Jason has for a resident to help him with Susan?"

"Don't tell me—Biotto?"

"You got it."

"How's that working?"

"Horribly. Biotto's got no idea how to handle this disaster. He's starting to regress. Keeps telling Jason to get in touch with his feelings about Susan. Jason wants to know how much prednisone to give her."

"Jesus," said Ryan. "I thought Biotto was coming along."

"I hate to say 'I told you so,' " said Brigid.

"How's Jason taking it?"

"To heart."

They went down to see Jason. He was in Susan's room. They had given her one of the two single rooms on the floor.

Jason was clearing Susan's CVP line when they walked in. He was happy to see Ryan.

"I hear you're coming back Monday."

"Yes."

"Susan's been doing just fine."

Susan was staring at Ryan and Brigid with an expression of unmitigated horror.

"Oh, God!" she shrieked, turning away. "They're so *ugly.*"

Jason looked at her, horrified. He looked up apologetically.

"She gets like this sometimes."

"Oh, please!" Susan shouted, pulling on Jason's sleeve. "Get them out of here!"

Jason looked at her helplessly.

"Please! Please!"

Ryan stepped out into the hall with Brigid. Jason came out.

"How long has she been like that?"

"Three days."

"What do the lupus mavens say?"

"It's either steroid psychosis or lupus cerebritis."

"That helps. You stop the steroids for one and increase the dose for the other."

"They said to stop the steroids by Monday if she's not better."

"What about her kidneys?"

351

"She needs the steroids for them, but the steroids make the blood pressure worse. It's such a mess."

Jason went back into the room.

"He was supposed to be off last weekend," said Brigid. "Spent it in her room."

"Have you talked to him?"

"I was hoping you might."

"What could I say?" asked Ryan. "To the extent that he's gotten past thinking only of Jason Adams, I guess this is all worth something."

"He's hurting more than is good for anyone, even an intern," said Brigid.

"I guess he needs talking to."

"Right."

"But what can I say?"

27

Monday, September 17

Caroline was in bed when Ryan arrived at nine that night. She looked tanned, but Ryan noticed her eyes were a little yellow, and she was puffy.

"Woods has me on steroids again," she said. "I hate 'em. They make me feel a little high, but they puff my face up."

"You look fine."

"Lovely yellow tint," she said. "I could puke every time I look in the mirror."

"When's the biopsy?"

"Don't know yet. There's been a delay. Something about my blood clotting. They're giving me vitamin K, through the IV."

"Don't get discouraged."

"Easy for you to say, white man."

28

Saturday, September 22

Nine o'clock Saturday morning, Ryan was awakened by the phone on his bedside table.

He did not officially begin on B-5 until Monday. He was done with the CCU on Friday, so it could not be business. He answered.

"Good morning." It was Diana. She never called on a weekend. Ryan allowed himself the fleeting hope she might be coming in, to spend the weekend with him.

"Good morning."

"Are you in bed?"

"Yes."

"Alone?"

"Distressingly."

She laughed.

"Where are you?" he asked.

"In bed." Then, lower, "Can I see you Monday night?"

"Of course," said Ryan. "You know you can. Whenever."

"I can't seem to get you out of my mind."

"Where's Alan?"

"Raking leaves. Such madness."

"He must be crazy, leaving you in bed."

"It's been done before," she laughed. "I'm used to it."

"Not really."

"Save Monday for me."

She hung up. She had called for the effect. Ryan realized that. But it worked. He could ride the entire weekend on that single call.

29

Monday, September 24

Diana was due around nine that night. Ryan was shaving after
a shower, a towel wrapped around his waist. Diana liked him that
way. Arch was out with Jane. The door buzzer rang, and Ryan
ran downstairs, razor in hand, shaving cream and towel his only
covering. He threw the door open.

It was Hope.

"Lucky I didn't bring my camera," she said. "May I come in?"

Ryan tried to think of a way to say no graciously, but could
not. Hope swept past him and up the stairs. Ryan raced after her.

He decided to take the offensive: "I've called you at all hours,"
he said. "Don't you sleep at home anymore?"

"Only when the spirit moves."

"Some answer."

"Some question."

"Agreed," said Ryan, deflated. He was trying to think of some
way to get her out.

"Actually," said Hope, "sometimes I just let it ring. I feel like
I'm just hanging in air where you're concerned."

"I know."

"But sometimes I just want to see you," she said, looking past
Ryan. A shocked look crossed her face. Ryan turned around.
Diana had walked into the doorway. She slipped into a chair,
crossing her legs with a flicker of a smile.

"Obviously, this is not the time," said Hope. She shot out the
door.

Diana looked at Ryan, without even following Hope's depar-
ture.

"I was going to ask about your leaving the front door open," she said.

Ryan felt sick. Hope had looked so crushed. Diana wasn't smiling either.

"I think I'd better leave," said Diana. "Looks like you have things to say."

"Please," gasped Ryan. "Don't go. Let me get dressed."

The act of pulling on clothes helped compose him. Ryan emerged from the bathroom ready to talk.

"Obviously," he said, "I was just as surprised as you."

"Well, no," said Diana. "You were surprised. I was astonished."

"She just appeared, out of the blue."

"Old girl friends do that kind of thing."

"Have you ever?"

"I guess my appearance rather ruined her scene," said Diana. "Rotten timing."

"I'll call her when she cools off."

"Something I am not likely to do," smiled Diana. "It seems like all weekend since I've had a taste of you."

30

Thursday, September 27

Ryan gave up calling Hope. It was just too difficult to call from work, using lines which nurses or other house officers cut into; besides, she wasn't answering. He dropped by her apartment, after work. He left the hospital, threw a raincoat over his whites, and got on an uptown bus.

He had never been to her new apartment, though he knew the address. It was one of those buildings with a buzzer system and no doorman. Ryan pushed the buzzer under Hope's name.

"Who is it?" she asked, her voice coming over the speaker near the door.

"Bill."

The buzzer rang, opening the lock on the inner door, and Ryan went upstairs. She lived on the sixth floor, and he was breathless by the time he reached her.

She opened the door and retreated to a wicker chair in the far corner of her one-room apartment. Ryan sat on her couch. She looked very fragile in the wicker chair. She was wearing blue jeans.

"I didn't hear what I didn't want to . . ."

"I'm sorry about the other night . . ." They both spoke at once. Ryan waited for her to begin again.

"I've got a large capacity for self-deception," said Hope. "I answered your phone and there she was. I could put it out of mind. But not her actually sitting there."

"Yes."

"Diana Hayes, right?"

Ryan couldn't see any point denying.

"Yes."

"A big honcho," said Hope flatly. "And married."

"Yes."

"You can really pick 'em."

Ryan shook his head.

Hope brushed her hair out of her eyes.

"Not that I've been all that faithful to you, you understand. But . . ."

She looked at Ryan and almost smiled.

"There I go again, with the games. I've been faithful, in my own way. Not that you ever asked, or cared."

"Hope . . ."

"It's true," she said. "I don't know why I've been so smitten."

Ryan looked at his shoes.

"Just promise me," said Hope, "that if I ever call you again" —she smiled—"you'll just hang up."

31

Monday, October 1

Thursday, Diana came over after dark, carrying her phone in her attaché case. Ryan had been trying unsuccessfully to read the latest *New England Journal of Medicine.* But he could never concentrate when he was expecting Diana.

She sailed past the door he held open, and up the stairs to his bedroom. She went straight to his bookcase, where he kept the anisette, and poured herself a glass. She always drank out of the glass with the Harvard emblem. She stripped to her panties.

"Now I'm comfortable."

Ryan sat on the arm of the wingback in which Diana nestled and kissed her. She did not let him up.

"I can't seem to get enough of you," she said.

"You control it well."

"I'm getting your chair all wet."

Ryan guided her bedward.

"I've missed you."

"Since Tuesday?"

"Too long."

"Leave Alan," said Ryan. "He'd never even notice."

"Eventually," she said.

"Eventually, you'll leave him?"

"Eventually, he'd notice."

32

Thursday, October 4

Ryan got paged during Morning Report. Nobody gets paged during Morning Report. People know better than to bother JAR's during Morning Report at the department office. It was B-5.

"Susan's had a grand mal seizure," said Jason.

"Get the neurologist."

"He's with her now."

"What's he think?"

"Bled into her head."

Jason hung up. Ryan called back. Brigid answered.

"She's a goner," said Brigid. "Better get up here. Jason's in bad shape. Don't know what he'll do."

"Report should be over in fifteen minutes. Call her parents."

"They're here."

"I'm off the floor half an hour and the place caves in."

"Come back soon."

"Wait a second," said Ryan. "Biotto's Jason's resident. Why am I getting called? Biotto's in the conference room, in Report."

"Jason specifically asked me to call you," said Brigid, losing patience. "Don't rub it in. Just get up here."

Ryan left Morning Report and met Brigid in the nursing station. They went to Jason, in Susan's room. They arrived just in time to see Susan arrest. Her heart monitor showed just a straight line where heartbeats should have been.

Jason pumped on her, and called for paddles to shock Susan's heart to life. She was gone. There was nothing left to save.

Ryan watched Jason pumping furiously on Susan's chest. Finally Ryan walked over and put a hand on Jason's wet shoulder.

"You can't help her now," he said. "Stop it."

Jason left the room. Brigid followed him.

She came back.

"He's in the bathroom, crying. I can hear him through the door."

"Where are her parents?"

"In the solarium."

Ryan went to see them. He got permission for the autopsy.

Ryan could not remember when a patient's death had changed things as much as Susan's. Deaths were frequently frantic, often saddening, but rarely did a patient's fate much affect the way the staff felt or acted toward each other. Ryan had hated Biotto briefly for telling him Mrs. Green had died. And there had been some heat over Mr. Suggs. But Suggs was the exception proving the rule. The staff members knew each other before and after the patients. No matter what became of the patients, the staff members still had to live and work with each other.

But Jason had called Ryan. Jason's resident had been Biotto. In a way, Biotto had always been Jason's resident, since Jason was just an embryonic doctor. But Jason had called Ryan. There could hardly have been a clearer message: Jason didn't trust Biotto. When it really mattered, he trusted Ryan.

Biotto's first reaction, after Susan had been pronounced dead, was outright pique. Jason had come out of the bathroom red-eyed, but composed, and looking only tentatively compensated. He went to see Susan's parents. Biotto took one look at him and decided to abstain from the obvious question.

"I know why he didn't call me," Biotto told Brigid. Brigid didn't want to hear this, and became absorbed in a chart. "Ryan's got 'em all convinced he's the action honcho when the chips are down. I'm flaky. He's Mr. Reliable." They were alone in the nurses station.

Brigid looked at him. "You blaming Ryan?"

"He could have stepped into the Report room and signaled me to come with him."

"I suppose he could have, at that," said Brigid, shaking her head. She went back to her chart, then looked up. "But I don't think Ryan was doing anything consciously to hurt you."

Biotto looked at her, then down at his shoes. "That's right. You're right. I'm hurt. My own intern doesn't trust me."

Ryan had been standing behind Biotto long enough to hear the last sentence. "It's not that at all," said Ryan. "He thinks the world of you."

"Then why did he call you, and make a point of not calling me?"

"Maybe you ought to ask him that," said Ryan. "Ask him later, of course. Not now."

"I'm no good in the clutch," said Biotto. "I don't have to ask him."

"Oh, stop feeling sorry for yourself," snapped Brigid. "And start thinking about Jason. Have you talked to him yet?"

"Not yet."

Biotto went to find Jason, who had accompanied Susan's parents off the floor. Now he was coming down the corridor, looking ashen. They went into the conference room, at the end of the hall. Biotto started to put his arm around Jason's shoulders as they went in. But Jason turned to close the door, and the gesture didn't work.

Ryan and Brigid watched, inconspicuously, from the nurses station.

"I should have talked to Jason way before this," said Ryan.

"That was Biotto's job," said Brigid. "Besides, what would you have said?"

"What's Biotto saying now?"

"That he's sorry," said Brigid. "I hope."

"For what?"

"For being a disappearing resident. For being Biotto. This has been coming. Today Biotto got the message from someone he listens to."

Ryan collapsed into a chair beside Brigid.

"What a way to start a day."

33

Monday, October 8

Caroline was crying when she paged. Ryan was trying to decipher a consult note in a chart on B-5. He sat with it in his lap, in the nurses station.

"What's wrong?" he asked, alarmed.

"It hurt."

"They did the biopsy?"

"Yes."

"It hurt?"

"Not hurt. It felt like I had the wind knocked out of me. I wasn't expecting that."

"Who did it?"

"A very nice old guy. A liver man. Hyman Bloomberg. Dr. Woods says he's the best."

"He's right."

"But Dr. Bloomberg told me the Hodgkin's might be in the liver. And he won't know until the biopsy is ready."

"You okay?"

"Would it be bad if it *is* in the liver? They all seem so concerned about its being there."

"Nobody wants it to be anywhere."

"But there's something special about the liver?"

"No," Ryan lied.

"I'm terrified."

"I'll be over tonight."

Ryan did stop by after Chart Rounds that evening, but Caroline was asleep, much to his relief. He had no good answers for her questions. She was on the eighth floor in Whipple, in Mrs. Green's room. He left her a note.

Didn't want to wake you.

34

Friday, October 12

October turned the leaves bright and brought the city to life. Ryan couldn't shake his own torpor. He thought about Diana and couldn't be moved to do much else. He even started following her.

One Friday evening he caught sight of her disappearing around a corner. She was carrying the attaché case she used for overnights whenever she stayed in the city. But she hadn't paged Ryan.

Ryan drifted along, a good distance behind, in the darkening street. She walked purposefully. She passed the building where she rented her room, and turned uptown at Second Avenue. She kept crossing streets until she got to Fifth Avenue.

She disappeared into a doorway, past a doorman.

The doorman lifted his hat and said hello.

Ryan was half a block behind and continued slowly toward the doorman, hugging the lengthening shadows of the building walls. The doorman jumped into the street to open a cab door. Ryan stopped. A figure emerged from the cab. A familiar figure. The doorman knew the man. But Ryan doubted the doorman knew the passenger's real name. Ryan knew it, though. It was Maxwell Baptist.

Ryan stood in a semiparalysis and licked at the metallic taste in his suddenly dry mouth. He was seized by one unshakable thought all the way home: he must live to confront Diana on Monday. After that grand scene he could crawl off into a corner and die.

There was no point trying to sleep Friday night, so he planned his trap. He rehearsed the scene until he had a response for every conceivable ploy Diana might try. The only tack she might take for which there was no satisfactory counter was absence. She usually came to see him Monday nights. But if she waited until Wednesday or Thursday this week, her perfidy would be less fresh. Ryan wanted the stain still visible on her hands.

Saturday he decided to call her in Nyack. She must have gone home after her night with Baptist to the doubly deceived Alan.

"Information. What city please?"

"Nyack."

"May I help you?"

"Mr. Alan Hayes. I don't know the address."

A distressingly long pause followed.

"I'm sorry, we have no listing."

An unlisted number?

"Try Dr. Diana Hayes." *She may have kept her maiden name.*

"Yes, we have that listing: 555-2424."

Ryan didn't call. The only thing he had was the element of surprise, and that would be neutralized over the phone. She could claim she couldn't talk, then plan her response all weekend. He had to hold off until Monday, then spring it on her.

35

Monday, October 15

The following Monday, Diana called.

Ryan managed to be outwardly cheerful.

"Can I see you tonight?" she asked.

"Of course," he said, smiling.

She glided into his study about six that evening.

"Oh, it's nice being with you," she purred, settling into his lap. She ran her fingers across his neck. She reaffirmed that Ryan was the light of her life, the true source of her most intense and abiding joy, and that Ryan was the man who thrilled her as no other had ever done. Ryan listened to the litany.

"How was your weekend?" he asked, innocently.

"Oh, the usual. We read the *Times* together on Sunday. Alan read me the entire 'Week in Review.'"

"Sounds like kind of a quiet weekend."

"My weekends usually are. It's the weekday nights I live for," she said, unbuttoning his shirt.

"Especially Friday weekday nights," said Ryan dryly, face flushed.

Diana's smile evaporated.

"Is it just Alan, me, and St. John, or is this just the tip of the iceberg?"

"What are you talking about?" said Diana, flushing, but not sure how damning the evidence was going to be.

"I broke all the rules and followed you Friday, to the arms of yet another light of your life."

Diana sprang out of his lap.

"He's no such thing."

"Just a little flicker?"

"What he is, is my concern."

Ryan uncoiled, and slapped Diana across the face sharply.

"I'll give you some time to cool down," said Diana. "Call me when you've thought about it."

She left without a slam.

Ryan paced around, then started to call Brigid. But that wasn't any good. He went downstairs and had coffee with Arch, who didn't know what had happened, but tried to cheer him up anyway. Ryan just felt more alone.

36

Friday, October 19

Ryan started to dial Hope's number but hung up. It really wasn't fair. Besides, it wouldn't help. He'd just keep thinking about Diana. Hope had asked him to step out of her life, and he owed her that.

He looked up Caroline's number at Whipple. It was ten o'clock, but Caroline never slept much at Whipple.

"Did I wake you?"

"Jest not," she said. "This is Whipple. Some grimy intern just left, with about three quarts of my blood."

"At ten P.M.?"

"That's what I said."

"You got a fever?"

"Now how did you know that?"

"Late-night blood-drawing. Blood cultures."

"Hundred and two."

"Whew!"

"They're gonna give me Tylenol."

"Don't you like aspirin?"

"Don't mind it. But there's some problem about my platelets."

"How's the liver?"

"I was going to ask you."

"Don't know."

"Will you find out for me?"

"Sure."

"No news is good news."

"Sleep tight."

"Okay."

Ryan hung up. He didn't like them giving her Tylenol. But she must have been uncomfortable. He knew he should go visit her during the weekend. He also knew he would not.

37

Monday, October 22

A week had passed, and Diana had not called. Ryan had seen her, sitting in the front of the amphitheater, at Grand Rounds. He had passed her on a stairwell, once. She said, "You look tired," and kept going.

She was right, of course. She owed him no explanations. Ryan had been presumptuous to feel deceived. He realized how indefensible his outburst had been. He had deceived himself far more than she had ever deceived him.

Ryan needed to talk with someone about Diana. He would have told Arch, but he knew Arch would never understand. Arch was too rational. The whole issue turned on whether or not she loved him. Ryan was wild about Diana and wanted whatever part of her life he could have. The only question was whether he could still believe she felt the same way about him, in her heart of hearts. Arch would say: Look at the evidence. She tells you you're the light of her life. What does she tell Baptist? She's a lady who cultivates manageable little passions. Diana Hayes was not looking for life-altering romance. She had no intention of absconding with Ryan to a little clinic in Scotland. She had life enough right here in New York.

Arch had already summarized his assessment of their relationship for Ryan: "You could walk in here some night and find her in bed with Biotto. And she'd tell you it wasn't happening. And you'd believe her."

Caroline had been right: nobody heeds good advice.

Somewhere in the highest centers of his cerebral cortex, Ryan knew all this made sense. It was rational. It fit the facts. But he did not and could not believe it.

Ryan believed the language Diana spoke with her body. No one could fake the feeling she flooded him with in bed. She told him love was never like this with anyone else, and he believed her. He believed her because it was that way for him. He was convinced by the flawlessness of her body, by her laughter. She loved him because he wore pink shirts with club ties. And because he was adorable. Every woman has one true love. Ryan didn't read novels for nothing.

Ryan would have to apologize.

The trouble was framing an apology. He considered calling, but she could hang up. Flowers were too conspicuous. It came down to a note, or a direct confrontation.

The opportunity surfaced in the form of a fifty-year-old lady with a noisy heart, who was admitted to Ryan's floor in need of a catheterization. Ryan went down to the cath lab right after Morning Report.

Diana was gloved and gowned, busy advancing the catheter into the patient's pulmonary artery.

"Please wear an apron," she said, never taking her eyes from the pressure monitor. "You may not value your progeny, but I do. I hope to . . ."

Ryan put on the lead apron, to protect future generations from the X radiation. His head spun with her oblique avowal that she might want to have his child. She did love him. There was no doubt of that.

Diana stepped on the pedal and the fluoroscopy machine clanked on, lighting up the TV monitor above their heads with a picture of the patient's heart, the catheter, and the contrast dye Diana was injecting.

Diana manipulated a catheter from the cutdown on the patient's arm and stepped on the fluro pedal again. Then she hit the X-ray switch with her knee and seven X rays fired by in rapid succession, under the patient.

"What did you think?" she asked Ryan. "Don't look at the pressure monitor."

Ryan had been looking at the pressures, but he wasn't thinking about the patient or her heart.

"Mitral stenosis."

"There's some aortic regurgitation, too," said Diana.

"Some what?" asked the patient.

"Nothing to worry about," said Diana. "We'll go over everything later."

She finished the case with Ryan wavering between retreat and inaction, hoping his beeper would go off for once when he needed it.

Diana sewed up and took off her sterile gloves.

"We'll go over the films," Diana told the patient. "Dr. Ryan will tell you all about the findings."

"Is it good or bad?" asked the patient.

"Not bad."

They stepped out of the lab, into Diana's office. She sat behind her desk.

"Missed you," she said.

Ryan gulped and stepped backward, one step.

"I'd like to believe that."

Diana sighed quickly.

"There's nothing I can do to make you believe, now."

"Guess so."

Diana's eyes drifted toward her office window, as if she were temporarily distracted by something passing by on the river.

"This isn't you. It's as if you're not really with me now. You're so far away. Can it ever be the same?"

"Depends on you."

"On me?"

"How you feel," said Ryan, "about me."

Diana caught him in a blue-eyed vice, half laughing, half crying.

"Isn't it obvious how I feel? Hasn't it always been?"

"Doesn't make sense."

"Make sense of this," she said, holding up the printout from the catheterization. "Don't try to make sense of me."

Ryan fastened on her eyes, unblinking. It was like looking at a cat.

"Sometimes I think I should blow your cover and tell someone about us. Biotto. Anyone. And about Max."

"Don't play with Max," she said flatly. "Just hope he hasn't gotten wind of you. Sometimes I think he's picked up your scent."

38

Wednesday, October 24

Ryan called Hyman Bloomberg.

"Ryan, my good man. What's cooking?"

"That's what I called to find out," said Ryan. "You did a liver biopsy on a patient and friend of mine, Caroline Smith."

"Oh, yeah," said Bloomberg, sounding suddenly unhappy.

"Is the pathology done yet?"

"She's got it in her liver."

"Shit."

"I'm sorry, Ryan," said Bloomberg. "She's a friend of yours?"

"Yeah."

"Woods is going to blast her. They'll do an EOD on her first."

"I thought she had an Extent of Disease workup just recently."

"This changes things."

39

Monday, October 29

During the week since Ryan had sought Diana out in the cath lab, he had not touched her. He had been on call, and she had called once or twice, but never when he could really talk. He wasn't sure he even wanted to talk.

He thought about her constantly, but that was nothing new. He imagined where she was, whom she was with, what she might be thinking. But the thought of Diana curled up with Baptist sullied the image. Somehow, the exquisite little pangs accompanying images of Diana wrapped around her husband made Ryan want her all the more. But the image of Diana with Baptist had the opposite effect.

Friday night had been bad. He couldn't be sure she was with Baptist. But he felt strangely relieved Saturday morning, feeling she must be heading home to Alan.

Some state of affairs. She's got me being grateful for Alan.

She called him that night.

"I really must see you," she said. "This is tearing me up."

"Why don't you try to forget about me?"

"Don't you think I've tried?" she said, all breathy. "Don't you think I've wanted to uncomplicate my life?"

"No," said Ryan, though he couldn't say why. She had seemed to enjoy her naughtiness. That was half the fun, the sneaking about.

"Think again," she said. "You're trouble."

"Then divest."

Diana knew all about silences, how to time them, how long they should last. She pulled one now.

"I will," she said. "If you really want that."

Ryan was never good when Diana called his cards.

"You know what I want."

"I'll do something," she said. "I know I have to make up my mind, and act."

40

Friday, November 2

Hope was on B-5, looking for Ryan. She found him in one of the patient's rooms, examining an old gomer with cirrhosis.

"Got to talk to you," said Hope. It crossed Ryan's mind, for one insane second, that Hope might be pregnant. That would be the fitting disaster for this period in his life.

"Guess who I specialed last night at Whipple?"

"Caroline?"

"She's really sick," said Hope. "When was the last time you saw her?"

"I talked to her just the other—"

"I said *saw* her," said Hope, cutting Ryan off.

"Been a while."

"You can't just desert her now."

"I know."

"When people stop coming by, she feels it. She's just sinking down."

"I'll stop by tonight," said Ryan.

Diana paged Ryan before he left the hospital.

"Can I see you tonight?"

"Of course."

"I've got to go home. But just for a few hours. Early. Six, okay?"

"Sure."

"I just can't behave myself," she said. "I really shouldn't. But before I catch my train. Just a taste of you."

Ryan didn't get through on B-5 until a quarter to six. He never

378

had time to stop by Caroline's bed in the Joan Green Memorial Room at Whipple. He fell asleep right after Diana left.

Friday, November 9

Ryan woke up with a headache on Friday. He felt a little nauseated by afternoon. He went by Diana's office. She wasn't there. So he sat for a while, looking at her big overnight attaché case.

She walked in.

"Have a nice weekend," he said unhappily.

Diana looked at him, unblinking.

"I want *you* to have a nice weekend," she said. "Don't think about foolish things."

"I hate Fridays."

"I'm not overly fond of them myself," said Diana.

"Then why don't you make other plans?" asked Ryan. "For your weekends."

"See you Monday," said Diana.

Caroline was writing notes when Ryan stopped by on his way home from the hospital.

"They're at it again," she said.

"More chemotherapy."

"Oh, yeah," she smiled. "But first they had to do their thing. Lymphangiogram. Whole lung tomograms. You name it—I got it."

"How're you holding up?"

"Like a champ," she said, a tear rolling down her cheek. "I'm going out like a champ."

"You're not going anywhere."

Ryan kept meaning to see Caroline, but she kept asking him questions for which there were no happy answers. The truth was, she was getting worse, very likely dying. Restarting chemotherapy was a real defeat. She had been weepy and depressed, and with Diana to think about, and his future in doubt, Ryan just

379

could not bring himself to cross the avenue and stop by Whipple.

She had paged him, apologizing, but increasingly desperate. The more desperate she got, the more he fell away.

"Ryan," she said hopefully, "I was thinking. Your place is only a few blocks from Whipple. It's so scary here at night. I've got a special some nights, your friend Hope. I guess you know."

"Yes."

"But I still get crazy at night."

Ryan waited for her to continue, to suggest the unthinkable.

"Maybe, you'd like to rent out a room."

"To a sundowner who gets crazy at night." Ryan tried to laugh, but it didn't come off.

"I'm not all that bad," Caroline started crying. "I'd be good."

"Caroline," Ryan said, sadly, "you've got to be here. It wouldn't be safe, right now."

"I'm dying, aren't I?"

"Don't be crazy on me. You're set back, but you'll do just fine."

"Okay," said Caroline, and then, "I haven't seen you for so long."

She was right about that. Ryan had been stopping by less and less.

"I can't fake it with her," Ryan told Arch. "She'll see it in my eyes."

"Better that than not seeing you," Arch said.

Ryan knew Arch was right. Easy for him to say. Arch could see Caroline and see nothing but a pretty albeit slightly yellow girl. Ryan couldn't help seeing the skull beneath the skin. Ryan watched Caroline with mounting horror, a horror he struggled to conceal. She held a cigarette in her hand as she always did, palm held outward. But now that palm jerked once or twice. It was called "asterixis." It heralded liver failure.

"What are you staring at?" Caroline asked, crushing out the cigarette. "You're such a *doctor,* sometimes, in the worse sense of the word. A girl can't even sneak a smoke."

"I didn't say a word."

"Didn't have to. I saw you looking at my cigarette." She laughed. "No great loss. I'm smoking more now and enjoying it less. Tastes awful."

Another sign of liver disease: loss of taste for cigarettes. And liver disease in Hodgkin's is so often a one-way street. Ryan had seen it this year. He'd seen the livers at autopsy. And he looked at Caroline and saw a liver full of lumpy lymphoma balls.

It was agony being with her. She wouldn't ask any terrible questions, like Mrs. Green. Ryan knew that. But he would have to be cheerful when he felt like burying his head in her sheets and crying. And that would be a lie, being bright and bucking her up.

The more he wanted to absent himself from Caroline, the more he wanted to flee to Diana. They were connected somehow. Ryan realized there was a connection. He perceived it had something to do with guilt. He shouldn't want to avoid Caroline. And he shouldn't want to be with Diana.

"I miss you," Caroline told him over the phone.

"I'll stop by," said Ryan. But he never seemed to find the time.

41

Monday, November 12

"I can't figure either one of them," Ryan told Jane. Jane and Arch were stretched out on the sofa in Ryan's study.

"Hope comes by, in person, but it's about Caroline. Hope won't go out with me, but she comes by the floor."

"How is Caroline?" asked Jane.

"Not good."

"How did Hope look?" asked Arch.

"Good. She always looks good."

"She's all class," said Arch. "I don't blame her for throwing over a bum like you."

"I can't be sure what she really wants."

"What's she say she wants?" asked Jane.

"To be rid of me," said Ryan. "But women never say what they mean."

"That makes life easy then," laughed Jane. "You can do whatever you please, if you believe that."

"Well, as long as Diana's in the picture, I guess Hope really means it."

"Did you ever have to make up your mind?" sang Arch.

"Great help, my friends," said Ryan.

"We can give you the world's best counsel," said Jane. "But you're only going to hear what you want to hear."

42

Friday, November 23

Diana stopped by the town house, carrying her big attaché case. Another Friday evening. But she was going out of her way now. She stopped by, rather than just disappearing.

"I know I have to do something," she said in her flattest tone, sounding drained.

Ryan looked at her silently, his chin on his hand. He was cultivating silence now. They looked at each other, unsmiling.

"I'm such a coward," she said. "We both know what I want. Why can't I just do it?"

Ryan continued his silence.

"Well," said Diana, getting up with an outrush of air. She smiled a sad little smile. The smile always worked, and Ryan went to her, holding her.

"Do you think it's snowing in Edinburgh this early in the year?" she asked.

"Not yet," said Ryan. "I think the season's changing still."

43

Around the beginning of December the buzz went up that St. John was calling people in for the senior residency cut.

"No news is good news," Biotto told Ryan.

"What's that suppose to mean?"

"Sometime this week, all but ten lucky residents will be called to St. John's to get the proverbial ax."

"It's this week?"

"That's the word."

"How do you know?"

"Ginny told me."

"St. John's secretary?"

"The same. They've been making up folders all week, one for each JAR."

Ryan's beeper went off. *Here it comes,* he thought. But it was an outside call. So he decided to answer it.

"Ryan, my good man," said Hyman Bloomberg. "Have you gone to your mailbox?"

"Jesus, is that how they do it?"

"Do what?"

"I thought they called you to St. John's office."

"What are you jabbering about?"

"I have it on the highest authority that I'm not making SAR. St. John's calling people in."

"Who is highest authority?"

"Ginny, his secretary."

"Unless you hear it from St. John, you haven't heard. Did he call you?"

"Not yet."

"Don't be absurd then. You're a giant. Besides, you're published, as of today."

"Where?"

"The *New England Journal,* schlepp. It's probably in your mailbox. That's why I called. *Lead* article, no less. *With* an editorial. Praising us to high heaven."

"No!"

"Yes."

"With an editorial?"

"Highly laudatory, of course."

"Incredible."

"Predictable. Now, what's this about your not making senior resident?"

"St. John hates my guts."

"Not to worry. You're a star now. He can't cut a star."

"Unbelievable," said Ryan, relieved, euphoric, and needing badly to pee.

Bloomberg hung up, disquieted. The meeting for the house staff cut was coming up. He hadn't planned to attend, but Ryan had worried him. He called his own secretary.

"Do I have any patients scheduled for Monday, December tenth?"

"Full house, morning and afternoon."

44

Friday, December 7

Caroline had called over to the Tower, trying to page Ryan, but never managed to connect. She was happy to hear his voice when he called.

"How are you, sport?" he asked.

"Okay," she said unconvincingly. "Well, actually, a little scared."

"Why?"

'Dunno. Just am."

"You're going to be fine."

"Will you come see me?"

"Of course, tomorrow."

"Good," said Caroline. "Oh, Ryan?"

"Yes?"

"They tell me I haven't been making sense all the time lately. You won't be upset?"

"When have you ever made sense?"

Ryan hung up, upset. Why had he forsaken her? Because he was chickenshit, that's why he had forsaken her.

Caroline's favorite aunt was visiting. They had been talking in their usual animated way when her aunt noticed that Caroline was just saying, "Yes, isn't that crazy?" to everything Auntie said.

"Caroline, are you feeling okay?"

"Yes, isn't that crazy?" Caroline smiled serenely.

Auntie called a nurse, Hope. Hope was taking Caroline's vital signs when Ryan walked in. Hope paged Caroline's intern. Ryan got some fresh frozen plasma into Caroline in the meantime, and Caroline's glazed eyes cleared.

"Was I making myself clear?" she said.

"You were most communicative, dear," said Auntie.

"But not wildly lucid," said Caroline, perturbed.

"You're better now," said Ryan.

"It's just a phase," said Caroline, not at all surprised to see Ryan.

"What do you mean, dear?" said the aunt.

"Do you remember when Granddad died, and Mother gave us all little white cards to address?"

"Yes, dear," said Auntie, smiling, but not liking the drift of the conversation.

"Well," said Caroline, "I think that you had better go get some white cards now."

Hope looked at Caroline and took her blood pressure. Wordlessly, she rolled down the head of the bed and opened the IV full tilt.

Stunned, Ryan and Auntie stared at patient and nurse. Ryan tried to think, tried to move, but nothing happened. Finally, his hand pulled his stethoscope heavily from his pocket. He listened to Caroline's heart. The sounds were muffled.

Ryan heard his own voice say to Auntie: "I wonder if we might have some time alone with her." But Auntie had already fled.

They tried, but Caroline just turned more and more gray. She arrested, and Ryan tried to code her, but her intern walked in and quietly countermanded the order.

No calls for help. The intern watched as Ryan worked furiously over the lifeless body, pumping the chest, intubating, pumping useless units of blood and bicarbonate into dead veins. Ryan grabbed the defibrillator and shocked her. But the monitor showed nothing.

"We were just talking with her," he said hysterically, to nobody in particular.

Ten units of bicarb later Ryan was still pumping and Hope bagging, and the intern was still standing behind them. The intern put his arm around Ryan's drenched shoulder.

"You can't help her, now," he told Ryan.

Ryan went to the toilet and sobbed. He thought if he stayed there long enough the intern might call Caroline's parents. But then he realized he had to tell them.

He had promised Caroline.

He told Auntie first, then went to sit with Hope, who was crying in the conference room. Ryan sat down inertly beside her. She put her arm around his shoulder, and they cried. Caroline's parents arrived an hour later.

45

Monday, December 10

Maxwell Baptist swept out of his inner office, past Ginny, around the corner, and into the conference room. His secretary watched him pass, and carried his morning mail into his office, stacking it on his desk. She put his new journals in the left-hand corner, with the *New England Journal* on top. She heard her buzzer ring.

"Ginny," said Baptist, "I forgot the folders. Bring them in here, will you?"

Ginny took the folders from the couch and carried them into the conference room.

By nine thirty everyone was there. Baptist, the attendings on the advisory committee, Diana, representing cardiology, everyone except Hyman Bloomberg.

The ten Selected folders would be approved first. Baptist took the first one.

"Biotto. Any comments, objections?" Baptist looked around. Everyone shrugged. "A good man," said Baptist.

They had gotten through the S's. Hyman Bloomberg slipped into the room, puffing his pipe, grinning his dolphin grin.

"Have they gotten to Ryan yet?" he whispered to one of the attendings.

"Must have passed him," he whispered back. "Already up to T."

There were four charts left in the Approved pile.

"Have we done Ryan yet?" asked Bloomberg, good-naturedly.

"No," said Baptist, slowly, his eyes shifting quickly between Bloomberg and Diana.

"Why not?" asked Bloomberg.

"He's not in the Selected group."

Bloomberg started.

"Why not?" asked Bloomberg.

"We'll discuss the Unselected after we finish the ten in the Selected group," said Baptist.

Bloomberg looked around the table. There were all the chiefs of the various divisions, most selected by Baptist, but there were as many private docs. He judged the numbers.

"I think we'd better discuss this now, while we still have a quorum. Some private docs will have to get back to their offices by the time we get to the Unselected," said Bloomberg slyly.

"I think it's more important to approve the residents who will be with us. We can discuss objections and additions later," said Baptist.

Bloomberg took his pipe out of his mouth and blew a puff toward Baptist.

"Max," said Bloomberg, "how many of these guys in your Selected group have a lead article in the *New England Journal* to their credit?"

Baptist's eyes shifted quickly around the room: the others were looking at Bloomberg.

"What are you talking about?" asked Baptist.

Bloomberg stood up, taking a rolled-up *Journal* from his inside coat pocket. He slammed it on the conference table. Everyone started.

"I'm talking about 'Gordiodiasis: Another Cause of the Gay Bowel Syndrome. Evidence for Venereal Transmission,' " said Bloomberg steadily. "By William Ryan, M.D."

The attendings surrounded the journal, swelling a buzz of approval. Diana smiled silently.

Baptist watched them point and laugh and register commendation. Then he reached over to inspect the journal himself. He looked at the article briefly, then tossed it back on the table with an expression of monumental indifference.

"That's William Ryan *and* Hyman Bloomberg," he said with great satisfaction. "Everyone knows who wrote that paper,

Hyman. You're an old softie. But giving Ryan the credit won't fool anyone."

"Quite the contrary," boomed Bloomberg, *"au contraire.* It was Ryan's work. I was grateful he included me as second author. He did the work."

"Really, now?" scoffed Baptist. "When did he get an idea about a gastroenterologic topic like that?"

"He had a case of mine when he was an intern. He dropped a duodenal tube and made the diagnosis. Imagine that. An intern thinking of a duodenal aspirate. I sure hadn't. It turned out to have Gordio. The rest is history."

"One paper does not a senior resident make," said Baptist. "Especially this one, all things considered."

"It's a great paper," said Bloomberg indignantly.

"If you're coauthor," said Baptist slyly, "I'm sure it is."

Before anyone could respond, Baptist went on, "Anyone else want to continue this digression?"

"He's a damn good kid," said Sidney Cohen, Mr. Sloan's doctor.

"My impression exactly," said Baptist. "He needs to do some more growing up. He just hasn't got the maturity for senior residency."

"He's done good work," said Bloomberg.

"Anyone else?" said Baptist.

Bloomberg looked imploringly around the table. His eyes fastened on Diana, who quickly became fixated on a scratch on the gleaming conference table. She ran her finger over and over the scratch, but said nothing.

46

Tuesday, December 11

St. John called Ryan in Tuesday morning. Ryan's folder was on his desk. Pictures of his daughters smiled brightly at Ryan from a bookcase behind St. John's desk. Ryan wondered whether the daughters were screwing older men.

"Well, Ryan, how are you enjoying this year?"

"Immensely," said Ryan.

Baptist coughed.

"Fine. Well, we have a problem about your senior residency. It seems we have more people than positions, if you know what I mean. We can't keep you."

Ryan was looking bad news in the eye, and not believing it. Baptist continued, "Of course, if an opening should develop. But it looks unlikely, if you know what I mean."

Ryan knew. He knew precisely what Baptist meant. No senior residency. And probably no other hospital in New York would take him. Baptist could see to that. Ryan would need a letter from his chairman, no matter where he tried to go in New York. And Baptist did not want Ryan in New York.

The fix was on. The results were in. Ryan was out. And there wasn't anything he could do about it.

Tuesday Evening

Arch was thunderstruck when he heard the news. Arch had thought that he and Ryan would always live in the town house. Where could Ryan go? Who would have him?

Biotto came by to pay his last respects. He couldn't believe what he had heard.

"You went to medical school here, trained here. They can't say you're not well trained. What the hell did he say?"

"He said there were more people than positions at Manhattan Hospital."

"Now I really feel bad," said Biotto.

"Why?"

"They kept me and booted you."

"Oh, that's just talk. Baptist hated my guts. He could have kept twenty guys on for SAR if he wanted."

"But you love this stinking place."

"Oh, I don't know."

"Sure you do. You tried to perfect it."

"They don't like that. You have to forgive them. Nobody likes being scolded."

"Well, I'm gonna fuck 'em in the end," said Biotto with a furtive smile. "I got myself a psych residency last week. Nobody knows. Not even Baptist. I can't wait to see the look on his face next July, when he hears one of his SAR's is deserting medicine for shrinkdom."

"Biotto," said Ryan, shocked to the the core, "don't give up medicine."

"Fuck 'em."

"Fuck who?"

"All of them."

"You won't be a doctor anymore."

"That's the best part."

393

"That's no kind of revenge."

"Don't say it. I know. *Illigetimum non carborendum.*" Biotto grinned. "I've heard you say that so often, I know it by heart."

"You let the bastards get to you."

"Naw. It's not Baptist, or any of that pathetic lot," said Biotto, fidgeting in his chair. "I don't know. I just don't like sick people. They're obnoxious."

"You're upset," said Ryan, consolingly. "You're outraged, and tired. You'll like it better this year. You'll be a prince."

"No," laughed Biotto. "You'll like it. I never will. I'm getting out."

Ryan looked at Biotto's wavering smile and thought of what Brigid had said when Biotto had begun his "transformation." She had doubted his character. She thought the change superficial.

"Ryan, do me a favor," said Biotto. "Don't tell Iggy, or anybody."

"I won't."

"For a long time I tried to blame Baptist and Soft Sam and all the rest," said Biotto, trying to answer the silent reproof he could see in Ryan's face. "But it wasn't really them. They just made a bad scene worse."

"Don't be angry at sick people."

"Coming from you . . ." said Biotto, but he didn't finish the thought. "I am outraged though. About you."

Ryan wasn't as outraged as Biotto. Ryan knew he hadn't had his mind on doctoring for two years. He had been kicked out for sleeping with the chairman's woman. But he deserved to be kicked out: guilt made it easier to accept.

He deserved the ax. He deserved it for neglecting Caroline.

What made it really smart was the sticky pang of shame no rational analysis could shake. Iggy would hear, and Brigid. Diana would have to be told. She might have already heard. From Baptist. He wouldn't be ashamed if it were just Diana. She would lay the blame on Baptist, where it didn't really belong. But still, she was the one who made it really hurt.

Ryan wondered whether he should just let the word get out, or tell people himself.

47

December 12

The next morning Ryan went by Diagnostic Radiology to tell Iggy. He'd tell Iggy, then Brigid.

Iggy was trying to wash some barium out of his blue Ralph Lauren shirt when Ryan found him in a hallway, outside a barium enema room. Ryan had his hands in his pockets, trying to look casual. But his palms had gone icy and wet.

Iggy glanced up from the hallway sink. He looked embarrassed. Something in that gaunt face told Ryan Iggy already knew. Iggy extended a bony hand to the bereaved.

Ryan was hesitant to offer his own wet paw, but took Iggy's hand anyway. Iggy started.

"They didn't kill you, prince," said Iggy. "It's just exile. No need to go around feeling like a cadaver."

Ryan laughed, relieved, and so did Iggy.

"You always know everything before I can tell you."

"Thanks for thinking of coming by to let me know yourself."

"Sure."

"What now?"

"Don't know," said Ryan. "Have to find another place."

"Bloomberg will find you one," said Iggy. "He loves you."

Ryan wandered toward B-5, not wanting to see Brigid, but feeling compelled at least to try. She was at her desk in the nurses station. She looked up, happy to see him, as always. She didn't know. Ryan could see that.

"Ryan, I've got a couple of interns up here you've got to whip into shape," said Brigid, getting up and dragging him by the arm into the privacy of the utility room.

"You're talking to the new, silent Ryan," said Ryan. "Low profile. I aim only to avoid offending."

"Oh, you can talk to a couple of erring interns," winked Brigid.

"I'm close-mouthed."

"In silence are the cruelest lies told."

Ryan looked at Brigid for meaning, then realized what she was saying.

"You know," he laughed, astonished, "you are so cagey. Never let on a thing."

"Baptist is such an old goat."

"You used to call him a pussycat."

"Changed my mind," said Brigid. "Taking out a personal thing on you." She stopped herself a little abruptly, giving it all away.

"What personal thing?" said Ryan, voice pregnant with suspicion.

"He's never liked you."

"You meant more than that."

"No, I didn't."

"Can't fake it now," said Ryan. "I can see it in your face."

"See what?"

"It's not like you to cover when you're called on a bluff."

"Oh, all right," said Brigid, exasperated. "I think Baptist is a goon to can you just because of Diana Hayes."

"You knew about us?"

"Everyone knew," smiled Brigid, blushing. "Christ, Ryan, this is Manhattan Hospital."

"Jesus," said Ryan.

Brigid looked at the floor.

"And you went out with me and all, all along."

"I like you, Ryan," she said, still looking at the floor. "I knew you'd see through her eventually."

Ryan took Brigid in his arms and kissed her forehead, and then, briefly, her lips, and went back to the town house. He would wait for Diana to call.

48

December 13

When another day passed, and she still hadn't called, Ryan decided it was finally time. He called her office and left a message. "Please stop by." She came by that night.

"I had a talk with St. John, just recently," said Ryan, from his wingback chair. Diana sat on his couch.

"Oh?" she said tightly.

"I guess he's forced us both to make some choices."

"What did he say?"

"He said that Manhattan Hospital isn't big enough for both of us."

"Jesus," said Diana. "Did he give any reasons, any justification?"

"No, but he made himself quite clear, if you know what I mean."

"You could go . . . somewhere else in the city," she said unconvincingly.

"Any ideas where?" asked Ryan. "I'd prefer some place where they wouldn't think to call St. John as soon as I fill out my application.

"No," he said. "Hyman Bloomberg just called. He's got me a G.I. fellowship at Hopkins, and I'm going to take it."

Diana crossed, and sat on the arm of Ryan's chair. She stroked his hair. Ryan regarded her steadily.

"You can come with me . . ." he said.

She looked at his hair as she spoke, so quietly she was almost inaudible.

"Where? To Baltimore?"

Ryan felt silly. Diana in Baltimore. It was unthinkable.

She spoke. "I couldn't do it to Alan."

"You couldn't do it to yourself," said Ryan, looking at the ceiling.

Diana sighed. "This will pass. We'll have our clinic in Scotland yet."

"No clinic," said Ryan softly.

"No clinic? Not even in Edinburgh?"

"No, Scotland's miserable in the winter. No central heating. I couldn't stand it . . . especially without you."

"We weren't talking about without—"

Ryan cut her off.

"Yes. We are talking about endings. It's not Alan who'd be lost if you came away with me. It's you."

"No."

"No? Of course, no. You've reached the stage of denial," said Ryan. "What else can you do but deny?"

Diana was silent. So many of her most effective retorts consisted of silence. Then she said, "I could repent."

"Repent? For what?"

"For not being what you imagined me to be."

"That's novel," laughed Ryan. "No, penitence doesn't become you. Besides, penitence is for salvation, and it was me who was looking to be saved."

"Saved?"

"By you."

"How could I ever have saved you?" asked Diana, somewhere between laughter and tears. "And from what?"

"From everything smelly and diseased, from the unaesthetic world of doctors and disease we know and love. By being all the fragrant, alive, clean, exciting things you are. A night with you erases the whole day of fecal impactions."

"You make me sound like an enema."

"Call it catharsis."

"Semantics," said Diana, half smiling.

She refused to leave that night. She wrapped herself in Ryan. In the morning she was in the kitchen when he awoke.

398

Ryan sat at the table, watching her. She couldn't find much to say. She just fluttered around the kitchen, putting away dishes, which drove Ryan crazy, because he had quite a lot of important things to say but got distracted watching her.

"Diana, anytime you're in Baltimore . . ." Ryan's voice trailed off. Anytime she was in Baltimore she'd be on Alan's boat.

"This July, I'm going to pack up. And we'll be two states and ten light years away from each other," said Ryan.

"I didn't want this to happen," said Diana.

"I know. You wanted us to go on forever."

"I don't know what I wanted. Ever since I met you I've had a bad case of chronic paralysis."

"Must be catching," said Ryan. "I had it, too."

"No," said Diana. "It wasn't infectious. We both know the cause."

"You're paralyzed, all right," said Ryan. "But not by other people."

Diana said nothing. She went over to Ryan and stroked his hair.

She knelt by his chair.

"How're you doing?" she asked.

"Okay."

"I thought you would be."

"Fool that I am, I like to think that, good or bad, nothing that happens to me is ever wasted."

"That's a very Catholic thing to say."

"Is it?"

Diana glided out of the kitchen and disappeared upstairs. A moment later she was at the door downstairs, where she paused. Ryan listened to her listen for him, but he stayed in the kitchen and played with his coffee cup. He heard the door click shut.

He went to the window. She had crossed to the other side of the street, and was heading east, toward the hospital. To look at her, sailing purposefully along, you could never have guessed that this morning was different from any other.

Afterword

It was the end of June, but still not really hot. And the humidity had been decent. Ryan had been down to Baltimore and found an apartment.

He hadn't seen Diana since Baptist lowered the boom that past December, except a few times in corridors, or at Grand Rounds. He had run into her in the cafeteria once, and she had asked him when he was moving. And whether or not he had a place in Baltimore. He had said yes, and stopped eating in the cafeteria.

On moving day Arch, Iggy Bart, and Biotto helped him carry all his boxes of books and his furniture down to the U-Haul in the street.

"Seen my checkbook?" asked Ryan.

"Found it in the breadbox this morning," said Arch, flipping it to him.

The U-Haul was finally packed. Ryan's rooms were bare. Arch and he strolled through the half-empty town house together for the last time. Outside, New Yorkers in cars and cabs were being typically gracious about the traffic jam caused by the U-Haul.

"For a momentous occasion, this seems pretty unmomentous," Ryan observed. "Just doesn't seem fitting. Almost a decade at The Manhattan Hospital, counting med school, and no send-off."

"When you pass on to Heaven, they'll mark the occasion," said Arch. "You're just passing out of state."

Arch produced a bottle of champagne and pressed a passing shopping-bag lady into service. She was induced to smash it on the U-Haul, and Ryan's expedition was christened.

Jane showed up to bid a tearful farewell.

"Chrissake, she's my girl," bawled Arch. "What was going on between you two?"

Ryan swung the U-Haul into midstreet and headed up toward Third Avenue. He watch Arch and Jane waving, in the side view mirror. At the corner he leaned out the window for one last look at the Tower. Then he swung the U-Haul onto the avenue and drove out of the city.